KNOT ON YOUR PUCKING LIFE

A SNOWVALE HOWLERS OMEGAVERSE NOVEL

HEATHER LONG

For you—
for finding laughter when there were only tears,
for making art in the dark,
for choosing to be yourself in a world that tried to reduce you to a diagnosis.
You've shown me what it means to make every word count, to tell entire stories in a single image, and to stay feral and luminous even when things are heavy.
You are one of my biggest cheerleaders, one of my constant inspirations, and even when I don't say the story out loud, I can still hear you whispering, "Do it."
So this book is for you, my beautiful, chaotic, Mayhem.

FOREWORD

Dear Reader,

Welcome to my very first Omegaverse.

Wren Foster and the Snowvale Howlers showed up rather impertinently while I was in the middle of another series, teasing me with a chase through the snow involving hockey masks. Yeah... that's where it started. They refused to leave me alone after that, and once the idea lodged itself in my brain, it became clear I wasn't getting any peace until I wrote their story.

I've never been one to write to a trend. I prefer to wait for the stories to grab me first, to let the characters settle in and start making noise. This is my first time stepping into the Omegaverse, but Wren and the boys moved in, went completely rent-free, and wouldn't go away—so here we are.

Now, the rules of Omegaverse can vary wildly from series to series, and I didn't lean into any established handbook for this one. These are the rules of *this* world. Suppressants exist, but they aren't especially legal the way Wren uses them. She also doesn't want to be limited by her designation—whether alpha, beta, or omega—when it comes to the work she's good at or the life she loves. And yes, she's surrounded by alphas all day long. So what does that look like? How does instinct collide with ambition, control, and choice? Those were the questions that kept circling in my head as I wrote.

As the story took over, a few core themes floated to the surface and refused to let go: autonomy versus instinct, found family, gender role reversal, the wildness of winter reflecting internal chaos, and mating as a chosen connection rather than destiny. Along the way, I gleefully embraced some of my favorite tropes—forced proximity, heat and chase scenes, fiercely protective alphas, a beta with dark horse emotional depth, hurt/comfort, a little mask kink, and primal energy. There's even a "not like other omegas" angle in here, but I did my best to approach it without tearing down anyone else to make Wren shine.

If you've read my books before, you already know this, but it bears repeating: consent has always been non-negotiable for me, and it's no different here. No matter how feral things get, choice remains at the heart of this story.

This is a complete standalone, so you can dive in with no prior knowledge of anything I've written before. I hope you enjoy Wren, the Howlers, the snow, the chaos, and all the wild, messy feelings that come with them.

And who knows... maybe there will be more tales from the Howlers someday.

I'll see you on the flip side.

xoxo

Heather

PS: Human voices only. All the work involved in this and

all my novels from the stories themselves to the covers, to editing, to the audio are human-produced materials and voices only.

CHAPTER
ONE

WREN

There were three unspoken rules in the Snowvale Howlers' locker room.

One: Don't touch the gear if you don't want to lose a hand.

Two: Don't mention the 2019 playoff choke. *Ever.*

Three: Don't flirt with the PR manager unless you're ready to get roasted in front of your teammates.

Guess which rule they broke the most.

"Foster," Rhett called out from where he was slouched on a bench, sweat-damp hair curling at the ends, pads half-off like he was auditioning for a thirst trap. "You ever get tired of pretending you don't wanna climb me like a tree?"

I didn't even pause my stride. "Only on days ending in 'never,' Navarro."

The guys hollered. Rhett clutched his chest like I'd mortally wounded him. "Cold. Ice-cold."

"That's the brand," I shot back, tossing a stack of media schedules onto the table by the fridge. "Try reading some-time, it builds character."

Across the room, Jay Kim didn't even look up from

where he was taping his stick with surgical precision. "Navarro doesn't have character. He's just noise in a nice jawline."

"As opposed to all your jealousy in a pair of too-tight compression shorts," Rhett countered.

"Jealous of what?" Jay asked dryly. "Your save percentage or your IQ?"

"Both," Rhett grinned. "You wish you could make a crowd scream the way I do."

Roan Whitaker snorted from where he was stretching out on the floor, foam roller under his back. "They're screaming because you can't stop dropping your stick mid-game."

Rhett flipped him off. Roan didn't flinch—he just looked at me. Quiet, steady.

"You okay?" he asked, voice low and private despite the chaos around us.

I gave him the same answer I always did. "Always."

And it was always a lie.

Because here's the thing about working this job as an omega: no one's supposed to know.

Suppressants made it easier—at least, they used to. My scent stayed muted, my cycle flatlined, and my body mine. No glowing skin, no come-hither hormones, no pheromones curling through the air like invisible snares. I was just Wren. Smart mouth. Sharp boots. Full control.

But keeping up that illusion meant knowing how to read the room.

And the Howlers locker room was a jungle. Sweaty pads, damp towels, leather tape, pine-scented body wash and alpha musk all stewing in a low-grade haze. I'd learned to walk through it like a minefield: don't linger too close, don't lock eyes too long, and never—*never*—breathe too deep.

Especially not around Roan.

Or Rhett, when he was laughing.

Or Jay, when he got that look in his eyes like he saw something you didn't even know you were hiding.

"Team meeting in five!" Coach Morrissey's voice boomed from the hallway. "If you're late, you run."

A chorus of groans followed. Helmets thunked back into cubbies. Sticks got propped up. Someone cursed about missing their protein shake.

I didn't even make it a step before the Coach eyed *me* with a nod and asked, "You joining us, Foster?"

"I'll brief you after," I said. "Owner's upstairs. Wants to talk playoff strategy—media coverage, not defensive lines. Sorry to disappoint."

"Don't be," he said, already distracted as he barked at Apa to tuck in his damn jersey. "You do your job better than half my rookies do theirs."

"That's because I don't get concussed weekly."

He chuckled as he walked off, and I headed toward the elevator, smoothing the front of my blazer. As much as the guys joked around, the real pressure came from up top. I didn't even make it another step before Roan stepped into my path.

Roan rolled his shoulders as he rose, the motion smooth and measured like everything he did—controlled. Deliberate. He stepped closer, eyes briefly scanning my face, then the small tension in my hands I didn't know I'd been clenching.

"You sure you're okay?" he asked again, voice lower this time. Closer. Something warmer flickered underneath the usual stoicism.

I shrugged like it didn't matter. "Just tired."

His gaze lingered on me, too perceptive for comfort.

"Then maybe take your own advice for once and rest," he said, dry as ever but softer now. "You're always on. Even wolves sleep."

I huffed out a quiet laugh, surprised. "Was that a poetic metaphor, Whitaker?"

"It was a threat to make you nap, actually."

He turned to leave, but paused mid-step. "We notice when you don't take care of yourself, you know."

Then he was gone, following Coach down the hallway with that long, steady stride.

I stood there for a second too long, but when I turned, Jay was watching me.

He was leaning against the locker just to the side, stick still in hand, tape dangling from his fingers. Calm. Unreadable. But his eyes—dark and sharp and cutting right through me—locked with mine. Not challenging. Not accusing.

Just *knowing*.

I maintained my professional mask, a faint smile with a hint of certainty that refused to be dislodged even by his silent, if intense, accusation. Didn't matter in the long run, though, I looked away before I strode out of the locker room.

Strode.

Not fled.

Yes, I was very good at lying to myself.

The Howlers' owner, Adrien Marchand, was exactly the kind of wealthy, sharp-eyed alpha who made people instinctively nervous—and he liked it that way. His suits were always immaculate, his words sparse, and his presence unsettling in that power-play, boardroom-heat sort of way.

"I hope they're not giving you too much trouble," he said as I stepped into his office. The view of the snow-drenched rink below looked like something out of a postcard, if the postcard came with a scent warning and blood-stains on the ice.

"They're puppies in pads," I replied, cool and crisp. "Loud, slightly untrainable, but manageable."

His mouth twitched. "Good. Keep them focused. This playoff run could make or break the franchise."

I nodded, did the PR dance, promised press coverage, coordinated talking points, and got out of there before his scent started digging claws into the back of my throat.

Because lately?

Everything was getting harder to ignore.

My skin had started to buzz in crowds.

A heavy-bass hum just beneath the surface of my bones, like I was a radio tuned half a frequency off. I'd found myself leaning in when Roan spoke, breathing slower when Rhett laughed near me, reacting—*viscerally*—to things that shouldn't have touched me.

Certain voices made my stomach twist. My balance slipped around stronger scents. I was waking up flushed and aching, mouth dry, sheets tangled like I'd been chasing something in my sleep and never caught it.

The worst part? I couldn't even tell if it was them, or me.

The locker room—*don't even get me started on that place*—used to be just sweat, banter, and chaos. But now it felt like a live wire. A sauna of unwashed gear, testosterone, and temptation I couldn't afford to want. Like my instincts were starting to hear a frequency I'd spent over a decade pretending didn't exist.

I was slipping. The act was fraying at the edges.

That was before I ended up sitting in a too-white, too-bright medical office, arms crossed, stomach knotted, while my doctor gave me news I hadn't wanted to hear three weeks earlier.

Dr. Maida clicked her pen. "Your readings are unstable. The suppressants aren't binding the way they used to."

I stared at her. "Then increase the dosage."

"We've already pushed past the safe threshold, Wren." Her tone softened, but it didn't help. "Your liver enzymes are elevated. You've developed a tolerance, maybe even a dependency. Your body's trying to override the meds."

My throat dried. "There's got to be something else."

"There is. Stop taking them." She leaned forward, gentle but firm. "Let your system reset. Let your body regulate."

"No," I said flatly. "You don't get it. I *can't*—"

"You don't have a choice. If you keep going like this, you could trigger a crash. Organ damage. Full burnout. You'd be hospitalized."

I looked away, jaw tight. Through the window, snow was starting to fall again—soft, quiet flakes spiraling against the glass. First storm of the season. I used to love snow.

Now it just made everything feel like it was closing in.

"Wren," she said, voice low. "Who are you hiding from?"

I didn't answer.

Because I wasn't hiding from *someone*.

I was hiding from *everyone*.

From two alphas whose scents were starting to pull something dangerous out of me.

From one beta who noticed too much.

From a life I didn't want—no matter how badly my body was starting to whisper otherwise.

I'd done the math, then waited another few days to stop taking the suppressants. It would take time to let them cycle out of my system. They had a half-life. The doctor had walked me through all of it. She even had brochures and recommendations for services that could help me once they were out of my system and my first heat in over a decade hit.

That wasn't today, though. I still had time. Time to get everything ready for the playoffs before I took a few days off. I only hoped it would be enough.

A message buzzed on my phone. Marchand's assistant asking for another thirty before I came up. Fine. I'd get other work done until then.

The lobby was empty, the ice behind the glass rink walls freshly resurfaced, gleaming like a frozen promise. Upstairs, the media suite was quiet, mercifully. I didn't think I could handle small talk or caffeine-laced gossip from the junior marketing assistant who was perpetually tracking the team's Instagram engagement like it was the stock market.

I pushed open the door to my office and froze.

Rhett was already inside.

Well—had *been* inside. The room was empty now except for the faint trace of his scent hanging in the air— cool eucalyptus, warm spice, and just a hint of something wild that didn't belong in a business setting. Of course he wasn't in here, he was with the team. I shook off the visceral reaction that had my skin pebbling.

There was a folded note on my desk, held down by a

puck he'd swiped from media day. My name scrawled across it in a messy black sharpie.

Wren.
If you're not okay, you know you can tell me, right?
—R

No joke. No flirt. Just... that.

I stared at it longer than I should have.

For someone who made everything a performance, Rhett had a nasty habit of slipping sincerity in when I least expected. It was a side of him he didn't show on purpose. And that? That was harder to shake off than the usual locker room crap.

I folded the note in half and tucked it into the drawer with my backup comms and a handful of granola bars I hadn't eaten since the preseason road trip.

Then I sat down, powered up my monitor, and braced myself.

Because the doctor hadn't given me a choice.

You need to stop taking the suppressants, Wren. Let your body regulate. When it's time, take a few days. Let it pass.

Right. Just "a few days." Like I was coming down with the flu and not about to fall into hormonal hell surrounded by two alphas and a beta who already watched me too closely. But she was right, at least based on my bloodwork. If I didn't stop now, the crash wouldn't be optional. It would be catastrophic.

I should have had a full three weeks, at least, but the window was closing on me far more swiftly than I expected. Particularly with my enhanced reactions. I had maybe forty-eight hours—*tops*—to get everything in order. Then I'd need to go.

Coordinate next week's playoff media push. Schedule Roan and Jay for post-practice interviews. Prep the owner's talking points. Update the fan engagement calendar. Answer twenty unread emails. Put out whatever dumb fire Rhett started next.

And—if I had time—bury my rising panic in a neat little email auto-reply that read: *"Taking a few personal days. No, I haven't been kidnapped. Please contact Head of Comms for urgent requests."*

I took a slow breath. Then another.

No more suppressants. No more pretending my body wasn't circling the edge of something dangerous.

I just had to survive long enough to outrun the fallout.

Easy.

TWO

WREN

Each day, my morning routine grew more challenging. No suppressants. No safety net. Just me, my to-do list, and a body I didn't quite trust anymore.

The morning started like usual. Alarm. Shower. Too much dry shampoo. Coffee I forgot to drink until it went cold. The only difference was the pill bottle on the bathroom counter—still full. Untouched. Waiting.

It was fine. I felt fine.

Okay, my pulse was a little fast. And I'd reapplied deodorant twice. But that could've been anxiety. Or the twelve deadlines I'd stacked on myself trying to beat my own body to the finish line.

I pulled my coat tighter as I stepped into the frigid arena tunnel. The sound of skates on ice echoed ahead—practice in full swing. I could already hear Rhett's voice over the others, loud and relentless, trash-talking Roan mid-drill like his life depended on it. He was one of the best defensive goalies in the league. Unfortunately, he also *knew* that and loved to rag on the others.

"Come on, Cap! I've seen faster footwork in synchronized swimming!"

Roan didn't respond. He just hip-checked Rhett into the boards and kept moving.

God, I loved this job.

I made my rounds—checked in with the social team, flagged the arena ops guys about the power glitch in the west-side spotlight rig, then headed down toward the benches, where the Howlers' post-practice interviews were supposed to start in fifteen minutes.

Practice was over by the time I reached the locker room, which smelled like hard work and bad decisions. Not unusual. But today, the usual scent-cocktail hit me like a slap. Not overwhelming. Just... sharper. Like someone had turned the volume up on the air.

I tugged at my scarf. Overreacting.

This was fine.

They were always sweaty and loud and too close. Today was no different.

Except it *felt* different.

Roan passed me first, towel around his neck, hair still damp, eyes catching mine for half a second longer than usual. Not suspicious. Not exactly. But my heart skipped anyway.

"Interview lineup's posted in the lounge," I said as he passed. "Don't disappear."

"I never do," he replied, low and easy.

Rhett came next, shirtless, of course, twirling a stick between his fingers like a baton. "Morning, PR Queen. You look—".

"Finish that sentence and I'm sending your college highlight reel to the team's TikTok."

He grinned, utterly unabashed. Terrible man. "You wound me."

"You're not deep enough to be wounded." But I did enjoy verbally sparring with him, it kept me sharp.

"Wrong. I'm deeply offended. Which, if you ask Jay, is the same as foreplay."

Jay, right on cue, stepped out of the shower hallway, hair so black it gleamed blue under the fluorescents when it was slicked back like now, damp, clean, and cool as ever.

"I don't do foreplay," he said. "I do exits."

"Great," I muttered. "Then you can leave first after your media slot."

He held my gaze just a moment too long. "Sure. Just say when."

I blinked. That had sounded... loaded. Or maybe I was reading into it. He often looked at people in that calculating, calm, vaguely threatening way that didn't make sense until hours later. He always seemed to know so much more than everyone around him. Or maybe he was just really good at pretending.

Me too.

The guys filtered into the lounge one by one. I followed, clipboard in hand, headset snug, pretending my skin wasn't prickling every time one of them got too close.

Roan sat on the edge of the leather couch, answering questions like a man who'd studied diplomacy in another life. Focused. Steady. Unreadable. But when the reporter leaned in—too close, too friendly—I caught Roan's eyes flick toward me. Fast. Flicker of something. Then gone.

Jay went next. Efficient. Dry humor. Didn't crack once. But when I handed him a mic, his fingers brushed mine—deliberately or not—and the contact crackled up my arm like static.

Rhett was last. Always the wildcard. Shirt still open, energy turned up to eleven. He threw his arm around my shoulder between interviews like he always did—but this time it lingered. Warm. *Heavy.*

"You okay?" he asked, mouth near my ear so no one else could hear.

I stiffened. "What do you mean?"

He paused, smile faltering for half a second. "I mean… you good? You've got that whole *Ice Queen with a secret* vibe dialed up to max."

I stepped out from under his arm, brushing him off with a laugh. "If I had a secret, you'd be the *last* one I'd tell."

"Ouch," he said, but there was something like concern under the theatrics.

By the time the interviews were wrapped, I felt like I'd run a damn marathon. And the worst part was nothing *had* happened.

No one said anything weird. No one looked at me like they knew. No sudden scent-spiral. No forced dominance. No accidental bonding marks or heat triggers or primal chase initiated by a coffee spill.

Just the team. Being the team.

And yet…

My head felt too full. My pulse kept stuttering. And every glance from one of them—Roan's flicker, Jay's pause, Rhett's weight at my side—felt like I was walking a wire I couldn't see the end of.

Paranoia. Had to be.

They'd always flirted. Always hovered too close. Always bantered and played and never crossed the line.

I was the one changing, not them.

But I also knew this wasn't even the hard part.

That came soon.

When the clock ran out.

When the real instincts kicked in and I stopped being able to pretend.

I was halfway through collecting the mic packs and mentally reciting my to-do list—schedule edits, budget approvals, cry in a closet somewhere—when the air changed.

Not dramatically. Not like a thunderclap or a scent spike. Just a *shift*. A pause in the noise. Like the room took a breath—and didn't exhale.

I looked up.

And there he was.

Walking through the open lounge doors like he owned the place, even though he hadn't worn our jersey in five years.

Beckett Rylan.

Former Howler. Now captain of the Bay City Vultures. Rival team. Big name. Bigger ego. Even bigger scent—dark cedar and ozone, the kind of alpha musk that belonged on magazine covers and late-night scandals.

He had the kind of face that made photographers forgive their lighting—handsome in a rough-edged, too-many-fights sort of way. A nose that had clearly met more than one right hook and lost. Jaw shadowed with stubble, mouth carved for sin, but the eyes ruined any illusion of softness—hard, assessing, always looking for an angle.

His grin slid toward me the moment our eyes met. Slow. Knowing. *Sharp.*

"Foster," he drawled. "Still looking like trouble in heels."

Every nerve in my body screamed not to react. I smiled —professional. Smooth. Like I hadn't just felt the tension in the room spike by a hundred degrees.

"Rylan," I said evenly. "Still not cleared to speak without a media handler, I see."

He laughed, deep and lazy. "Some things never change."

Behind me, I practically *felt* Roan shift his weight. Subtle. Controlled. But I didn't have to look to know his jaw had locked tight.

Rhett, less subtle, stepped up beside me like he might physically block Beckett from getting closer. "What the hell are *you* doing here?"

Not for the first time, I was grateful for the heels on my boots. I needed to get taller ones. It kept them from towering, especially when they went all alpha like Rhett was now. His personality seemed to flood around me, making him seem even bigger, stronger... *hotter.*

Beckett lifted a hand, mock-innocent. "Easy, goalie. I come in peace. Marchand invited me."

Of course he did.

Adrien Marchand loved a spectacle—and Beckett *was* a walking PR headline. Bringing him in during playoff press week? Classic power move. Even if it was a reckless one.

I put on my best diplomatic smile and stepped between the testosterone minefield before it exploded. "Well, if that's the case, welcome back. You're just in time to charm the press. They're still packing up."

He winked. "Didn't know I needed an audience to see you again, but hey—bonus."

Don't react. Don't engage. Don't let him scent blood in the water.

Jay moved next, quiet and precise, his eyes tracking Beckett with a chill I hadn't seen in him before.

"Thought you burned this bridge on the way out," Jay said coolly.

"Thought you were mute," Beckett shot back.

Jay smiled, razor-sharp. "Only when I'm bored."

Roan was still silent, but I could feel the tension radiating off him like heat. His shoulders drawn, his stance just a little wider. If Beckett noticed—and of course he did—he didn't seem intimidated.

He just looked back at me.

Like he could *smell* something.

Like he knew I was a little off. That the balance I held so tightly was slipping just enough to be interesting.

I took a breath and shifted my stance, reclaiming control. "You're welcome to stay for the rest of the media rounds, Beckett, but only if you keep out of the way."

"Wouldn't dream of interfering," he said, flashing teeth. "Just here to observe. Maybe stir the pot a little."

He turned and walked toward the press pit like he belonged there, like he hadn't just set a lit match down in a room full of gas.

I glanced at Roan. His jaw was clenched, eyes locked on Beckett's back like he was calculating how fast he could check him into a wall without causing a PR crisis.

"Let it go," I muttered under my breath.

He didn't answer.

Rhett's hand twitched at his side, fists curling, but his voice was bright when he spoke. "If he breathes on you wrong, I'm breaking both his kneecaps."

I arched a brow. "Is that a goalie thing or just your love language?"

"Yes," he said flatly.

Jay was last to pass me as the guys filed out, still watching Beckett like he was waiting for an excuse.

When he brushed past, he murmured just loud enough for me to hear: "He's sniffing for changes."

My heart stuttered. But I didn't flinch. Didn't pause.

Just stood there, spine straight, breath shallow, smile sharp even as I kept silently counting the hours until this week was over.

The boys filed out in a loose pack, leaving the room ten degrees colder in their absence, and somehow Beckett still managed to take up all the air.

He didn't follow. He lingered by the press table, casually flipping through a branded press booklet like he actually gave a shit.

One of the junior reporters from a local sports blog hovered nearby, badge tilted, mic clutched a little too tightly.

I saw it coming before she even opened her mouth.

"Mr. Rylan—just a few quick questions? For our coverage on the playoff dynamic and your former role with the Howlers?"

He smiled, teeth like a wolf in a well-tailored coat. "Sure. Anything for the home crowd."

His voice dropped into that rich, media-polished alpha tone that always came across well on camera and even better in clickbait quotes. The reporter swooned a little—visibly—and I resisted the urge to roll my eyes hard enough to sprain something.

The easiest journalists were the betas. They could probe and press without aggravating the situations. Omegas, when they weren't in heat and their partners didn't mind, were good for eliciting less *ethical* reactions. Particularly if they wanted to set the players up.

I preferred the alpha journalists, though. They didn't play these stupid games. They just pissed off their targets to get the clickbait they wanted. It was why I was so damn careful about *who* I gave credentials too.

"I imagine it's strange being back," Molly prompted.

She didn't carry much of a scent mark at all. Neutral beta. Though she was cute. "Especially with your new position across the ice. Any tension with your former teammates?"

Beckett's gaze flicked to me. *Lingered.*

"Let's just say... the temperature's different," he said. "But some things are worth the heat."

The reporter blinked. "Could you clarify—"

"I'm sure he *could*," I cut in smoothly, stepping forward with my best 'wrangle the chaos' smile. "But I'll be reviewing all quotes before they go to print, per Marchand's media policy."

Beckett tilted his head, amused. "Still cleaning up after us, huh?"

"Someone has to be the adult in the room," I said sweetly.

Before he could reply, a new voice joined the room—smooth, expensive, and laced with calculated authority.

"Wren. Beckett. Excellent," said Adrien Marchand, owner of the Snowvale Howlers and professional puppet master. "Just the two I was hoping to find."

He glided into the lounge like a man who'd never once been denied anything. His coat was cashmere. His shoes were suede. His smile didn't reach his eyes.

"We're due in the owner's box for lunch," he continued. "Come."

I opened my mouth to politely decline, already bracing for my out: work, scheduling, blood pressure, but Marchand lifted one manicured hand, already anticipating me.

"I need you there, Wren. Beckett's return needs framing. Context. You're the best at shaping narrative into digestible bites."

His *return.*

"He's coming back to the team?"

"Maybe," Beckett said, his breath teasing my ear as he leaned a little too close to me.

"That's why you and I are going to have lunch with him. You're going to help me persuade him." There it was. The compliment as a command. The leash in a velvet glove.

I forced a breath through my nose. "Of course."

"Excellent." He turned, already walking. "Let's not keep the chef waiting."

Beckett smirked at me as we followed. "You always were the one holding the leash around here."

I shot him a look. "Keep testing me and I'll tighten it." *Until it strangles you.* I didn't add that last part out loud though.

His grin widened. "You promise?"

I didn't answer.

Mostly because I wasn't sure if my next words would be professional or a snarl.

I still had a couple of days to go before I was officially a problem.

THREE

RHETT

I should've been feeling good.

Practice was clean. Interviews were smoother than usual. I hadn't punched anyone.

And yet, walking down the hall away from the press lounge, my whole damn body was buzzing like I'd missed something big.

Jay was quiet beside me, which wasn't unusual. What *was* unusual was the way he kept glancing back over his shoulder.

"Spit it out," I said finally, stripping off my jersey and half-tossing it at the laundry cart.

He didn't answer right away. Just slowed his steps and tilted his head slightly, like he was tracking a sound no one else could hear.

Then he said, low, "Did she smell... different to you?"

That stopped me dead.

I looked at him, heart already picking up speed. "Wren?"

He gave a small nod.

I tried to laugh it off like I should've. "She always smells good. That's kind of her thing."

"That's not what I meant," Jay said, voice flat. "Not perfume. Something else."

I opened my mouth. Closed it again.

Because the truth was, I'd noticed it earlier too. Not strong. Not like someone in heat—or at least, not like any heat I'd ever scented before.

Just... a pull. Subtle. Magnetic. Dangerous in a way I didn't have language for.

That intoxicating aroma had been coming from *her*.

"Could be nothing," I said. Even I didn't believe it.

Jay shrugged, but it looked more like he was mentally filing it away to dissect later. I'd seen him do that before games—take mental notes on opposing players like he was pre-writing how to dismantle them.

"Maybe," he said. "But Beckett noticed it too."

I clenched my jaw. "Yeah. I saw."

We didn't need to say more than that. We *hated* Beckett Rylan. Always had.

Not just because he was a dirty player or a smug asshole or the kind of alpha who walked into a room like he owned it and left it smelling like trouble.

No—we hated him because of the way he used to look at Wren when he still wore our jersey.

Like she was prey.

Roan met us at the end of the corridor, already half-dressed in civvies, arms crossed over his chest. He didn't ask what we were talking about. He didn't have to. "You two done over-analyzing?" he asked, cool and sharp.

Jay lifted one brow. "You noticed it too."

Roan didn't answer. His mouth pressed into a tighter line.

I stepped in. "She just... felt off. Not in a bad way. Just—different."

"She's under a lot of stress," Roan said. "Marchand's pulling media stunts. Playoffs are close. It's her job to keep this thing from blowing up."

"That's not what this is," I muttered. "You felt it."

Roan turned away. "Doesn't matter what I felt. She didn't ask us for anything."

"That's not the same as saying she doesn't need us," I shot back.

He didn't look at me. "If we cross a line—"

"We're not animals, Roan."

Jay didn't say anything, but his gaze flicked sharply to the stairwell at the other end of the arena and the door opening at the top.

Then I saw her. Wren. Her dark coat sharp against the neutral tones of the arena halls. Head held high, tablet in hand, stride clipped and professional as always in her knee-high boots that always looked damn good on her.

And right beside her?

Beckett.

Flanking her on the other side—*Marchand.*

I stilled.

The way Beckett leaned just a fraction too close. The way he was smiling like he knew something we didn't. The way Wren's spine stayed too straight, like she was bracing herself through the whole thing.

Roan must have tracked what I was looking at. His body tensed, subtle but unmistakable.

"Where are they going?" I asked.

"Owner's box," Jay said.

"For lunch," Roan added. His voice was flat, but his fists were clenched at his sides.

"Did she agree to that?" I asked. "Or is she being used to spin whatever dumbass narrative Marchand's cooking up this time?"

None of us had an answer for that.

And none of us moved.

We just stood there—three guys who'd spent years pretending we didn't notice her. That we didn't *feel* anything. That it was all just banter and team dynamics and maybe a crush or two we'd outgrow.

But right now?

Right now, I wanted to storm up there and plant myself between her and that smug bastard like a goddamn wall. Judging by how tense Roan was next to me, I wasn't the only one.

Jay broke the silence first. "You still think this isn't our business?"

Roan didn't answer.

Because deep down, he had to know—something was shifting. It wasn't just Wren.

We stood there too long until all three were out of sight.

None of us said anything for a beat—not until the elevator doors swallowed them up.

Then Jay said, "We staying or heading out?"

Roan ran a hand down his face. "We're grabbing lunch."

That wasn't what he *meant* though. It was dismissal. A clean cut.

"Seriously?" I said, turning to him. "You saw that little power play Marchand just pulled. You're the captain. If he's trying to woo Beckett back to the Howlers, you should be in that room."

Roan didn't blink. "No."

"You don't think it matters?"

"I think showing up uninvited gives Marchand exactly what he wants."

Jay tilted his head. "You could at least call. Or text. Plant a seed. Let him know Beckett's not welcome here."

Roan's jaw tightened. "No."

There was that damn word again.

Jay squinted. "Why the stonewall?"

Roan's answer came like a slap. Quiet, sharp, undeniable. "Boundaries."

I barked a short laugh. "You're kidding."

He wasn't.

"I'm not feeding Marchand's ideas," Roan said. "Beckett being here might be nothing. A PR favor, a photo op. If I react, it makes it *something.*"

"What if it already *is* something?" I shot back. "You know how this works. If Beckett's sniffing around, Marchand's got a reason. Wren's being dragged along for the optics. Again."

Jay crossed his arms, still cool, but watching Roan carefully now. "You're not wrong. But Rhett's not wrong either. This feels off."

Roan shook his head, stepping back like that would create enough distance to keep everything tidy. "She's not ours."

That stung more than it should've.

"You think I don't know that?" I snapped. "You think I'm trying to *claim* her?"

Roan didn't answer, which meant he didn't believe it either.

I paced a few feet, hands flexing at my sides. "Fine. If you won't poke the bear, I will."

Roan's head snapped toward me. "Rhett—"

But I was already pulling out my phone.

Jay raised a brow. "What are you doing?"

"Calling in a favor."

"From who?"

"Sabrina. She's working press for CBC this week." I thumbed through my contacts and hit the dial. "Just a little curiosity call."

Roan looked like he wanted to snatch the phone out of my hand. "Do *not* stir shit right now—"

I held up a finger as the call picked up. "Brina." Her sharp indrawn breath was so audible, I could almost *smell* the arousal. Not possible over the phone. Also, not the point… I didn't need a hookup. In fact, I definitely didn't *want* one with *her* either. "Hey, hey, relax—it's not one of those calls. I just had a quick question. Off the record."

Jay mouthed *off the record,* like that ever meant anything. I ignored him as I waited for Brina to get it together.

"Off the record?" The skeptical note in her voice definitely carried more than a hint of distrust.

"Yep. Off the record. You didn't hear anything from me and you aren't getting any quotes either."

"Uh huh," she said slowly. "Just a little chat between friends?"

Oh, she was intrigued. "Yep. You got time for me?"

"No time like the present." Got her.

I kept my tone light. "You hear anything about Beckett Rylan maybe jumping ship? Word around here is Marchand's rolling out the red carpet. Thought the Vultures were riding him all the way to finals, but hey—maybe he's got other plans?"

A pause.

Then a quiet, "Wait, what?" Oh, I had Brina's number.

There was definitely *relish* in her voice despite the way she tried to smother it.

"Oh yeah," I said, oozing charm like syrup over a blade. "He's up in the owner's box right now. Marchand's being all mysterious. Wouldn't *want* anyone to think he was stabbing his current team in the back, though... unless, y'know, there's a contract already signed. Then it's old news."

Another pause. The sharp indrawn breaths, and equally harsh exhales betrayed her excitement. Yes, Brina was panting after the story the same way she did when I had edged her orgasms.

"...I'm gonna need to make a few calls."

Huh. That was wild. Normally the sound and the thought it provoked would entice me. She was fun enough in bed, but nope... My dick didn't even twitch. Weird.

Still, I grinned. "Appreciate you. Lunch on me if it hits the wire first."

Click. She didn't even bother to respond. Just hung up.

Roan looked like he wanted to strangle me. "You didn't just do that."

I slid the phone into my pocket. "Relax—I didn't say a thing. Just asked a question."

"You dropped a bomb." Roan's voice went quiet and hard, the kind of quiet that smells like war. Being alpha didn't mean we were above trying to throttle each other; it just meant we could usually laugh about it later. I wanted to sock him—good-natured rage, not lethal.

"Not my fault if it blows up," I said, like it was the most casual thing in the world.

Jay let out a low whistle, half-impressed. "If Beckett doesn't have a contract yet, he'll be pissed."

"Good." I didn't want that douchecanoe back on the ice or the team or anywhere that brought him near us much less Wren. Then again, if I accidentally broke his ass during practice...

Roan was already shaking his head, but I didn't miss the glimmer of reluctant approval in his eyes. Just for a second.

Sure, maybe I crossed a line. That was on me. I'd take the fallout from it.

But I also wasn't going to sit around while Marchand played chess with *her* like she was just another piece on the board. I used to think he was a tough alpha, a tough businessman, and even tougher owner.

I used to respect the hell out of him too. But the past couple of years?

I'd started to notice how often he pulled Wren in to "fix" things. Not just clean up our image or our statements or our messes. The last person I'd expected to see in the midst of our post-playoff win orgy two years prior had been Wren, but there she was walking through that minefield of hedonistic scents in her prim skirt, button-down blouse and jacket so straight and pressed that it practically threatened any wrinkle that wanted to muss her up.

The attraction that hit me at that moment had been delivered with a mallet.

The protectiveness that followed it, though, had threatened to drown me. How dare Marchand pull her into that... How dare he bring her somewhere she might have been mistaken for the entertainment...

I'd abandoned my partner mid-coitus and strode across the room, dick still wet, and the look Wren had favored me with had almost made my balls shrivel up into my body. Most guys would probably have crawled off with their tail between their legs, I was made of a lot sterner stuff.

Or maybe I was just stubborn as fuck. I'd grabbed a

towel, wrapped it around my waist and become her shadow to keep her safe until she was done.

No one was allowed to touch her. Not then. Not now.

I'd kill Beckett Rylan first.

No ands, ifs, or buts about it.

"So..." Jay said slowly. "Lunch?"

FOUR

WREN

The owner's box at Howlers Arena looked like every expensive room owned by a man who wanted people to think he didn't *need* to show off. Glass walls. A quiet, panoramic view of the ice. Sleek black furniture. A buffet catered by whatever private chef Marchand had on speed dial this month.

It was quiet.

Too quiet.

I kept my tablet in front of me like a shield, scrolling through media schedules and pretending I didn't feel Beckett Rylan's eyes on me.

He sat opposite me at the long table, legs spread wide, one arm draped over the back of his chair like he was holding court. His suit was perfect, his ruddy-brown hair artfully tousled, and that shit-eating grin of his hadn't slipped once since we walked in.

Marchand sat at the head of the table, wine glass in hand, smile thinner than usual. Calculating. Relaxed in the way only rich predators could be.

"You've done well for yourself here, Beckett," he said

smoothly, lifting his glass. "Captain of a playoff-bound team. Clean PR record—well, mostly."

Beckett laughed, low and warm. "You know me. I aim to impress."

I didn't look up from the tablet. "Funny. I thought you aimed to get suspended every other game."

"I missed your mouth, Foster." He chuckled, low and throaty, with an edgy kind of sensuality that made most women throw their panties at him.

Most women. Thankfully, I wasn't most. I had never been and would never be one.

I didn't flinch. "You won't when I start using it."

That earned a low laugh from Marchand. "Always sharp. You two had such... interesting chemistry back in the day."

My stomach tightened. There it was. The first thread pulled. More than once, Marchand had put me in charge of keeping Rylan from going off the rails. Too many read that as we were dating. We had not.

"This is a professional lunch," I said calmly. "I'm here to make sure any quotes that come out of it won't require a mop and a PR fire extinguisher."

Beckett leaned in just slightly, and God, he smelled like cedar, smoke, and bad history.

"Can't we have both?" he asked. "It's been a while, Wren. You look good."

I finally looked up. Made eye contact. Held it.

"One, you're in a public arena," I said. "Flirting with the Howlers' PR lead while still under contract with the Vultures. So unless you're planning on pissing off two teams in one afternoon, I suggest you cool it."

"And two?" Rylan all but dared me to continue.

He needn't have bothered. "We've never had anything *but* a professional relationship. That isn't changing. Period."

Marchand sipped his wine, perfectly content to let the tension build.

That's when it hit me. This wasn't just a PR reunion.

Marchand wasn't dangling a contract in front of Beckett.

He was dangling *me*.

My pulse jumped, but my face didn't move.

"Let's not pretend we're here to reminisce," I said lightly before I shifted my attention to the real predator in this room. "What do you need, Adrien?"

Marchand set down his glass with a soft clink. "I need headlines that make people forget how many injuries we've racked up. I need a narrative shift. Drama. A return to roots. Our bad boy coming home, perhaps. And you—" he gave me a smile so polished it should've come with a warning label—"you've always known how to spin chaos into gold."

My skin went tight.

Beckett smiled at me like he'd already been promised something.

I sat back in my chair, carefully crossing one leg over the other. "Bringing back a player who left under more than a bit of bad blood as well as a cloud of controversy is not a simple re-entry. You'll need a full brand reset. Interviews. Fan engagement. Rebuilding trust."

"I have full faith in your ability," Marchand said.

Of course he did.

Because I wasn't just the handler.

I was the bait.

Beckett's return wasn't about stats or strategy. It was about headlines. Attention. Familiar tension. Somehow, I didn't doubt that Marchand was betting that the *chemistry* he kept hinting at would be enough to close the deal.

Beckett watched me in that way he always had—too direct, too amused, too sure of himself. Like he knew something I didn't.

I pressed my fingers to my tablet screen to ground myself.

This wasn't new.

I'd walked this edge before. I could do it again.

Even if this was actually the absolute *worst* time for this.

Even if my scent was changing.

Even if my skin felt too tight and my body too aware and the wrong alpha was sitting across from me smirking like he could *taste* the shift in the air.

I could do this.

Professional. Composed. No weakness. No tell.

Period.

Beckett didn't stop smiling as Marchand took a call and stepped out onto the terrace—some power play, no doubt, letting us stew alone together. Across from me, Beckett lounged in his chair like he owned the room.

Like he already knew how this story ended.

"So," he said, voice low and amused. "Are you the one who lured me back here, Wren?"

I didn't even blink. "Don't flatter yourself."

"Too late. You're here. Looking like that. Sitting across from me like you're not dying to ask what I'm thinking."

"I know what you're thinking," I said coolly. "It's the same thing you're always thinking."

He grinned. "Touché."

I went back to my tablet, scrolling through a schedule I already knew by heart. "This isn't high school. If Marchand brought you here to stir up headlines, then let's talk about what he's actually offering you. A one-season deal? Two? Is it PR or a real play for your contract?"

For the first time, something in Beckett's face shifted. The grin didn't fade, but his posture changed. Less cocky. More intent.

"I've got options," he said. "Vultures aren't exactly happy I'm here, but they'll live. Marchand's offering more than just a number on a paper. He wants a story. A comeback. Something flashy to drag the Howlers into a headline run. And maybe a little... unfinished business."

He said that last part while looking right at me.

I folded my hands over my tablet. "You have an agent?"

He gave a low laugh. "I've got *you.*"

I stared at him. Deadpan. Not playing. "That's not how this works."

"You're the best mouth this team's got." His tone dipped suggestively. "You always knew how to manage me. I can definitely tell that hasn't changed."

"That was never my job."

"It should've been."

There was something serious under his teasing now. Something that made my skin go cold even as the back of my neck prickled with heat.

He leaned forward, forearms on the table, eyes steady. "You're better than this place, Wren. You always were. The way you run this team's image? It's a joke they haven't made you GM."

"And yet here you are," I said. "Crawling back to the team that traded you."

"Because you're here."

That stopped me.

It shouldn't have. Beckett flirted like breathing. He didn't mean half the things he said, and the other half were designed to get under people's skin. But right now, something in his scent—sharp, focused, threaded with... something indefinable or at least something I did *not* want to define—made my stomach twist.

I hated that I felt it.

"I'm not here for *you,*" I said. "If you think Marchand's offering you a fair deal without an agent, you're either dumber than I thought, or a lot more desperate."

He tilted his head, watching me too closely. "You always take care of your players this personally?"

"Only the ones who're about to self-destruct in public."

"You care." He made it sound like a damn accusation.

"I manage." I clipped the words off, kept them absolutely neutral without a hint of skin in this game. His. Mine. Anyone's.

He smiled again, but it was slower this time. Not a smirk—something almost genuine. *Almost.* I refused to let him fool me.

"I missed this," he said softly. "You pretending not to care. Me knowing better."

My throat tightened. I hated that it almost sounded real. That my body felt hot and restless and wrong, and that the shift in my scent was no longer subtle—not in this enclosed space, not with an alpha tuned to me the way Beckett always had been.

But I kept my expression cool.

Professional.

Unshaken.

"You have five minutes," I said. "Then I need to get back to my team." I let the emphasis linger on the word *my.* Not enough to dare him to act, but more than enough to send the message. The Howlers were my team.

Not him.

He leaned back again, all lazy confidence. "Five minutes is more than enough."

I smiled, sharp and cold. "I've heard that about you." If he wanted to let his guard down and leave me an open shot, I would definitely take it.

That finally shut him up—for a beat.

Long enough for Marchand to step back inside, smiling like he hadn't missed a damn thing.

"Everything good in here?"

I stood, already gathering my things. "Depends on your definition."

Marchand looked at Beckett, then at me. "Let's reconvene soon. This is just the beginning."

I hated how certain he sounded.

How much he believed he'd just won something.

I was halfway to the elevator when I heard my name.

"Wren."

I turned, fixing the neutral expression back onto my face like armor. "Yes, Adrien?"

Marchand stepped into the hallway with the air of someone who'd already decided how the next week would go. His smile was pleasant. Polished.

Predatory.

"I'll need you on-call for the next few days," he said smoothly. "If things go the way I'm hoping, there will be optics to manage. Interviews to coordinate. Headlines to... massage."

Which meant he expected Beckett to accept the offer and wanted me ready to spin gold out of gasoline.

"Unlikely," I said. "I'm due for a few days off. Cleared it with admin weeks ago." Even with the playoffs *coming*. We had a little over ten days until the first playoff game. Originally, the down time was just so I could decompress before going hell for leather. We had *time*. Before it had been time I needed. Now, it was time I *had* to have. No way I could survive coming off them here. No way in hell. Not. Negotiable.

Marchand tilted his head slightly, as if surprised I'd say no to him. "You can push that, can't you?"

"I can't," I said, keeping my tone easy. "I've got appointments."

That wasn't a lie. Just not the kind he thought.

His smile faltered just a hair.

"Wren—"

"I'll be available for written statements if things move forward. Otherwise, I trust you'll use your years of experience and good judgment not to let him blow anything up before I'm back."

I pressed the elevator button and held his gaze. Few others could maintain with Adrien Marchand. I'd noticed that. Even the other owners, all alphas in their own rights, tended to backoff. Flick their eyes away, just once, but still away.

I didn't.

Never had.

Right now, he'd irritated me enough to make a point that he couldn't make me back down. It was the only thing alphas understood when they weren't getting their way. When the doors slid open, I stepped inside by walking backwards just *two* steps. Not once did I look anywhere else, even when his nostrils *flared* and a flush touched his face.

Two steps.

Then my phone *buzzed*.

Once.

Twice.

Then in a flood.

Time elongated, but Marchand's irritated inhale was enough. I won that skirmish.

I glanced down—half dreading, half curious—and saw the first message.

JANA (CBC):

> You need to get ahead of this—somebody just dropped Beckett's name as a Howlers prospect and it's going viral. Was it you??

I blinked. Just before the elevator doors closed, Marchand's phone went off.

So did Beckett's.

Simultaneously.

Shit.

Another message lit up my screen.

COLIN (TEAM COMMS):

> Wren. Damage control. NOW. CBC, TSN, and Vultures' press all blowing up. What the hell happened?

Then another—

The doors opened to the ground floor and I strode out, before I checked the next message.

JANA:

> Looks like Navarro stirred the pot? Some "innocent" question and now the rumor is everywhere. You better get ahead of this before it spirals.

I stopped dead in the hallway.

People were already looking at their phones. Whispers

floating. Somewhere nearby, a monitor was playing a segment I didn't even need to see to *know* it was about us.

About *Beckett*.

About him coming "home."

Too late to get ahead of it now.

The wildfire had already ignited.

I was standing in the middle of it, one step from meltdown, one tick from exposure, with exactly zero backup.

My suppressants were already trickling out of my system.

My control was slipping.

And now the press had blood in the water.

Perfect.

FIVE

JAY

The waitress had freckles and fangs, her braid looped into a knot at the base of her neck, and a wedding band that glinted every time she reached for a glass.

Omega. Bonded. Her arms were tatted up and on full display. Her scent said *happy*, *safe*, *fuck off*, *claimed*—in that particular cocktail only true mating could pull off.

So, of course, Rhett flirted with her anyway.

In the harmless way.

"Baby, if you ever want to switch teams—"

She whacked him with a bar towel before setting down our drinks. "Navarro, if you want to keep your kneecaps, you'll cut that out."

I smirked into my water. Roan gave a huff that might've been a laugh. Barely.

Rhett held up his hands. "I'm just sayin'. I'd treat you right."

"You'd treat me pregnant," she shot back, already turning toward the booth behind us.

Roan scowled. "Do you *ever* shut up?"

"Why would I?" Rhett said, sipping his soda like he hadn't just joked about knocking up a bonded omega in a public bar.

The place wasn't packed, but it was full enough and familiar. A half-dozen guys from the team were posted at the long high-top near the back, beers in hand, posture easy. That tension you only noticed when you *knew* the difference between casual slouching and barely-contained rage.

I noticed.

Then, I noticed everything. Especially the shift in the air when someone's phone lit up. A mutter. The scrape of a stool. Then—

"Yo, what the *fuck* is this?"

Roan looked up instantly. Rhett did too, slower, but alert.

I didn't move.

Yet.

The guy who'd spoken—Devon Laskey, winger, third-line grinder, built like a truck and just smart enough to get pissed when his spot felt threatened—was shoving his phone toward the others. Everyone leaned in.

Dammit.

I knew before they even said it.

Before Roan's phone buzzed.

Before Rhett's did.

Before mine did.

GROUP TEXT – TEAM PR & CAPTAINS:

CBC Sports BREAKING: Former Vultures captain Beckett Rylan spotted at Howlers Arena. Sources say reunion with PR manager Wren Foster may be part of the pitch.

There was a photo.

Of Wren, in the owner's box, gaze on Beckett.

Framed like a date. Posed like a fucking *scandal*.

"Oh, hell no," Devon growled. "They're gonna bring that asshole back? What, so they can bench me during playoffs? Is that the plan?"

"Relax," Roan said.

"Relax?" Devon snapped. "You see this shit? She's practically drooling over him. You think this doesn't make her look compromised?"

That did it.

Rhett sat up so fast his glass nearly spilled. "Watch your mouth."

"I'm just saying—"

"Say it again," Rhett said, voice low and sharp, dimples gone, brown eyes gone flat. "Call her compromised one more time."

Roan was already moving. "Enough."

But I was watching everything. The bar. The other guys. The waitress freezing mid-step, sensing the shift. The way Devon's nostrils flared as he scented the alpha heat rolling off Rhett and started bracing like he might throw a punch.

I stepped in before he could.

"Let's not pretend you care about Wren's professionalism," I said calmly. "You care about your contract."

Devon's gaze snapped to me.

Good.

"Don't make this about her," I added. "She didn't leak the story. She doesn't *want* him here."

"You don't know that."

"I know her better than you do." Of this, I had zero doubts.

My certainty made him blink.

Even Roan looked at me—quick, sharp. Like I'd said too much.

Maybe I had.

But I wasn't about to sit here and let Wren take the hit for a PR ambush we *all* knew was Marchand's style. That photo didn't leak by accident. And it sure as hell didn't leak from her.

Rhett was still bristling beside me, but at least he wasn't standing. Roan's jaw was tight enough to crack.

Devon muttered something under his breath and stalked off toward the back.

Roan finally broke the silence. "Well," he said. "That blew up faster than expected."

Rhett raked a hand through his hair, then cursed and leaned back in the booth. "She's gonna kill me."

I didn't disagree. But something else was tugging at me. Something colder. It wasn't just about Wren's image. Or Beckett's smug attempt at a return.

It was the scent shift I'd clocked earlier—subtle, strange, wrong. Not bad. Not even unpleasant.

Just... new.

When the food hit the table later, and none of us touched it right away.

Roan pushed his grilled chicken salad around like it had personally offended him. Rhett picked at fries and muttered to himself. I ate my burger, because someone had to act like a functioning adult.

None of us said what we were really thinking.

Wren.

That photo.

That smirking bastard sitting across from her.

The quiet calculation in Marchand's timing.

Ten minutes later, we paid and left, the late-afternoon

sun hitting too hard as we stepped out onto the sidewalk. The air was crisp, brittle with early-season frost. The kind of cold that teased snow but hadn't committed yet.

We walked a half block in silence.

Then Roan said, "You shouldn't have called the press."

Rhett didn't even look at him. "I asked a question."

"You started a fire."

"Which was already lit." Rhett finally turned to face him, steps slowing. "You really think Marchand wasn't planning this already? That Wren *wasn't* going to get dragged into it no matter what?"

"I think making it worse didn't help her."

"Yeah? And hiding away in your fucking corner does?"

Roan stopped walking.

Dead stop.

The two of them faced each other like opposing lines on the ice, shoulders squared, postures tight. People passed by without stopping, but the tension crackling between them was magnetic—pulling, stretching, sharp.

"She set boundaries," Roan said, voice low. "We *respect* them."

"And if respecting them means letting her get eaten alive by press, or Beckett, or *Marchand?*" Rhett's voice dropped too. Not volume, but his tone. Rough, raw. "You gonna keep standing back and letting her handle it all alone?"

"She's *always* handled it," Roan snapped.

"Yeah," I said, stepping between them before they could escalate further. "That's kind of the point, isn't it?"

They both looked at me.

Not angry.

Worse.

Guilty.

Roan turned first and started walking again. Slower this time.

I didn't move. Just stood there with Rhett while Roan created distance like he always did—quiet, cold, deliberate.

"He's not wrong," I said eventually. "You're not either."

Rhett made a frustrated sound. "Then what the hell are we supposed to do?"

I didn't answer.

Not right away.

Because the truth was, *I didn't know.*

Wren Foster was the most self-contained person I'd ever met. Not just cool under pressure—*untouchable*. She handled interviews like combat. Skated around flirtation like it was sport. Shut down rumors with a raised brow and the threat of a headline no one wanted to explain.

And her scent?

Controlled.

Perfectly modulated.

Never inviting. Never angry. Just... sharp. Clean. Professional.

The first time I met her, I'd assumed she was an alpha. The kind who chewed up anyone who tried to put a leash on her and spat out the bones.

She still felt like that now.

Even knowing what I knew—or what I thought I knew — and right now, something niggled at the back of my mind. A fact that wanted me to notice it but I couldn't quite see the shape of it.

It wasn't like alpha/alpha pairings didn't happen. Hell, alpha/beta did too, more than most people talked about. We were raised on mating charts and textbook biology, but instincts didn't always play by the rules.

Still.

Wren had never allowed *any* of us—even Roan—to get close enough to pretend.

Every line she drew was carved in stone. And every time one of us stepped too close, she pushed back. Calm. Brutal. Final.

And now?

Now, for the first time, she looked like she might *break*.

Roan was already a full half-block ahead, walking fast enough to outrun guilt, maybe.

Rhett finally shoved his hands in his pockets and exhaled hard. "I just want to help her."

I nodded. "Then stop making this about what *you* want."

He flinched.

Didn't deny it.

Didn't argue.

Just turned and followed Roan toward the arena.

I waited a beat before walking after them, eyes scanning every reflection in the glass, every alert on my phone, every tightening thread in the fabric of this team.

Because something was unraveling, and for once, I wasn't sure Wren could hold it all together.

Not without tearing herself apart.

Roan stalked through the front entrance like the glass doors had personally offended him. Rhett was two steps behind, radiating heat like a furnace with a blown seal.

I didn't rush to catch up.

They had fire.

I had questions.

More, something gnawed at the back of my mind like a dull toothache. A shadow I couldn't quite pin down.

I followed them into the lobby, let the motion sensor close the doors behind me, and slowed even more once we hit the east corridor. The heavy chill of the rink's back halls settled in—concrete, fluorescent lights, the faint chemical sting of gear soap and wax.

The guys peeled off toward the locker room, voices low and tight, likely picking up the same argument from earlier.

I didn't follow.

Not because I wasn't pissed.

I was.

But anger didn't solve things.

And it didn't explain the itch under my skin.

Where was she?

Everything I knew about her said she hadn't vanished. She didn't. It just wasn't who she was. Others might go for duck and cover when the shit hit the fans, not Wren. She orchestrated. She directed. She held the team like string between her fingers and made us all dance whether we knew it or not.

But right now?

She was *gone*.

And I didn't like it.

Not the silence.

Not the space she left behind.

Not the scent trail so faint it barely clung to the corners of the hallway.

I caught it near the PR office. Not the clean, crisp notes I was used to—but something older, deeper. Like ozone before lightning. Like leather in heat.

I paused. Breath stilled. That was the thing, wasn't it?

I wasn't an alpha. Never had been. I didn't ride the highs of instinct, didn't lose control in scent-drunk spirals or rage spirals or rut. My head was always clear. Always focused.

Except now it *wasn't*.

There was something different in her scent.

Subtle.

Wrong.

Or... maybe too right.

My hand brushed the edge of the office door. Locked. Empty. But her scent had been *here*, curling like smoke around the furniture, warming the air in a way I hadn't noticed before.

My pulse ticked up.

Annoying.

Unnecessary.

But not unfamiliar.

Because at the end of the day?

I fucking *liked* Wren. Not just respected. Not just wanted to protect. I liked *her*.

Liked the way she knew how to say no without ever saying the word. Liked that she was smarter than half the coaching staff combined. Liked the way she dressed like she could gut you with her heels and make you thank her for it.

So, yeah, I wanted to be her friend.

If she'd let me.

But lately...

Lately, something dark and feral had been whispering in the back of my skull. Quiet. Steady. Insistent.

Not just *be near her*.

Not just *protect her*.

Hunt her.

Taste her.

Explore every sharp edge and hidden place she'd never let anyone near.

I clenched my jaw and dragged my palm down my face.

Beta.

I was *beta*.

This wasn't supposed to *happen.*

But whatever she'd been hiding—whatever had been *shifting* in her, *rising*—it was starting to show. And if I could feel it?

The others would too.

Rhett already did. Roan had gone stiff the moment she entered a room. Even Beckett—

My fists clenched.

Beckett knew.

He'd always been a predator, but now?

He was circling.

And Marchand was using her to lure him in.

"Fucking hell," I muttered and turned on my heel.

She wasn't in her office.

But that didn't mean she wasn't somewhere in the arena.

And if something was wrong?

I'd find her.

CHAPTER

SIX

WREN

The ice was quiet this time of day.

No drills, no blades carving lines. Just the low hum of the refrigeration system beneath the surface and the occasional thud of a puck from a few rookies messing around at the far end of the rink.

I stood just outside the team bench tunnel, arms crossed, coat still on, the press corral half-visible from where I was positioned. Two cameras. One tablet. Four hungry little monsters in puffer coats pretending to check their notes instead of tracking me like prey.

Marchand stood beside me.

Too close.

His scent was clean and sharp—cologne, a hint of pine, and that underlying alpha static that never went away no matter how many boardrooms he sat in or how much silk he wore.

I didn't look at him. Didn't need to in order to know what he was about to say.

"I could have a word," he said calmly. "Shut it down."

Bad idea. "No."

His smile was mild. "No?"

"You shut it down, it becomes a story. You comment, it becomes a *statement*."

"Right now, it's a *rumor*. A damaging one."

"So let it burn out."

He turned to face me more directly, his posture casual but sharpened. "You've been compromised, Wren."

I felt it then, like a nerve had been pulled tight just under my skin. Too hot. Too fast. I should have had another week. But I couldn't ignore the changes surging through me. My blood hummed. My scent shifting inexorably.

I shouldn't want to snarl at him the way I suddenly *did*.

I kept still. I always did. But my voice dropped lower. Colder. The calm I'd perfected over a decade of suppression. "The only person in that box," I said, "with motive, opportunity, and access to that photo was *you*."

Marchand's eyes narrowed. Slightly. "Careful."

"No." I finally turned to face him. Met him head-on. "*You* be careful."

The air between us vibrated. Not loud. Not visible. But *charged*.

It wasn't alpha to omega anymore.

It was something else.

He straightened just a hair, and it felt like the kind of shift that preceded either a boardroom war or a blood-scented fight.

"Fire me," I said, voice still even. "If you think I'm compromised. Go ahead. Make that call. Leak *that* to the press while you're at it. Or—" I leaned in just enough to lower my voice further, just enough that it would reach *only* him, "you listen to the one person in this organization who knows how to manage *your* messes."

Silence greeted my challenge, though his jaw flexed.

It wasn't capitulation. Not yet. So, I pressed harder.

"They're going to speculate. That's what they do. They're going to say Rylan's leaving the Vultures, that he's signing with us, that we're offering him part of the fucking *branding* package. They're going to pitch stories and slap on fake sources and chase whatever headline gets the most clicks."

I stepped past him, slow and precise, until we stood side by side again.

Calm. Poised.

"Do you know what we don't do, Adrien?"

He didn't answer.

"We don't give them *anything else.*" I looked straight ahead, toward the rink. Toward the weight of the playoffs pressing against the boards. "We stay quiet. We stay steady. We talk about *our* players. *Our* wins. We let the Vultures spin out, not us."

His silence continued, however, it was no longer passive. Instead, it had turned calculating.

The press lingered fifty feet away, still pretending they weren't trying to see our dynamic or hear what we were talking about.

From the outside? We probably looked like two professionals discussing media angles and sponsorship deliverables.

No raised voices.

No flared tempers.

No blood in the water.

But inside the space between us, there was fire. Rage. An almost unbearable weight of *containment.*

I was shaking with it. Barely. But I was.

He didn't speak again until I turned to walk away.

"I assume," he said, his voice as flat and cool as mine had been, "you're still taking care of yourself, Wren."

I paused.

Not for long.

But long enough for him to know he'd landed the hit.

Then I smiled, sharp and blade-thin over my shoulder. "Of course, sir. Everything's under control."

Liar.

Marchand walked away without another word, his footsteps echoing sharp and even across the concrete. No backward glance. No parting threat. Just the cold, controlled exit of a man who thought he'd won something.

He hadn't.

Then again, neither had I.

I stayed by the boards until I heard the outer door click closed behind him, waiting five long seconds more to be sure he wasn't doubling back.

Only then did I let my shoulders drop.

Just for a breath.

Then I turned toward the press corral, where four bored-looking reporters tried not to look *too* eager.

One lifted a hand. "Wren—just a second?"

I offered a tired smile. "If you promise not to ask me about what Beckett orders for lunch."

They laughed—too easily. Probably relieved I wasn't slamming the gate shut in their faces.

The youngest of the group—an intern maybe, or one of the new podcast boys—asked first. "So is the Rylan rumor real?"

I blinked at him, all innocence. "You know how rumors are. They like to feel important."

A second voice—more experienced, more familiar—

jumped in. "But he *was* here today. With you. With Marchand."

"He stopped by." I shrugged like it meant nothing. "Our owner likes to talk business. He talks to a *lot* of people."

A third tried a sharper angle. "Any comment on the speculation that he's been offered a slot with the Howlers for next season?"

I smiled wider, smooth as ever. "My comment is that Roan Whitaker is laser-focused on this year's playoffs, not next year's headlines. And that's the only narrative we're running with."

Another flash of fake chuckles. Another round of polite nods.

I kept walking.

Out of the press' line of sight, the air was colder, emptier. The heels on my boots echoed in the hallway. My legs felt heavier than they should've.

Still time. I still have time.

It had only been a couple of weeks since I stopped taking my pills. The little white capsule that I'd lived on every single day for nearly ten years. Ten years of white-coat secrecy, of hush-hush refills and behind-closed-doors blood work. I'd timed everything down to the minute.

It shouldn't be shedding this fast.

My muscles felt lead-lined. My thoughts kept fracturing at the edges, every passing scent or sound pulling focus in ways I couldn't afford. My nerves were lit like fuse wire.

I turned the corner near the east hall—

And stopped short.

Jay was there.

Leaning against the wall, arms crossed. Casual. Sharp-eyed. Dangerous in a quiet, surgical way.

He pushed off the wall when he saw me, gaze sweeping

me head to toe like he was assessing for injuries no one else could see.

"What are you doing here?" I asked, keeping my voice easy. Light. The kind of tone I used when I wanted people to think I was fine. "Shouldn't you be upstairs icing Rhett and Roan's bruised egos?"

"I could ask you the same," he said. "You were supposed to be out of here hours ago."

My lips parted as I glanced at my watch, then shut again. I hadn't realized how long it had been.

He tilted his head slightly. Just enough that a lock of black hair fell into his eyes. "You okay?"

I blinked.

Normally, I would've laughed. Deflected. Told him I was insulted he'd even ask.

But something about the way he looked at me—so *direct*, so unflinching—it short-circuited the script in my head.

"I'm fine," I said anyway.

He didn't move.

Didn't blink.

Didn't *believe* me.

That made something in my stomach tighten in a way I didn't like. His scent, normally clean, neutral, just a whisper of spice beneath steel, hit me too hard. Like I'd stepped too close to a furnace without realizing it was on.

I swallowed.

Hard.

Jay was a beta. There wasn't supposed to be a reaction. Not from me. Not from him. He was the *safe one*. The one who didn't crowd, didn't posture, and didn't pull at my instincts in that dangerous way alphas did.

But now?

Now I could *smell* him.

Not just clean and sharp, but warm. Alive. Inviting in a way I had no business noticing.

I turned my head slightly, trying to blink the weight off my vision.

"Don't look at me like that," I said.

"Like what?"

"Like you're waiting for me to fall apart."

"I'm not." His voice was low. Controlled. "I'm waiting to see if you're going to ask for help before you do."

Goddamn it.

My throat went tight. Just for a second.

That wasn't fair. That was *too close.*

"I don't fall apart, Jay."

"No," he said softly. "But you might *implode.*"

That hit harder than I could have imagined.

I looked away before he could see whatever flickered across my face. My skin felt too thin. My control was too brittle. His presence—his scent—too loud in the air between us.

"You should get back to the team," I said, turning slightly, putting a few inches of distance between us. "We've got enough mess on our hands without adding another headline."

"I'll walk you out."

It wasn't a question.

For once, I didn't argue.

My rapid decline seemed to be spiraling faster and faster with each passing moment. The heat under my skin was starting to boil. And I didn't know how many more minutes I had before it started showing in more dangerous ways.

I was glad I'd packed up before Marchand summoned

me to the ice. My laptop, files, tablet—everything was already stashed in the back seat of my car, zipped away in a sleek black bag I could pretend meant I had plans to work from home or wherever.

I didn't.

Not tonight.

Not tomorrow either, probably.

Maybe not for a few days.

But the illusion mattered, even if it was just for myself. I kept the keys tight in my hand and let the echo of my heels against the parking structure floor be the only sound I focused on.

Jay walked beside me, silent.

He always seemed to know when not to talk.

Still, I caught him watching me from the corner of his eye. His hands were in his pockets, but his shoulders were set just slightly tighter than usual. He was thinking. Calculating. The way he did before big games or before Roan lost his temper or Rhett did something reckless.

I almost asked what he was trying to solve.

Instead, he spoke first.

"So," he said mildly, "days off, huh?"

I arched a brow but didn't look over. "That's what the calendar says."

"Planning something exciting?"

"A three-day nap, maybe."

"Wild."

"I'm known for my partying."

A pause. The silence stretched again, then—

"You going anywhere?"

I could feel him watching me again, not as casual this time.

I kept my expression neutral. "Not far."

"Hot springs? Cabins? Hotel with room service and blackout curtains?"

"Sounds expensive."

"Sounds earned."

I allowed a faint smirk. "You always dig this hard when people take time off?"

"No," he said. "Just you."

That pulled a flicker of something across my chest. I wasn't sure if it was warmth or warning. Probably both.

"I'm leaving late," I said, changing lanes in the conversation. "I should get on the road."

"You shouldn't be driving if you're—"

I stopped. Turned. "If I'm what?"

His jaw flexed, just once.

But he didn't finish the sentence.

Didn't have to.

We were at my car now—corner space, back edge of the lot. Tucked into shadow.

That's when I saw it.

A square of white, tucked under the wiper blade. Not the official arena parking kind. No logo. Just a thick card folded in half and wedged like a cliché.

I didn't need to touch it to know who it was from.

But I did anyway.

My stomach clenched before my fingers closed around the paper.

Rylan.

His handwriting was unmistakable with its tight, sharp slashes, like everything he said was either a challenge or a dare. I didn't read it.

I didn't need to.

I tore it straight down the center, then again, again, again—until it was nothing but scraps between my fingers.

When I turned to Jay, he didn't say anything. Just held out his hand like he'd been waiting for me to break.

I handed him the pieces.

He slipped them into his coat pocket without a word.

That... did something to me.

Took the last thread of control I was holding and pulled it too tight. It wasn't even *what* he did—it was *how*. Quiet. Solid. No demand for explanation. No pity. Just a quiet offer to carry what I couldn't hold. Didn't want to hold.

And it nearly undid me.

I swallowed hard, but the lump in my throat didn't go anywhere.

"Thanks," I managed. "For walking me out."

His eyes didn't leave mine.

There was something *fierce* behind that quiet now. A low thrum of tension. Not protective, exactly.

Possessive.

I broke the eye contact first.

Not because I was afraid.

Because if I didn't go now, I was going to fall apart in a parking garage with someone who saw *too much*.

My hand found the door handle. I pulled it open, every movement sharper than I meant it to be—because *too much* was still too close.

"Wren," Jay said, voice low.

I froze.

Just for a second.

It was stupid how hard it was to glance back at him—like the motion alone might unravel me. But I did it. I made myself do it. I even curved my mouth into something like a smile. Managed to summon a flicker of dry humor, because that was what I *did*.

"Yes?"

His dark eyes were steady. "I'm here, if you need me."

No push. No pressure. No expectation.

Just that rare, dangerous kind of kindness that didn't ask anything in return.

"Remember that, okay?"

God.

It hit harder than if he'd reached out and touched me. Harder than scent. Than instinct. Than any primal drive still clawing under my skin.

And I wanted to joke—I *wanted* to deflect with something clever and biting and perfectly dismissive, the way I always did.

But I didn't want to make fun of what he'd just given me.

So I went with the truth. Quiet and small and barely hanging on.

"I will," I said. "I'll remember."

It wasn't much.

But it was all I had.

I climbed into the car, shut the door, and started the engine without letting myself look back.

CHAPTER

SEVEN

ROAN

I was going to kill Rhett.

Not in the fun, locker-room, "you dumbass" kind of way, either. No, this was more the *how many strings I would have to pull to have his phone banned from league press lists* kind of murder.

Because even hours later, the fallout from his little stunt hadn't slowed. My phone continued buzzing with updates—half speculation, half denial, and somehow all fire.

And for what?

Some ego-fueled tantrum over Beckett fucking Rylan walking into our rink?

Get in line.

I stood outside Marchand's office door, arms crossed, debating whether or not barging in without an appointment would be worth the blowback. The man had a knack for baiting power plays, and I wasn't in the mood to be tested.

Not when every bone in my body was telling me to do something else entirely.

63

Go check on her.

I clenched my jaw, forced the thought out of my head. It was pointless. She'd made it clear—again and again—that she didn't want that kind of attention. That we were *not* going to cross any of the lines she'd drawn.

But those lines hadn't accounted for Rylan. Or the headlines. Or the *look* in her eyes earlier.

Something was wrong. Deeper than PR, deeper than press.

I didn't need to scent it to know. Still, I didn't move. I wasn't going to disrespect her by pushing. No, I was just... going to make sure. Pivoting, I was already halfway down the hall, striding for her office.

Just a quick check. A knock on her door. A chance to offer—

"She's gone."

I turned even as I halted, immediately on edge.

Jay stood just down the hall, dark hair mussed from the wind, that same unreadable expression locked across his face.

"What?"

"She left," he said simply. "Car's gone. She packed up before she met with Marchand."

"When?"

"Ten minutes ago. Maybe fifteen."

I didn't move. Not at first. Rhett would've exploded—rushed out into the parking lot, scent wild and ready to fight a ghost. I held the reaction under my ribs like something sharp, pressing against bone.

"Did she say anything to you?" I asked.

Jay's gaze didn't flinch. "She said she needed to get on the road."

That was it. Not where. Not why.

No heads-up. No promise to check in.

She just left.

And the air in my lungs felt heavier for it.

I rubbed the back of my neck, exhaling slow. "She say when she's coming back?"

"No."

Of course not.

"She looked..." Jay hesitated, then dropped his gaze for the first time. "Tired. She said she'd remember."

That made no sense.

But it sounded exactly like her.

I ran a hand down my face, thinking.

Remember what? To take care of herself.

This wasn't how she handled stress. She didn't bolt. She worked—gritted her teeth, filed statements, steamrolled press, kept the world from spinning out. *Leaving* was not her default.

Unless something was wrong.

Really wrong.

I didn't say any of that.

Instead, I asked, "Rhett know yet?"

Jay snorted softly. "Would we still be standing here if he did?"

Fair.

I stared at the empty hallway behind Jay. At the space where she *should* have been. Where I'd planned to find her —to talk to her. Not about boundaries or rules or any of the hundred reasons I kept my distance.

Just to ask if she was okay.

Now it was too late.

And the worst part?

I wasn't sure she *wanted* any of us to follow.

"Let's get out of here," I said instead of the myriad of other thoughts I had.

"What about Rhett?" Were we going to tell him? That was what he really meant.

"Not tonight." Mostly because I didn't want to deal with him. "If he does something stupid—"

"When," Jay corrected unhelpfully and I barely managed to restrain a glare. Jay wasn't being combative, just honest. Normally, his steady personality and vibe were more than enough to soothe me at my worst.

Not today.

Not growling, I said, "When he does something stupid, we'll have to manage the fallout and him."

"You're not in the mood." Without a hint of irony, he nailed it with one sentence, so I just nodded. We walked in silence back to the locker room. Rhett was on the phone, but when I glared he mouthed "my brother" and I blew out a breath.

Talking to his family was fine. If I caught him talking to the press, I might break his phone then his jaw. The rising tide of fury threatened to boil me inside out. I grabbed my gear from the locker before jerking my thumb at the door.

Jay nodded with a flick of a look at Rhett. He was gonna keep an eye on him for us. Good.

"See you guys tomorrow."

They had apartments in my building, all three of us owned the top floor. It gave us plenty of space, and security when we needed it. The separate apartments also allowed us our privacy when we wanted that too.

Right now, I needed it.

All the way to my SUV, however, I kept having to glance around. Cause there was a scent...

One I couldn't quite identify, but it tantalized and teased right there at the edge of my comprehension. It was also making me crazy.

Maybe I should call someone… there were plenty of beta girls out there who wouldn't mind a straightforward hookup. Maybe I could ease the ache in my stone hard cock, and get rid of some of this aggression.

No sooner did I get in the car than I dismissed the idea. As much as I could use the release, the idea of calling any of those women just didn't appeal.

"Focus," I told myself, resisting the urge to punch the steering wheel. "Focus on the playoffs."

Maybe if I said it enough, it would work.

THE NEXT DAY, the agitation under my skin wasn't any damn better. I stared at my phone for a solid minute. Her name sat at the top of my screen. Untouched.

No message typed. No call placed. Nothing but the weight of decision bearing down on my thumb like a trigger I wasn't sure I had the right to pull.

Just check in.

That's what I told myself. Simple. Professional. Polite.

But I knew better.

Calling her now wouldn't be a courtesy—it would be a line crossed. One she'd never forgive if I made the wrong move.

Fuck me, that was the *damn* problem.

I don't trust myself to make the right one anymore.

Not after dreaming about her all goddamn night. Dreaming about the half-curve of her knowing smile, the glint in her eyes when she put me in my place or even better, when she got Rhett. The husky sound of her laughter when something genuinely amused her. The razor sharpness of her tongue when she was *displeased*.

It had left me so damn hungry for her, I woke with my hand outstretched and a roar in the back of my head because she wasn't *there*. Wasn't where she should be. Where she belonged. Except... Except that Wren Foster had never once even seen my bed much less been in it. As attractive as she was, as playful and fun as she could be, that was a firm line she had always maintained. We could flirt, she would shut us down.

End.

Of.

Story.

All of a sudden, that was just not good enough. Fuck that ending. I wanted a better one. For her. For me. For us. I *wanted*...

That... that furious desire-fueled possessiveness was new. Too new. Too... consuming.

Before I could deal with that or even decide what to do with it, the locker room door cracked open and Ozzie stuck his head in. "Coach wants everybody on the ice. Ten minutes."

I nodded. He was already gone.

Jay had disappeared down the hall right after we got here, probably headed back to suit up. Rhett was god knows where, hopefully *not* talking to another reporter. And I was still here, with a phone in my hand and a choice I wasn't ready to make.

I dropped the phone in my duffel. Slammed the zipper.

We had a job to do.

Even if the walls were cracking under the weight of it.

PRACTICE STARTED STIFF AND FAST, like Coach felt the tension too and wanted to bleed it out early.

Didn't work.

The second the blades hit the ice, the mood soured. Fast.

Lines were sluggish. Energy was wrong. A couple of guys looked like they hadn't slept. A few others were just *pissed*.

And I didn't have to ask why.

Wren was gone.

For the first time in years, her absence wasn't logistics. It wasn't travel or a split meeting or one of her carefully compartmentalized "off-the-grid" days.

This was *visible*.

Speculated.

And some of these assholes thought they knew why.

"You see the damn photos?" Nate muttered when we skated by the boards. "Beckett and her, all cozy? Press calling it a 'quiet lunch between old friends.' Yeah, I bet."

I didn't answer.

Didn't need to. Jay, on the far edge of our formation, looked like he might actually snap his stick in half.

But it was Akshay, of all people, who cracked first.

During our fourth drill, after a missed pass and a bad check, he spun on Nate hard.

"Maybe if you paid more attention to puck control and less to Wren's love life, we wouldn't be eating shit out here."

Nate shoved him.

I got between them before it could escalate, arms out, voice sharp.

"That's enough."

Nate growled, low and hot. "She's supposed to be *our* PR lead, not getting cozy with some rival alpha who's about to take someone's contract."

The subtext hit the ice like blood.

His contract. Nate thought this was all about him.

I stared him down. "You think Wren's the one making those calls?"

"She's in the room."

"Then you should know better than to question her loyalty."

Nate's jaw ticked, but he didn't push further. He backed off.

Everyone did, eventually. We skated hard. Longer than usual. Coach pushed drills like he wanted someone to snap. He wasn't subtle.

But I didn't break.

I didn't yell. I didn't slam a stick or throw a punch or even check someone with a little extra weight.

I just did what I always did.

Held the line.

But that didn't mean I wasn't burning underneath it.

By the end of practice, my muscles were screaming, my shirt was soaked, and my patience was damn near gone. I waited until the locker room was loud again—banter, slamming lockers, a round of trash talk starting up between the rookies.

That's when I reached into my bag, grabbed my phone, and finally opened the message thread with her name on it.

Still blank.

Still silent.

Still hers.

You okay?

I typed it. Deleted it.

Tough day. Let me know if you need anything.

Deleted that, too.

Finally, I typed something else.

Keep your head down. We've got you.

I stared at it.

Simple. Unassuming. Safe. Yet still way too close to something that wasn't supposed to exist.

I hit send anyway.

Ten minutes and one shower later, the message still sat on my screen.

Unseen. Unread.

The locker room had settled just enough to be dangerous again—quiet enough that anything could ignite it. Towels snapped. Gear hit the benches. Cold water hissed through pipes and cracked open soda cans. The tension hadn't gone anywhere. It had just slipped beneath the surface like a shark.

Rhett stalked back in five minutes after I got back to my locker. Hoodie halfway off, face flushed, curls wild like he'd been running a loop of the arena—or pacing the fucking roof. His phone was in his hand, but he wasn't looking at it.

Not yet.

He headed straight to his locker, stripping the hoodie the rest of the way off before he dropped it on the bench. Sat. Didn't speak. Then he unlocked his screen. And it was like watching a bomb go live.

First, the silence. Then the inhale. Too slow. Too sharp.

Then the snap of his locker door slamming back against the hinge.

"She's *gone?*" His voice cracked against the tile.

Jay, still pulling on socks a few feet away, didn't look up. "I told you."

"You said she left," Rhett snarled, turning on him. "You didn't say she *left-left.*"

"She didn't tell me where she was going, Rhett. You think she's sending postcards now?"

I rose. "Cool it."

But it was too late.

"You don't get it," Rhett barked, stepping toward Jay.

Jay, credit to him, didn't move. Just lifted his head and looked right through him.

"I get more than you think," he said, voice cold as ice.

Rhett scoffed. "Yeah, sure. Coming from the guy who doesn't even feel heat—"

That's when Nate muttered something under his breath. Something low, bitter, and just loud enough.

"Maybe if you two weren't so damn obsessed, she wouldn't have run."

Rhett froze.

Turned.

"Say that again."

Nate stood, his own fists clenched, half dressed. "I said maybe she left because the rest of us are sick of being in the middle of your leash fight. You think she doesn't know how you two look at her? You think it's not *obvious*?"

The second he said it, I knew he regretted it.

But regret didn't stop fists.

Rhett launched.

I moved.

But not fast enough.

He slammed Nate back into the row of lockers, one fist gripping the front of his jersey, the other cocked high and trembling.

"Say it again," Rhett growled, teeth bared, scent flaring hard and hot. "*Say it again.*"

Nate didn't.

Not because he backed down—because I was between them now, one arm shoved into Rhett's chest, the other braced to hold them apart.

I met Rhett's eyes. "Enough."

His nostrils flared. Jaw tight. He didn't move.

"Let go," I said.

He didn't listen.

Jay stood beside me suddenly, calm as always, but there was something *sharp* in his stance now. Coiled. Ready.

"This isn't the way," Jay said quietly.

That got through.

Barely.

Rhett let go. Not with grace. With a jerk, like his own body betrayed him by listening. He stepped back, hands still twitching, eyes still lit with the kind of fury that made alphas dangerous.

Nate adjusted his jersey. "He needs to get his head on straight before playoffs."

"Shut up," I warned, and he did. Fast.

Rhett's chest heaved. His mouth opened—like he had more to say—but the words never came. Instead, he turned and walked out.

No bag. No hoodie. Just his keys in one hand and fury in the other.

Gone.

Jay looked at me.

I didn't say anything. Because *what the hell was there to say?*

We were unraveling.

Not because of the press.

Not because of Beckett.

Because Wren wasn't here—and none of us knew how to handle that without making it worse.

What I hated most was I couldn't protect her if I didn't know where she was. I couldn't help with... whatever she needed assistance with and though I had no evidence, a part of me was dead certain that she *needed* something.

Fresh anger ripped through my veins and I glared at the lockers. It took me a minute to get that wave of aggression under control, but by the time I did, the locker room was empty except for Jay.

He watched me with eyes as calm as a midnight pond on a still day. "Better?"

"No." That was the truth. "But I'll deal with it. Let's get out of here."

I dragged on my clothes in a hurry, ready to be out of the locker room, the arena—fuck the goddamn city. Jay snagged Rhett's hoodie and bag along with his own while I finished. Once I had my duffel and turned to face him, Jay lifted his chin.

"We could go look for her."

It was absolutely the last thing I expected him to say. "What?"

"We could go look for her," he repeated, not an ounce of emotion bleeding into his voice or shifting his stance.

Hunting her down crossed a line. We weren't invited and she hadn't even left us an in case of emergency notification. I glanced down at the still unread message on my screen.

"She's an adult," I said, reminding him. Reminding me. "Not really—"

"She's our friend," Jay said cutting me off. "We're worried about her. You're worried. Rhett's frantic. If we check on her and she's fine, she can be pissed at us. But we'll know."

He had a point.

"And if she isn't okay..." Jay didn't even have to finish that thought.

"Where the fuck do we start?"

CHAPTER

EIGHT

WREN

Less than twenty-four hours after I got to my destination, I'd already run out of things to organize.

Not for lack of trying.

The cabin was small, tucked into the side of a wooded slope just east of Yellowstone—barely a dot on any map, and even less on cell service. The snow made it beautiful. The silence made it perfect. The remoteness made it *safe*—from cameras, from gossip, from men with sharp eyes and sharper instincts.

But mostly, from myself.

I'd gotten in late the night before, half-frozen and fully wired from the drive. The first few hours alone had been easier than I expected—almost peaceful. There'd been no buzzing crowd, no scent-thick locker room, no weight of alpha gazes dragging across my skin. Just trees. Cold. Stillness.

I thought it would help.

I was wrong.

Because now, on day two, my skin itched. Not in the

way you scratch and move on—in the *bone-deep, nerve-bright, jump-out-of-your-own-body* kind of way. The kind that kept me pacing across the hardwood floor like a caged animal.

I wasn't in heat yet. I knew what that was. I'd *been* through that twice. The first time had been absolutely brutal, and the second had been a misery. Forty-eight hours of hell and eventually it passed. I'd started on the suppressants not long after that second heat.

Despite all these years, I hadn't forgotten the build-up, the excruciating experience itself, followed by the come down. This wasn't heat yet.

This was the build-up.

This was the beginning of what my body had been trying to do for years—shove past the drugs I'd force-fed it, rip down the walls I'd built, and flood me with everything I'd spent a decade pretending I didn't need.

My scent was already different.

I could smell it in the throw blanket I hadn't meant to curl up in the night before, in the collar of the worn hoodie I'd pulled out of my bag this morning. *Not theirs.* One of mine. Clean. Neutral.

But it didn't stay that way.

Everything I touched started to smell like *me* again—and I hated it. Not because I wasn't used to it, but because it felt... *loud.* Like I was shouting into the empty cabin, calling out to no one.

The worst part?

I kept *answering myself*.

I folded the same towel three times before I was satisfied with the corner. Rearranged the firewood. Sorted the snacks. Stacked the books I'd brought by topic, then by size, then color-coded the spines until I wanted to scream.

This wasn't nesting.

Not really.

I wasn't *fluffing pillows with purpose* or scent-marking surfaces like some omega fantasy story.

I was just trying to feel *normal.*

To keep moving before the ache swallowed me whole.

I hadn't slept more than an hour the night before. Couldn't. Every time I closed my eyes, my body kicked. Hot one minute. Cold the next. My jaw ached from clenching. My thighs ached from nothing at all. And my thoughts kept drifting back to the guys.

To Roan, arms crossed, always calculating.

To Jay, too quiet, too perceptive.

To Rhett—smiling like he wasn't constantly two steps from combusting.

The way they looked at me.

The way I wanted them to look at me again.

No.

I shut the thought down.

Walked to the kitchen. Opened a cabinet I'd already checked twice and stared into it like something new might appear. It didn't.

Outside, wind shoved snow across the windowpane in slow, silencing waves.

I pressed my palms to the edge of the counter and exhaled. Long. Shaky.

"I'm fine," I said to no one. "This is fine."

The problem was, I wasn't entirely sure who I was trying to convince. It was the lack of activity that was driving me mad. Work, I told myself. Get it done. There was plenty to prep for the playoffs. It was why I'd brought the laptop in the first place.

I managed half a page.

Maybe less.

I stared at the screen long enough for the cursor to mock me, blinking steady and bright in the middle of a sentence I didn't remember writing. My outline sat untouched beside me. The comms calendar was open, color-coded, and somehow still blurry.

None of it made sense.

None of it *mattered*.

The Howlers could set themselves on fire and I couldn't string three damn thoughts together right now. Every part of me was too aware of my own body—tight skin, flushed nerves, scent bleeding into the air with every breath. I couldn't focus. I couldn't sit still.

I shoved the laptop away and stood up again.

Shower number two.

The first had been this morning—early. Before the sun was all the way up. I'd scrubbed like it would clear my head, like the water could drown out the pulsing scent rolling off me, the one that had started curling its way into every soft surface I touched.

This one? This one was desperation.

The water was near-scalding. The steam fogged the mirror before I'd even stepped in. I braced one hand against the tile and stood under the spray with my eyes closed, trying not to think about how hollow my chest felt. How restless I was. How the heat didn't help the ache—it just *warmed it.*

The scent faded—*slightly.* Washed down the drain for now.

But not gone.

And not the only thing haunting me.

It started small. Like déjà vu.

The first time I met Roan, he'd just come off the draft.

Fresh-faced and pissed off for reasons no one could pin down. His rep came first—ferocious on the ice, dead silent off it. The only player Marchand bragged about like he'd landed a goddamn wolf king.

He walked into the room and every single person went still.

Even me.

Not because he was the biggest alpha I'd ever seen—but because he was *quiet*. Still. Calm like a blizzard before it broke.

But his scent?

God. His scent had wrecked something in me.

I hadn't even let it show. Not a twitch. Not a breath. But something in my chest had tilted sideways that day, and it *never really reset.*

It didn't help when Rhett and Jay came on a season later—both of them chaotic in their own way. Rhett was louder than life from the first handshake. Called me "boots" for a solid month and winked every time he got away with it. Jay, on the other hand, had barely said three words at first, but the way he *watched* everything, every shift of tone, every change in expression? It was surgical.

They weren't quiet about liking me. None of them were. Not even Jay, when you knew how to translate the silences.

But Roan?

Roan never said a word.

Not once.

Even when Rhett flirted too loud, when Jay made one of those dry comments that landed like a scalpel in silk—Roan just stood at the edge of the storm, arms crossed, watching.

Managing.

There I was, watching him right back.

I wasn't stupid. I saw it long before anyone else did—

the way Roan *eased* around them. How the hot-headed rookie who barked at refs and broke sticks on the ice suddenly stopped pacing. How he started laughing—*actually laughing*—when Rhett lost a glove mid-practice and yelled "naked hand" like it was a goddamn emergency.

Jay would roll his eyes. Roan would smirk.

The three of them were chaos and gravity. Orbiting each other like planets. Pulling everyone around them into their strange, perfect rhythm.

Including me.

I told myself I didn't care.

Most of the time, I *didn't*.

I had work. I had rules. I had a plan.

But the memories didn't give a shit about that.

Now, in this cabin, alone, exhausted and sore and strung out on a biological clock I couldn't hold off anymore—those memories were *everywhere*.

I left the shower and sat on the edge of the bed in a towel, hair dripping, laptop still open on the table across the room. My scent was back already. Warm. Sweet. Edging darker by the hour.

Not full heat.

Not yet.

But it was close enough that I couldn't lie to myself anymore.

I wasn't focused.

I wasn't fine.

I wasn't *alone* in my head—and that might've been the most dangerous part.

～

I DRANK another glass of water.

Third in an hour.

The giant flat I'd hauled in from the back of the SUV was half-drained now, bottles scattered like fallen soldiers around the cabin. Water was supposed to help. Hydration, balance, grounding. Or whatever bullshit mantra my doctor had tossed me before I left.

It didn't help.

Neither did the protein bar I chewed like cardboard, jaw aching, stomach curling away from the idea of food. I *wasn't* hungry. Not for that.

I paced.

The movie I'd tried to start was still running in the background—some indie romcom I didn't have the energy to absorb. Too many soft looks. Too much chemistry. Too much of everything I couldn't let myself want.

The blanket I'd wrapped around my shoulders fell to the floor again and I left it there.

My body was hot.

Not just flushed—but *hot*. Skin too tight. Too sensitive. Every movement against fabric scraped across nerve endings I didn't know I had.

Even the hoodie I'd put on earlier felt like too much now. I stripped it off and threw it across the back of the couch, one bare arm wrapping around my ribs like I could hold myself together.

Touch-hunger, they called it.

I'd heard other omegas talk about it, years ago. Whispered, half-mocking stories about their first heat after suppressants—how their brains short-circuited when they couldn't scent anyone else, couldn't feel the comfort of a bond or pressure of skin-on-skin.

I'd rolled my eyes at the time.

But now?

Now I couldn't sit down because the couch didn't *hold* me. Couldn't stop moving because the air was too empty. Couldn't stop *aching* because my body didn't want space—it wanted contact.

Not sex.

Not yet.

Just... *touch*. Heat. Scent. *Them.*

I closed my eyes and immediately regretted it.

Because I could *feel* them again.

Roan, all silent presence and iron will, scent like cold smoke and snow-damp cedar.

Jay—sharp, clean, quiet. A whisper under the chaos. A blade sheathed in silk.

Rhett—loud and sun-warmed, always moving, always two steps from wrapping himself around someone like it was his job.

My hands curled into fists. My breath caught.

This wasn't fair.

I'd fought so hard to keep distance. To be neutral. To stay *contained*. Yet, here I was and my body was rebelling like it had never agreed to any of those terms in the first place.

I made it to the bed out of exhaustion more than intent. Curled on top of the covers with another bottle of water beside me, half-finished. My legs tangled. My body burned. My thoughts refused to stay quiet.

The window was cracked, letting in a sliver of night air to cool the rising heat. I closed my eyes again and told myself I'd just rest for a minute. Just long enough to reset.

Sleep didn't come gently.

It came like drowning.

～

THE DREAM STARTED in the arena.

Empty. Echoing.

The lights above the ice humming like insects.

I stood barefoot at center rink.

And then they were there.

Roan first—helmet off, skates half-unlaced, watching me like I was the only thing in the building.

Jay, gliding silent from the bench, gloves off, eyes too dark to read.

Rhett, breathless and grinning, already close, scent thick and teasing, curling around my ankles like smoke.

"You ran," he said, brushing my hair off my neck. "You didn't have to run."

"I didn't—" My voice caught.

Jay's fingers grazed my wrist, feather-light. "You always run. Even when you're standing still."

Roan didn't speak.

He just stepped closer.

I *let* him. What was I doing? I was... oh, it was a dream. I didn't have to fight it. I didn't have to lie. I didn't have to keep the leash tight around a body already slipping.

Roan's hand touched my jaw, firm and steady.

Jay leaned in, his scent cutting clean through the fog. "Let go, Wren."

Rhett whispered at my back, warm lips brushing my ear. "We'll catch you."

I wanted to say no. But that wasn't what came out of my mouth. No, a very simple word. Maintain the boundaries. Keep my distance. Be contained.

That was what I should have done. But what did I do?

I said *yes.*

～

I woke with a gasp, drenched in sweat.

Blankets kicked off. Skin burning. Muscles clenched.

The air in the cabin was cold. Too cold. My body didn't care.

I sat up, heart pounding.

My scent was *everywhere*.

It was no longer subtle. No longer manageable. It was full and heady and soaked into every surface. I could barely breathe through it.

My hands trembled.

This wasn't heat.

Not yet.

But it was coming.

Fast.

I wasn't ready.

For the first time since dismissing the doctor's recommendation of hiring a pro, I wanted to scream at myself. Saying no to that had been automatic, intense, and necessary. The idea of someone else...

No. I survived those first two heats. I'd survive this one. I dragged myself to the bathroom, still half-dazed from the dream. The cold tile beneath my feet was a jolt, but it wasn't enough to shake off the lingering sensations. I splashed water on my face, the shock of it barely registering against the fire beneath my skin.

The mirror reflected back a stranger—eyes too bright, cheeks flushed, lips parted like I was already panting. I looked like I was in the throes of it, even though I wasn't. Not yet. But the signs were all there, screaming at me that I was on the edge of something I couldn't control.

Already naked, because even the sheets had already been too much touching my skin, I stepped into the shower again. The water was ice-cold this time, a desperate attempt to cool the inferno raging inside me. I stood under the spray, teeth chattering, but it didn't help. The ache was too deep, too insistent. It wasn't just physical; it was a need that went beyond my body, a craving for something I couldn't name.

Dialing the water up to something warmer, I reached for the soap, my hands shaking as I lathered it over my skin. Each touch was electric, sending sparks through my nerves. I couldn't get enough. I couldn't get clean. The scent of my arousal was thick in the air, clinging to me, marking me.

I slipped my hand between my legs, fingers gliding over slick flesh. The sensation was intense, almost painful, but I didn't stop. I needed release, needed to ease the pressure that was building inside me. I worked myself faster, harder, chasing the orgasm that would give me a moment's respite.

It came in waves, crashing over me, leaving me gasping and trembling. But it wasn't enough. It never was. The ache was still there, gnawing at me, demanding more. I leaned against the wall, water cascading over me, and slid to the floor, too exhausted to stand.

I stayed there, curled up in the corner of the shower, until the water turned cold again. Then I dragged myself out, wrapping a towel around my shivering body. I stumbled back to the bed, collapsing onto the mattress, too tired to do anything but lie there and stare at the ceiling.

Sleep eluded me, but I didn't fight it. I let my mind drift, let the memories and fantasies take over. Roan, Jay, Rhett—their faces, their scents, their touches. It was a dangerous game, letting myself go there, but I was past caring. I was past everything but the need.

I reached for the bottle of water, taking a long drink, trying to ground myself. But there was no grounding when my body was on fire, when every thought was consumed by the approaching storm. I closed my eyes, letting the darkness take me, hoping that this time, sleep would bring some relief. But even as I drifted off, I knew it was just a temporary escape. The heat was coming, and there was no running from it now.

I wasn't gonna sit around and do another lap on the ice like it would fix anything.

Roan could bark orders all he wanted—*"keep your head in the game, Navarro"*—but that ship sailed the second I realized she wasn't just *off the clock.*

Wren was *gone.*

Not answering her phone, her private line, her backup number. No location pinned on her work calendar. No car in the arena garage. No familiar scent lingering near the media rooms or tunnels or even the stupid vending machines she hit when she forgot to eat.

She hadn't just left for the day.

She'd *left.* Period.

Twenty-four hours later and no one seemed to know where the hell she went.

Except maybe...

I took the stairs two at a time, not even trying to hide the fact that I was headed to her office. If security wanted to stop me, they could try. I had a key. Technically. Sort of.

Maybe it wasn't *mine*, but I'd borrowed it once during that preseason charity shoot, and Wren had never asked for it back.

So that was her fault. Kind of.

I reached the top of the stairs, heart pounding hard enough to feel it in my throat—and froze.

Her office door was already open.

Light on.

Someone inside.

I stepped in fast, ready to throw down if it was Beckett or Marchand or some dumb rookie with a death wish—and found Jay.

Sitting calmly in her chair, desktop computer on, his fingers moving with surgical precision across the keys. His black hoodie sleeves were pushed to his elbows, expression unreadable, mouth a thin, focused line.

"What the hell," I blurted. "You hacked her computer?"

Jay didn't flinch. "Didn't need to. Her access card was still in the drawer. Backup one, the spare she keeps in case her main gets demagnetized."

He didn't even glance at me. Just kept scanning.

I stepped farther into the room, shutting the door behind me. "And what—you're just going through her stuff?"

He finally looked up then, brows lifted like *really, Rhett?*

"She's gone." His voice was low, clipped. "Why are you acting like you didn't come here to do the exact same thing?"

I didn't answer.

Because he was right.

Jay turned the monitor so I could see her screen. "Calendar's clear after yesterday. But look—her upcoming out-of-office entry? 'Personal medical leave.' Starts today. Runs five days."

"Five days," I repeated, the words catching in my throat. "You think she's in heat?"

But she wasn't an omega. Why the fuck did my brain go straight to her being in heat?

Jay didn't blink. "I think we don't know what we don't know."

Which wasn't a no.

"She's not an omega." I tested the words out, my understanding of them, and my knowledge of Wren. If anyone was an alpha, it had to be her. Right?

"You asking me or telling me?" Jay was such a cool-headed prick sometimes.

I scrubbed a hand down my face, pacing a slow line across the office while Jay clicked through her email tabs with surgeon-level calm.

"She's too careful," I muttered. "She wouldn't just go off the grid like this. Not unless—"

"She didn't want anyone to know where she went."

Jay's voice cut through mine, clean and sharp.

I stopped pacing.

"She's been planning this," he added. "Check the sent folder—she rescheduled meetings, reassigned her PR rotation to the assistants, cleared the schedule for every major player interview through the weekend."

"But she didn't tell us," I said quietly.

Jay's mouth pulled tight.

In that moment, I saw it too.

The *hurt*.

He was the calm one, the sane one, the guy who never lost it—but that didn't mean he didn't *feel* it. His silence wasn't indifference. It was control.

And it was cracking.

"She didn't trust us to handle it," I said.

Or she was scared.

Or ashamed.

Or trying to protect us from something we didn't even understand.

"She didn't want witnesses," Jay said.

I turned toward him, mouth open to argue—but then I caught the way his hands hovered just above the keyboard, not typing. Not clicking.

Just... *tensed.*

"It has to be a heat. She's close," he said, more to himself than to me. "Or maybe she thinks she will be. Then she didn't want anyone to see it."

"What if she went to help another omega with their heat?" The minute I asked the question, I kind of hated myself a little. Because the idea of her touching anyone else, even a needy omega just pissed me off. The anger was flash fire hot and incandescent.

"If she was helping an omega, she wouldn't have to hide it." Jay sounded so damn certain.

"How do you know?"

His shrug, even as tense and controlled as it was, wasn't an answer.

I flattened my hands on the desk and glared at him.

It was like my temper just rolled off him, water against a rock. Frustrated, I straightened. "She's not helping someone else. This is about her."

"She wouldn't go to this much trouble to hide her activities if it was anything else."

My chest tightened.

"Fuck," I whispered.

Jay stood up slowly, ejecting a flash drive from her computer before he shut it down. "We need to find her."

"Where's Roan?" We hadn't spoken since the blow-up with Nate in the locker room.

Jay didn't answer right away.

He slid the flash drive into his pocket, calm and clinical as ever, then finally said, "Roan's looking into some things on his end."

"What kind of things?" I asked, sharper than I meant to. "You think he knows more than we do?"

Jay tilted his head slightly, studying me like he was debating whether to tell me the truth or feed me something soft to keep me from blowing up again.

"He went to talk to Marchand," Jay said finally. "Figured if anyone knows where she went—or why—he would."

I scoffed. "Marchand doesn't give a shit about any of us unless there's a dollar sign next to it. He probably *sent* her off somewhere, just to keep her from being a distraction during the press storm he created."

With a half-shrug and a raised a brow, Jay said, "Then Roan's the one who might be able to get the truth out of him. So let him do his thing."

My hands curled into fists. "His *thing* is being a cold, controlling asshole who refuses to admit he cares about her."

Jay's expression didn't shift, but I caught the faintest pause in his breathing. Just a flicker.

"We all care about her," he said.

"But we don't get to show it, right?" I threw my arms out. "We have to pretend she's just the PR rep who talks shit and wears leather boots and doesn't drive us completely *fucking feral*."

Arms folded, Jay leaned back against the edge of her desk. "You think I like this?"

"You're acting like you do."

He exhaled through his nose—*barely* a reaction, but enough to know I hit something.

"I'm not pretending," he said. "I'm just waiting until I know what the hell is actually going on. Losing it isn't going to help her."

"You really think Marchand's going to tell Roan the truth?" I asked, bitter. "That he's just going to open a file and hand him a map and say, 'Here's where your missing PR manager is hiding while she explodes into an unclaimed omega heat'?"

Jay's eyes flicked toward me.

And *that*—that little flash of narrowed, knowing focus—

"You *do* think she's an omega." I said it low.

Jay didn't answer right away.

He didn't have to.

"Fuck me," I muttered, sinking down into the guest chair opposite her desk.

Blowing out a breath, he sighed. "I don't know for sure. I'm not saying I do. But... she's been different lately. Scent's been off. She's been twitchy. Quiet. And now she's vanished for 'medical leave' with no location listed and every trace of her presence scrubbed like she's preparing to disappear."

"She didn't even tell Roan," I said.

"She *especially* didn't tell Roan."

That... hurt more than I wanted to admit.

I ran both hands through my hair and exhaled. "Okay. So Roan's talking to Marchand. You and I are hunting records, emails, calendars. Maybe she used a team card to book gas or a hotel?"

"I already pulled up travel receipts for the last thirty days. Nothing yet." Jay nodded to the flash drive. "But there's one thing I haven't checked. Marchand's approval logs."

"You think he signed off on something and thought no one would see it?"

"Or she tricked him into approving something vague that didn't flag as personal."

I stood. "Let's dig."

Jay followed. "You check logistics. I'll check her flight records. If she used a corporate connection, I'll find it."

"And Roan?"

Jay's tone cooled. "Let him deal with Marchand. He plays the long game. We don't."

I paused at the door and glanced back.

"She's out there," I said. "And if she's about to go through what we *think* she is..."

I turned back to the desk and gripped the edge like I needed something to hold me to the floor. My mind was moving too fast now, connecting things I didn't want to connect.

"She's *not* an omega," I said again, quieter this time. She couldn't be. It was damn impossible to wrap my head around it.

Like saying it gently might make it more true.

Jay didn't bother to respond. Just waited, still and sharp, like a knife laid flat.

I laughed once. Hollow. Bitter.

"Fuck." I scrubbed my hands down my face. "You know who was just here? Beckett fucking Rylan."

Jay's eyes narrowed instantly. "What are you talking about?"

"The day she left," I said. "Remember? He showed up.

Like some smug bastard out of nowhere. Said Marchand invited him. But that wasn't the weird part." My chest tightened. "The weird part was the way he *looked* at her."

Jay didn't interrupt, he just watched me with that all-seeing sharp gaze.

"I thought he was just being his usual territorial dick-head," I kept going. "Like trying to get a rise out of Roan, or needle me into snapping."

"He was always like that," Jay said slowly. "But…"

I nodded, catching his train of thought. "But this time it was different. He didn't look at her like a guy messing with a PR manager. He looked at her like a—"

Anger flickered through Jay's veneer of calm. "Like an unmated omega."

The whole idea tasted like blood in my mouth.

I straightened and started pacing again, one hand fisted tight in my hoodie sleeve. "You're telling me none of us noticed? Not once? Not in years?"

Jay tilted his head, frowning slightly. "If she was on suppressants…"

"She *was* on something." The memory crashed into me —*her scent changing*. The near-misses, the flashes of heat under her skin. The way she started avoiding the locker room, keeping distance, making excuses not to get too close.

Like she was trying to *hide* from us.

From me.

From all of it.

I stopped pacing. "What if that photo? The one with Beckett in the owner's box? What if *he* knew?"

His stare sharpened. "You think he was trying to stake a claim?"

"He was scenting the air near her when we passed him

in the hall." My voice went flat. "I thought he was just being gross."

Shoulders tense, Jay stood a little straighter. "If he picked up on something we didn't…"

"He'd go after her." I didn't hesitate. "Especially if he thought she was going to go into heat and wouldn't have anyone around to stop him."

All at once, Jay's voice dropped into something far colder and far more dangerous. "Do you think Marchand knew?"

"I think he didn't care," I growled. The man only ever cared about his bottom line and the reputation of the team. Even the latter was negotiable. "Or worse—he saw the leverage and wanted to use it."

He went still again. Thinking. Calculating.

But I was already halfway back to the door.

"Where are you going?" he asked.

"I don't care if it's a long shot—I'm going to find her. I'll drive every icy road from here to Alaska if I have to."

Jay followed me into the hall. "Rhett."

I turned back.

"If you go rogue, you might spook her. Make it worse."

"I'd rather her be pissed at me than alone in a cabin with some *feral asshole* circling her like prey."

He didn't argue, because he knew I was right. All he said was, "Then we do this smart. I'll keep digging. You check the highway cams. Look for traffic logs, gas receipts. Roan might have something soon, and if he doesn't—he'll come looking too."

I swallowed hard.

Everything inside me was howling now. Not just anger.

Need.

Fear.

Something *older*.

She's in heat.

She's alone.

She's *ours*.

"Okay," I said. "Okay."

But I was already moving.

Because if Beckett Rylan thought he could lay one hand on her, he was about to learn exactly how feral *I* could get.

CHAPTER

TEN

ROAN

I didn't go looking for Marchand without a plan.

Not because I wasn't pissed — I was. I'd spent the last twelve hours drowning in it. I'd nearly broken my stick over the boards during drills. Almost snapped at Nate when he chirped about Wren being "too cozy" with Beckett during that owner's box lunch.

If Jay hadn't intercepted me after practice to give me the latest — that Wren hadn't just taken off, she'd cleared her calendar for five days of *medical* leave — I might've gone full caveman.

But this wasn't a situation I could punch through. And Wren?

She didn't need a feral alpha charging into the storm.

She needed someone who could outmaneuver it.

So, before I made my way to Marchand's office, I'd already done two things:

1. Called my agent.
2. Started drafting a very strategic leak of my own.

99

Just enough to put pressure on Marchand without making it traceable. A whisper campaign — the kind that asked questions without making accusations.

Things like:

"Is Beckett Rylan really in talks with the Howlers?"

"What does that mean for team dynamics and player safety?"

"Sources say one player already left the facility right after his visit — temporary medical leave. Coincidence?"

I wasn't dumb enough to name names. Not mine. Not Wren's. If only Rhett were as discreet.

But the suggestion would be enough to make any decent PR department sweat. Particularly when their master of spin—Wren—was not here to fix it. Marchand was going to have to deal with this on his own or make someone far less qualified cope. Either would be painful for Marchand and it would make him sweat, or worse, he'd make mistakes. Marchand *hated* sweating.

How sad.

For him.

His assistant tried to head me off at the door. I gave her a look that said try me and she wisely decided to find somewhere else to be.

I walked in without knocking.

Marchand was on a call — no doubt trying to spin something — but he put the phone down when he saw me.

"Roan," he said with that fake-as-shit smile. "You're not scheduled. What can I do for you?"

"You can start by telling me what Beckett Rylan was doing in our box yesterday."

The smile didn't move.

"That's a front office matter," he said smoothly. "Not your concern."

I stepped forward slowly, keeping my voice level. "He's a known locker room risk. He's got a record with the league, and we've *all* seen the way he acts around Wren."

"Wren," he repeated, tasting the name. "She's on leave. Not really your concern either, is she?"

My jaw ticked. "I don't give a damn about what's *technically* my concern. I'm the captain. I care about what affects the team."

"Then you'll be happy to know I'm doing my job — building the roster, exploring our options. That includes free agents."

"That includes someone who *predatorily hovered* around our PR manager while the press was in the building?"

He leaned back in his chair, folding his hands. "You're making some heavy implications for a man with no proof."

I took a breath. *Control, Roan.*

"I don't need proof to know that if something happens to her, it won't just be a PR problem. It'll be a *player* problem."

His smile cracked then, just slightly, like he hadn't expected me to go there.

Good.

"I've already spoken to my agent," I continued. "About next year's contract. About trade options. About locker room cohesion. You know, all the things a captain worries about."

Marchand's eyes narrowed. "You threatening me, Whitaker?"

"No," I said, calm and clean. "I'm *warning* you. We're heading into playoffs. The team's holding on by a thread. If you're bringing in Rylan to stir shit up and bait Wren into some kind of meltdown, you're not just risking your PR. You're risking the *entire season.*"

He didn't answer right away.

So I dropped the last nail in.

"There are already whispers in the press. You might want to check your alerts."

His phone lit up on the desk, vibrating once, then again.

I didn't smile or react in any emotional way. The point of the play was to keep the puck on the move. Marchand seemed to have forgotten that I'd made my career on my instincts.

This right here would be the first ripple.

If Marchand thought he could play dirty, he was about to find out just how sharp my game could get. He stared at the vibrating phone on his desk, then flicked a finger to stop the second call from coming through. He didn't check the screen. Didn't pick it up.

He didn't need to, because he knew exactly what it was.

"Leaks like that don't stay whispers for long," he said, voice colder now, quieter. "They have a way of mutating. Becoming something no one can control. Sponsors pull out. Fans riot. Players spiral."

I didn't blink. "Then it's a good thing you've got someone like me holding the locker room together."

"You're our captain." He smiled, all teeth and no feeling. "That used to mean something."

"It still does," I said, holding his stare. "Just not the same thing it used to."

He leaned forward. "You planning to walk, Whitaker?"

"Depends."

"On what?"

I shrugged, easy. "How much shit you plan on stirring before playoffs are even underway."

He scoffed, a low breath of disbelief. "You think you're untouchable?"

"No. I think I'm *valuable.*" I let the silence stretch for a beat, then added, "And I think you know what happens to this team if I go."

Marchand didn't reply.

But his jaw twitched.

Because it was true.

I was the axis the Howlers spun on, not because I scored the most or ran the flashiest plays, but because I kept the whole damn machine from breaking apart. I managed egos. Tempered the wild ones. Balanced the line between bloodlust and brilliance.

You lose that? You lose the team.

He finally sat back in his chair, eyes narrowing in thought. "You've got one year left. Maybe less, depending on the playoffs. You really want to burn it all down over *her?*"

I didn't flinch.

"She's part of this team," I said. "And unlike you, she doesn't treat people like pawns."

"She's not your responsibility."

"She's *mine,*" I said before I could stop myself, quiet, certain, and final.

Something flickered across his face at that. Recognition. Surprise. Maybe even a little amusement.

"You're really willing to go free agent?" he asked, like he needed to hear me say it out loud.

I met his gaze dead-on.

"If you push this? If you keep dangling Rylan like he's not a loaded weapon? If you let Wren take the fall for your backroom schemes?" I leaned forward, resting my palms on his desk, close enough he'd smell the promise in my voice. "I walk. And I won't do it quietly."

He went very still.

For the first time since I'd entered the room, I saw it hit him. It wasn't fear, not exactly, but calculation. Marchand wasn't afraid of people. No, but he was terrified of *risk*. He hated messy headlines, contract lawyers, and a fractured locker room right before playoffs.

He dreaded *chaos*.

What I had just promised him was an absolute and unavoidable fucking tempest of it.

The phone buzzed again.

A third call.

He ignored it.

I straightened. "You've got a decision to make. I'd make it soon."

Then I turned and walked out, never once looking back. Because when it comes to bluffing? The best one is the one you're willing to follow through on.

And me?

I was more than willing.

The elevator doors shut behind me, the echo of Marchand's office still ringing in my ears like post-fight adrenaline.

I'd won that round.

Didn't feel like it.

I was halfway down the corridor when my phone buzzed. Not the team line — my personal. Only a few people had the number.

JAY:

We're heading out.

JAY:

Got a lead. Call you when we're closer.

I stilled and cold settled into my chest.

Not *a* lead.

Her.

I didn't need to ask who they were talking about. Rhett had been vibrating with frustration since she vanished, Jay too quiet to be innocent. I knew that look in their eyes—restless, starved, on edge.

If they were heading to Wren?

That was a line they couldn't uncross.

I called Jay. He didn't answer.

Figures. Asshole.

The moment I hit the parking level, I cut across the west corridor, took the side stairs, and ducked out a door few knew was even open. The one that would give me a shot at catching them before they peeled off into the city or worse, off the grid.

It wasn't just that it was reckless. Or selfish.

It was that Wren had made herself clear.

Don't follow me. Don't cross this line. Don't ask.

She'd always been explicit about her boundaries.

Even now, when every part of me ached to find her, to *see* her—to scent her and just know she was okay—I wasn't going to disrespect what she'd so carefully protected. What she'd survived to maintain.

But the others...?

Rhett was a fucking wildfire on a good day. Jay could out-calculate most analysts mid-play, but the second emotion bled into logic, he was a blade looking for a target.

If they showed up at her door?

She'd never forgive it.

What was worse for me—yes, I would be selfish about this—she'd think *I* sent them.

That thought alone had my feet moving faster.

I pulled out my phone, hit Rhett's name.

Straight to voicemail.

Goddamn it.

I was halfway to the auxiliary lot when the wind cut across my jaw and dragged the memory up from nowhere.

The first time I saw her.

Not on paper. Not in the team reports. Not the dry HR onboarding where they tell you who does what and who to nod at on the way in.

No, I mean *really* saw her.

I'd just been signed. The press conference had ended, sweaty and hot under the lights, with the owners posturing about the "future of the Howlers." I'd been handed a fresh jersey. Cameras still flashing.

Then the crowd had parted, and there she was.

Boots planted. Black coat sharp as hell. Clipboard in one hand, coffee in the other. Sunglasses still on indoors, mouth curled into something too amused to be polite.

She took one look at me and said, "If you ever call me sweetheart, I'll have your trade paperwork filed before you finish blinking."

No scent flare. No hesitation.

Just cold wit and sharper eyes.

I'd never seen anyone carry that much command without raising their voice.

More impressively, I'd never forgotten it. It was the rare alpha who could put me in my place so thoroughly. My dominance was just too damn much. I'd learned to temper it to make it easier for others, but with Wren?

She'd blown right through me like that breeze.

Even now, as I jogged across the lot and spotted Rhett's ridiculous cherry-red muscle car parked half out of its lane, I remembered the way she'd tipped her head that first day. Measured. Like she could already tell I'd be trouble.

She'd been right.

If I didn't stop these two idiots, we'd all be in deeper than we knew.

I caught them halfway to the car.

Rhett's keys were already in hand, Jay a few steps behind, scanning the lot like he half-expected her to materialize out of thin air with her sunglasses in place and a familiar, if tolerant, smirk on her lips. They hadn't seen me yet, and for a second, I debated letting them drive off. Let them make idiots of themselves, get it out of their system.

Then I saw the look in Rhett's eyes—too bright, too wild. And Jay's—cool, yes, but with the tightness of someone balancing a storm inside his ribs.

They weren't just restless. They were about to do something very, *very* stupid.

So I moved.

"Going somewhere?" I kept it calm. Level. Like I was asking about lunch plans instead of stopping two grown men from detonating both their careers.

Rhett froze, his whole posture coiling, before he turned with that trademark half-grin that always meant trouble. "What, you gonna stop us, Captain?"

"Didn't say that." I slid my hands into my pockets, put on a smile that didn't reach my eyes. "Just making sure no one thinks the three of us are about to start a brawl in broad daylight. Bad for optics, you know."

Jay got it immediately. His chin tipped, the faintest flicker of acknowledgment. Rhett, though—shocker— clearly *wasn't* in the mood for subtle.

"Optics?" he repeated, voice sharpening. "You think I give a damn about optics right now?"

"Yeah," I said. "You do. Or you will. After you cool off."

I kept my tone easy, the kind that played well on camera, the kind Wren herself used when corralling one of us mid-meltdown. Hell, I'd *learned* it from her.

But Rhett just stepped closer. "She's out there somewhere, Roan. Alone. And you're telling me to cool off?"

"She probably needed space and a break." If I had to deal with Marchand daily as well as the rest of us, I'd already be bald from ripping out my own hair.

"She didn't *say* anything," Rhett shot back. "That's the problem."

Jay's head turned slightly toward me, a quiet warning in his eyes. He could feel it too, that edge creeping in under Rhett's words, the kind that carried scent, power, challenge.

"Back off," I said quietly. "You start digging without her permission, you'll make things worse."

"Worse than her disappearing?" Rhett's laugh was sharp, disbelieving. "You really think she'd vanish like that without a damn reason?"

"I think it's her call."

"And I think," Rhett said, stepping right up into my space, "you're scared to admit what we both know."

Jay murmured, "Rhett—" but it was too late.

Rhett's smile turned wolfish. "What if she's an omega?"

The words hit like a puck to the sternum.

My jaw locked. "*What?*"

He didn't stop. "What if that's why she left? What if she's in heat right now—alone, trying to keep it together, because she didn't want any of us to find out?"

My pulse roared in my ears.

No.

No, that wasn't—she wasn't—

But every memory slid into place like dominoes lining up for the fall.

The calm composure that always felt a little too deliberate. The way she controlled her scent — or rather, the near *absence* of one. The edge to her voice when someone got too close. Her rigid boundaries, the refusal to ever let any of us step beyond that professional line.

And the one time, two years ago, when she'd vanished for a week mid-season, claiming the flu.

No one questioned it.

God help me, I'd dropped off soup at her building and left it on her doorstep because she wouldn't answer the door.

Her voice, when she called to thank me later, had sounded... frayed.

Breathless.

Sweet.

The realization rolled through me slow and hard and primal.

If she was an omega—

If she was in heat—

Every instinct I'd spent years mastering suddenly wanted to claw free.

Rhett saw it. The faint widening of his grin said he did.

"Yeah," he said softly. "You feel it too, don't you?"

My hand flexed at my side. "Watch yourself, Navarro."

"Why? Because I said what you're thinking?"

"Because you don't know what the hell you're talking about," I said, even though my voice came out lower, rougher. Even though my body betrayed me.

"Enough," Jay said, his tone low but firm as he stepped between us, calm as ice. "We're not doing this here."

Rhett's jaw worked. He was breathing fast, too fast. I

recognized that look. He was on the edge of a fight he'd regret. I'd make him regret it.

Gaze flickering between us, Jay maintained his neutrality. Though it was also peppered with his own tight anger and need. "You both need to remember who she is. What she means to this team. You think this helps her?"

That cut through. Barely.

Rhett looked away first, swore under his breath, then chucked his keys against his own car hood. "Fine. Whatever. You're the captain, right? So lead."

I exhaled slow, steady. My heart hadn't slowed at all.

Jay looked at me a long second before he said quietly, "You believe him?"

I didn't answer.

I didn't have to. Because now that I'd tasted that idea, really *felt* it, I knew the truth. The truth I'd let her conceal with—whatever she'd used—and respected her boundaries. If she was in heat, and she'd taken leave for it—no, none of *that* mattered. What mattered was if she needed us.

Needed me.

ELEVEN

JAY

Roan was ice.

Rhett was fire.

I sat there in the passenger seat, just sane enough to hold the line while everything else frayed

None of us spoke as we pulled away from the arena, the engine humming low beneath Roan's knuckles, white on the steering wheel. Rhett had folded himself into the back-seat like a storm cloud, radiating heat and twitchy, fight-me energy. The kind of coiled aggression that begged for a target. Or a reason.

Too bad I wasn't in the mood to give him one.

Roan had argued the moment I'd said it—*We shouldn't go there. We don't know what we're walking into.*

Yeah. That was the point.

And maybe I *should've* backed off. Maybe if this had been anyone else—any other staff member who dropped off the radar—I would've let it go. Waited for a call. Trusted the system.

But this was *Wren.*

We didn't have that luxury.

"If we're wrong," I told them in the garage, "then I'll take the heat. I'll eat every ounce of her fury. But at least I'll know she's okay."

Neither of them could argue with that.

Not out loud.

It was the second half of my sentence that turned Roan's head—*especially with Rylan sniffing around*—and after a long, icy pause, he just said, *We're taking my car.*

So now, here we were.

Trapped in a car together for the next twenty-two minutes as we crossed town to her townhouse. It was a cute place located in a nice area. She had neighbors on one side and on the other, she sat right next to a greenbelt. I'd been to her place all of once before, but Roan didn't even need GPS.

Not commenting on that for the moment, I focused on holding the line. While Roan clearly exerted his own brand of control, Rhett was *not.* Since they weren't fighting at the moment, I'd count that as a win.

Her neighborhood was just like I remembered it. Clean. Quiet. One of those HOA places where every lawn was manicured and every porch had some kind of decoration for whatever season it was. Wren's was the only one without anything. Of course.

Still... I caught myself wondering if she *ever* did it. Goth up the place for Halloween? A single snowflake in the window at Christmas?

Hard to picture.

Even in her office, holiday cheer was strategic—tasteful and minimal. The barest suggestion of celebration. Like everything else with her, it was curated. Intentional.

She showed the world the version of herself she wanted us to see. No more, no less.

Roan pulled into a spot right in front of her unit. Detached garages were tucked around the back, but the front had open street parking. I was already out of the SUV before he came to a full stop. Rhett was half a step behind me, tension thrumming off him in waves.

"She lives here?" Rhett asked, surprise briefly flashing across his face before it vanished under something darker. "How do you know where she lives?"

I didn't answer. Neither did Roan.

He locked the car and strode up the short path to her front door. The breeze rolled down from the greenbelt, cool and earthy. Pine. Damp leaves. A little woodsmoke from someone's chimney nearby.

Roan raised a hand to knock.

Then the wind died.

And Roan went still.

So did I.

Two steps away—and I *felt* it more than I *smelled* it at first. A shimmer of tension down my spine. Heat behind my teeth. Then the scent hit fully, and it was like the bottom dropped out of the world.

It was her.

But not *just* her.

It was Wren's scent, stripped down to something *feral*. Softer in places, sharper in others. Complex and layered and... *undeniably* omega.

My breath caught.

Rhett stopped beside me with a sound between a grunt and a growl. His nostrils flared, eyes going sharp.

"Holy *fuck*," he breathed.

Roan didn't say a word.

He stood like a statue in front of the door, hand still raised, but he didn't knock. Didn't move.

Because what the hell were we supposed to do now?

None of us spoke it, but the truth crashed over us like a thunderclap.

She was in heat.

She had been hiding it.

And she was close.

The scent marker on the door was faint, but it was *fresh*. A warning to stay back. A primal signal that shouldn't have belonged to *her*, yet it did.

I swallowed hard. My brain went static.

For years we'd known her as alpha. Professional. Composed. Untouchable.

But now?

There was no *pretending* anymore.

Rhett's hand hit the siding next to the door with a low thump. "She's alone in there," he ground out. "She's alone and she's—she's fucking *glowing*—"

"Stop," Roan said.

His voice wasn't loud, but it cut like ice.

He finally lowered his hand, his whole frame rigid with restraint. Not a single ounce of scent leaked from him, but I saw it in his shoulders—the pressure, the *tightness*.

He was unraveling just as much as we were.

But he wouldn't show it.

Because he *couldn't*.

"Don't even think about crossing that line," Roan said, looking straight at Rhett.

"Why?" Rhett snapped, his voice too raw. "Because it's hers?"

"Yes," Roan said simply. "Because it's *hers*."

That shut Rhett up.

I stared at the door. At the house that still smelled like her underneath the newly laid heat markers. Like cold steel and late nights and too much coffee. Like tension and intelligence and hunger repressed so tightly it left claw marks.

But that new layer...

God.

It *sang* to something in me.

Even as a beta, I wasn't immune. Not to *her*.

Roan turned away, jaw clenched. "Back to the car."

"You're serious?" Rhett said, incredulous. "We're just going to walk away?"

"No," I said, clearing my throat and dragging my focus off the door. "We're going to give her time. We're going to give her space. And then we're going to find a better way to do this."

"If Rylan comes sniffing around?" Rhett's voice was low, tight.

"Stop borrowing trouble." Roan looked back at the townhouse once. Just once.

Whatever flickered through his eyes made my pulse skip. I buried that kneejerk reaction. "He isn't the problem," I said by way of agreement. "This is about Wren, not Rylan."

Expression taut, Rhett looked like he was about to argue, but he surprised me when he didn't. Instead, he just blew out a harsh breath. This whole thing seemed to be provoking their territorial sides. So, I leaned into keeping my breathing even, no good would come from all of us losing it.

We were quiet as we climbed back into the car.

Roan didn't start the engine right away. Just stared out through the windshield like the answers might be hiding in the shape of the clouds.

"She's not here," he said finally.

I blinked. "What?"

"The scent markers are here," he said, voice low, reluctant, "but they're stale. Not today. Not even this morning. Two days old... at least."

I frowned. That was subtle. I hadn't picked that up. Rhett, based on his expression, hadn't either.

Didn't say much for the fact that none of us had caught her omega status before, either. That, however, was a fight for another day.

"She's gone," Roan added, confirming what we were all thinking.

"If she's in heat," I said, "and she isn't *here*..."

"She went somewhere to ride it out," Roan finished grimly.

Rhett didn't hesitate. He was already digging his phone out of his jacket. "Okay. Okay, okay, hang on."

I turned in my seat. "What are you doing?"

He didn't even look up. "May or may not have logged into her cloud once."

Roan turned slowly in the driver's seat. "You *what*?"

"It was a *dare!*" Rhett said, eyes locked on the screen, thumbs flying. "One time. Preseason last year. I logged in, I logged right back out. Didn't touch anything. But she never changed the password."

I just stared at him. "You broke into her cloud on a dare?"

"Technically not *broke*," he muttered. "More like... tapped gently."

Roan just grunted, exasperation radiating off him in waves. "What's the password?"

Rhett hesitated for half a beat. Then: "notyouralpha99. All lowercase. No special characters."

There was a pause.

Roan's brows lifted.

"That's so her." I snorted. "She *knew* we'd try." A weird little spark of fondness cut through the tension in my chest.

Rhett grinned, wicked and sharp, even as his fingers flew. "Exactly. You think you're special? You're not. Get in line, cowboy."

Roan looked like he wanted to roll his eyes, but didn't give Rhett the satisfaction. "So? What are you looking for?"

"Anything tagged travel," Rhett said. "Or remote. Or vacation. Or *heat bunker deluxe*, if we're lucky."

I sighed. "You think she left a digital trail."

"I think she's human," Rhett said. "And she was under pressure. People slip when they're scrambling."

Though he looked unconvinced, Roan said nothing.

I twisted so I could watch as Rhett navigated folders and files and backups.

"She covered her tracks," he muttered. "Mostly."

"Mostly?" Roan asked, voice sharp.

Our resident hellion grinned. "Found a PDF itinerary in her deleted items. Cabin rental. Mountains. Four-hour drive. No return date listed."

Jay whistled low. "You get an actual address?"

"Yep. Near Yellowstone."

Roan sat back hard against the seat, muttering a curse under his breath.

I stared out the window, the weight of it all settling across my chest.

She hadn't just hidden this.

She *ran*.

Far.

Now that we knew, the question wasn't if we'd go after her. It was how fast we could get there. Roan didn't say a word. He just reached over, hit the start button, and shifted the SUV into gear.

The moment the wheels hit the road, he thumbed the control on the steering wheel to dial out through the car's Bluetooth.

Two rings.

Then: *"Yeah, Whittaker?"* Coach's gravel-edged voice filled the cabin, tension already vibrating beneath the words.

Roan didn't flinch. "We're taking the next four days off."

The silence that followed was so loud it made the air feel heavier.

"Excuse me?"

Roan didn't blink. "The whole team needs to breathe. We'll be back after that, ready to focus on the opposition. But the tension in the locker room? It's past critical mass. You want them on the ice like this, Coach? You want that fire turning inward?"

I shot a look back at Rhett, his mouth twitched like he was biting down on something he probably shouldn't say. Damn. I was almost impressed by his restraint, but I was absolutely stunned at Roan's absolute audacity.

It wasn't just the boldness of Roan's tone—it was the calm. He didn't sound like a player making a request. He sounded like a man who'd already made a decision.

"This coming from you?" Coach finally said, voice tighter now. *"You're the one who always wants more ice time—"*

"I'm telling you," Roan said flatly. "This isn't negotiable."

"Four days, Whittaker? We've got the damn playoffs—"

"And we'll be ready. We always are. But if you push them now, you're going to break something. Or someone."

Coach didn't respond right away. We all waited—me,

Rhett, and Roan—locked in that thin strip of highway sound and the background hum of Bluetooth static.

"You're skating a fine line, Captain."

Roan's hands didn't tighten on the wheel. His voice didn't shift. He just said, "I know. Thanks, Coach."

Then he ended the call.

No one said anything for a minute after that.

Then Rhett, voice low from the back, said, "Guess that's why he gets the 'C'."

Roan didn't answer.

But I saw the twitch of his jaw. The way his eyes didn't leave the road. He wasn't patting himself on the back.

He was bracing for the next step.

"Address," he said and Rhett didn't fuck around, he read it off and at the next traffic light, Roan entered it into the car's navigation.

It gave us four hours and forty-one minutes to arrival. Goddamn that seemed like forever. As fresh agitation ripped through me this time, it was accompanied by an almost impossible sense of tranquility that paved over the restlessness vibrating in my blood.

Because whether Roan admitted it or not—we were heading straight into a storm named Wren. As eager as I was, I found that I could wait because I knew she'd be at our destination.

Time would tick down to us seeing her.

The longer we were in the car, the more the silence felt like it might crack open.

Roan hadn't looked at either of us since we got on the highway. His hands never left ten-and-two, knuckles rigid, jaw sharp.

Rhett, on the other hand, hadn't stopped moving since we left. His leg bounced, fingers drumming against his thigh, and every so often he let out a long, frustrated breath that made my temples throb.

"You need to calm down," Roan said without looking at him.

"I'll calm down when we know she's safe."

"She's not stupid, Rhett."

"Didn't say she was. I said she's alone."

The corners of Roan's mouth tightened before he said, "And we don't know if she even wants us there."

I leaned my head back against the seat. "Would either of you have stopped me from going?"

Roan cut a sideways glance at me.

"Exactly," I muttered. "So stop acting like you have the high ground."

No one replied.

The car settled into another tense quiet. My fingers itched for my phone, not to track her—there was nothing to track—but to hear her voice, to *do something*. But she hadn't answered a single message. Not even the last one I sent that wasn't a question, just a promise: *Whatever it is, I'm here.*

Still—nothing.

Rhett's voice cut into the silence again, softer this time. "You think she's scared?"

Roan's grip on the wheel shifted.

I said, "I think she's hiding something that hurts. That doesn't mean she's scared."

"I think she's in heat."

Roan's jaw flexed.

I closed my eyes, because hearing Rhett say it again still made something *shift* in me.

I'd been to enough heats—been there for omegas in the worst and best ways—to know what the scent of one did to an alpha. Hell, even to a beta.

And Wren...

If that was what was happening—if she'd been masking it this whole time—

The burn in my chest wasn't lust. Not really. It was something deeper. Thicker. *Older.*

I didn't want her because of a heat. I wanted her because she was Wren. Complicated, disciplined, terrifying Wren. With her steel trap mind and mouth full of dry fire and that fucking scent—whatever part of it she'd *let* through over the years—it always hit harder than it should've.

Now I wondered if that was deliberate. If we'd only ever gotten what she allowed.

Rhett's knee bumped the back of my seat. "It's like I can feel us getting closer."

"Then keep your shit together," I said without opening my eyes.

"You gonna tell me you haven't felt it?"

"I didn't say that," I muttered. "I said keep it together."

That was the difference between me and them.

They burned loud. I burned *quiet.*

Even now, while I kept my body still, my thoughts were anything but. Images flickered behind my eyes, all of them her—pacing her office, hair pulled up tight, lips red from biting back her temper, her scent caught in the thread of her scarf.

I didn't need to see her slicked and needy and gone to know what I wanted.

I wanted her *here.* In her chair. In control. Snapping at us in that low, cutting voice of hers like she always did.

If she *was* in heat and *hiding* it, then she was scared someone would see her come undone. That someone might find out what she really was.

Maybe that someone had already tried. Anger flash-fired through me with brutal effect.

Roan spoke suddenly. "Rylan doesn't touch her. That's not up for debate."

The car went even quieter.

I turned my head toward the window and said, "Agreed."

Rhett's voice came low. "He tries, I'll kill him."

Roan didn't argue.

Neither did I.

The truth of that silence was heavier than anything we'd said.

CHAPTER
TWELVE

WREN

The phone buzzed again.

And again.

The muted thrum of it against the thick knit blanket I'd tossed over the kitchen table sounded like thunder against my skull. I didn't have the energy to reach for it, didn't have the clarity to care. I'd turned the alerts off, or thought I had. But somehow, the breaking news pings still came through.

Probably about me.

Probably about the photo.

About Rylan.

About the team.

Maybe about Roan. Maybe Rhett. Maybe Jay.

Each time the device shivered, it pulled at a thread I didn't have the strength to follow. The fog in my skull was dense now, burning at the edges. I'd given up on food hours ago—protein bars and electrolyte drinks lay scattered across the kitchen counter, some half-eaten, others untouched.

I'd torn off my hoodie somewhere between the bathroom and the firewood stack. Now I was curled into a corner of the old leather couch in just a tank and sweats, wrapped in a quilt that didn't stop the cold or the shivering.

Or the scent.

My scent.

Everything smelled like *me*. Too sharp. Too strong. Too much.

And outside...

God, the *snow*.

The first flakes had started falling hours ago—soft and harmless at first. Now it was relentless. It hissed as it hit the windows, rasped like whispers across the roof and deck. Not loud, not really, but persistent. Scraping against my brain like claws.

It sounded *wrong*. Like it wasn't falling—it was coming for me.

The world was so quiet out here, it amplified everything.

Too much.

It was all *too much*.

I'd taken the last suppressant forty-eight hours ago. Seventy-two was supposed to be the mark. The real turn. But my body had its own schedule. It always had. And now it was tightening the screws, locking me deeper inside a skin that didn't fit. The heat was no longer a whisper beneath my skin.

It was wildfire.

I couldn't sit still. Couldn't lie down. Couldn't focus. Couldn't *breathe*.

I'd tried to work. Failed. Tried to read. Failed harder.

The shower hadn't worked.

The water had gone from blistering hot to ice-cold, and I'd stayed there through both.

I'd braced my hands on the tile, the heels of my palms digging in like that would somehow ground me. I'd bitten my lip until I tasted blood. Let the steam curl around me and tried to pretend it was enough.

That *this* would be enough.

But it wasn't.

It never was.

Now, the couch creaked beneath me as I shifted again, one leg tucked up, the other half off the edge. I pressed the heel of my hand between my thighs, biting back a sound that felt more like frustration than need.

I tried again.

The palm of my hand, then fingers. I slipped a hand past the waistband of my sweats. The thin cotton of my underwear was already damp, and not from the snowmelt I'd tracked inside earlier.

It should've worked. It *used* to work.

Back before.

Back when I didn't have three very real, very untouchable reasons imprinted on the inside of my skull.

Roan, who watched the world like it was a threat and carried it like a burden.

Rhett, who deflected and charmed but had a storm living just under his skin.

Jay, who never touched unless invited, but looked like he *could*… and would… if you let him.

I ground the heel of my hand harder, chased the flicker of pleasure and came up short.

Every breath I took was ragged. My pulse thudded behind my eyes. I shifted again, pulled the blanket tighter, tried to block out the cold and the noise and the fire eating its way through my blood.

There were toys.

I'd packed them.

Had a whole bag with neatly folded towels and supplies and items I'd researched as I prepared everything for this break. Basic heat wasn't fun without a partner, but survivable. Lube, heat aids, even scent-masking candles could all help.

But they were in the other room. In a drawer.

And that was *too far*.

Too much.

I didn't want to go get them. Not when reality sank into my bones that I'd planned for everything—*everything*—except one key issue. Battery-operated toys, no matter how nice or cleverly designed, weren't *them*.

Nothing I brought would work. Nothing I touched would scratch the itch. Not when every cell in my body had apparently decided *now* was the moment it wanted... them.

I curled tighter into the blanket, furious at myself.

This wasn't supposed to happen like this. I was in control. I *had* been in control. I had *planned* for this.

I had done everything right.

Still, this aching, hollow, trembling need had bloomed like fire in my lungs and in my bones. I couldn't focus. Couldn't breathe. Couldn't even get myself off.

I bit the inside of my cheek hard enough to ground myself, but it barely worked.

My phone buzzed again from the other room.

Then again.

I didn't move.

Didn't look.

Didn't *want* to know.

Because if one more headline had my name in it—if one more notification lit up with their faces or some new speculation—I was going to lose the thread entirely.

Another breeze scraped against the cabin's window, a low moan through the wood.

Outside, the snow was falling faster.

Inside, I was coming apart by degrees.

And no one even knew.

Or... maybe they did.

Maybe that's what scared me most.

Sleep came in shards. Broken things. Sharp things. Beautiful, *cruel* things.

Every time I drifted off, I dreamed of them.

Roan's hands — steady, sure, bracketed on either side of me, holding me still while he looked down like I was something dangerous he couldn't quite put away.

Rhett's laugh, low and hot against my skin, all mischief turned molten.

Jay's voice, that cool precision melting into something that sounded like a command: *look at me, Wren.*

I'd jerk awake gasping, slick with sweat and want, sheets twisted around my legs. The change in location didn't help, not that I remembered moving. The cabin was too hot and too cold at once. I'd kick the blankets off only to drag them back up seconds later, the air biting at my skin.

Every dream ended the same way — a climax that didn't come, a voice that sounded *real*, and the crushing awareness of being alone.

Except now... I wasn't sure I *was.*

Somewhere between one breath and the next, the walls began to hum. The faint rattle of the windowpanes sounded too much like footsteps on the porch. The faint thud of snow slipping off the roof — too much like someone brushing against the door.

I sat up fast, heart hammering. The low light from the

embers in the fireplace painted everything in amber and shadow. My pulse was a drumbeat against my ribs.

There was *nothing* out there.

There *couldn't* be.

Still, I got up.

My knees almost gave out the moment I stood. Every inch of my body ached with need, a raw, throbby, living thing that pulsed in time with my heartbeat. I shoved the blanket aside, staggered toward the main door. My fingers fumbled on the lock before I twisted it shut. One. Two. Three times. The solid click of the deadbolt gave me a flash of relief that vanished as soon as I exhaled.

Then I heard it.

A voice. Soft. Rough-edged. Familiar. "Wren..."

My name. Whispered through the walls.

My stomach twisted.

"No," I muttered. "You're not here. You're not—"

"Wren." Another voice this time. Lower. Rougher.

It was Rhett's cadence, Rhett's *tone*, the teasing lilt sanded down by something darker.

My breath hitched, eyes darting toward the frosted windows. The glass was fogging. Slowly. Like breath pressed against the outside pane.

I stumbled back. "No. No, you're not—" My words cut off as another voice joined the others. Calm. Steady. Threaded with command.

"Open the door." *Roan.*

My throat went dry.

They weren't here. They couldn't be here. There was no reason for them to be here.

Except... the scent in the air shifted again, thickened, coiling with my pulse. My body *believed* them, even if my mind didn't. The room tilted.

I backed away, bumped into the corner of the sofa, then half-ran for the hallway. I slammed my bedroom door, twisted that lock too, pressed my forehead against the wood.

The sound outside the cabin intensified — a scuff, a low thump, something dragging through snow.

The fog on the windows was thicker now. I could see it from the crack under the door — dim light flickering against it. My imagination painted silhouettes in the haze. Shapes moving. Waiting.

A whimper escaped before I could stop it. Not fear. Something worse. Something needier.

"Go away," I whispered, but it didn't sound convincing. Not even to me. "Please…"

The silence that followed stretched too long. My pulse thundered, blood singing in my ears. Then—

A knock. Low. Heavy. Deliberate.

It rattled the whole cabin.

I staggered back until the backs of my knees hit the bed. My scent spiked and I *felt* it all thick, lush, and impossible to hide. The world narrowed to the hammering of my pulse, the phantom echo of their names still in the air.

I curled onto the bed, dragging the blanket over my head like it could block out the sound.

But the last thing I heard before I drifted under again, half-delirious and trembling, was a voice I couldn't mistake for a dream.

"Wren, open the door."

The wind had picked up.

At least, I *thought* it had. The sound outside deepened, a low rush that could've been a storm building… or footsteps crunching through fresh snow. The kind that didn't echo so much as *pressed* against the air.

I didn't look.

Couldn't.

If I looked, I'd see shapes and if I saw shapes, I might *believe* them.

Dragging the blanket tighter around my shoulders, I curled tighter on the bed, forehead pressed to my knees. My whole body pulsed in waves—hot, cold, electric. Every nerve ending felt wrong, exposed, like the world was rubbing raw salt into me just by existing.

"Stop it," I whispered, though I wasn't sure who I was begging. "Stop it, stop it, stop it—"

Outside, the wind howled, catching on the edge of the roof. Something thudded softly against the siding. A tree branch? A boot?

My chest seized.

This wasn't how heat was supposed to feel. Not this *deep*. Not this *lonely*.

The suppressants should've eased me out gently—years of careful dosing, of keeping everything quiet, contained, professional. I'd prepared for side effects. I'd *planned* for restlessness. A few sleepless nights, sure. Some craving, maybe.

Not this.

Not this complete unraveling of self.

Every breath tasted like lightning and salt and something half-feral. My body didn't know whether to fight or *beg*. I could smell my own scent—thick and sweet, clinging to the walls, bleeding into the air. I hated it.

It filled the cabin like proof.

Proof of everything I'd buried.

Proof that I wasn't built to be untouchable after all.

Outside, the snow whispered again—soft, slow. Too steady. Too *heavy*.

I jerked my head up, staring at the window.

The glass was completely fogged now, every inch blurred to white. But movement shifted behind it—a darker smudge crossing the pane. Another followed. Then another. My pulse spiked so fast I tasted metal.

It was a hallucination. It *had* to be.

I'd heard of this—extreme heats could trigger sensory distortions. You could imagine scents, sounds, touches. Your brain filled in what your body screamed for.

That was all it was.

Except...

When I pressed my palm to the wall, it *thudded.*

A weight on the other side.

A shadow of motion again, nearer the front door this time.

I wanted to sob. I wanted to claw out of my skin. I wanted to open the door and *run.*

But my body wouldn't obey.

Instead, I whispered, "This isn't how it's supposed to be."

My throat broke around it. "Why is it—hurting—why is it—"

My voice died under the sound of another thud, closer, like a shoulder or a hand against the porch railing.

Then silence.

The kind that pressed against your eardrums, thick and absolute.

My heart beat too fast, my breaths too short. Every inch of me trembled, heat pulsing through my veins like poison. I couldn't tell anymore if the world was really shaking—or if it was just me.

The air shifted again. A scent—faint but distinct— curled beneath the door.

Clean ice. Cedar. Smoke.

For one impossible moment, my instincts surged with recognition. My body *knew* that scent, wanted to drown in it, even as my mind screamed that it couldn't be real.

My lips parted. My voice came out cracked. "Roan?"

No answer.

Just the wind.

Just the snow.

Then there was me, half-delirious, half-wild, pressing my hand to the locked door as if I could stop my own heart from breaking through it.

For a while, there was nothing. Just the wind. Just the sound of my heartbeat, too loud in the stillness.

Then...

"Wren."

Soft. Familiar. Rhett.

That easy charm stripped bare, all smoke and hunger. His voice slid through the cracks in the door, brushing my skin like a whisper of heat.

"Wren, hey—look at me..."

My throat closed. I *could* hear him. I could *feel* him. I could almost *smell* him—warm amber and spice, the scent that always clung to his gear, to the crease of his grin.

But it was too vivid. Too real. A hallucination. It had to be.

I pressed my palms to my temples and tried to breathe through it.

Then another voice threaded in, cooler, deliberate.

Measured down to the breath.

"Wren, you need to open your eyes."

Jay.

The precision in his tone carved through the haze like a knife. I could almost *see* him in my mind—arms crossed, expression unreadable, those dark eyes cutting through every layer of my defenses.

And with it came the scent—crisp ozone and ink and something sharper, something male and grounding. My body reacted before my brain could deny it. My pulse *jumped*.

"No," I whispered, shaking my head. "You're not here. You're *not here*."

But the air was thickening again.

The heat pulsed harder.

Under it all—steady, deep, calm in a way that terrified me—came *him*.

Roan.

Not in sound at first. Not even in sight.

In scent.

Clean ice and cedar, steady as breath, the smell of control itself. It wrapped through the others, anchoring everything that threatened to splinter apart.

"Wren."

His voice was low this time. Close enough that it vibrated in my chest, in my *bones*.

I blinked, eyes blurring, and for one impossible second, I *saw* them—three shadows outlined through the fogged glass, tall and solid, shapes that could have been born from my worst or best dream.

My whole body locked. They couldn't be real. They *couldn't*.

But I could scent them.

All three. Layered together. Threaded through the snow. Crackling in my lungs.

Rhett's heat. Jay's ice. Roan's gravity.

My fingers trembled on the doorknob. I wanted to reach for it. I wanted to tear it open and *know*.

But my voice came out wrecked and small.

"Stop. Please. I can't—"

Then—

A single knock.

Hard. Sharp. Demanding.

The sound thundered through the cabin walls and straight into me.

The air stilled.

Through it, clear as the next heartbeat, came Roan's voice, real or imagined, I couldn't tell anymore.

"Open the door, Wren."

THIRTEEN

WREN

I couldn't think. My head spun, the world shifting beneath my feet, but I heard them. I felt them, and that, more than anything, was what made my hand move.

My fingers twitched against the cool handle of the door. I pressed my palm against it, steadying myself, even as the world seemed to tilt. *No.*

No. No.

They couldn't be here. Couldn't be.

I turned the knob. My vision swam—blurred. My pulse felt like it was thundering in my throat, thick and heavy, as I pulled the door open just a crack.

The shadows outside looked like them—like *them*—but they were ghosts, vague shapes.

It was too much.

Rhett's warmth washed over me, a low simmering storm, thick and spicy. I didn't know whether to *fight* or *collapse* into it, because every inch of my skin *ached* for it. And Jay—God, Jay was cold, so cold, like ice and earth, sharp enough to freeze the air around him, while Roan—

Roan was steady, pulling gravity in on itself until all I could feel was the space between us and how much I craved it.

Everything was *too much.*

I couldn't breathe.

"Wren," Jay said, his voice strained, but it was like the words were coming from miles away.

I wanted to *lean* into him. I wanted to feel his quiet strength wrap around me.

But I couldn't.

"Are you real?" I whispered, my throat raw, even though it was the stupidest question I could have asked.

A low chuckle from Rhett, and his voice rumbled in that damn way that made my insides twist.

"Yeah, baby. We're real." He took a step forward, but Roan was faster, his arm snapping out to shove Rhett back before his fingers could even graze my skin.

Rhett's growl was low, but Roan didn't even flinch. He just locked eyes with him, something like a warning flashing between them.

"No," Roan said, voice low and steady. "Not yet. Not without her permission."

Rhett sneered, but I saw the tension between them, the way Roan's words *landed* on Rhett. It made my stomach turn in knots, a whole mess of hunger and need.

I wanted them. I wanted to feel them. *All of them.*

But I couldn't even focus. The fog in my mind was too thick.

Roan's gaze moved to me. And as if the world had shifted, he came into sharper focus, his shoulders, the set of his jaw, the dark intensity of his eyes. He didn't move closer, though. Not yet. Just stood there, towering, calm, in a way I didn't understand.

I was burning from the inside out. And it *hurt.*

"Wren."

His voice broke through the haze, steady and controlled, everything about him like *ice* in the fire.

The scent of them—of *all three*—was everywhere, seeping into my lungs, flooding me. It didn't feel *real*, it felt like too much, too *fast*.

I reached for the doorframe. My fingers ached, my legs weak beneath me.

"I don't... I don't know..." I was whispering, barely able to even form words.

But Roan was there in an instant, his body filling the space between us, blocking out the rest of the world. He wasn't touching me, but he was close enough to make my whole body pulse with that illusion of contact.

"You don't need to know yet," he murmured, low and reassuring, like he was trying to anchor me. "You're okay."

But the closer he got, the more I needed—needed to be touched, needed them to prove they were *real*. But I didn't know how to ask for it.

I *couldn't*.

Jay took a half-step forward, watching me like he was waiting for something. For a cue. For *permission*.

But Roan stopped him. "Not yet."

Jay blinked, but nodded slowly, his breath coming in quiet pulls. He was calm, calm in a way I *wanted*, and I hated the way it made my chest ache.

"Wren," he said, quieter now, the edge gone from his voice. "You're not alone."

It was too much.

I couldn't take it. Not yet.

The flood of emotion, the hunger twisting in my gut, the ache between my legs—it was all too much.

"I can't..." I broke off, tears I didn't know I was holding back slipping down my face.

"I can't do this."

Rhett leaned against the doorframe, his eyes softening as he watched me, and something shifted in his expression —*understanding*. He didn't push this time. Neither did Roan.

But I could feel it. The *want*. The need.

All of them, waiting. Watching me.

And I wanted to scream.

But what would I scream for?

I was burning, and they were here. And yet, I couldn't have them. Not like this. Not without breaking something inside me.

Roan spoke again, his voice soft but insistent.

"Wren," he murmured, "we'll wait. When you're ready, we're here. But only when you're ready."

I closed my eyes, and it felt like everything in me *unraveled* at once.

I stumbled back.

Away from the door. Away from them.

My legs didn't want to work right. My knees were soft, my spine a weak reed of heat and panic and too much *need*. My shoulder hit the wall and I followed it down until I was crouched on the hardwood floor, my cheek pressed to the cool paneling near the baseboard.

It helped.

Not enough.

They didn't come after me.

Some part of me noticed that. *Registered* it.

They stayed outside. Even with the door cracked. Even with the scent of my heat pouring into the air between us like a siren's call. Every breath I took filled my lungs with the three of them, and it was so potent, so thick I could *taste* them.

Yet they still. Didn't. Move.

No footsteps. No door creaking open farther.

Just the low rasp of breathing and the fire in my chest as tears slipped down my cheeks.

This—*this*—was the exact moment I'd tried to avoid. The reason I'd run. Because if they saw me like this—wrecked, raw, undone in a way that couldn't be hidden—they'd see what I really was.

And I hated that.

I hated *needing*. I hated *breaking*.

And still... they came.

They *found* me.

How?

The word slipped out in a rasp I barely recognized as my own. "How?"

The door creaked a little wider although no one stepped through, but Jay's voice drifted in, calm and steady.

"We found reservations you didn't delete all the way. You left some digital breadcrumbs." The words didn't make a lot of sense. Then I couldn't really process anything digital or not.

Then he was moving, slow, careful.

A single hand reached around the corner of the doorframe. A bottle of water, still sealed.

"Here." His voice was gentle. "You should hydrate."

I stared at the water, then at the floor. I didn't trust my hands not to shake when I took it. But I did. I reached for it, and Jay let it go the second my fingers brushed plastic.

No contact.

No push.

I twisted the cap with shaking fingers and took a drink,

forcing it down. My throat burned, my stomach clenched, but the coolness helped. I drained half the bottle, and my hands were steadier by the time I set it down.

Still, they didn't come inside.

They could have. Any of them could've crossed the threshold. I was in heat, disoriented, needy and far from rational. I hadn't even locked the door. I'd cracked it open like an idiot because my body had begged for them and my instincts had won.

And yet...

"You're not coming in?" I asked, still breathless.

Roan's voice answered, level and smooth as slate. "Not unless you ask us to. Clearly. And only if you mean it."

That broke something in me. Not because of the words he used but because of his *control*.

I could *feel* what it cost him. What it cost *all* of them. The thick weight of their restraint pressing against my skin more than any touch ever had. The fact that they hadn't stormed in. Hadn't scooped me up or pinned me down or tried to kiss away the sweat-slick desperation from my skin.

They were white-knuckling it.

All of them.

I peeked up again.

Jay was closest to the door, kneeling now, his forearms resting on his thighs, still calm, still steady, though the cords of muscle in his jaw were tight. Rhett paced behind him, moving in small tight loops, like his skin didn't fit. And Roan—

Roan stood like a sentinel.

Arms crossed, braced in the doorway, like a dam holding back a flood. Eyes locked on me. Not my body. *Me.*

That look slowed everything down. The snow fluttering down behind them like an animated background, the golden glow of the porch light shining on them, crowning his hair with shimmering effect.

The more I stared, the more I *saw*. Like his control bled into the space between us, pressing back the fever inch by inch.

Giving me room.

Giving me *air*.

I didn't know how he was doing it, but with every second I stayed in that place, grounded by his presence, the fog receded just a little more.

I could *breathe*.

I drew in a shaky breath. "I didn't want this."

Jay nodded, solemn. "We know."

"I didn't want to hurt anyone. Or... put you in this position."

"No one's hurt," Roan said, quiet but firm. "We're here because we *chose* to come."

"Because we care," Rhett added, voice rough and hoarse. "Not because we're trying to take advantage."

God, the effort it must have cost him to say that.

My chest caved a little as another wave of something close to grief, but far closer to hope, washed through me.

Roan didn't take his eyes off me. "But we won't touch you, Wren. Not unless you ask us. Not unless it's *what you want*. Not heat-driven. Not instinct."

Just... me.

They would wait for *me*.

And the brutal honesty of that undid me more than anything else.

Tears welled up again—but this time they didn't feel sharp. They just *were*.

Real.

Because this was real.

They were *real*.

For the first time since the heat started, I felt like I wasn't completely alone.

I kept breathing. In. Out. In again.

Each pull of air scraped my throat raw, but it helped. It gave me something to count, something to hold on to.

They stayed where they were. Still. Steady.

That steadiness helped me push up from where I lay against the floor. Supported me as I took another long drink from the water, draining it. Lifted me when I put a hand on the wall and climbed to my feet. Gave me the strength to string words together.

"Can you..." I swallowed. "Can you handle being inside?"

The question came out half-directed at them, half at myself. Could *I* handle them being inside? The answer pulsed somewhere deep in my chest, hot and aching—*no*, but also *God, yes*.

I looked at the doorway, at the edges of their silhouettes blurred by the light snow that had started to drift past them. Tiny flakes clung to Roan's shoulders, melting as they touched his skin. Jay had a faint dusting of white in his hair, and Rhett... Rhett looked like a furnace barely leashed.

The cold felt *good* on my overheated skin, but they were standing out there in it, and it was stupid. I forced another breath through my nose. "You'll freeze," I murmured. "It's —stupid. I should let you in."

Roan's mouth curved, a small, almost tender smile that didn't reach his eyes. "We're not likely to freeze to death, Wren. We've played in worse."

That flicker of humor caught me off guard, and I almost laughed, almost, but it died before it left my throat.

"We can stay in the car if we need to," he continued,

voice quiet and even, the way he always sounded right before a puck drop. "You don't have to worry about us."

But that landed wrong in my chest. I *was* worried. Not just about them standing in the snow.

"No," I said, shaking my head. "That's not fair to you."

The words tumbled out before I could stop them. I was talking to them, but also to myself, as I began pacing unevenly in the tiny front room as if I could think my way through the heat burning beneath my skin. "It's just—the cabin's small, there's only one main room and the bedroom's—"

I broke off, realizing how insane I sounded, how fractured.

I wanted them close, but I didn't trust myself. I wanted *control*, but the longer they stood there, the more my body begged for things I'd spent a lifetime denying.

Roan's presence was still my anchor—steady, heavy, a solid weight in the storm—but the heat pulsed underneath all of it, a molten thread that made my skin prickle and my breathing stutter. Every time I inhaled, their scents tangled through mine—sharper now, more distinct—and it made it impossible to stay detached.

Jay's voice was the one that broke the silence next, soft and careful. "We can go," he said. "We'll stay close. Just to watch out for you. But if you'd rather we—"

"Don't." The word came out a whisper, but it cut through everything as I faced them, locking my legs so I didn't sway or fall.

I met his eyes. Then Roan's. Then Rhett's.

"Don't leave."

The plea escaped before I could smother it. No command, no mask, no control, just raw, honest need that trembled through every syllable. I would lose it if they left.

That knowledge poured through me as fiercely as the violent craving roiling inside.

For a heartbeat, none of them moved. The air between us went thick and quiet, full of things I couldn't name.

Roan's jaw flexed once, his gaze flicking to Jay, then Rhett. Then back to me.

"Okay," he said simply. "We won't."

Somehow, those two words steadied me more than anything else could have. Taking a deeper breath, deeper than any since the neediness took me over, I said, "Then come inside?"

CHAPTER
FOURTEEN
RHETT

I'd never wanted anything the way I wanted her.

Not a playoff run. Not a game-winning goal. Not even blood on the ice, and *that* was saying something.

Because normally? I could keep shit light. Flirty. Playful.

A joke here. A smirk there. Push the line, then pull back before it burned.

But not now. Now I was on fire from the inside out.

The only thing holding me together was the sheer *force* of Roan's presence. Not because he was growling or throwing weight around—not even close. He hadn't said a damn thing since we crossed the threshold. But his dominance radiated off him in steady, grounding waves. Not aimed *at* me, not meant to shut me down. Just *there*.

A low, thrumming reminder. Something to *grip onto* when I wanted to lunge.

Any other time, I would've taken that kind of ferocity as a challenge. But this wasn't about challenging Roan. This wasn't about power or pride.

This was about *her*.

Wren.

Wren, who stood barefoot on the worn wood floor, swaying just a little, like she couldn't decide if she wanted to bolt or drop to her knees.

Wren, who had her arms wrapped around herself like she could hold her own body together while her skin flushed golden in the low light.

Fuck, she was so beautiful it hurt.

Midnight blue-black hair in tangled waves, the kind of wild mess that begged for someone's hands in it—mine, preferably—but even disheveled, she looked unreal. Ethereal. Like something made of shadow and fire.

And those eyes. *God.*

Honey-colored, warm and sharp, but rimmed in that almost metallic gold that likely only showed when she was like *this*.

Not a mask in sight.

She kept running her fingers through her hair—agitated, restless, pacing—and I couldn't stop staring at the way her skin shimmered under the soft glow of the cabin lights. Not literally, no glitter or sparkle. But it was *there*, like golden honey dust swept over her collarbones and throat and arms and the delicate edges of her jaw.

It made me ravenous.

Made my mouth dry.

Made the primal part of me, the part I usually kept leashed, *howl*.

And I wanted—*Fuck, I wanted.*

Wanted to sink my hands into her hair, taste that glow on her skin, drag my tongue along the sweet hollow beneath her throat and see if it melted like sugar.

But I didn't move. Not even a step.

Roan was still and silent behind me, a mountain of

control and unreadable strength, and Jay... Jay hadn't spoken once since she'd told us not to leave. He stood just inside the door, not too close, not too far. Watching. Waiting. Like he always did. Like he could *read* the room better than any of us.

I couldn't read anything right now except the way Wren's scent had changed.

The sweetness of it. The dizzy, golden-bright pull of her.

It was *wrong* how good it was. Wrong how *perfect*. It made my gums ache, made my fingers twitch.

Made it hard to breathe.

So I stayed where I was. Tensed. Hot. Unmoving.

Holding the line because Roan hadn't told me to step back, but he hadn't told me to move forward either. His restraint bolstered my own, even as Jay's serenity seemed to calm the stormy waves slashing against me inside. If there was even *one* breath of uncertainty in Wren, then we were staying exactly where we were.

God help me, though. If she *asked*. If she whispered my name with *want* instead of fear— I didn't know if I could survive it.

Because I didn't just want her scent, or her heat, or her permission. I wanted *her*. All of her.

There wasn't a damn thing playful about my desire or the primitive demand unfolding in my soul. A demand I'd *never* experienced once in my life and wasn't entirely certain I was prepared to cope with right now.

Jay moved first.

Quiet. Measured. Controlled like always. The kind of control that didn't *ask* for attention but *commanded* it anyway.

He didn't look at Wren as he moved through the room.

Didn't crowd her. Didn't even glance her way too long. He just started collecting—blankets first, then the towels crumpled at the end of the couch, a water bottle knocked on its side, her laptop halfway out of its case, like she'd tried to work and couldn't focus.

The normalcy of it should've been grounding.

But the second he lifted the first blanket, the *scent* hit me.

Hot and heady. Intimate in a way that made my heart stutter in my chest. That blanket had *held* her—probably for hours. Maybe days. It was soaked in her, steeped like tea, and *fuck me,* it was glorious and devastating and *not mine.*

I reeled back half a step, sucking air in through my teeth.

Not enough. Not *clean.* Every breath I took was full of *her.*

"I'm sorry," Wren said suddenly, her voice small and raw as she crossed her arms over her chest. "I should've washed them—I meant to, I just— I can't seem to keep my scent under control anymore."

The pain in her voice sliced straight through my ribs.

But before I could say something—*anything*—Roan answered. Firm. Calm. Steady. "Don't worry about it."

And what the *hell*—how was he this composed?

He didn't even blink. Didn't shift his weight or clench his fists or *react* in any of the ways I knew his body was probably screaming to.

It was like his dominance built a wall around him, and somehow Wren's need didn't pierce it the way it was gutting me from the inside out.

How was he *not* unraveling?

I had no goddamn idea.

Jay took the blankets and towels to the kitchen and opened the tiny stacked washer-dryer in the closet. His movements were smooth, practical. I didn't even think he was trying to scent-mark or assert some kind of claim—it wasn't that.

He was just *taking care* of her.

"Wren," he called gently as he dropped the last towel in and started the wash cycle. "You need more water. And something to eat."

Caretaker voice. I'd seen Jay use it before, usually on rookies who'd collapsed after an overlong training skate or got heat exhaustion on an away game. It was clinical. Cool. Compassionate without inviting pushback.

And I realized—

He wasn't holding the line *for* her.

He was holding it *with* her.

Maybe I was the only one seeing it. The way he folded into that role without question. Without hesitation. Not weakness. Not a passive thing. He was just... *there*.

Like he always was.

Wren gave a shaky laugh—sharp and brittle and too real.

"Oh my god," she said, pressing a hand to her forehead. "This is either the worst moment of my life or the most humiliating. No, wait—maybe both. I'm going for the double."

The sound of it—it was beautiful and *awful*, a little wild and a little too close to a sob.

Roan finally moved, just a step forward, arms still loose at his sides, his body language a masterclass in non-threatening.

"Focus on the funny part," he told her. "The rest is just noise."

And *shit*—the fact that his voice didn't even tremble—

That was what held me together.

So, I leaned into it. Into the only thing I *could* offer in that moment.

"Hey," I said, throwing on a grin even if my voice came out rougher than I wanted. "You think this is bad? At least you're not stuck in a cabin in the middle of nowhere with three guys trying not to spontaneously combust like badly written fanfic."

Wren blinked. Her mouth twitched.

I grinned wider. "Seriously. All we need now is a conveniently timed blizzard and someone to shout *'there's only one bed!'*"

That did it.

She let out a startled laugh—*real*, this time. It punched through the tension in the room like sunlight through storm clouds.

Bright and loud and *alive*.

It lit her from the inside out and brightened her *glow*. Lit *me* up too, like every cell in my body remembered how to breathe.

For one perfect second, the fevered ache of wanting her wasn't unbearable.

It was just *want* and it was beautiful. Wren's laughter was like getting punched in the chest and kissed on the mouth at the same time.

God, it was a *relief*.

A pure, gut-deep, holy shit we didn't lose her kind of relief. That sound soaked straight into my bloodstream, carved through the tension, and reminded me she was still *her* under all of this. Still the Wren who outmaneuvered media sharks with one hand and kept three overclocked alpha athletes in check with the other.

Even if her legs were shaking.

She eased herself onto the couch, spine curved, shoulders trembling with the aftermath of whatever strength it had cost her to stay upright this long. But she didn't collapse.

She didn't break.

And that meant I could keep my goddamn feet planted where they were instead of crossing the room to touch her the way every instinct inside me screamed to.

Her smile lingered, faint and almost wry, her eyes glassy but glowing like melted gold as she looked between the three of us.

"There's only one actual bed," she said, too solemn for the words to be anything but a tease. "I think the sofa folds out into another. And I can always make a pallet on the floor somewhere."

I *snorted* before I could stop myself. "Yeah, okay. Good luck with that. You think *any* of us are gonna let you sleep on the floor?"

Jay let out a soft huff of agreement behind me, and Roan didn't say anything, but his jaw tensed in that way that said *absolutely not happening.*

But since Wren seemed in the mood to play—*and dear god, let her stay in that mood*—I cocked my head and offered, "Okay, but what about the blizzard? Any bad weather in the forecast? Because I gotta say, I'm committed to the fanfic plot line now."

She licked her lips absently and lifted one shoulder in the smallest shrug. Even that simple movement—hair falling across her cheek, the shimmer of her skin, the curve of her collarbone—was *erotic* as hell. Like she was built to utterly undo me with nothing but the tilt of her head.

"I have no idea," she murmured, voice soft and rough and full of suggestion. "Should we check?"

That was all I needed—hell, I was about to start pulling up weather apps on my phone when—

"Only if we get to bet on what the weather says," Roan said, deadpan.

And *that* made me freeze.

Jay, too.

Even Wren blinked, lips parting as she turned those luminous, heat-drenched eyes on him.

A long pause.

Her voice was low. Curious. "What are we betting for?"

Roan didn't answer immediately.

But his gaze stayed locked on her like a tether—like if he looked away, the whole room would fall apart again. I had a sudden feeling whatever he said next... was going to matter.

"Are you open to negotiation?" Roan asked, voice quiet but unshakably firm.

Wren blinked, something catching in her breath. Her fingers curled a little tighter around the edge of the throw blanket she hadn't realized she'd pulled over her lap.

"The captain wants to negotiate?" she asked, tilting her head slightly, and her tone was somewhere between amusement and caution.

Roan didn't miss a beat. "Not a captain here," he said, and there was an edge under the words that turned them into something more than just a clarification. "You're not our PR goddess who takes care of everything, and we're not the ice jockeys. This isn't about offense or defense."

Okay. *Okay.* I had to give it to the guy. That was a damn

strong move. The kind of statement that slowed everything down and made the air feel thick. Wren's mouth parted like she might argue, but instead she blinked once, slowly, and stayed quiet.

"So," I said, stepping into the silence because someone had to, "are we all negotiating then?"

Roan shot me a look. One of *those* looks—half *do not test me*, half *you better follow through now*, and somehow also a little bit amused. Encouraging, even.

Fine. I could play serious, too. At least until my brain got steamrolled by the visuals currently setting up camp behind my eyes.

Jay, of course, was the first to speak up.

"Good." His voice was that calm, anchoring baritone again. The one that let you breathe even when your skin was too tight. "If I call it, I want Wren to let me run her a bath."

Wren inhaled sharply.

Jay went on, evenly. "You're trembling. I can see it, and I imagine your legs are cramping. You need heat—not just internal, but real, steady warmth. So that's what I want if I win."

Roan didn't move.

Wren stared at Jay like she couldn't quite believe him. Not because it was too much.

But because it was... *exactly right.*

She didn't say yes. Not yet.

So I stepped up, because how could I *not?*

"If I call it," I said, hearing my voice come out rougher than I meant it to, "I want you to let me feed you."

Wren's gaze whipped to me, stunned. Probably because I hadn't even meant to say it.

"No skin-to-skin," I added quickly. "Just me... cutting up the fruit. Feeding you pieces. That's it."

That wasn't what I meant to offer.

Not even close.

But apparently it *was* what I wanted.

She blinked again, a little slower this time. Her lips parted. She looked at me like I'd just handed her a warm coat in a snowstorm.

Then her gaze shifted and landed on Roan.

She swallowed once, then asked, soft but steady, "And you? What do you want?"

Roan looked at her like he saw *everything*. Not just her flushed skin or trembling limbs. Not just the curve of her mouth or the way her scent was filling every inch of this cabin with honeyed fire and desperation.

But the way she was still holding the line.

Still trying to choose.

He didn't speak right away. The silence was nearly unbearable.

Then—

"If I win..." he said slowly, "I want you to let me help you sleep."

A breath hitched in Wren's throat.

Roan continued, low and steady, every word anchored in something that had nothing to do with lust and everything to do with *care*. "Let me sit next to you. Let me keep the others back. Let me be there while you rest. Just that. Nothing else. Not unless you ask for it."

Wren's eyes shimmered, and fuck, *my* throat closed up, just a little.

There were a hundred things I wanted. Needed. A thousand ways I wanted to touch her, to lay claim to her scent now tangled with mine, with all of ours. But Roan...

Roan just wanted to guard her sleep.

And that...

Yeah. That did something to me.

To all of us.

Wren's breath stuttered. Her lashes lowered. Her voice, when it came, was barely more than a whisper. "So who gets to call it?"

FIFTEEN

The clear-headedness was like a thread in water—visible for a second, then gone.

But I grasped it with both hands.

Rhett's teasing helped. His playful charm cut through the suffocating swirl of need that had pinned me to the walls of my own body. Jay's concern anchored me, practical and quiet, never crowding, never asking for more than I could give. And Roan...

Roan was bedrock.

I watched them now from where I sat, still trembling, still aching, but not drowning.

Not *yet*.

They stood in a loose triangle a few feet away from me, angled slightly toward one another, not speaking. But something passed between them. A look. A shift of breath. A weight of silence that said more than words ever could.

And I realized, all at once, that I'd never *really* seen them before.

Not like this.

Not like someone who *wanted* them.

Roan stood the tallest, broad and cut from glacier stone, pale blonde hair immaculately short, steel-gray eyes as sharp as ever—but softer, too. There was something in his stillness, in the calm he wrapped himself in, that felt like a shield thrown over all of us. That calm had always impressed me professionally.

Now, it burned.

The *control* he wielded over himself... the discipline of a man who had locked away his instincts for years. I could feel it, pulsing under his skin like heat beneath ice. And still, he didn't move toward me. Didn't even shift his weight. His restraint wasn't rejection—it was reverence.

And maybe that was the worst part.

Because I could *feel* how badly he wanted to move.

My eyes dragged to Rhett, standing just slightly off to Roan's left, coiled and twitchy. All fire and honey-brown skin, his dark curls a little unruly from the hat he'd worn, brown eyes still sharp despite the aching edge of desperation beneath his usual swagger. He was beautiful in a way that always made people turn around twice—and when he smiled, it was lethal.

Right now, he wasn't smiling.

But the wildness in him wasn't hostile. It was *devoted*. He vibrated with the need to protect, to touch, to *give*. His lips were parted like he was holding back words—or something more primal—and his hands were fists at his sides.

He'd go feral if I asked him to.

God help me, that idea made me shudder.

Then there was Jay.

Dark where the others were light, sharp where they were broad. His black hair fell in a slant across his brow like it had been styled that way by intention, not wind. His lean frame moved with quiet grace as he adjusted something on the counter—some clutter I hadn't realized I'd left. His hands were elegant, long fingers deft as he cleaned without fanfare.

He didn't look at me. Not yet.

But he was listening.

Jay always listened.

The beta.

Or... maybe not.

Because when my scent rose again—slight, unwilling, but undeniably mine—I saw the shift in his spine. The way his head tilted, slow and deliberate, like a predator catching the edge of something they weren't supposed to crave.

He didn't show hunger.

He showed *awareness*.

Of me.

Of us.

And still, none of them moved.

Not toward me. Not toward each other. Just three distinct storms caught in the same current. All of them watching. Waiting.

For *me*.

I exhaled slowly. My body was still burning, still on fire in places I could barely stand to notice. But the pulse of it had slowed, just enough for thought.

Just enough for desire to settle into fascination.

My gaze moved from Jay to Rhett, then to Roan—and back again.

This was the situation I'd been hiding to avoid. Not just the heat. Not just the loss of control.

It was *them*.

And what I might mean to them.

And yet...

They came.

They *found* me.

For a long moment, none of us moved.

Not even to breathe.

But I had asked them to stay.

And they had.

No hesitation.

Just quiet, restrained chaos pressed into male bodies, all three of them wrestling with their own urges and instincts and *not* touching me—because I hadn't said they could.

And because Roan wouldn't let them.

That authority didn't come with loud declarations. He hadn't had to growl or posture or throw his weight around. It radiated from him like gravity—quiet, dense, unshakable.

It steadied them.

It steadied *me*.

Enough to breathe through the worst of the heat flare. Enough to let my body settle into a strange place—still needy, still aching, but no longer frenzied.

Still mine.

Which was maybe the most important part.

My breath came easier now, even if my body still trembled. I took another sip of water, knees drawn up toward my chest on the edge of the sofa. They'd all given me space without needing to be asked. Even Rhett, who looked like someone had tied him to the floorboards and whispered *don't move* straight into his bloodstream.

I glanced up at them.

Three men. Three monsters.

My monsters.

Don't think like that.

"Okay," I said slowly, voice hoarse but clearer than it had been. "If I remember correctly... we were placing bets on the weather."

Rhett lit up like I'd handed him a loaded squirt gun and pointed at a room full of suits. "Hell yes, we were. And I stand by my guess, blizzard. The kind where you can't see the road signs, and someone loses a boot trying to check the mail."

Jay rolled his eyes and leaned a hip against the counter. "It's not even snowing that hard right now. My guess is light snow overnight, clear by morning."

Roan's gaze slid from one to the other, then to me.

"Four more inches by midnight. Wind advisory. Ice warnings on secondary roads. Your basic shut-it-down storm."

I blinked at him.

"Are you... quoting the forecast or making your bet?"

His mouth twitched. "Just a guess."

Of course it was. He probably *was* the forecast.

I blinked again, brain catching up. "Wait... does *anyone* have a phone?"

"Just you," Jay said, his voice mild as he straightened. He reached into his hoodie pocket and handed it over. "It started pinging again about twenty minutes ago. I silenced it."

I stared at him. "How did you...?"

"You left it in the kitchen." A pause. "Under a towel. Not exactly state-of-the-art hiding."

I took the phone from him carefully, our fingers not touching.

The heat in me pulsed, deep and slow and unrelenting.

But it didn't spike.

Okay. Okay...

I unlocked the screen with a shaky thumb, ignoring the dozens of notifications lining my feed. Sports updates, PR pings, news alerts, and—

Yep. There it was. Weather app already open in a background window, probably from earlier in the week.

I refreshed it.

Then looked up.

"Well?" Rhett asked, leaning forward like a very excited golden retriever trying to solve a murder mystery.

I raised a brow. "Anyone want to change their bet?"

Roan just gave me that patient, unreadable look.

Jay tilted his head.

Rhett made an exaggerated "nope" gesture with both hands.

"Alright then," I murmured.

I read the screen out loud.

"Current temperature, twelve degrees. Wind chill bringing it down to two. Snowfall expected to continue through the evening. Accumulation: four to five inches. Icy road warnings in effect through tomorrow morning..."

I looked up at Roan.

"You win."

His smile—small, faint, just the barest uptick of his lips —still somehow hit me low and hard.

"Of course he does," Jay muttered, pushing off the counter. "He's probably telepathically linked to the fucking Doppler radar."

"Don't be jealous," Rhett said, but he was already grinning. "We'll just beat him in the next round."

Roan looked at me then, and even from across the room, I *felt* the quiet weight of his attention. "So, Wren. We placed our bets."

My pulse tripped.

"Time to collect," Rhett added, a little too bright, a little too sharp.

And I realized—

This was what it felt like to be wanted by all three of them.

No pressure.

No demands.

Just open hands and simmering patience and *want* so deep I could feel it anchoring me to the earth.

And the only one who got to decide what happened next... was me.

I could still feel the heat curling inside me, but something about Roan's steady presence gave me a buffer, made it if not easier, then possible to breathe. His quiet confidence and his patience acted like an anchor. It was so easy to sink into that, to let him take control in the way he knew best. *How he always knew best.*

Of course, Roan had won. It was so *him*—never take a bet he wasn't sure about. Never do anything half-assed. It didn't matter if it was on the ice or in a game of odds about weather. Roan *knew.*

Yet, even now, as I tried to hold onto a fragile clarity, I was still left strung tight. His quiet dominance was soothing in one moment, but in the next, it felt like too much. The weight of everything pressed down on me again, like it always did when I allowed myself to truly *feel* the space I was in with them. The presence of their bodies. The scent of them—fresh, masculine, burning-hot, and unyielding.

"Are you going to help me sleep?" I asked before I could stop myself, and even as the words left my mouth, I was surprised by the vulnerability that bled into my voice.

Roan's eyes softened, but his jaw remained taut. "That was the bet," he answered, his voice just as even, just as controlled as ever. But then he added, "Do you want to take a bath first? Eat something?" He raised a brow, clearly offering the decision to me.

I blinked, caught off-guard. *He's giving me control.*

No one had ever done that before—not like this. Not with so much *care* woven into the offer. I could see the surprise flicker in both Jay and Rhett's eyes. Neither of them had expected this from Roan—*Roan* Whittaker, the man who always had a plan, who was always the rock.

But he was handing it over to me. All of it. I could feel the weight of it. *What does that mean?*

Part of me wanted to give in. Wanted to let him take care of everything, to fall into the quiet, open strength he was offering me. But I didn't—couldn't—give in that easily. My thoughts were a tangled mess.

"Maybe... sleep first?" I said slowly, testing the waters. "I don't know that I can really eat, and I've showered so much already... maybe a bath later?"

Roan's face softened further, the sharp lines of control in his expression melting away. He nodded, just once, as if it was already decided.

"Sleep it is," he said, his voice gentle but firm. "Let's get you into bed."

As he moved toward me with that purposeful grace that always had a way of putting everyone else on pause, I felt myself pull back. Not in fear, but in uncertainty. The flood of everything swirling inside me made it hard to know what was *right* anymore.

Rising, I forced deeper breaths. My legs felt weak, and for the first time, I didn't want to be alone. Not with the heat still coursing through my veins, not when the temptation to give in to everything was this strong.

I paused in the doorway that separated the main room from the bedroom.

I wasn't sure what to say—*what I should say*—but in the end, the question slipped out of me, unexpected, almost reckless. "Will you stay?" My voice was soft, fragile in the air between us, but I didn't care anymore.

I knew the consequences of what I was asking. The consequences of needing them so badly. Of wanting them too much.

But I still asked. "I know if you stay... it might mean you're trapped here with me."

Roan's gaze never wavered. His hand settled on my back, the blanket and the tank top I wore, keeping his skin from touching mine. Everything about him remained steady and calm, but his eyes? They were sharp, full of something that made me feel seen, understood. His voice rumbled low in the room. "I'm staying."

Then Jay spoke up, his voice carrying a seriousness that cut through the earlier tension. "We all are."

Rhett, too, didn't hesitate. "Yeah. I'm not leaving."

They didn't even flinch at the thought of being stuck here with me. It was something—something that shouldn't have been this simple, yet *was*.

I didn't have to make the decision for them. They had already made it for me. For a fleeting moment, that sensation of relief flooded me all over again.

They were staying. They were here. For me.

I couldn't explain why that felt so monumental, but I didn't need to. All I knew was that for the first time in... *forever*, I wasn't alone.

Maybe, just maybe, I could stop pretending I could do it all myself.

Roan's hand slid to my shoulder as he gently coaxed me into the room, his presence grounding me. Rhett and Jay remained in place, just outside the door, but I could feel them. Even without looking, I knew they were there.

It was a strange sort of peace, surrounded by all of them—my strength, my security, my *monsters*.

I stepped into the room, feeling the weight of everything shift again, but this time... in a way I couldn't explain. Or maybe I didn't have to.

I wasn't sure of the future. But I was sure of this moment.

I wasn't alone.

Not anymore.

CHAPTER

SIXTEEN

ROAN

She was trembling by the time I got her to her room.

Wren didn't weigh much—barely anything at all—but the determination in her kept me from just sweeping her up in my arms. She carried so much more right now than just this burning need. The weight of everything she'd hidden, everything she was still trying to hide, even from herself.

I was careful and minimized the contact to just hovering close in case she stumbled. Maybe I was too careful, but I didn't think *that* was possible. I didn't let my skin touch hers, not once. I had gloves on, sleeves pulled down, jacket buttoned to the collar. She was a bonfire, and I didn't want to go up in flames.

Not without permission.

She was quiet, mostly, but twitchy. Her body fought between exhaustion and instinct, nerves shot from the overexposure of the day. Her scent—gods, her scent—was thick, syrupy sweet, soaked in suppressed heat and tangled anxiety. It clawed through every restraint I had like it was looking for a way in.

I straightened the blankets as she stared at the bed, almost belatedly realizing they were wrecked from her restlessness. Once she'd laid down, I pulled them up to cover her. Her eyes were already half-closed, whether in sleep or just lost in the haze, I wasn't sure. Still, better to just tuck her in.

"No," she murmured. Her fingers fluttered out, reaching—not consciously, not quite—but the motion sent a jolt through me. Her hand was bare. My instincts surged, pushing past the walls I'd spent years building. I jerked back and snatched the throw blanket at the end of the bed, wrapping it around her in one swift motion before her fingers could graze mine.

Her eyes blinked open, hazy and confused. "Why can't I —" she shifted again, frowning. "You're so warm. Why can't I touch you?"

Because I wouldn't survive it.

"You agreed to let me help you sleep," I said, voice low. "That's all we agreed on."

She opened her mouth like she might argue, but then the scent of her deepened again—warmth, frustration, longing. It caught in my throat like smoke. I forced myself to breathe through my mouth.

"You're hiding yourself," I said before I could stop the words. "Suppressants?"

Wren didn't answer right away. Her eyes flicked to mine, sharp despite the haze, and for a moment I saw the real her—omega, fighter, survivor. Then her lashes lowered, and she nodded.

"Over a decade," she murmured. "They're not illegal. Not really."

"No," I said, jaw tight. "They're not endorsed either. There's a reason for that."

"They let me survive," she whispered. "They let me... live the way I needed to."

And gods help me, I wanted to be angry. I *was* angry. At her. At the system. At whoever had made her think suppressing something so fundamental was the only way she could be safe, be free.

But she was barely holding on. Her face turned into the blanket, cheek pressing into it like she was trying to disappear again, burrow away from the reality she'd peeled back just enough to show me.

"Sleep," I told her. It came out more like a command than I intended.

She fought it. Of course she did. Her body was wound tight with lingering adrenaline, tension, scent. But the exhaustion was winning. Slowly, her muscles loosened, her breath slowed.

I sat with her, holding her carefully—arms circled *around* the blanket, never under it. My head tilted back against the wall behind her bed, and I stared at the ceiling like it might offer me some way out of this storm.

Her breath feathered against the side of my throat. Her warmth soaked into my chest through layers of fabric and resolve. Every inhale was torment—sweet, sharp musk that wanted to sink its teeth into me and *stay*.

I stayed still. Locked it down. Iron-fisted control.

She'd let me in this far. That was all she'd consented to. And I'd earned that much—barely. I wasn't about to betray it.

But the more I held her, the more I thought about all the ways she'd kept this hidden. The more I reframed every look, every tense breath, every time she flinched away from her own biology.

And the angrier I got.

I kept that locked down, too.

Because this wasn't about me. Not yet.

She'd taken risks—unnecessary ones. Dangerous ones. The kind that could have hurt her. The kind that had clearly hurt her already.

I had questions. Too many. But now wasn't the time.

She was asleep now—fitful, restless, caught in half-dreams, murmuring things I couldn't quite catch. Her fingers flexed in the blanket. I didn't loosen my grip. I didn't let myself respond.

One day, I'd ask her why. Why she chose this path. Why she thought she had to walk it alone. One day, I'd earn the right to those answers.

But not tonight.

Tonight, I would just hold her and burn.

She shifted again in my arms, a soft exhale warming the side of my neck, and I focused on the rhythm of her breathing. Slow. Uneven. But deeper now. Sleep was claiming her, if only in pieces.

Through the thin walls, I could hear Rhett pacing. His footsteps were steady, but erratic in pattern—he was struggling but thinking and worrying. I could hear Jay too, lighter on his feet, his movements purposeful. Cleaning, as he always did when he couldn't fix something with his hands.

I didn't blame either of them. This wasn't something we could fix. Not easily.

My senses had been sharpening for days—maybe longer. Since we started tracking her, something inside me had started pulling tighter, tuning sharper, like a blade honing itself. At first I thought it was stress. Then instinct. Now... I wasn't sure it wasn't something else entirely.

I concentrated on my breathing—controlled, even—

and felt it ripple outward. A steadying anchor. I let it bleed into the air around me, the way I'd done with the team more times than I could count. When adrenaline threatened to fracture cohesion mid-game, when panic clawed at the edge of someone's focus—I could pull it down, spread calm like a blanket.

It was working now too. Rhett's steps slowed. Jay's cleaning settled into a softer rhythm.

Even *I* could think more clearly.

I looked down at her—at *Wren*. The stubborn, sharp, guarded omega curled up against me, wrapped in a barrier of cloth and walls she'd built around herself for so long, I wasn't sure she remembered how to step outside them. And still she'd let me do this. Trusted me to hold her. To *not* act on every instinct clawing at the inside of my ribcage.

I'd earned that much. Maybe not more.

But I'd *earn* the rest. I had to.

My thoughts drifted, unbidden, to that night—two years back, after the championship. That party had been chaos. The kind that always came with victory: loud music, expensive liquor, and bodies pressed too close under the hot haze of triumph and sweat.

Most of the team dove in headfirst. Celebration in its rawest, wildest form.

I'd lasted maybe ten minutes before I'd peeled away from the crowd. The noise, the press of scents, the heat—it was all too much, too fast. Too hollow.

She'd been there, of course. Wren.

Working.

Wearing a dark suit with her hair twisted up and her sharp mouth set in that firm, unshakable line she wore like armor. Her tablet had been in one hand, her stylus twirling absently in the other as she monitored the event like it was a top-notch spy mission or something.

I could still picture the way her eyes would flick across the room, calculating the danger of every half-drunk millionaire and rising rookie with poor impulse control. It was adorable, in a way. Impressive, too. She was good at it. Always had been.

I sat beside her, nursing a drink I didn't finish. She glanced at me, brow arched.

"No harem of admirers waiting for your attention?" she asked dryly.

"They can wait," I said. "You're the most interesting thing in the room."

She'd rolled her eyes, but I caught the flicker of amusement she didn't hide fast enough. That smile, biting and real, had stayed with me longer than I'd admitted at the time.

A woman had flung herself into my lap not ten minutes later—beautiful, eager, everything a man was supposed to want after a win like that. I'd stood, put her gently on her feet, and excused myself with a kind smile and a shake of the head.

Wren had looked at me, slightly bemused. "You *do* know it's legal to enjoy yourself after a win?"

I'd held her gaze, unflinching. "I *am* enjoying myself."

And I had been. Sitting beside her. Listening to her tear into the absurdity of the team's spending habits, her dry commentary laced with subtle fondness. She never once tried to outshine the room. She didn't have to, she just *was* the brightest part of it.

I should have known then.

A part of me *did* know. But I buried it. For her sake. For

the team. For the lines we weren't allowed to cross and the futures we thought we were protecting.

I looked at her now—soft in sleep, but not peaceful. Her face twitched faintly, like even in dreams she was battling something. It wasn't fair. That she'd had to fight so long. That she'd taken suppressants for a decade just to survive the world as it was.

Suppressants weren't illegal, no. But they weren't safe either. Not really. Not for long.

Some studies suggested that they masked more than scent. They dulled *everything*. Even instincts. Even pain.

What had she given up to live like that?

As aggravating as that thought was, I wanted to know what had I missed—by letting her?

My grip tightened fractionally around her blanket-wrapped form, but I didn't let myself move. Didn't let myself feel the way her breath still danced over my throat, the way her warmth soaked into me.

I let myself look at her now. Really *look*.

I'd stopped avoiding the truth. I was done pretending I didn't know what this was between us. What it had always *been*.

When her heat passed, we were going to talk. No more guessing. No more hiding. No more letting her carry it all alone.

Whatever it was—whatever she'd been afraid of—I'd take it. Piece by piece, if that's what she needed.

But not tonight.

Tonight, I held her.

I held her and I waited.

The door creaked open with the softest whisper of hinges, and I didn't need to look to know it was Jay.

His scent hit first, all cool linen, tea tree oil, and that quiet steadiness that was as much a part of him as his pulse. He moved carefully, silently, like he understood exactly how delicate this space was. Which, knowing Jay, he probably did.

He held two bottles of water and a bag that smelled like something warm and savory—bread, broth, maybe rice. Nutrients she'd need when she woke, and more that he clearly meant for me.

I looked up as he crossed the threshold, then back down at Wren, who hadn't stirred. Her brow twitched once, but the fitful sleep held. For now.

Crouching low, Jay set the food down on the desk without a sound, then straightened and passed me one of the bottles.

"You need to eat," he said, his voice pitched low, barely above a whisper. "And drink. Especially if you're not planning to sleep."

I took the bottle, twisting the cap one-handed and drinking half in one go. I hadn't realized how dry my throat was. "I will," I said.

Jay gave me a look. Not skeptical—just firm.

"I will," I repeated, then nodded toward the wrapped bundle of omega warmth in my arms. "When she's deeper under. I don't want to shift her right now."

He glanced at her, his expression unreadable, but his nostrils flared just slightly. That was the first confirmation. The second came a beat later when his jaw tightened, just a flicker of strain that most wouldn't catch, but I wasn't most people.

"White-knuckling it?" I asked, just enough edge to my voice to let him know I saw it.

Jay exhaled slowly. "I'm not immune, Roan. None of us are. But I'm *trained*. I'm fine."

He *was* trained and had years of mental discipline, medical knowledge, scent desensitization drills, the works. Still. Wren's heat was potent, even suppressed. The fact that a beta like Jay was feeling it said a lot about how far things had progressed—and how much she must've been suppressing.

Before I could press the thought, Rhett's voice drifted in from the next room.

"I've been doing some research on suppressants."

Jay's eyes flicked toward the door. I didn't answer. Just nodded once, slow and steady, letting Rhett know to go on.

He didn't come in. Just stood there, pacing again, voice pitched the same as ours—low and careful.

"It's not great news," Rhett said, and there was weight behind the words. It cost him something to even say it. "There are studies... not many, but enough to be concerning. Some suggest the longer someone is on suppressants, the more likely they are to experience lasting effects."

I didn't speak. Just held Wren a little closer, felt her breath brush against my throat. My arms tightened around the blanket. Around her.

"Lasting," I said eventually. "As in permanent?"

"Some cases, yeah." Rhett hesitated. "It can alter hormone receptors. Neural pathways. Change how the body processes its own instincts. And it can make things worse when they *do* come off it."

Jay's mouth tightened beside me. "Define 'worse.'"

"Heats that are more volatile. Less predictable. Stronger. Sometimes painful. There's reports of emotional instability, pain responses heightened... even scent distortion in some cases."

I didn't move. Not visibly. But something in me went stone-cold.

"She's been on them for *over a decade*," I said.

Rhett didn't answer.

Because what *could* he say?

Wren stirred again, a soft noise escaping her throat—more a whimper than a word, muffled by the blanket. I shifted my grip, settling her without skin contact, my movements practiced, precise.

She calmed. For now.

Jay moved back to the desk, picking up the container and unsealing it just enough to let some of the scent out—hopefully enough to rouse her gently when the time came. He didn't look at me, but I felt the tension in him.

"Roan…" he began, hesitating like he wasn't sure if he wanted to finish the thought.

I beat him to it. "Yeah. I know."

This was bigger than we thought. And more dangerous.

Still—still—I wouldn't leave her. Not now. Not again.

My voice was steel when I spoke again, barely audible.

"When she wakes up, she'll need food. Water. She'll also need to know she's not alone in this."

Jay nodded once. Quiet agreement.

Rhett's voice came again from the hallway, this time quieter. "Whatever she needs, we're here for her."

I glanced at Wren, then at the door. At the men I trusted with my life. I gave a small nod. Gratitude, maybe. Or warning.

Because whatever came next—however hard it got—we weren't going back to the way things were.

Not now that I knew what she'd been carrying.

Not now that I *felt* it.

When this was over, when she was through the worst of it, Wren and I were going to have a very real conversation.

Because I wasn't running from this anymore and like hell I'd let her run either.

SEVENTEEN

WREN

I surfaced slowly—like rising from deep water, every movement heavy, every thought too slow to catch.

The air was warm. Too warm. My skin prickled with sweat under the blanket wrapped around me, the weight of it a barrier between me and the fire still burning low in my belly.

I was still in my room. I could tell by the ceiling, by the scent of clean linen, by the faint hum of a ventilation unit that probably hadn't worked properly in years. But that wasn't what held me still.

It was him.

Roan.

He was beneath me—or rather, *behind* me, the solid wall of his chest pressed lightly to my back, arms looped around me on the outside of the blanket, cradling me without touching me. Protective. Steady. Impossibly careful.

His head rested back against the wall, tilted slightly to one side in such a manner that could not possibly be comfortable. His eyes were closed, his breathing deep and even.

Asleep.

The realization hit me like a strange, unearned gift. Roan was here. *Still* here. He hadn't moved, hadn't left, hadn't run—not even when my body had been all scent and heat and confusion. He'd stayed.

I let my eyes linger on him, drinking him in without shame.

Gods, he was beautiful.

Tall and broad even in rest, his frame always took up more space than he seemed to realize. The pale blonde of his hair—cropped short, always neat—stood out against the darker shadows of the room. His features were sharply defined, aristocratic almost, if not for the quiet strength they held.

Roan had always been handsome, but never *soft*. He wore calm like armor. Carried himself with the kind of precision you didn't teach—you *trained* it into bone. And still, now, in sleep, his expression was peaceful. Guard down.

Steel-gray eyes hidden behind thick lashes. Brows relaxed. The tension I'd seen in him for days—maybe *years* —finally smoothed away.

He always looked like this in moments of stillness. Like the world could fall apart around him and he'd pick up the pieces with those capable, unshakable hands.

A tactician. A protector. A leader.

An alpha who never once threw his weight around. If anything, he overcorrected—stepping back, pulling inward, avoiding dominance like it might hurt someone. Like *he* might hurt someone.

It made me ache in a way I wasn't prepared for.

Worse—it reminded me brutally that my heat was still here. Still alive and simmering in every part of me. What had been dulled by exhaustion and shock was now brightening again, fueled by proximity, by scent, by the slow realization that *Roan* was the source of so much of the need clawing through me.

It surged the longer I stared at him. My skin flushed hot, my throat tightening. A little sigh slipped from me before I could stop it. I closed my eyes and turned my head, trying to will the desire back down. Trying to focus on anything *else*.

That's when I saw him.

Jay.

Sitting just across the room, quiet and watchful in a chair I hadn't even heard move. Elbows resting on his knees, hands clasped, his expression unreadable—but not unkind.

He didn't flinch when I met his gaze. Didn't pretend to look away like he hadn't seen every second of that private, hungry moment I'd just had with Roan's sleeping form.

He was just... *there*. Patient. Steady.

Waiting for me to notice him.

It hit me in a moment of blinding clarity that he'd been doing exactly that for a while.

Watching. Waiting. Protecting us both.

I swallowed. "How long—?"

"A while," Jay said, voice soft. "You needed the rest."

My cheeks burned, and not from the fever of my body. Still, I didn't look away.

I couldn't.

Because something in his gaze told me that this wasn't pity. It was something else. Understanding and maybe—if I was brave enough to name it—respect.

I shifted under the blanket, muscles stiff and skin too warm. It took effort to focus past the heat coiling low and tight in my core. Everything felt slow. Hazy. Like waking from a fever dream only to realize I was still dreaming.

Jay didn't move, but his gaze softened, just slightly.

"How long have I really been asleep?" I asked, the past two days had been such a blur for me and I couldn't recall how much, if any, real sleep I'd had.

"Six hours," he said. "Give or take."

Six. Not nearly enough. But far more than I expected.

My eyes flicked to Roan again, then back to Jay. "Has he... has he taken a break at all?"

"No." Jay gave a slight shake of his head. "Won't let either of us near you for long. You were restless. Kept reaching out in your sleep." He didn't say what I already knew, that it had been Roan I was reaching for.

"And he stayed." Wonder unfolded inside of me. Humbled wonder because what alpha did that without question or reward? They were just as much at the mercy of their biological instincts as I was, but here he was.

"He stayed," Jay confirmed. "Hasn't eaten much. Hasn't moved. Not even to lie down. Just sat there. Like that."

Like *this*. With me. Arms around me like a barrier, his body the still center of something I couldn't name.

I swallowed again, throat dry. My stomach growled weakly, a cramp blooming in my side like it had just remembered I was human, too.

"Good timing." Jay's lips quirked, the ghost of a smile. "You're due for food."

He stood, moving silently to the desk and returning with the container I'd smelled earlier—broth, rice, maybe some root vegetables. Something easy. Comforting. Warm.

He crouched next to the bed, setting it down on the

nightstand before reaching for a spoon. I went to lift my arms—and stopped.

The blanket.

Roan had wrapped me so securely I couldn't get either hand free without unwrapping myself entirely. And there was no *way* I was doing that with my heat still burning and him still holding me like I might break apart if he let go.

My jaw clenched slightly. "I can feed myself."

Jay tilted his head, amused but gentle. "I believe you. But you're also mummified."

"Roan's fault." I glared at first the man holding me in place, then the man offering to feed me. Honestly, I couldn't even hold that fierce look for long. They were *here*. They didn't deserve my temper.

"You tried to touch him," Jay said, like it was a known fact. "And he didn't want to take chances. You wouldn't stay under otherwise."

I muttered something under my breath—he didn't ask me to repeat it. Instead, he just sat back down on the edge of the mattress, spoon in hand.

"Let me help."

I hesitated. Every part of me balked at the idea of being *fed* like I was fragile. I wasn't. I was still strong. Still me.

Just... wrapped in a comforter and burning from the inside out.

Jay waited, spoon poised.

I sighed, shifting minutely so my head rested more comfortably against Roan's chest, and nodded.

"Fine."

The first bite was warm and salty, the broth rich but mild. My stomach lurched at the sudden intake, then settled, welcoming it.

Not saying anything, Jay just fed me in slow, unhurried

motions—giving me time between bites, letting me reclaim what little strength I could one spoonful at a time.

I hated how good it felt. The care. The quiet. The safety of it.

"I'm not usually like this," I muttered between mouthfuls.

Jay lifted an eyebrow. "You mean, letting someone take care of you?"

I narrowed my eyes, and he chuckled, all soft and kind.

"I know," he said. "It's fine, Wren. You don't owe me pride. You just need food, sleep, and, hopefully, to not burn yourself out trying to out-stubborn biology."

I let out a small breath through my nose. "Easier said."

"I've noticed," he murmured, offering another bite.

I took it. The burn inside me didn't lessen, but something about the food and the rhythm dulled the edge. Gave me enough presence of mind to think. To notice how carefully Jay moved, how he never leaned too close, how his scent—neutral, grounded—was just far enough from triggering to let me breathe.

"You're good at this," I said quietly.

Jay glanced at me. "Good at what?"

"This," I gestured vaguely with my chin, the only part of me free to move. "Caretaking. Managing alphas and omegas in denial. Betas aren't supposed to notice heats like this."

His face remained still for a moment. Thoughtful. "I notice *you*," he said simply. "That's different."

The words dropped between us, quiet and not meant to do harm. But they caught, somewhere deep.

I didn't answer. Couldn't. Not with Roan breathing steadily behind me and Jay feeding me soup I hadn't asked for but needed.

I was too full of want, of shame, of *longing*. This without having even looked Roan in the eye since waking.

I didn't know if I *could*, but I would. Eventually. Because if I knew nothing else, I was aware that when this heat passed, I wouldn't be able to keep running. Not anymore. Not now that they knew.

Jay kept feeding me in calm, deliberate intervals. Like he had all the time in the world.

He probably did.

There was never any rush in his movements. Every action was purposeful, grounded. The kind of control that wasn't rigid. It was just there, woven into his being. Not dominance, not passivity, just... quiet strength. Reliable.

He held out another spoonful, and I took it without protest. The heat still pulsed through me in relentless waves, but eating helped. So did Jay's scent. Clean, low, neutral. Not challenging. Not provoking. He made this possible.

When he offered the bottle of water next, I took it with my teeth and a huff of thanks.

He didn't even blink.

"You always this good with invalids?" I asked between slow sips, the coolness soothing my throat.

His mouth twitched. "Only the difficult ones."

"Lucky me."

"Lucky *us*," he said, not quite teasing.

I stilled. The silence stretched just long enough for my mind to start running ahead, so I asked the next thing that came to me. "Where's Rhett?"

"Out," Jay replied, his tone still gentle. "He went for more supplies."

Something pinched in my chest. Not sharp. But deep. "Oh."

Jay must've heard it whatever leaked into that single syllable, because he set the spoon down gently and met my gaze. Calm. Direct. Unyielding.

"Don't worry," he said. "He's coming back."

I looked away, but only briefly. His voice didn't leave me room to argue.

"You're not alone, Wren. None of us are leaving you. We just need things like medical supplies, more water, food. He's handling it."

I nodded slowly. I believed him. Mostly. But the ache didn't leave. Not entirely.

Jay didn't press.

When I finally gave a low exhale and mumbled, "I'm full," he nodded and set the container aside. Then, predictably, he held the bottle of water up again.

"More."

I gave him a weak look. "My bladder already hates me."

A faint grin tugged at his mouth. "You'll live."

"As long as Roan's got me hostage in this blanket trap, I'd rather not test the limits."

Chuckling under his breath, Jay recapped the bottle and nodded. "Fair enough."

The warmth from the food curled low in my belly, not in the same place as the heat, but adjacent to it, like a reminder that I was a body *and* a mind. Still whole. Still me.

Jay didn't move right away. Just sat with me. Watched me. That patient silence of his returned—but now, it felt heavier. Like it was no longer waiting for my needs, but for something *else*.

Finally, he asked, "Will you tell me?" His voice didn't change. Still soft. Still even. "Why the suppressants? The secrets? All of it?"

I blinked.

Slowly, I turned toward him again.

He wasn't smiling. He wasn't pushing. But the focus in his eyes sharpened like a blade slipping free of its sheath— so quiet I almost didn't feel it until it was already there. Laid bare between us.

"You don't have to lie," he added. "You don't even have to explain everything right now. But I want to know. I *need* to know."

Gods, there was nowhere to hide from that. He didn't flinch or look away. He just waited.

The longer I stared back, the more impossible it became to pretend I wasn't already unraveling. I couldn't answer him immediately, even if I'd wanted to just confess it all. The words, the experience, *my life* all backed up inside of me.

The question hung in the air between us all soft and almost ephemeral, yet heavy like a shackle. Jay didn't move, didn't speak again. He didn't *need* to. His stillness was the question's echo, waiting for me to fill it.

My tongue felt thick, my throat tight. The warmth of the food in my stomach soured with nerves.

"Why the suppressants," I repeated softly, mostly to buy myself time.

He didn't nod, didn't press.

I looked down or tried to. The blanket held me too tightly, so all I could do was lower my eyes, staring at the faint pattern in the fabric near my chin.

The first words came out before I could stop them.

"Because I couldn't afford to be an omega."

While Jay didn't react, something in his breathing changed. A fraction deeper. Listening harder. I let out a shaky exhale, staring past him now, at nothing.

"I was twenty when it started to… manifest." My voice

was barely audible. I'd been such a late bloomer. Most omega and alpha tendencies showed up during puberty. Only betas tended to find their niche a little later. "I'd spent my whole life thinking I was a beta. Hell, so did everyone else. My tests always came back inconclusive. Then one day, it wasn't inconclusive anymore."

I swallowed hard. "I was working for a company that didn't tolerate… complications. Female employees were fine. Betas, even better. But omegas? Liability. Distraction. Weak link. There wasn't a place for one on a security team, and I'd just fought my way into mine."

His expression didn't change, but his eyes softened.

"So, I made it go away." I laughed a little—bitter, small. "Found a man who knew a man who knew a chemist. Paid too much. Didn't care. The first batch burned like acid, but it worked. I passed for beta again."

The memory made my throat ache. "After—I just… kept doing it. Year after year. I told myself it was safer. Smarter. That I was protecting my job. Protecting *them*."

I risked a glance at Roan—still sleeping, still steady, oblivious to the storm breaking in whispers beside him.

"I didn't want anyone to see me differently," I said. "Least of all him."

Thankfully, Jay didn't do the one thing that would have broken me. He didn't offer comfort or understanding, only patience as he *listened*.

"Eventually, I started to believe the lie. That I was just a slightly off-kilter beta who got headaches and insomnia sometimes." I gave a hollow smile. "It was easier than admitting I'd spent ten years poisoning myself to keep a secret no one had asked me to keep."

His gaze sharpened to the point I could almost feel the

way it sliced into me, seeking. "You say it like it was past tense," he murmured.

My chest constricted. "Because it is," I whispered. "I stopped this week."

That silence came again, deep and long. I couldn't tell if the look in Jay's eyes was sorrow or respect—or both.

"You knew what it would do," he said finally.

I nodded once. "Yeah."

"You did it anyway."

"Yeah."

It wasn't defiance. It wasn't shame. It was just... truth.

A muscle in his jaw flexed, but Jay's voice remained calm. "Then you knew this was coming."

"I didn't know it would be *this*," I said. "I didn't think I'd —" My voice caught, and I bit down on the rest. *I didn't think I'd drag all of you into it.*

Jay reached out then, not to touch, just to rest a hand near the edge of the blanket. A quiet gesture. Solidarity without intrusion.

"Alright," he said softly. "That's enough for now."

But I could still see the questions behind his eyes, the rest of what he wanted to ask, what he probably *needed* to. Like, why *this* week? Why *now*?

I wasn't ready to answer that. Not yet.

More, I wasn't ready to answer what happened after.

So I closed my eyes and leaned back against the steady weight of Roan's chest, letting the slow rise and fall of his breathing anchor me.

For the first time in years, I'd told someone the truth.

At least the first piece of it.

Despite the exhaustion and the heat still clawing at me, that admission gave me my first real breath in years. "Jay..."

"I'm here," he said as if he needed to reassure me. Maybe he did.

"I really don't know how to do this."

"This?" At his prompting, I opened my eyes to look at him again.

"This." I nodded to him, then looked up at Roan and found his eyes open and focused on me. The realization struck all the air from my lungs in a visceral blow as the bloom of heat inside me expanded to a torrent of fire.

Fuck... *How am I going to deal with this?*

With *them*.

CHAPTER

EIGHTEEN

ROAN

I woke slowly.

Not because I was tired—but because I didn't *want* to wake.

For the first time in what felt like weeks, the weight in my chest wasn't crushing. The room was quiet. Warm. My body was heavy, arms wrapped around the solid heat of a blanket-wrapped Wren, her weight pressed just enough against mine to anchor me. I could still feel the echo of her restlessness from earlier, the way she'd shifted in her sleep —how even unconscious, she seemed to seek me out.

And I had held the line.

Hadn't touched skin. Hadn't let myself give in, even when every instinct screamed for contact, scent, *closeness*. I'd stayed exactly where I needed to be.

Until now.

Because now—now her voice was cutting through the haze of sleep, low and raw and husky with disuse and heat, and every cell in my body responded to it like a shot of lightning to the spine.

I didn't move. Kept my breathing even. Eyes closed.

191

But inside, my awareness snapped into brutal clarity.

She was speaking to Jay. Her voice was quiet, but the acoustics of the room—plus the heightened edge of my senses—let me hear every word.

"I was twenty when it started to... manifest."

The sound of her voice. That tone. The *truth* in it. It did things to me I wasn't proud of.

I gritted my teeth, fisted my restraint tighter. Tried not to focus on the curve of her body wrapped in my arms. Tried not to breathe too deeply—her scent was still thick in the air, impossibly sweet, persistent, *dangerous*.

I didn't *want* to hear her confession. But I couldn't turn away from it either.

"I'd spent my whole life thinking I was a beta. Hell, so did everyone else. My tests always came back inconclusive. Then one day, it wasn't inconclusive anymore."

My fists curled tighter, careful not to shift even a millimeter against her back. Her voice—gods, her voice— was breaking in all the wrong places.

I could feel the words vibrating in her chest against my arm.

"I was working for a company that didn't tolerate... complications. Female employees were fine. Betas, even better. But omegas? Liability. Distraction. Weak link. There wasn't a place for one on a security team, and I'd just fought my way into mine."

A muscle jumped in my jaw. *Complication. Weak link.*

I wanted to find whoever taught her that word belonged to her and break their goddamn spine.

"So I made it go away."

That hit me harder than it should have. Even knowing —*suspecting*—what she'd done, hearing her say it so plainly gutted something in me. The way she laughed—small, bitter, like the joke had always been on her—tightened something in my throat.

"Found a man who knew a man who knew a chemist. Paid too much. Didn't care. The first batch burned like acid, but it worked. I passed for beta again."

She'd poisoned herself.

For a job. For safety. For *us*.

"After—I just... kept doing it. Year after year. I told myself it was safer. Smarter. That I was protecting my job. Protecting them."

Them. She meant us.

I opened my eyes—just barely—and looked down at the curve of her shoulder, where her head tilted toward Jay. She was still wrapped tightly in the blanket I'd cocooned her in. Her body was flushed, slick with heat, but not trembling. Not fighting me anymore.

"I didn't want anyone to see me differently. Least of all him."

The last hit me harder than a puck to the gut. I didn't react. Couldn't. Not without shattering every ounce of calm I'd clawed together since this began.

She'd meant *me*.

And I hadn't known. I should have. I should've *seen* it. Her quiet strength. Her control. The way she never slipped —*never* let anything through unless she wanted it seen. I'd thought it was professionalism. Temperance. Maybe even pride.

But it had been survival.

Jay didn't say anything, didn't move, and that—gods, that was exactly right. Exactly what she needed. Not comfort. Not pity.

"Eventually, I started to believe the lie. That I was just a slightly off-kilter beta who got headaches and insomnia sometimes. It was easier than admitting I'd spent ten years poisoning myself to keep a secret no one had asked me to keep."

I could feel her heart beating. The faint, uneven flutter of it against my arm. Like it wasn't quite sure what it was allowed to do anymore.

"You say it like it was past tense," Jay murmured.

Her answer came soft. Almost broken.

"Because it is. I stopped this week."

And that—*that*—told me everything I needed to know about what we were really dealing with.

She *knew* this heat would come.

She knew it would hurt.

She knew it might kill her—and she did it anyway.

"You knew what it would do."

"Yeah."

"You did it anyway."

"Yeah."

"Then you knew this was coming."

"I didn't know it would be this. I didn't think I'd—"

She didn't finish.

She didn't have to.

I didn't think I'd need him. Need you.

That's what I heard.

All I wanted in that moment was to touch her. Just my hand. Just one second. Her hair, her back, anything to let her know I was awake and I was *here* and I wasn't going *anywhere.*

But I didn't.

I stayed still.

Because what she needed right now wasn't my reaction.

It was *space*. The kind she hadn't had in a decade.

When she was ready—when the heat passed and her body stopped screaming—I would ask the questions burning through my chest. The ones I had *every damn right* to ask now.

But not until then.

Not while she was still fighting the fallout of survival.

She'd trusted someone with the truth.

Even if it wasn't me, not yet... that mattered.

When she was ready, I'd be here. Arms open. Patience intact. But not blind. Not anymore.

She went quiet again.

For a long moment, the only sound in the room was the subtle rustle of her breath against the blanket, the whisper of cloth as Jay set the water bottle aside.

Then, just as I thought she might close herself off again, she said it.

Soft. Unsteady. The closest thing to lost I'd ever heard from her.

"I don't know how to do this."

That was it.

Not whispered like a secret. Just laid bare. Raw. No walls left.

I opened my eyes.

Jay saw it first. His head turned just slightly, like he'd known all along I was awake and had been waiting for me to step forward.

Wren didn't notice as swiftly, then she glanced up and met my gaze. It was a physical blow that reached right into my soul. Once I knew I had her attention, I answered her earlier statement. "Then we learn."

She jolted a little in my arms, instinctively trying to turn —only to remember the blanket still wrapped her in place. The same blanket I'd used to keep us both safe.

She tilted her head to look at me again, wide-eyed, pupils still blown wide from the heat. Her cheeks flushed, hair sticking to her forehead. She looked exhausted. Overheated. Vulnerable in a way I'd never seen her.

I held her a little more firmly, just to keep her steady.

"I—" she started, then swallowed hard. "How long have you—?"

"Long enough," I said quietly. "But not as long as I should've."

Her throat worked as she looked at me, and I could see the walls trying to rebuild themselves—brick by brick.

I didn't let them.

"You think we haven't been watching you tear yourself apart for years?" I asked, keeping my voice low, careful. "Jay. Rhett. Me. You've carried so much alone, Wren. You never had to."

She didn't answer.

Didn't deny it, either.

Jay didn't speak. He stood, quietly collecting the empty food container, moving to give us space without being obvious about it. But his eyes met mine for a second— something silent and sharp passed between us.

He nodded once and stepped away.

I turned my focus back to her.

"You don't have to know how to do this," I told her. "You've spent a decade surviving. I don't expect you to switch that off just because you're finally safe."

Her brows knit together like she didn't know whether to argue or cry—or maybe both.

"Is that what this is?" she asked hoarsely. "Safe?"

"Yes."

She shook her head, just a little. "It doesn't feel like it."

"Because your body's at war with you. You're too close to the fire to feel anything else."

"And when I'm not?"

I hesitated, but only for a second.

"Then we'll talk. All of it. Suppressants. Secrets. What this means. You won't have to guess."

Her breathing hitched.

I reached up and gently tucked a piece of damp hair behind her ear—careful not to touch skin. She let me. Her eyes didn't leave mine.

"Wren," I said, quieter now. "You didn't fail us. You protected yourself the only way you knew how. I wish you hadn't needed to. But I don't blame you for surviving."

Her eyes shimmered—not with tears, not quite. But close.

"You should be angry with me."

I was.

But not for the reasons she thought.

"I will be," I said, honest. "Later. When you're not burning up. When you can stand and argue with me. But not now. Not when you're hurting."

That seemed to break something in her—not a collapse, but a release. Her shoulders slumped, some of the tension bleeding out of her limbs. The fight in her quieted. Not gone, but resting.

Finally, she closed her eyes again.

"I don't know what to do with you," she murmured.

"You don't have to," I said. "I'm not going anywhere."

None of us were. Not for anything.

Though she went quiet, she didn't fall asleep right away.

Even though her body was spent, and the food had taken the edge off, the burn of heat still rolled off her in thick, feverish waves. She shifted slightly in my arms, just enough to press the crown of her head against my throat again. Her exhale was a long, shaky sigh.

Then her voice, soft and hoarse.

"I could have... handled this differently."

My arms tightened instinctively around her. "You did what you had to."

"No." Her laugh was quiet and flat. "I mean now. This week."

That pulled my attention sharp. I glanced down. Her eyes were open again, staring across the room, unfocused but restless.

"The doctor I see—the one who advised me to take a break from the suppressants... she warned me what was coming. She recommended a couple of... services."

Something cold and dark opened in my gut. "Services," I repeated, though it came out low. Flat.

Wren heard it anyway. Her lips twitched — not quite a smile, more like something bitter surfacing. "Professionals. Companions. Paid and trained to help omegas through heat."

I went still.

Too still.

"She gave me names," she added, voice distant, "vetting. Medical profiles. I could've hired someone to get me through it. Would've made it easier. Faster. Supposed to burn through the worst of it in twenty-four, maybe thirty-six hours with the right—attention."

My breath hissed out between my teeth before I could stop it.

Someone. Touching her. Kissing her. Inside her. Skin on skin. Even if it was sanctioned. Professional. Even if she'd asked for it. The primitive, feral part of me responded like a match to dry grass.

I locked it down so hard it nearly made my vision blur.

She noticed. Her voice softened, threading with that weary amusement that never quite reached humor.

"I didn't," she added quickly. "I didn't want that."

I didn't trust myself to speak.

"I thought about it," she admitted, turning her face slightly toward my neck. "When the fever started and the headaches were bad... I almost called one of them. But I couldn't." Her eyes slid shut. "I didn't want to just lie there. Let someone *do* things to me. No matter how polite or skilled or highly recommended."

A small, bitter breath escaped her. "I didn't want to feel helpless. Not with a stranger."

And there it was.

The truth. Quiet. Raw.

Not shame. Not prudishness.

Control.

Wren had lived her entire adult life dragging her instincts down into silence. Choosing who got access to her. Choosing when and how. Or not at all.

The idea that she might have sacrificed all that for convenience made me feel—

No. Not feel.

Burn.

Yet underneath the fire, deeper than instinct, something else sat cold and heavy in my chest. *She almost went through this alone.*

Wren. In this kind of pain. In this kind of danger. With no one she trusted. No one to hold her. No one to make sure she made it out the other side.

I breathed deep. Steady. Careful. When I finally spoke, my voice was barely audible. "I'm glad you didn't."

She blinked.

"Not just because it would've..." I stopped, teeth gritting. "Because it would've killed me to know someone else—"

I shook my head. No. That wasn't fair to lay on her now.

I tried again.

"I'm glad you waited," I said, quieter. "Even if you didn't know it was for us."

She looked up at me then, eyes heavy, but clear. No masks. No pushback. Just that tired, honest woman I'd been chasing since the moment I realized she was missing.

She didn't say anything. She didn't have to.

I shifted just slightly, careful not to loosen the blanket around her, and pressed my forehead gently against hers. Skin to fabric. Nothing more.

"I've got you," I murmured.

She let out a breath, this one less shaky. More surrender than struggle. Finally, *finally*, she closed her eyes.

Wren finally gave in to sleep.

Her breathing evened, the tension in her body melting one slow inch at a time until her weight went fully slack in my arms. I didn't move right away—couldn't. My body was a live wire, raw and burning. Every breath of her scent scraped against the inside of my skull, pulling tight every thread of control I'd laid down.

But I had it.

Barely. Just enough.

I shifted her carefully, still swaddled tight in the blanket like some fragile, priceless artifact. She made a soft sound in protest, instinctive, but didn't wake. I eased her down into the nest of pillows we'd built earlier, adjusted the edge of the blanket at her shoulder, then stood.

Just being vertical hurt.

The blood pumping through my body felt molten. Like every nerve was screaming her name.

I made it to the bathroom in seven long strides.

Turned on the faucet. Cranked it to cold.

Bent down and threw two full handfuls of freezing water straight into my face.

The shock didn't help as much as I wanted it to. My skin still burned. My lungs still ached.

I gripped the edge of the sink and leaned into it, head bowed, trying to exhale through the fire. My back muscles were tight. My thighs throbbed. Everything in me was *demanding*—answers, action, contact.

But it wasn't mine to take. None of it. She hadn't asked for a claim. She hadn't asked for *me*. Just help. Just safety. I gave her that. I'd keep giving it until she no longer needed it and then—

I didn't finish that thought. Instead, I did something stupid. I glanced in the mirror.

The man staring back at me looked like he hadn't slept in days. His jaw was clenched so hard it pulsed, eyes rimmed with red, pupils still too wide.

Pathetic.

I splashed another handful of water across my face. Entertained—for the briefest second—the idea of stripping down and throwing myself into the snow outside. It probably wouldn't help either.

But the ache would at least be honest.

After I used the damn toilet, I rinsed my hands, and then braced both palms on the counter. She was going to come out of this. I was going to make damn sure of it.

And when she did… when she was steady and thinking clearly again…

We were going to talk. If I reminded myself of this enough, it would help me maintain the control we needed.

I left the bathroom and stepped back into the bedroom.

She was still asleep. Curled slightly to the side now, face half-buried in the blanket, one hand peeking out from the folds. Vulnerable and flushed and so damn beautiful it hurt to look at her.

I stared at her for a long moment. Let myself have that. Just that.

There were so many things I wanted to say.

And so many more I knew I couldn't.

Not yet.

The sound of the front door opening snapped me out of it.

I turned sharply. Moved to the bedroom door and stepped through, easing it closed behind me until the latch clicked quietly into place. Jay stood in the kitchen, his expression tight and fierce. I tracked his gaze to where Rhett was already pacing, his hair damp and littered with flecks of snow.

He'd left his boots by the door and dropped his jacket too, but energy just surged off of him.

I didn't get a chance to say a word. He turned as soon as I came out. His energy was wrong—tight, barely contained.

"We've got a problem."

My stomach sank even as my spine straightened.

"What kind of problem?"

NINETEEN

WREN

I had no idea how long I'd slept.

The room was steeped in shadows, the last light of the day bleeding faintly through the edges of the heavy curtains. But there was light in the next room— muted, pale, artificial. Not morning light.

The bed was empty.

Not cold, though. Roan's warmth still lingered in the blankets, pressed into the dip of the mattress where his weight had been. But he was gone now. And I wasn't alone.

Their energy—the three of them—was still here. I could feel it. Like static crawling over my skin. Familiar. Wild. Controlled but charged.

Even muffled behind the bedroom door, the pulse of them was unmistakable.

I drew in a breath and sat up slowly, my head swimming, legs trembling with the effort. Everything ached in that dull, lingering way—like I'd been sick for days and was finally coming up for air.

I didn't feel *better*, not exactly. But I could *think*. That felt like something. I got to my feet and padded to the bathroom, my steps unsteady. My legs hated me. My hips hated me more.

When the hell had *heat* made me feel so... broken?

That said, I managed the essentials, though. Peeing took longer than I wanted to admit—my bladder was staging a full rebellion. I splashed cold water on my face, brushed my teeth slowly. Even found a comb and wrestled it through my hair, working out the tangles with grim determination and sharp little winces.

A shower was out of the question. I could admit that. I didn't trust my legs to hold me up for that long.

Instead, I found a robe slung over the back of the door. Soft fleece, unfamiliar but clean. I pulled it on and belted it tight, hoping it would help dull the sharp edges of my scent.

It didn't. Not really. But it made me feel *less* exposed, and that counted for something. I was almost to the bedroom door when it opened from the other side.

Jay stood there, a solid shadow framed by light. Calm. Composed. Unflinching as always. His gaze swept over me once, clinical and quick.

"You sure you should be up?"

"No," I admitted, breathing a little harder than I wanted. "But I needed to move."

His eyes softened just slightly at the edges.

"I'm thinking clearly," I added. "Mostly. That's a good sign, right?"

He didn't answer that—just tilted his head toward the light behind him.

"Come on. You should be part of this."

That was the second sign something was wrong.

Jay didn't extend invitations. He laid out logistics.

I followed him into the living room.

Rhett and Roan were both on the far side of the space, standing by the wide window that looked out over the snow-covered trees. They weren't speaking, but the silence was sharp-edged. Tactical.

Roan's arms were folded tight across his chest. Rhett's fingers were twitching near his belt like they wanted to be wrapped around a weapon.

The instant I stepped into the room, both of their heads turned toward me.

Roan's eyes—*steel gray, cutting and bright*—landed on me first. They skimmed over me from head to toe and then back again, expression unreadable. Not cold. But contained.

My heart kicked up. Not from heat.

From instinct.

I didn't waste time with pleasantries.

"What is it?"

No one answered right away.

Jay moved to stand beside me, a quiet line of support at my side. Roan glanced once at Rhett, then back to me.

Rhett was the one who spoke. "I did some research and made some calls."

To be honest, I had no idea what I expected him to say but that wasn't it. Fidgeting with the belt tie on the robe, I frowned. "Okay?" The word came out rough, a little hoarser than I liked but still, clear. "How is that a problem?"

Because I needed more information.

Raking a hand through his hair which caused parts of it to stick up in places, Rhett gave me a frustrated look. "I was looking into the suppressants, and the research and... stuff."

My stomach bottomed out, but I fought the trembling by folding my arms. "I'm listening."

The stone stillness from Roan betrayed more than Rhett's almost jittery upset. My gaze kept tracking back to

Roan's gray eyes but I needed to focus on Rhett so I didn't miss anything.

"I don't know which ones you were taking and I couldn't find them...probably should have done a deeper search of your place but I didn't go in and they weren't in your office."

I left Rhett's admission of snooping in my office alone. Right now, that wasn't important.

"There's a variety of suppressants out in the world, very few that are considered legal or advised for any long-term use. Most seem limited to once or twice a year *at most*."

Agitation marked Rhett's delivery as he began to pace again. If I were to guess, he wasn't angry—he was *terrified*.

That had me taking a couple of slow steps forward to the sofa and sitting. "Just... tell me what you found."

Rhett stopped pacing for a moment, his eyes darting between me and Roan, like he wanted to make sure we were both paying attention. The space between us had thickened, and I could feel the weight of every word he was about to say.

He opened his mouth, then closed it again, as if unsure how to start. Finally, he pushed through.

"Some of these suppressants, the ones that aren't regulated or that people get off-market, they're... they're dangerous." He raked a hand over his face, his usual confidence gone. "Long-term use, particularly if they're not dosed properly or monitored—can fuck with the body in ways that can't be undone."

My stomach twisted, my eyes narrowing. I wasn't sure I wanted to hear this, but I needed to. I *needed* to know what was coming.

"Permanent damage?" My voice was softer than I intended, but the words were there, heavy and weighted.

My doctor hadn't mentioned that, but she had ordered extensive bloodwork, and she'd also insisted that I needed to go off of the suppressants for at least one heat.

Was this what she was looking for? Did she say nothing because she didn't want to muddle the results?

Rhett's lips pressed into a thin line as he nodded. "Exactly. Some of the changes are hormonal, neurological —shit like that. But there's one problem that kept coming up in my search... It can mess with your body's response to heat." He grimaced. "In some cases, it can make it *worse*."

I felt the air around me get even heavier, but I refused to flinch. The words were gnawing at the edges of my mind, but I didn't want to hear them. I couldn't.

Still, I asked, because I had to know. "How much worse?"

The man was going to wear a groove into the wooden floor, with his pacing. With a sharp exhale, he stopped once again. "I'm not sure. The studies I found were incomplete, but... they suggested it could make heat cycles longer, more intense. It can turn what should be a 24 to 36-hour flare into something that drags on for days. Or worse, become chronic."

Days.

I didn't know how to respond. My body felt like it was on fire, and everything in me was telling me to get up and run, to move away from this conversation, but I couldn't. I was stuck in the thick of it, all of it, all at once.

Days.

I looked at Roan, his face unreadable, still as stone. I could see his hands clenched into fists at his sides. Every muscle in his body was tense, but I couldn't read the expression on his face. It was like he was holding himself together by sheer force of will, just like I had been.

But the air between us had changed. I could feel the weight of it now, like the tension had spiraled tighter since the moment I'd opened my eyes. It wasn't just heat I was dealing with anymore.

It was something else.

Rhett cleared his throat and continued. "You're not the only one, Wren. This isn't just a rare occurrence. People who've been using suppressants for years... they're seeing the effects, especially if they were on non-regulated ones. It's a growing concern, but it's also dangerous territory. The more I looked into it, the more I saw how little we actually know about long-term effects."

I swallowed hard, my throat feeling tight as I tried to process everything. The truth of it, the weight of it.

"They don't have a lot of conclusive research," I admitted. "The doctor told me that. Most... most people don't use suppressants for that long."

"No," Rhett said, taking two steps toward me. "They're not supposed to use them long-term, in fact, you should be getting regular checkups, bloodwork, and monitoring...at least having one to two heats a year to let your system reset."

Oh, there was anger in Rhett now.

"How the hell could *you*, of all people, be so careless and stupid?" The question landed like a blow, and I didn't have it in me to mask my flinch.

"Rhett," Roan snapped his name like a command.

"I have a right to know," Rhett argued, but he whirled and focused his temper on Roan. "We all do. She's been *hurting* herself."

That muscle ticking in Roan's jaw increased in speed and ferocity. Jay shifted his stance until he was nearly standing between me and the other two.

"I didn't know," I said before anyone else could launch into this argument. "I still don't." The last came out far wearier than the first. "Your research is what? Internet articles? MD sites? Health journals?"

Arms folded, Rhett grimaced before he said something I didn't quite catch.

"What?" I frowned.

"I called my cousin." That came out clearer, but there was a faint note of sheepishness. I didn't get the reference. Rhett came from a fairly large family, but he'd never seemed especially close to any of them.

Roan pinched the bridge of his nose. "You called your *cousin*?"

"We needed answers." Rhett sounded defensive now.

"You asked your cousin, the *doctor*, about suppressants and omegas?" Maybe it was how quiet and even he sounded, but the shock punching through the words declared how appalled he was.

"I asked carefully," Rhett argued and I raised a hand as Roan started to round on him. To my utter shock, all three went still and the weight of their regard slammed into me like a fierce wind.

"Rhett..." My voice was hoarse, raw, but I couldn't seem to smooth it out.

Jay moved abruptly and returned before I finished getting my thoughts together with a fresh, and very cold, bottle of water. I took it gratefully, unscrewing the top and drinking down several gulps.

"Thank you," I murmured, and Jay nodded.

The world was starting to blur at the edges, there was almost a lens flare effect. Not only was the room filled with my scent, but I could taste theirs now and it was in every single breath I took.

So much for getting past the heat. I blinked slowly, trying to recover where my thoughts went. Oh. Heat. Meds. System reset. Another drink of water then I focused on Rhett again.

"We can worry about this later," I said slowly. "I can call my doctor tomorrow. She has my records. She—she can of course check."

"Did she warn you about this?" Roan asked, his intensity so visceral it was like he wrapped around me again and where it had muted the throb beneath my skin before, it only seemed to enhance it now.

"Not this, specifically. She just said..." I tried to remember her exact wording, but the syllables were slipping away before I could fully grasp them. "Fuck..."

The last word came out a groan because Jay had drifted closer, and the rich amber of his scent was so heady, that I swore I was damn near drunk. He smelled so good. They all did really.

"Don't touch her," Roan ordered. Who was he talking to? Then I realized my eyes were closed, so I forced them open again. Jay was a half step from me and on one knee, his whole body seemed to be leaning in my direction.

"She's hurting." The protest from Jay was remarkable enough to make me focus again.

"Not... pain." It came out reedy, and winded, like it had taken me a lot of effort to push those words out. "You're just pretty."

Jay blinked and he wasn't alone. Rhett's lips twitched, but Roan's entire being seemed to turn to stone.

"You're all so damn pretty." There was no hiding the shaking now. Maybe I should call the doctor now? When I couldn't even think of her name, I had to discard that idea.

The men were moving around me, and I frowned as Roan lifted me. "What are you doing?"

"Taking you back to bed," he said.

"Oh… will we get naked there?" Some part of my mind said I probably shouldn't have asked that, but the rest of me just threw up my arms with a why the fuck not? My nipples were tight, my cunt slick and pulsing, my body on fire, and Roan hadn't even touched me for real yet.

Skin-to-skin… that's what we needed.

I fumbled with the tie of my robe.

Roan let out a little growl. An actual *growl*. It was the kind of aggrieved sound he only used when he was truly aggravated. The need bloomed inside of me like a gas explosion racing through to consume all the oxygen.

I was going up in flames.

"Stop," he told me in a voice that was a low rumble, power and need vibrating in the single syllable. I turned my gaze up to him, trying to push away the sting of that rejection.

"You don't want me?" The question broke free before I could stop it—barely a whisper, more wound than words.

Roan didn't answer right away. His grip shifted on me as he carried me toward the bedroom, his arms like iron bands, his jaw locked so tight I could *feel* the tension in him. Every step he took was deliberate. Controlled.

Too controlled.

That only made it worse.

"I didn't say that," he ground out at last.

"Then say what you *do* want," I whispered, fingers curling in the soft fabric of his shirt. My heart was a thunderclap behind my ribs. I could smell myself—my heat, my need—and beneath it, the way he was trying to cage every shred of his own instinct.

The restraint in him was maddening. Dignified. Terrible.

Because I could feel it—under his skin. The want. The war.

He laid me back down in the bed with excruciating care, like I might break apart if he moved too fast. I wanted to scream. I wanted to pull him down with me. I wanted—

"I want you whole," he said, voice low and gutted as he leaned over me. "Not like this. Not because your body's on fire and you're desperate for relief. Not because you can't help it."

"But I can," I breathed. "I *do*. I'm still me, Roan. I know what I want. Even now."

His eyes flared, heat igniting behind steel. For a second, I thought I'd broken through. For a second, I thought—

But then he reached down and tugged the robe back together with a care that was somehow more intimate than anything else he could've done. His fingers brushed the hollow of my throat before they moved away entirely.

"You're not asking me to choose you," he said, voice rough with restraint. "You're asking me to take advantage."

"No," I said, voice cracking. "I'm not—"

"You don't understand how hard this is." His hands clenched into fists again. "How much I *want* you. But if I cross that line now, I don't know if I'll be able to stop. Not when you need my control."

Tears stung behind my eyes, hot and frustrated. "What if I don't want you to stop?"

He shook his head and stood up straight, stepping away from the bed like distance might help him breathe again. It didn't. He still looked like he was barely holding it together.

"I want more than this," he said.

I blinked. "More?"

Roan stared at me like the words were being carved out of his chest. "I want *you*, Wren. Not your heat. Not the chemical wildfire you're riding out. *You.* The woman who slices through my plans with one line of logic. The one who watches over all of us like we're her mission. The one who never needed me—but still always had my back."

Every word landed like a blow. Like a balm. Like both.

"Then why does this feel like punishment?" I asked, curling in on myself as much as the ache would allow. "Why does doing the right thing *hurt*?"

Roan turned away before I could read his expression again, voice barely audible as he said, "Because I want you too damn much."

And then he was gone.

He pulled the bedroom door shut behind him like it weighed a thousand pounds.

I was alone again. Only this time, it wasn't the fever that was burning me alive. It was the truth.

CHAPTER

TWENTY

RHETT

The door closed with a quiet *click*, but it echoed like a gunshot in the back of my skull.

Roan stood just on this side of it, fists clenched, chest rising like he'd just run a damn marathon. His ironclad control seemed a hair's breadth from cracking.

And I wasn't much better.

I scrubbed my hands down my face and turned away, trying not to breathe too deep. Not to *inhale* her. Like that ever worked. Her scent was everywhere. Seeped into the walls. Saturating the fabric. In the fucking floorboards.

Thick. Wild. Sweet.

She wasn't just in heat, she was in *distress*. Her body was screaming for relief, and every damn one of us could feel it in our bones. And worse, every instinct in my body wanted to give it to her.

Again and again and again until the scent faded, until her thighs stopped shaking, until her body melted into ours with exhaustion instead of suffering.

I'd never felt anything like this. I'd been around omegas

215

in heat before. I'd seen the effects. Smelled it. Wanted it, sure. But not like *this*.

Not *her*.

I dropped into the nearest chair, hands gripping my knees, trying to lock my joints to hold myself still. My voice was low when it finally came.

"We may not be able to wait."

Roan turned toward me, slow, like even that movement took effort. His face was pale, lips pressed together, jaw tight enough I thought his teeth might crack under the pressure.

"I heard her," I added, quieter this time. "What she said. She's breaking apart in there, and you—" I cut myself off and looked away, guilt flaring. "You're holding it down, but Roan... if *you* fracture, the rest of us are gonna shatter."

He didn't deny it. Didn't look at me, either. Just stared at the floor, unmoving.

I pressed the heels of my hands to my eyes. "Her scent is *worse* than when we got here. Stronger. It's not fading."

"Because she's getting deeper into it," Roan said, voice a low rasp. "The suppressant damage...you said it altered things and dragged it out. She's stuck in it."

The unspoken truth hit like a freight train.

She might not *get out of it*.

Not without help.

I lifted my head and stared at him. "You know what that means."

Roan didn't answer.

My throat burned. My gut twisted.

"We're past the wait-it-out plan. Past moral high ground and noble restraint. She needs an alpha, she—hell, she probably needs *all of us*. If you think I'm just gonna sit here while she—"

"She didn't *ask* for us." Roan's voice cracked like thunder, sharp and final. "She didn't invite this. She didn't consent."

"No," a calm voice said from the kitchen where he'd shifted after Roan carried Wren away. "But she's also not throwing us out."

Jay.

He moved back into the room like a shadow, posture steady, composed—like always—but there was heat under his skin. I could see it now. He was *white-knuckling* the same restraint Roan was, the same leash I'd been chewing through since we got here.

How fucking bad was it if Jay, a *beta*, was struggling? No wonder I was in hell. Roan turned his head slightly, not quite meeting Jay's gaze.

"She doesn't have to ask," Jay said simply. "She's *letting us stay*. She's letting us *touch her*. She's been naked under your hands, Roan, and you wrapped her up like you were covering a damn flame. She *let* you."

That sat between us like a line drawn in ash.

Not permission. Not consent.

But not refusal either.

Jay folded his arms, voice quiet and solid as granite. "We're not here to take advantage. But if we wait too long, it *won't* be a choice anymore, for her or us. You know that."

Silence spun out.

No, if it continued at this pace, it would be absolute madness. The primitive, biological drives would take over. I didn't even question whether or not I would be susceptible to it. Wren touched me in ways no one ever had—alpha, beta, or omega. The fact that her need was a keening demand in the air called to me on the most fundamental level.

I stood slowly, because sitting wasn't helping anything. Neither was pretending that my hands weren't shaking, that my breath didn't hitch when I thought about her voice breaking, about her looking at Roan like he was the only damn lifeline she had left.

I swallowed hard.

"You've always led us," I told Roan. "So lead now. Tell us what the hell we do."

Roan didn't answer right away.

His shoulders stayed tight, spine straight, like if he let his posture give even a little, the whole dam inside him would crack open. I could see the war on his face, the tension riding every muscle. The alpha in him was *screaming* and he was denying it with everything he had.

And I knew why, for the same reason I was. It wasn't about ego or pride, but Wren. This was our *Wren*. That possessive hit like a Mack truck.

Ours.

She was *ours*.

The woman who drank her coffee blacker than sin and smiled like a knife's edge. Who kept us out of scandals and fights and jail cells. Who'd been our handler, our babysitter, our sharp-eyed guardian long before any of us even noticed *who* she was underneath.

Roan had *noticed*. Maybe longer than the rest of us. Maybe *too* long.

"She's not some omega in heat," he said finally, voice tight with barely checked strain. "She's Wren."

"*We know that,*" I snapped, too fast, too hard.

His head jerked slightly like I'd hit him, but I didn't back down. The pressure had been building in me since we walked through that door and smelled her on the air like wildfire. And I wasn't proud of the temper coiling through my gut, but I wasn't ashamed of it either.

"If she *wasn't* Wren," I went on, louder now, "we wouldn't be here. You think I'd be fighting every goddamn instinct in my body right now for just *anyone*? You think Jay would be sitting on his hands, burning from the inside out, if *she* wasn't *her*?"

Roan turned to me slowly, and I saw the flicker in his eyes. Pain. Conflict. Guilt.

"She matters," he said, so quietly it barely made sound.

I stepped in closer, jaw clenched. "Then stop acting like she only matters to *you*."

That did it.

Something behind his gaze flared hot, challenge, or maybe grief.

Jay didn't move, didn't even breathe loud, but I felt him right behind me, that steady presence grounding me before I went too far. But I wasn't finished—not yet.

"She's important to *all* of us," I said, voice quieter but sharper than before. "You're not the only one who sees her. Who's seen her for *years*. She's not your burden to carry. She's not some line you have to walk alone while Jay and I pretend we're not coming apart at the seams."

Roan's hands flexed open at his sides, then clenched again.

"She didn't ask for this," he said.

"No," I agreed. "But she's *in* it now. She's suffering. And if you think standing in this room while she burns alive in the other one is the noble fucking choice, then maybe you're not thinking as clearly as you believe you are."

Roan's nostrils flared. His mouth opened—then shut.

The silence that followed was tight and charged.

Jay broke it, his voice low, certain. "We can't fix this by pretending it's not happening."

Roan finally looked up at us both. Really *looked*.

Then he dragged a hand down his face, exhaling like it gutted him.

"Damn it," he muttered. "Damn it, *damn it*."

He didn't argue with us anymore.

For the first time since this whole thing began, I saw the exact moment Roan *stopped* trying to fight his nature—and started trying to figure out how to *control* it, for her sake.

Not to deny what she was.

But to *meet* her in it.

To meet *us* in it.

Roan dragged both hands over his face, like he could scrub the war out of himself by force.

Then, voice low and raw, he asked, "What exactly did your cousin say? About... the heat. How bad it could get? How long?"

I blew out a breath and rubbed at the back of my neck. "Not much. That's the problem. No one really *knows*. There aren't enough controlled studies because no one's *supposed* to use suppressants that long. But what research exists says there's a pattern. A dangerous one."

Roan's stare locked onto mine, and it hit like a steel bar across the chest.

"She's already past the 36-hour mark," I said quietly. "And her reactions are intensifying. You saw her—this isn't tapering off. This is climbing."

"And if it keeps climbing?" he asked, jaw clenched.

"Then it's going to get worse." I hesitated, then added, "There's no map for this, Roan. No clear line. No guarantee. All we can do now is what *she* wants. What she needs."

Roan's expression turned colder, sharper. "That's not an answer."

"It's the *only* answer we've got," I shot back. "We don't decide how this plays out. *She* does."

He didn't like that, obviously. Roan thrived on control, on strategy, on being the one with the plan. But there was no plan here. No command post, no playbook. Just the heat and the ache and *her*.

Jay's voice came from the far side of the room, calm and deliberate. "You don't have to stay, Roan."

That pulled both our gazes to him, sharp and fast.

"She wouldn't blame you if you left," he said. "None of us would."

"The hell I wouldn't," I muttered.

Jay ignored me. "You've been shouldering this since the second we smelled her. You've been trying to protect her, protect us, *and* keep yourself in check. But if you can't be here for what she actually needs, then—"

"I'm willing," I cut in sharply, eyes locked on Roan. "Whatever she needs—however she needs it—I'm *in*." I paused, just long enough for the lie to come out with teeth. "And if she pushes me away after, if she never looks at me again? I can live with that."

We all knew that was bullshit.

Even *I* didn't believe me.

Then Roan looked at me, really *looked*, and something in his expression cracked.

"I'm not going anywhere," he said finally, voice low and solid. "Don't care if it kills me. I'm staying."

That admission hit like a shot of adrenaline, lighting something up in my chest. Not relief, not exactly. Just... certainty.

Jay tilted his head slightly, like he was studying the two

of us. Then, after a long moment, he said, "Then we stop pretending this is normal. We stop tiptoeing around it."

Roan arched a brow. "And do what, exactly?"

Jay's lips curved, just slightly. "We make it sport."

We both stared at him.

"Sport?" I repeated.

Jay shrugged, as if what he'd just said wasn't completely insane. "She's a professional. A fighter. Strategist. She's always had the upper hand with us, always out-thought us, out-maneuvered us. If she wants this—*wants us*—then we don't just give in. We don't coddle her. We make her *earn* it."

Roan crossed his arms slowly, wariness creeping in. "Earn it how?"

"We hunt her," Jay said simply. "We let her try to escape, try to outsmart us. But she knows what happens if she gets caught."

He said it with that maddening beta calm, but there was *heat* under it. The kind of quiet, building promise that made the room feel smaller.

"This is insane," I muttered, but I could already feel my instincts snapping to attention.

My pulse kicked. My skin buzzed. My mouth went dry.

Every alpha instinct I had screamed *yes*.

Roan looked over at Jay, then down at the floor like he was checking his soul for cracks. Then, finally—his voice a rasp—he asked, "Are you *sure* you're a beta?"

Jay smirked. But before he could answer, a soft click split the tension in half.

We all turned.

The bedroom door had opened behind Roan, and she stood there—barefoot, robe hanging off one shoulder, hair a wild halo around her flushed face. Her eyes burned gold, glowing in the low light, and her skin shimmered with sweat and scent and something more.

She didn't speak. She didn't have to. Every molecule in the air shifted. And my heart. Fuck. It *stopped*. Then came roaring back to life, all at once. Wren. Bedraggled, beautiful, blazing.

More perfect than I had ever let myself admit.

Roan was frozen in front of her, tension radiating off his back like a living thing. Jay had gone still too, his expression unreadable—but *ready*.

But me? I took a step forward, because I knew. The game had already started.

"I'll do it." The words fell from her lips like a match hitting gasoline.

Every single molecule in me *ignited*.

A low, guttural sound rumbled out of my chest before I even realized I was making it. It wasn't human—wasn't civilized. It was raw, primal, *mine*. The kind of growl that came from someplace buried so deep in me I hadn't heard it in years.

I barely resisted the urge to fist pump like some kind of lunatic. The sheer adrenaline, the electric punch of *yes* that ripped through me, was too much. Too hot. Too consuming.

She'd said yes.

Not to safety. Not to retreat.

To *us*.

To *this*.

The possessiveness that slammed through me hit with the same force as the need—hard enough that I had to curl my fingers into fists before I reached for her and ruined everything before it started.

Jay, of course, was the only one whose voice stayed

steady. Calm as always, even when every line of his body betrayed the same pulse of hunger that had me half-feral.

"You have to really run, Wren," he said, tone low, deliberate. "You can't just let us catch you. If you give in—if you surrender—then we won't do anything."

I wanted to *goggle* at him for being able to say that like it was simple. Like his restraint wasn't hanging by the same thin thread mine was.

But I got it.

Hell, I respected it.

He was giving her agency—her choice. That *mattered*.

Even if every instinct in me was screaming to skip the whole damn chase and bury myself inside her so deep that we'd never figure out where I ended and she began.

The fog in my head thickened, wrapping around thought and sense until it was just scent and sound and need. Then Roan moved. A sharp slash of his hand through the air—fast, decisive.

It was like he'd sliced through the tether of her scent, forcing a breath of clean air into the haze. I gasped in something deeper than oxygen.

"Are you sure this is what you want?" Roan asked, voice low but firm. The words were jagged steel, forged in control. "Tell me you understand what we're saying. Tell me you understand what will happen."

Wren's chin lifted.

God, that *chin*.

Eyes blazing, mouth soft but sure. That bright intelligence in her stare, sharp enough to cut through every drop of logic I had left, met Roan's head-on.

The queen in her had woken.

"I run," she said, voice steady and clear, though the air

around her vibrated with heat. "You hunt. If you catch me, you can have me."

Roan's jaw flexed, but she wasn't done.

Her gaze cut to me, then to Jay, then back again.

"But you *each* have to catch me," she added, her tone almost wicked.

For a second, I forgot how to breathe.

Oh, she was good.

She was adding *rules*. A challenge. A layer of control laced with pure, devastating temptation.

"Just because one of you does," she continued, "doesn't mean the others get me. But if you do succeed..."

She paused—long enough that the silence in the cabin turned thick and alive.

"I want everything," she said finally. Her voice had gone husky, molten. "I want your knots. I want to feel you marking me. I want..."

Her gaze flicked across each of us, deliberate, scorching.

"...you."

The word detonated inside me.

That she said *you*—and meant all of us—was a blazing, neon *go* sign that hit my bloodstream like liquid fire.

Roan tilted his head back, nostrils flaring as he inhaled deeply, like he needed the confirmation of her scent to believe what he'd just heard. His voice, when it came, was roughened with heat and tension.

"Fine," he said. "Then get dressed."

My pulse hammered.

"It's cold out there," he went on, eyes locked on her. "You get a thirty-minute head start."

The faintest smile curved her lips. Dangerous. Wicked.

"Thirty minutes," she repeated. "That's generous."

Roan's mouth twitched, but his voice was pure command. "You'll need it."

She tilted her head, that smile deepening—then turned and disappeared back into the bedroom, the sway of her hips doing obscene things to every nerve in my body.

The door clicked softly behind her.

For a long, heavy moment, the only sound was our breathing—ragged, uneven, charged.

Then Jay let out a quiet, almost reverent exhale.

"Well," he murmured, lips curving. "Game on."

TWENTY-ONE

WREN

The crisp air bit at my skin as I stepped out of the cabin, each breath sharp and cold against the heat simmering beneath. Snow crunched underfoot, the ground a blinding white canvas that seemed to stretch endlessly into the woods, the trees standing like silent sentinels.

The cold wasn't enough to cut through the wildfire inside me, the heat that still thrummed in my veins—a constant reminder of my body's primitive needs, the biological imperative that was currently consuming me.

The bite of the wind barely registered as I walked, boots sinking into the snow with each step, the rhythm of my pulse matching the crunching beneath me. The woods were quiet, peaceful in a way that made the tension in the air feel all the more pronounced.

They're watching.

Roan, Rhett, Jay—each of them a force, a presence. Each of them an ache I didn't know if I could survive. They were watching me and the weight of their regard was a physical caress against my senses. Liquid heat pooled between my thighs and soaked my panties. I had no doubt that it would soak through my leggings, but at least the snow suit was water proof.

The rub of the fabric of my bra against my nipples was a new torment. Masturbating did nothing for me now. And I tried after Roan left me in the bedroom as need vibrated through me. Vibrantly aware of them out there, I'd tried to stroke my clit to get to orgasm.

No matter how much force I applied or how I rotated my fingers against the swollen bundle of nerves, it didn't *work*. I clung there, right on the edge, *hearing* their voices like the most tantalizing moments of edging, but it wasn't enough. The orgasm wouldn't come and all it did was leave me aching and hungry for *more*.

For *them*.

I was starving for *them*.

My thoughts scrambled more and more as I moved deeper into the woods, my body on fire and yet so *cold*. The storm raging inside me now was as much a battlefield as a sensation. Imagining their touch clung to me, and I couldn't escape it. The way they'd looked at me, spoken to me—the things they'd promised, things I wanted.

But it wasn't just about the heat anymore. It wasn't just about the hunger that made my blood burn. It was *them*. Their connection to me, the raw, undeniable attraction. I needed to test it. Needed to know just how far it could stretch before we all broke.

Though if they'd just taken me right there...

Eyes closed, I pressed a hand against a tree and stopped to suck in icy cold gulps of air. Oh, I could *feel* how good it would have been. At the same time, Roan told me to make them work for it. To make them capture me. It appealed to all parts of me, even the one who wanted to just lay down and spread my legs until they filled me over and over.

Shoving away from the tree, I tried to chase the images away at the same moment. The scent of them was inside of me now, I could taste their musk and their need like it was my own. I wanted more though. So, legs burning with effort and the trees closing around me like a maze, I pushed on.

I was leaving a trail a toddler could fucking follow. A glance over my shoulder revealed where I'd plodded through the snow, sinking up to my mid-calves over and over. Pausing again, I frowned. The fog clouding my thoughts parted briefly as I tilted my head and began to sweep the area around me with a studying gaze.

A trail that blazingly obvious would not provide them with a challenge. In fact, it was an open invitation that just said, here I am, come and get me. Irritation sparked off the dark, delectable voice that pointed out, "the sooner they find you, the sooner you get fucked."

Except, I reminded both that bitchy inner monologue as well as myself, Roan made it clear if I didn't at least attempt to give them a challenge, I wouldn't get shit.

One of us snorted. Then I giggled. I had to slap a gloved hand over my mouth at the sound. I didn't giggle. Or titter. Or make little girly noises of any kind. My cunt clenched on emptiness. It would continue to flex around that great, big fat nothing if I didn't make them work for it.

Decide. I told myself. *Decide if you really want them. Cause you can just give up right now, go back to the cabin and live through this hell until it's over. It won't kill you.*

It wouldn't.

Heat *sucked* to just ride it out. Might suck epically after all these years on suppressants. But I *would* survive it. The only drawback is all four of us would be in this sensory hell instead of just me.

"No," I whispered against my gloved hand as I took another searching look at the area around me. I *wanted* more. That meant I had to make them *work* for more. To do that, *I* had to work smarter. I closed my eyes, braced a gloved hand against a tree and took three, long, controlled breaths and released them.

The icy cold air washed through me. The breeze shifted and it filled my nose with the fresh scents of pine, snow, and cold. There were hints of an oncoming storm. More snow. Every breath flushed out some of the haze.

How long would it last? I had no idea. The forest was beautiful, serene in its harshness, but there was no peace for me here. Not anymore. Not—

A rustle behind me, a whisper in the wind...

I turned, searching the area but nothing moved save for the wind nudging the trees. The pines waved. The clouds had crowded out the sun, and it was growing darker. Holding, still, I let the air movement bring me scents from the direction of the cabin.

Nothing but snow, trees, and...

I needed to move. Shifting my weight, I angled uphill and away from the hollow I'd been wading through. The snow drifts tended to be shallower up here. I wound my way through the trees. The trickle of water over rocks drew my attention.

The river.

There was an arm of it that cut through here, the shores on both sides were rocky. They would be slick with the ice, but the water movement said it wasn't totally frozen. If I could make it there, I could muddy the scent trail.

Adrenaline-fueled excitement spilled into my blood and I found a fresh burst of energy.

It was barely more than a creek in most places—fed from the mountains, icy even in summer—but in winter, it was a calculated gamble. The rocks along the banks would be slick, the water running just fast enough to stay partially unfrozen. The temperature alone would be a shock to my system, but if I made it across without eating shit or breaking something, it might be enough to throw them off. At least for a while.

I cut my way through the trees, moving faster now that the terrain sloped up and the snow wasn't swallowing my legs with every step. I slid, stumbled, but kept pushing forward. The cold scraped at my cheeks, biting deep into the exposed skin, but that pain kept my head clear.

Focus. Stay sharp. Keep moving.

There were eyes on me again.

I couldn't hear anything. No footsteps. No breathing. But my instincts screamed. The skin between my shoulder blades prickled like a hot brand had been pressed there. Something was behind me. Watching. Tracking.

I glanced over my shoulder. Nothing.

But I felt it.

They were getting closer.

The raw need that had settled into me—the firestorm licking through my veins—flared hotter at that thought. They were hunting me. Their blood was up. Their need as visceral and feral as mine.

I wanted them to catch me. I wanted to feel their hands, their mouths, their bodies...

But not yet.

My boots hit rocky earth, the snow thinner here, scattered between broken stone and skeletal branches. The river cut across the forest like a jagged wound, steam rising faintly from the frigid surface. The sound of it—the steady burble and splash of water over rocks—muffled the forest's natural silence.

I picked my way down the incline and slipped once, knees cracking against the frozen ground, breath hissing between my teeth. I caught myself on a low branch and crawled to the edge.

The water was deeper in the center, moving fast enough to bite. I could see the places where it had frozen in sheets along the edges, and I wasn't stupid enough to try stepping on them.

Still... I had to move. I had to throw them off.

I waded in.

It took time for the temperature of the water to slice through the waterproof clothing. Normally, I was not a fan of knives being sliced over me, but it helped keep my mind clear. By the time I was midstream, the icy current threatened to crest the high waist and that would suck as the cold water would soak down the inside of my clothes. Still, I pushed through as my whole body kept threatening to go rigid at the idea.

On the far side, I slipped again, nearly went down face-first, but caught myself. My gloves were holding up—barely. Some water crept under the elastic hem of my ski pants and soaked into the top of one boot. A part of me could practically hear the crunching of ice. The only thing keeping my limbs moving now was pure will and the lingering bite of my heat, still buzzing through my system like a live wire.

I paused long enough to circle back, doubling over my tracks and stepping across fallen logs to confuse any trail. The wind helped, too—shifting behind me, carrying scent away from the direction I moved.

Smart, Wren, I told myself, even as my teeth began to chatter. *Keep it smart.*

Adrenaline surged in my system, sharpening my focus and giving me some clarity of thought I'd begun to believe I'd lost entirely. Not knowing how long it would last, I just went with it.

The sun had nearly dipped below the horizon now. Dusk swallowed the forest in deepening shades of blue and gray. The wind picked up, whispering through the branches above, and for the first time, I felt the first real warning bite of another storm moving in.

Good. That would help, too.

I kept heading west, using the sun's dying glow as it slid beneath the clouds as a guide. The hills rolled in that direction, and if I remembered the map correctly, there was an old hunting cabin tucked between a couple of ridges. One that had been available for rental like the one I'd taken.

Shelter. Maybe even a fire if I could get one going. That would be the smart play.

But wariness crept in again. I hadn't heard them—hadn't seen them—but that *sense* hadn't left me. The one that said I was prey. Being watched. Being stalked.

No matter how clear-headed I tried to be, my body betrayed me with every step. I was cold. Damp. But I still ached for them. Still throbbed between my thighs with every jolt of footfall.

This wasn't just heat anymore. It was something *bigger.* Something *deeper.*

That something was getting harder to ignore.

I didn't stop moving. I couldn't. Not yet. But my limbs were getting heavier, my breath shorter, and the pull of the heat inside me was turning into a dragging weight. Like it wanted to pull me down. Make me collapse into the snow and *wait* for them.

But that wasn't the deal. That wasn't the game.

They had to earn me. Each of them.

Just before I crested the next ridge, I glanced back—and I *knew*. There, across the white expanse, one of them had stepped out onto the riverbank. Far enough to make it a challenge still. Close enough that my heart slammed into my ribs.

I couldn't see who it was. Their snow gear squared out his shape, and the hockey mask was enough to give me a jolt of fear-laced desire. The shadows concealed the rest of him, but my body recognized his, whether my mind could name him or not.

The hunger.

The promise.

The challenge.

This one, at least, was getting closer.

Exhilaration sprinted through me as I smiled and turned, forcing my tired legs to run again, breath fogging in the cold, heart racing. The cabin couldn't be far now.

But neither was he.

Come and get me.

The figure caught me just as I reached the cabin, his grip like a vise around my waist, his hard arms wrapping around me with a force that left me breathless. The roughness of his arousal pressed insistently against me, a promise of what was to come. He managed to get the door open with one hand, his other never leaving my body, and pushed me inside with a fierce urgency that left no room for doubt.

Inside the cabin, the air was thick with anticipation and the lingering scent of pine. He said nothing, his breathing heavy and ragged, as his hands moved with rough, efficient movements punctuated by sound of zippers being tugged down to strip down my snow suit. The fabric tore under his urgent touch, and to my utter thrill, he ripped my soaked leggings down, along with my panties, exposing me completely to his hungry gaze.

Then, with a single, hard thrust, he entered me, making me scream. The sound echoed through the small cabin, a primal cry of need and desire that seemed to shake the very foundations of the building. I clawed at the table with my gloved hands, the wood rough and unyielding beneath my fingers, as he fucked me hard and fast. Each thrust was a claim, a promise, and a demand all at once, and I met him with equal fervor, my body arching to meet his.

His hands were everywhere, teasing and tormenting me with expert precision. Hard fingers found my clit, circling and teasing it with a ruthless intensity that had me gasping for breath. Another hand slid up under my jacket, pinching my nipples with a force that sent jolts of pleasure-pain straight to my core. I was on fire, every nerve ending alight with need and desire, and I knew I was his to command.

It was brutal, passionate, and everything I could have asked for. The release detonated through my system, a wave of pleasure so intense that it made me sob. But even after I came, he stayed stiff inside me, his body demanding more. As my breathing returned to a semblance of normalcy, he began to power into me again, and I realized that he was going to keep fucking me until we both couldn't take it anymore.

Laughter-infused tears spilled down my face as I pushed back against him, meeting his every thrust with a fervor that matched his own. It was everything I had ever wanted, a primal dance of desire and need that left no room for anything else. The sound of the door opening and the wash of cold air alerted me to a new arrival, and I heard the muttered oath as my captor continued to fuck me relentlessly, the rhythm of our bodies never faltering.

A new presence in the room only heightened my arousal, the knowledge that we were not alone adding a new layer of intensity to the encounter. My captor's grip on my hips tightened, his thrusts becoming more urgent, more demanding, as if he was determined to mark me as his own before anyone else could claim me. I met his every move with equal intensity, my body on fire with need and desire, until we both reached the peak of pleasure once more, our cries of release mingling in the air.

As the waves of pleasure subsided, I collapsed against the table, my body slick with sweat and my breath coming in ragged gasps. But my captor was not done with me yet. He flipped me over, his eyes dark with desire and determination, and lifted my legs over his shoulders. With a single, powerful thrust, he entered me again, his body demanding more, always more.

I met his every thrust with equal fervor, my body arching to meet his, as we danced on the edge of pleasure and pain. The new arrival watched us with a hunger that matched my own, his presence adding a new layer of intensity to our encounter. I was lost in a sea of sensation, my body alive with need and desire, as we fucked with a ferocity that left us both breathless and spent.

When we finally collapsed, our bodies slick with sweat and our breaths coming in ragged gasps, I knew that I was forever changed. This was more than just sex; it was a claiming, a promise, and a beginning. And as I lay there, my body still throbbing with the aftershocks of pleasure, I knew that I would do it all over again in a heartbeat.

The man fucking me stilled, his cock still deep inside me, and I could feel his release pulsing into me, a drug that sent waves of pleasure coursing through my veins. A grunt of sound escaped his lips, a primal, satisfied noise that sent a shiver down my spine. I was lost in the sensation, my body on fire with need and desire, when I realized that the third man was there, his presence a silent promise of more to come.

The second man approached me, his pants open and the long, hard length of his cock in his hand. He brushed it against my lips, and I opened for him without hesitation, a soft "Oh, fuck yes" escaping my lips. He pushed into my mouth, his grip on my hair tight and demanding, as he began to fuck my throat with a fierce intensity that matched the man still buried deep inside me.

A moment later, the third man replaced the first, his cock sliding into me with ease, coated in the generous cum left by his predecessor. I screamed around the cock in my throat, the sound muffled and primal, as the third man began to thrust into me with a relentless rhythm. The roughness of it was a kind of beauty, hard, fierce fucking that left me breathless and wanting more.

They pushed and pulled me between them, their bodies moving in perfect sync as they claimed me, used me, and filled me with a pleasure so intense that it was almost painful. I fought to stay focused, my mind a whirlwind of sensation and need, as hands slid under my jacket, palming my nipples with a rough, demanding touch.

The pleasure was blazing and consuming, a fire that burned through every nerve ending, every fiber of my being. For the first time since the heat struck, I felt whole, complete, as if every piece of me had finally clicked into place. The men were relentless, their bodies demanding and taking, and I met their every move with equal fervor, my own need matching theirs in intensity.

The man in my throat hit the back of it, his grip on my hair tightening as he held me there, his cock pulsing with his impending release. The man between my legs was just as demanding, his thrusts growing more urgent, more desperate, as he chased his own pleasure. I was caught between them, a plaything for their desires, and I reveled in it, my body alive with sensation and need.

As they both reached their peak, their releases filling me, I felt a sense of satisfaction, of completion, that I had never experienced before. It was raw, primal, and perfect, and I knew that I would do it all over again in a heartbeat. The men pulled away, their breaths coming in ragged gasps, and I collapsed onto the table, my body slick with sweat and my mind a blur of pleasure and satisfaction.

In that moment, I was theirs, completely and utterly, and I wouldn't have it any other way.

TWENTY-TWO

JAY

My body trembled from the force of my release as she choked on my cock, her throat working as she swallowed every last drop of my cum. I stared down at her, my breath coming in ragged gasps, not saying a word because Roan had ordered us to maintain silence when we caught her. We would give her everything, but no names, no declarations, let her have the pleasure of anonymity. And I wanted more of that.

Rhett was bracing his hands on the table, still buried deep inside her, his body tense with the effort of holding back. None of us were naked, but that's all I wanted—to strip her bare and have her over and over again. Roan moved around us, his control a thing of legends, but suddenly he was in front of her, waving me away.

Her lips were swollen from sucking me, her beautiful mouth red and puffy, and she stared up at Roan, dazed, as he pushed his cock against her lips. He was absolutely ruthless in fucking her throat, his hips moving with a fierce, demanding rhythm.

For all his control, his demand had my cock stiffening all over again. I watched as Roan took his pleasure, his grip on her hair tight and unyielding. Rhett and I locked eyes through the masks, a silent communication passing between us. We did rock, paper, scissors, and when my rock crushed his scissors, I could practically hear his swearing. But he pulled out, his cock glistening with her arousal and his own release, and I moved to fuck that sweet cunt of hers.

She was absolutely filthy from them both, her body slick with sweat and cum, and I gathered up the evidence of their pleasure, pushing it back inside her before I thrust in. Her body bucked upward, a gasp escaping her lips, and I used my fingers, sticky with their cum, to begin to tease her asshole. She was going to need to be able to hold both of their knots, and that started now.

I could feel her resistance, her body tensing as I pushed a finger into her tight, virgin hole. But I was relentless, my touch firm and demanding, as I prepared her for what was to come. She moaned around Roan's cock, the sound muffled and primal, and I knew that she was lost in the sensation, her body alive with need and desire.

Rhett moved behind me, his hands on my shoulders, his breath hot against my ear as he whispered, "Fuck her hard, Jay. Make her take it all." And I did, my hips moving with a fierce, unyielding rhythm as I claimed her, used her, and filled her with a pleasure so intense that it left us both breathless and wanting more.

As I thrust into her, I could *see* Roan's cock pulsing in her throat, his release imminent. It was erotic as hell. We were all on the edge, teetering on the brink of pleasure and satisfaction. And I was determined to push her over that edge, to make her scream and sob and beg for more, until we were all spent and sated, our bodies slick with sweat and cum, and our minds a blur of pleasure and desire.

Her wild need for us was intoxicating, her body a playground of primal desire that I couldn't get enough of. She was fucking gorgeous, all shattered and broken from her heat, her eyes glazed with lust and her skin flushed with arousal. The way she responded to us, the way she took everything we gave her and begged for more, was a sight to behold.

I wanted to mark her, claim her, make her mine in every possible way. The thought of her belonging to us, of her being ours to use and pleasure, drove me wild with need.

Her inner muscles clenched around me, her body on the edge of another orgasm, and I was close too. The sight of her, so beautiful and debauched, her body slick with our combined releases, was almost too much to bear. I wanted to watch her come undone, to see her fall apart in our arms, and I knew that we would all be there to catch her, to hold her, to love her.

As we reached the peak of pleasure together, our cries of release mingling in the air, I knew that this was just the beginning. We would have her over and over again, in every way possible, until she was completely and utterly ours. And I couldn't wait for the next time, for the next chance to lose myself in her, to drown in the primal, all-consuming need that she aroused in me.

The heat of my breath against my mask was almost too much as I pulled out. I gathered up more of our come, using it to lubricate my fingers as I returned to working on her ass, scissoring to loosen her up. The knot from either Rhett or Roan was going to be a tight fit, and I wanted to make sure she was ready for it.

Her resistance was palpable, her body tensing as I

pushed a second finger into that tight puckered hole. She kept clenching violently against me, pushing out and pulling at the same time. A low, husky sound escaped her as I relentlessly readied her. Yes, it was different and overwhelming, but fuck I wanted her. No pain for her, not that we couldn't ease.

She was panting, her eyes glassy as she began to toss her head from side to side, writhing on the table, lost in the sensation. The sight of her, so wild and abandoned, was almost too much to bear.

Roan caught her by the throat, his grip firm but gentle, as he whipped off his mask, then pinned her with a long, deep kiss that had her moaning so hard, I could feel my cock stirring to life once more. The sound of her pleasure, the sight of her surrendering to him, was intoxicating, and I wanted to join them, to lose myself in her once more.

Taking my cue from Roan, I ripped off my own mask. The cooler air was a relief against my face. Rhett had the fire going, the crackling flames casting a warm, inviting glow over the room. I was really glad that we had made sure to rent this place. It was the closest to the cabin she'd rented and no way in hell did I want unexpected visitors. Not when we could indulge in our wildest desires, where we could explore every inch of her body and every depth of our need.

As Roan broke the kiss, his breath coming in harsh gasps, he looked over at me. For all that her need and his body's own demands held him fast, he wasn't bowing to it fully. He held part of himself back, maintained control—command.

Right now, what he wanted was for me to get her ready. Because despite her orgasms and our own releases, she was already starting to move. Her heat was like a star going super nova, intense, consuming, and utterly devastating.

"I have it," I told him, my voice sounded rough to my own ears. Then he lifted his head to glance at Rhett. The other man was already there. At some point, he'd stripped his clothes off and between the three of us, we removed the rest of Wren's. She arched her back, her nipples hard points of dark pink perfection. I paused to bite the side of her breast, sucking hard against the softness until she let out a hiss and tangled her fingers in my hair.

The mark darkened slowly against the golden gleam of her skin. My mark. That satisfied me. Once she was naked, we shifted her, lifting her until we could settle her on Rhett's waiting cock. Another moan left her as he filled her. She dug her nails into his shoulders and I wanted her to do that to me.

With quick movements since my cock was already hard as a stone and dying to be back inside of her, I stripped the rest of my clothes and moved to stand behind her.

When Rhett glanced up at me, there was a wild grin that was almost a grimace tightening his mouth. He wanted to let go and just rut, but not yet. We had to take the edge off, and get her ready— With a grunt, he stabilized her hips as he began to pump his in a fierce, unyielding rhythm to drive up into her.

I used more of the cum he pushed out of her to lube up my dick and her ass once more before I pressed the tip of my dick against the tight rosette of her hole. Her whole body tensed as I began to push in, but Rhett distracted her with his thrusts.

Her slick coated my thighs from where I'd had her earlier, and the scent was the darkest, sweetest aphrodisiac to my system. Relentless, I pushed past that first ring of muscle. Far from truly loose, she still took and took as I fucked into her. The grip of her ass was unimaginably intense. Even as I bottomed out, I wrapped her hair around my fist. The thin barrier separating me from Rhett let me feel his cock moving inside of her.

"Fuck," Rhett swore, as we kept her in place and on his next thrust, I began to move. We seesawed her between us, moving in sync with a rhythm developed on the ice but Wren was so much more than a puck or a championship—

So.

Fucking.

Much.

More.

Tightening my grip in her hair, I pulled her head back so she would arch her body—fuck, right there. The position was perfect and I kissed her. It was the first time my mouth brushed over hers. Like a drug sliding into my system, the taste of her wound through me, leaving a fiery trail to mark her path. The brand soaked into my skin, my muscle, and scored my bones.

"More," she cried against my lips. "More."

Happy to oblige, we increased our tempo, our thrusts, our force and her cries were the symphony of pleasure I craved. The bloom of her scent...

Her scent in heat was a rich, intoxicating lushness that wrapped around me like a velvet cloak, drawing me in and ensnaring my senses. It was a heady mix of musk and honey, a primal aroma that spoke of untamed desire and unbridled passion. The air around us was thick with it, a heady perfume designed to drive even the sanest man mad.

Her heat was a living, breathing thing, a tangible force in the room with us. It pulsed and throbbed through her body, tore at ours as she cried out in need. The fire crackled in the background, the sound a staccato beat to underscore the slapping of flesh on flesh.

The sudden clamping of her muscles was my only warning of her orgasm. I dragged my head up, releasing her mouth as my hips stuttered. The release this time was almost a dry one, it hurt and felt so fucking amazing at the same time. The perfection of pain because this was Wren.

Our Wren.

Rhett let out a roar as he came. The gush of his release and her slick made a hell of a mess between us. He cupped her face and pulled her down for a devouring kiss. The moment expanding until it blocked out the world.

We were in a bubble of pure passion illuminated by the flames licking over the logs in the fireplace, perfumed in musk and need kissed by the cedar of the cabin itself. The three of us seemed to suspend there, panting. Sweat dripped down my spine. Hers glistened on her skin and I licked up the line of her throat before I bit down on the side of her neck.

She gave a start, her inner muscles clenching so tight she threatened to squeeze every last drop of my release. It was hers. All hers. Every fucking thing I had was hers. Rhett let out a low groaning growl as the respite proved almost too short. A little mewl of sound escaped her as she began to writhe again and his cock stiffened.

"Water," Roan ordered. "Clean up."

The words sliced right through the haze of need starting to cloud around us and I pulled back, slowly. Wren began to shake, tears tracking down her face.

"Shh," Roan ordered, his hand replacing mine in her hair as he began to pet her. Rhett started to thrust, but a snap of a look from Roan stilled him. I hated leaving her body and it grasped at me, wanting me to stay, but Roan was right.

If she was this needy already, this desperate...

She needed their knots.

On shaking legs, I backed up and grabbed a bottle of water. Unscrewing the top, I drained all of it while watching Roan and Rhett coax her into drinking. Then Roan was lifting her off Rhett's dick. The other alpha bit back a snarl but Roan was already carrying Wren toward the bedroom.

Since we'd planned to bring her here, we'd brought stuff over while Roan tracked her in the woods. Then we'd gone to join in the hunt. Like some giant hunting cat, Rhett was on his feet and prowling after them.

Roan had been busy while we fucked her. The bedroom was prepared, the sheets drawn back, a cover peeking out from under the fitted sheet. The sight of Wren sprawled on her back, legs apart with all of our come glistening between her thighs made my mouth water.

Then Roan was there with a cool cloth and she let out a cry and tried to escape him cleaning her up. I joined them in holding her still, wiping her down and then rolling her over to clean her ass as well.

"Drink," Roan ordered, pressing the bottle to her lips. Wren's eyes flashed fire and for a moment, the woman we adored was right there, glaring back at him. "There you are..." He brushed his knuckles down her flushed cheek. "There you are."

"Roan," she whispered his name in a rough croak. Then her gaze slid to me. "Jay..." When Rhett reappeared, she let out a sigh. "Rhett."

Languor infused her frenetic movements and she blew out a long breath. Some of the cloud in her eyes drifted away and when Roan cupped her cheek, she covered his hand with hers even as she reached out a hand toward me. When she would have twisted, Rhett came to sit on the bed next to her.

"We're here," I promised. "We're not going anywhere."

TWENTY-THREE

WREN

The desperation began to climb once again before they even finished wiping me down. Exhaustion and need twined through me to begin fanning the flames that seemed barely quenched, despite the ferociousness of their taking. Flushed and burning beneath my skin, I wanted *more*.

What control I'd found on the run to get here—was gone. Utterly destroyed. Every bit of it shattered like thin ice under their blades. My throat, my cunt, even my ass were all well-used and the orgasms still echoed in the ripples of my body even as the taste of them lingered on my tongue.

You'd have thought that was enough. But no, the fever climbed. Jay rubbed my arm, the contact should soothe but it just made me shift as need curled under my skin, demanding, prescient and fierce.

Roan stood there, one knee on the bed as he held out another bottle of water toward me, a god carved from stone and willpower. The weight of him dominated the room, even as Rhett eased onto the bed on my other side.

His wet hair, and red-flushed skin betrayed the shower he'd taken. I hadn't even realized the water was on, but Jay pressed a kiss to my shoulder before he slid off the bed and I tracked his passage to the bathroom.

The water came on again as Rhett lifted me until I was in his lap, my back to his chest—the contact of skin on skin sent me up in flames. I couldn't have stopped the moan I released even if I had wanted to, and currently, it wasn't even a distant thought on the horizon.

A soft laugh escaped Rhett as he pressed a line of kisses along my throat and I tilted my head to give him access even as my gaze latched onto Roan's. His chest rose and fell slowly, his eyes drinking me in as I unraveled.

"I'm fine," I said, though my voice didn't sound like mine. Too breathless. Too hollow.

"You're not." He closed the distance between us in a slow, almost sinuous motion. The touch of his finger to my cheek another point of pleasurable burn so intense it almost hurt. My body was already going softer, melting into Rhett even as I reached up to clasp Roan's wrist. They felt so good. "You're dehydrated. Your blood sugar's tanking. You need food."

"I need you." The words ripped out of me before I could stop them. "I need you so fucking bad—"

"Eat first," he said, firm and unrelenting. "Then we talk."

"I *don't want to fucking eat*," I snapped, desire transforming into fury. Couldn't he feel the fever in my skin? The slick already coating my thighs? The demand of the hunger wrenching me inside out? "I'm dying, Roan, I *hurt*. You have no idea how much—"

Rhett's cock was against my ass and so hard, all I had to

do was rise up a little and I could fill myself with him. Gorge on him.

Roan shifted his grip so fast, I didn't see it coming. He fisted my hair, yanking my head back just enough that I gasped. Rhett's fingers flexed against my hips, the bite of them as sharp as the pain against my scalp.

"Stop." Roan's voice was low. Lethal. "Listen to me."

My heart slammed against my ribs, but I went still. Even the writhing under my skin went quiet, quiescent... playing dead at his command.

"This is going to get worse before it gets better. You think you're desperate now?" His fingers tightened slightly in my hair. Not cruel. Controlled. "You need strength to survive this. If you pass out or crash or go into shock, you think I'm going to let anyone touch you then? You think *I* would? You want this? Then you keep your body functioning first. You keep your mind here with us."

I blinked up at him, caught in the weight of his gaze. The words were harsh, but his scent—God, his *scent*—wrapped around me like warm smoke, grounding and infuriating at once.

My lip trembled. I hated how close I was to crying. Hated how deep this need carved through me. He was right. I *did* need strength. But more than that, I needed *them*.

Roan held me still, his dark eyes never leaving mine. "Do you understand me, Wren?"

I swallowed, throat tight. "Yes."

He didn't release me immediately. Just watched me, making sure the answer came from more than my lips. That it rooted somewhere real. As I stared up at him, locked there under the heat of his gaze, I realized something sharp and aching, I hadn't even really *seen* him yet.

Not the way I wanted to. Not the way I *would*.

Not when I was so strung out I could barely hold a thought between my legs screaming for him. Not when I'd spent the last week fighting this, avoiding it, denying myself—denying *them.*

But I would. I'd see them. All of them. I'd learn every detail. Every scar. Every piece of history etched into their bodies. I would *take* them in every possible way.

That was my promise, as I slowly reached up and touched his face.

Roan froze as my fingers brushed the coarse stubble along his jaw. The rasp of it had raked over my own cheek earlier. The contact had marked me and somewhere deep inside, in a place I didn't want to examine too closely, I reveled in that knowledge. His breath hitched, just enough for me to catch it. He was holding on, too.

"I haven't even gotten to appreciate you," I whispered, fingers trailing to the corner of his mouth. "Not really. Not the way I want to."

His jaw flexed, nostrils flaring. His pupils blew wide as I dragged my hand down the center of his chest, feeling the heat radiate from his skin.

"But I will," I whispered. "Every inch."

The way he growled—it was soft, but primal—sent a ripple of heat down my spine. He released my hair, but not me. His hands caught my cheeks, steadied me even as I swayed toward him.

Rhett bit down on my shoulder in a move that held me still, but didn't hurt. A reminder that he was there too and I reached with my free hand to grip his thigh. His muscles went tense, and his cock was even harder, if that was possible. The pressure of it along the crack of my ass a sensuous promise.

Oh... Jay had taken my ass. That revelation slipped out

from under the haze of need trying to cloud my mind, but Roan stood like a barrier. Jay had been so careful, but he'd given me no quarter and I could feel where every inch of him had been. There would be no knot with Jay, but when...

A delicious shudder went through me as a cascade of images spilled through my mind. Wanting and caring about them had always been a part of me, even if I kept it locked down and under control. Some lines you didn't cross. But we had now and I didn't think there would be any going back...

"You eat first," he said again, but this time, his voice was ragged. Thinner. "Then we'll see how long you can survive what you're asking for."

My body already *had* surrendered. It wanted to surrender again. More, my mind was ready to give in and just fall, trusting him—them—to hold me together even as everything inside me tried to split apart.

And I did trust him.

"I'll eat," I said, throat raw.

"Good," he replied. "Because when we start this time, my beautiful, tempting, so fucking incredible omega, I'm not stopping until you beg for mercy."

His possession swept through me, knocking aside old doubts and past objections. Those were from then, this was now. I would beg, no doubt existed within me. But not yet. Not until...

"Make sure she eats," Roan said in an almost guttural growl that had my cunt clenching, my toes curling and my ass shifting against Rhett. His hitch of breath reminded me that I wasn't alone in my need and that had my gaze dipping to where Roan's cock stood erect, long, beautifully curved and the tip so red it was damn near purple. Every vein was visible, as carved and beautiful as the rest of him.

Oh, I would definitely be begging.

"I have her," Rhett said, then he bit down carefully on the juncture where my shoulder met my throat and I went liquid. The hold was declaring his intentions to claim. Closing my eyes, I leaned my head back, baring my throat to them both without a care. They were telling me what they were willing to do and I wanted them to know I was ready for it.

"Fuck," Roan said a moment before his mouth closed over mine. The kiss was hot, fierce, all teeth and tongue and heat, then he was gone as he practically ripped himself away. Jay was back, a towel hitched around his naked hips, but it did nothing to disguise the tent made by his cock.

"You finished showering," I whispered as the water came on again. Oh, and Roan was in there.

Jay chuckled as he carried the tray over to the bed and Rhett shifted me, then his cock was right at my entrance and I glanced back at him as he grinned.

"For fuck's sake..." Jay started but Rhett and I had already gripped his cock and I sank down on it. We both hissed out a long breath and my inner muscles went tight, flexing around his thickness as he stretched me perfectly.

"Not fucking her yet," Rhett said as he seated himself fully. This angle made him a lot, and he was already a lot. Once there, though, he wrapped an arm around my waist, a band to keep me still. "Just giving her cunt something to hold onto while we feed her. 'Cause her scent is going to drive me insane."

And Roan was in the shower.

That knowledge sank into my bones even as it hit Jay. I clenched around Rhett's dick, flexing my inner muscles and when he bit me this time, it did hurt. The teeth left a mark and he spread one of his hands over my breast. Then he twisted a nipple until the pain definitely edged over the pleasure.

"Behave," Rhett growled. "Eat before Roan comes back out here and punishes all of us."

There was something utterly intoxicating about that idea. Instead of arguing, however, because Rhett was inside of me and I was spread wide so Jay could see every inch of my flesh, I reached for one of the fruit slices. The apple was cold and crisp. Then Jay lifted a cracker layered with a slice of sharp cheddar and smoky ham.

Each flavor exploded on my tongue, a decadent experience. Gaze locked on Jay's, I took another cracker as he fed it to me, then stroked my lower lip with his thumb. He put the tray on the bed next to us and took a seat where he could feed me. Rhett fed himself, though and in between bites, he would thrust a water bottle to me.

The simple pleasure on Roan's face when he came out of the bathroom absolutely arrested me. He watched as I drained a bottle and nodded in satisfaction. The warmth that bloomed in my chest had nothing to do with the need in my body, a need that was already beginning to build even with Rhett's cock buried inside of me.

We weren't moving other than the boys feeding me. Rhett's cock had stretched and filled me. The thickness helped to quiet the need, even if it made my internal muscles tremble. Still, I was far from satisfied and the fact I recognized it was... different. At least for me. If I was aware of my own scent, then they had to be.

When Jay held up another cracker, this one boasting more sharp cheddar with a kiss of blackberry jam and a salty cashew, I took the whole bite and sucked off his fingers. His eyes darkened instantly.

Playing with fire?

Check.

Prepared to get burned?

Double check.

At the same time, something felt... off.

I looked around the room, brow furrowing. This wasn't the cabin I'd rented. Rhett shifted beneath me, pushing up ever so slightly and the stretch bumped the head of his cock inside. It—was distractingly wonderful.

Aware of Roan's watchfulness, I finished chewing my bite of food before taking the fresh water bottle and washing it down. Then I said, "This isn't my cabin. Not the one I booked."

Jay stretched out beside me like a lazy cat, one hand tucked under his head, the other trailing along the inside of my thigh just because he could. His grin was slow and smug, wicked in a way that made my stomach twist—part nerves, part anticipation.

"Nope," he said, popping the 'p' like it was a joke we were both in on. "Yours was cute, but empty. I took care of it."

"Took care of it?" I echoed, not sure I wanted to know what that meant.

Rhett leaned forward, nipping my ear this time. The sharpness of his teeth sent a zing rebounding through my system. My nipples went to points even as my cunt clenched around him like a fist. His hiss was pure decadence to my ears.

"There was another one a little further out," he said, his voice low and calm. "We rented it, too."

I blinked. "You rented... both cabins?"

Jay chuckled, stealing a berry off my plate like a thief. "No one for miles," he said, popping it into his mouth. "Just us."

Something in my chest tightened. It wasn't fear, not exactly. Yet, there was an inescapable thrill at the idea that I was trapped with them. Trapped in a position where my heat would drive us all mad and we were already lovers, whether it lasted past this moment—whether the moment took days or not—I didn't have an answer.

Frankly, I didn't care. Not right now. Not when they were everything I could want. Maybe I hadn't invited them. But I certainly didn't want to escape either.

Then Roan turned to look at me.

He'd been quiet this whole time, lounging at the foot of the bed, watching. But when his gaze met mine, it hit like a live wire—sharp and hot, like it could burn through me if I didn't look away. I didn't. I couldn't.

All that power he wore like a second skin focused down to a single, smoldering point.

"You're all ours," he informed me, his declaration every bit as intentional as Jay's bite. The liquid heat spilled into my blood like fire and then there was room for nothing else. No air, no thoughts, nothing.

With three words, he'd given my body permission to let go and the torrent that spasmed through me had Rhett growling, Jay's pupils swelling to drown out the iris and made Roan's slow, devastating smile grow.

"Yes," I whispered, giving in to what we all wanted right now. "Yours."

CHAPTER

TWENTY-FOUR

ROAN

She tasted like honey and heat.

The kisses we'd shared so far had all been in the fiery heat of the moment, all possession and control to bring her back to us when the heat eroded every inch of her control. The orgasms had been intense and ferocious.

Feeling her pretty little mouth on my cock was a memory I would keep close. More, I wanted a repeat. I wanted to bury my face between her thighs, lick her cunt up like my favorite ice cream until she bathed me in her slick and her cries. Then I would sink into her and fuck her into the mattress until she took my knot and my claim.

All of these thoughts, this hunger, this primal instinctive need to grab and hold onto her was a firestorm in my blood. Even as the scent of her heat perfumed the air with the intrinsically feminine sweetness of her scent, the musk a heady taste on my tongue, I recognized just how easy it would be to slip the leash.

But not this time. No, this time it was all about getting her through the experience. Helping her and easing her

259

aches—if that took our cocks, then so be it. Jay couldn't knot her, but he could give her orgasms and a solid place to stand. Too many overlooked what a beta brought to the relationship.

They didn't knot and they didn't go into heat. They were less a victim to their own instincts and more a tempering of our own. A good beta was worth a dozen mediocre alphas and then some. Jay was more than "just a beta." He was our friend and he cared about Wren every bit as much as we did.

I hadn't missed the fact that Rhett was getting his cock warmed in Wren's cunt or how she leaned back into him. The tiny little flexations of her muscles rippled along her thighs and her abdomen. She was soft and curvy in unexpected ways. I'd always appreciated her form, but she often wore these narrow cut dresses, pantsuits, and jackets.

They emphasized her height, her leanness and drew the eye away from the softness of her breasts, the way her hips flared, and the gentle little pillow on her abdomen. My cock was so hard it hurt, and still I drank in the sight of her. Jay was running a hand up and down her leg, a soothing petting motion.

"Rhett," I said, almost growling. Just because I could control myself didn't make me any less feral where she was concerned or diminish how much the need to have her gripped me.

The other alpha met my stare and when I gave him a single nod, I could practically taste his relief. He moved, rising with Wren still mounted on his cock and put her on her hands and knees.

"Kiss Jay," Rhett ordered as he closed his hands on her hips. There was no gentleness in him as he began to piston into her. Her earthy cries were music to my darker side. I wanted to hear every sound she could make. Jay twisted to kiss her and he swallowed each moan and groan that Rhett drove into her.

The slap of skin where his hips met her ass added to the rhythmic beat. The scent of her soaked into everything, the bed, the walls, the carpet—my soul. Rhett answered her rising siren call with wild dominance—raw, instinctual, hungry.

Jay's fingers slid under her as he deepened the kiss. The wet licks of their tongues added a separate music to the pound of Rhett's hips. I could almost *feel* it when Jay found her clit, desperately aware of every tiny bit of her.

Her scream bounced off the walls. Not even Jay's fiery kiss could muffle the sound of her pleasure. With one deep inhale, I drank in her scent. I wanted to roll in it, cover myself in her musk until she was so deeply embedded no one could question who any of us belonged to.

Later, I promised myself. That was for later. Her orgasm continued and finally Rhett let himself go, hips stuttering as he dug his fingers into her hips. He would leave marks on her. But we all had already. Little bruises from kisses, bites, and strokes. I had a few of my own.

And I wanted *more*.

She could mark me up, use me, and I'd walk around shirtless to show it off if she'd allow it. As much as I wanted the world to know I was hers and she was mine, it really only mattered if we could claim each other.

Spent, she and Rhett both collapsed. The swift rise and fall of their chests betrayed the reaction as did the combination of their release. Jay stroked her hair and glanced at me.

"Orgasms aren't going to do it much longer."

No. Her need wasn't subtle—it was a living force, *thick* in the air, pulsing with heat. It expanded like a storm surge, flooding the room with the heady, unmistakable scent of her arousal. It clung to the walls, sank into skin, made it impossible to breathe without tasting her hunger.

I hadn't kissed her yet—not properly—not the way I wanted, but we weren't going to have that time yet. When I closed on the bed, Rhett eased away. His cock glistened with her release, but he was already hard again. Both of us were, she called to every part of me from my alpha nature to the man I wanted to be for her.

She drove us all to the edge, and even sinking into her wasn't enough, not anymore. "Wren," I said, releasing my grip on my own power, my own dominance and letting it uncoil to meet hers.

With eyes that shimmered with light, she gazed up at me. "Roan... please."

"You never have to beg," I promised her, no matter how decadent the sound of it was. "Never." I stroked her hair, it was damp with sweat. Her whole body gleamed with it. It had already been hours since we got here and we had hours yet to go.

"Then what—" She croaked, her mouth dry and her throat rough. Jay tipped a water bottle to her lips and she drank thirstily before whispering, "Thank you."

He just winked at her.

"We need to knot you," I told her. There was no escaping it, not anymore. Whatever had been done to her body chemistry just rutting wasn't going to satisfy her. "Both of us."

The combination of her sharp gasp, dilated eyes, and bitable swollen lips were a drug for my system. A drug I was already addicted to and had no intentions of ever recovering.

"At the same time?" Her scent grew once more, a cloud of need and invitation. But she wasn't asking, she was reveling. "Oh, please." Half writhing, she rose to her knees and reached for me. I made no attempt to push her away.

The slide of her skin against mine was both a torment and a gift.

"I want you so badly," she confessed. "It's killing me."

"Kiss me," I told her, no command or request. Just the simplicity of the words and she wrapped her arms around my neck as her mouth found mine. A teasing brush of her lips against the corner of my mouth, then a sharp sting of her teeth as she bit me.

I almost laughed at the invitation and repudiation in the same moment. My Wren was still inside the desperate omega who needed her body filled. She chided me for my commands even as she gave me everything I could ask for and more.

When I teased the seam of her lips with my tongue, she opened for me. I alternated between sucking her tongue and stroking it. Her breasts rubbed against my chest, and the burn of contact spread with every caress. When I slid my hands to her ass and lifted her, she wrapped her legs around me,

The wet heat of her cunt enveloped my dick. With no encouragement she began to writhe against me, bathing me in her slick and Rhett's release.

"So fucking filthy," I exhaled the words against her lips as I slid two fingers into her. The spasm of her muscles and ease of the glide told me she was more than ready, she was eager. I teased her clit and she arched, biting my lip again until it stung.

"Fix it," I ordered, the growl in my voice more a purr than a warning. With sexy kittenish little licks that would drive a man to pure madness, she eased the sting. When I held up two fingers coated in our release, she sucked them into her mouth without hesitation.

The pupils of her eyes had expanded until the black covered her irises fully. There was no color, no glitter of gold, no honey or whiskey. When she fisted my cock, I gave into her demand. She positioned me and I thrust home. Her head arched back, a cry escaping her as I pounded into her from this angle.

"You feel so fucking good," I told her, nipping her throat, laving little kisses to each tiny mark I left. Soon, I was going to bite down and so would Rhett. We would bite her, mark her, and knot her.

My cock swelled further, but I fought the urge to knot. It wasn't always possible, but I'd mastered it a long time ago. When I knotted a woman, whether she was alpha, beta, or omega—she would be the one for me.

This was Wren. She was the one I'd been waiting for.

Taking her down to the bed, her legs stretching up until I had her calves against my shoulders, giving me the perfect angle to fill her over and over. I rocked my hips. She fisted my hair and kissed me. Or maybe I kissed her.

On some level, I was aware of Jay and Rhett moving, getting ready. This moment was to take the edge off, and I needed it. Needed her.

So did Wren.

"I want you so much," Wren confessed in a half-sob. "Fuck me, Roan. Please..."

Another kiss to steal her breath and quiet that pleading. Over and over, I drove into that silken sheath, reveling in how her body rippled for me. When she clamped down in a fierce orgasm, I held off, then drove into her again as she began to float down.

My cock hurt from needing her, but I wanted her ready. All too soon, her heat rocketed up and she thrashed from my thrusts. They would hurt as much as they felt good. Snapping my head up, I looked at Rhett. His eyes were as feral and hot as my own.

"She's ready."

"Thank fuck," Rhett said, his eyes as dark as hers. He was already reaching for her and I snarled. It came out before I could lock it down and Rhett went still, and watchful, even as Wren let out a little whimper.

"It's alright," Jay said, the rationality in his voice settling all of us and I threw him a grateful look. I pulled out of Wren and cupped her face when she tried to pull me back.

"Shh," I whispered. "Hold on for me a little longer."

As much as I said I wouldn't command her, I did now. She needed comfort, and reassurance. At her nod, I rose and then lifted her. Rhett moved toward the center and between us, we lowered her down onto his angry, red, and standing fully erect cock, They both hissed out a breath.

Jay tossed me the lube and I used it and some of her slick to loosen her ass. Our little flame pushed back on my fingers as I worked her and Rhett gritted his teeth as she writhed on him. Her neediness rose though, pushing a volcanic force of desire to plume around us.

Inhaling the sharp spiciness of her scent, I put the blunt tip of my cock to that ring of muscle and gave in to her now. This was Wren—our Wren—and soon to be our omega. "Hard and fast, little flame?"

She tossed a look so full of gratitude and desire at me that it hit like a mallet. "Yes."

It wasn't her scent, her words, or even her expression that convinced me. It was the awareness in her eyes. I pushed into her, not giving her any relief until I was seated into her ass and I could feel Rhett through the thin skin separating us.

Our gazes locked as Wren began to keen. As one, we moved. We moved her between us as easily and cleanly as we would the puck, sailing over the ice. Wren moved with us, her hips rolling as she took Rhett to the hilt then back as she pulled me into her.

Her nipples were hard points that I could palm and tease as Rhett kissed her bitten lips, their hard gasps coming in unison. The ferocious intensity built and built. It wasn't just an orgasm that was coming—it was everything.

My balls dragged up tight, the pain almost exquisite in its agony, and then the leash fell away as I bit down on her shoulder right at the juncture where it met her neck. Rhett bit her at the same time and her scream was a joyous thing that rang in my ears.

The feel of my knot ballooning was an ecstasy I'd never experienced. She writhed between us, moving like she either wanted to escape or pull us closer, utterly at the mercy of her body as we were ours.

"Fuck," Jay said on a harsh note and I could smell his release. He'd probably been jacking off as we moved and I almost laughed. Rhett's knot was as firm as mine and we were sealed to her. The taste of her was in my mouth, the smell of her in my lungs, and the feel of her... she was tattooed on my bones.

We lay there panting in unison, breath and bodies in sync. Eventually, she let out another dizzying laugh and I smiled before laving my tongue over the signature I'd made on her neck. It declared my claim as effectively as scent marking her.

"How long?" Her voice was hoarse, wrecked, and so damn wonderful it stroked over my senses.

"Could be a half-hour," Rhett answered her. "Maybe longer."

"Oh." Surprise filled her voice. "That long?"

"That's the longest I've ever heard of," Rhett admitted. "The omegas I've helped before, maybe ten minutes."

Interesting. I was still turning that over in my head when she said...

"No one has ever knotted me before." The wonder that punched through me at that confession unraveled me completely.

"No one?" Jay asked as he leaned onto the bed next to us. With Wren secured between us, he could only stroke her hair where she lay with her head against Rhett's shoulder. I had my arms braced so I wasn't sinking all of my weight onto her.

The fact her ass held my knot so damn fiercely wasn't lost on me. Nor that she'd sealed Rhett to her as well. Not once in my wildest dreams had I ever imagined something as right as this, as the four of us, in this profound moment.

"No," Wren whispered. "I was hiding, remember? The heats I had never lasted longer than twenty-four hours... they were never like this. Never this intense. This desperate."

"Is it better now?" I had to know, the curiosity consumed me.

"Yes," she admitted. "I can feel you both and it's wonderful. But I can also think again. I—"

"You?" I prompted. "Don't hide from us now, my little

flame. I promise you, nothing you tell us will go beyond us and no one will ever hold your honesty against you."

I didn't even have to check with Jay or Rhett, they were equally devoted.

"I almost hope it isn't all satisfied yet," she whispered, scarlet deepening her already flushed cheeks. "I want to do this again when I can think and feel..."

"Yes," Rhett answered.

"Absolutely," Jay swore.

When she looked at me, I just smiled. "We have a few more days before we have to be anywhere..."

Her eyes widened and then she spasmed like the promise was enough. But she was right, I was ready to knot her all over again.

I *never* gave in before, but for Wren, I would give everything. In fact... I gave her *me*. "This is my first time knotting anyone too."

Shock registered on Rhett's face and I could feel Jay staring at me, but it was Wren's reaction I craved.

"You too?"

I nodded. "I never wanted to knot anyone before."

"But..."

"I wanted you to have my knot, Wren. It's always been yours." It always would be and when these days were over, I would make that very clear. "I'm yours."

"As am I," Rhett joined me.

Jay was right there. "Me three..."

Her grin buoyed my heart and gave it wings. So did her little sigh and how she tucked her head down when I pressed a kiss to my mark. Wren was ours and I'd kill anyone who tried to take her.

She gave another little shudder, but her body didn't release us and I was in no hurry. I could stay buried in her forever. An hour later, as our knots finally relaxed, she began to move again, the need hitting her hard.

We took turns teasing her to orgasm, making her drink, and when she was ready, we knotted her again. My cock burned, and it hurt as much as it felt good, but I wouldn't stop until she'd been satisfied.

None of us would.

TWENTY-FIVE

WREN

The water had long gone warm, edging toward cool, but I didn't move. I just let myself drift, barely touching the surface of awareness, my limbs floating loose in the oversized tub. Jay sat behind me, his arms bracketing my hips gently, chin resting on my shoulder like he'd been there forever.

It was the first time in two days that no one was touching me with *need*.

And yet, I felt them all.

Roan was in the shower in the other room—the hiss and pulse of the spray rising above the low hum of the bath jets. Rhett's voice carried through the cracked bathroom door, warm and lazy, laced with mischief.

"We're gonna have to burn the bed," he called out. "Maybe the whole damn cabin."

My face went instantly hot. I sank deeper into the water, up to my chin.

Jay laughed softly against my neck. "Ignore him."

"I can't," I muttered. "He's loud. And I'm pretty sure I ruined that mattress."

Jay pressed a kiss to my temple. "It's not ruined. It's well-used."

God.

Two days. That's all it had been. Two days and I'd stopped counting knots after the fourth—or was it the fifth? I'd lost track somewhere between the last wave of heat and Roan dragging me half-conscious into the shower to cool down while Jay shoved a protein bar in my mouth and Rhett made me drink electrolyte water like I was going to evaporate without it.

Now the storm had passed, and I was left in the stillness.

Sore didn't even begin to cover it.

Every inch of me ached. I was stretched, marked, claimed in ways I hadn't been able to comprehend until it was over. I'd slept in between, in stolen hours. I'd eaten when they'd made me. I'd let go of everything I'd once thought I could control—my body, my heat, my scent, my *self*.

Yet, I could still feel them.

Under my skin. In my chest. Like echoes.

"You're thinking too hard again," Jay said gently, rubbing slow circles on my stomach. His touch was always soothing. Never rushed. Never forced. Just there, grounding.

"I'm fine," I whispered.

For a long beat, he said nothing. Then, almost whisper quiet, he exhaled the words against my temple, "You've lost weight."

I blinked. "What?"

Nuzzling kisses down to the side of my neck, he half smiled against my skin. "You're strong. You handled it, all of it. But your body's wiped. You're dehydrated. Your pulse is still running high. You didn't have enough reserves going into this."

"You're worrying again." I turned my head slightly, meeting his gaze over my shoulder.

"Not just me," he said, and I could tell from his tone that he was choosing his words with care. "You'll see your doctor when you get back?"

I nodded, slower than I meant to. "Yeah. I will." At the same time, I could almost hear the question he *didn't* ask. *Will you go back on the suppressants?*

Jay didn't push. He never did. But his fingers hesitated at my hip, and I felt the weight of it, the way he was trying not to look like he was bracing for an answer.

I didn't have one.

Not yet.

And I couldn't lie to him, not when his scent was all around me, not when my body was still humming with his touch as well as Roan and Rhett's knots. Their voices, their mouths—everything they'd poured into me like I was something meant to be filled until I overflowed.

They did it, and then some. Filling in gaps inside of me that I hadn't realized were even there. Maybe they hadn't been, before the heat shattered my control and broke me open like an egg. The Wren I was before hadn't ever experienced the *need* like I had this past week. It had been a week —five days almost— since I left to take a couple of days and ride out my heat.

Somehow, if they hadn't come when they did, I had a feeling, I would still be locked in that hell. That was more than a little unsettling. To be so at the mercy of urges beyond any control. The heats I'd experienced when I was younger hadn't been nearly this intense.

I didn't even realize I'd gone silent until Rhett appeared

in the doorway, hair damp, shirtless, his jeans unbuttoned and hanging low around his hips. His grin was cocky and devastating.

"Well," he said, "you two look indecent and exhausted. I'm proud of us."

I groaned and buried my face in my hands. "You're the worst."

"I'm the best," he corrected. "And," he added with a flourish, "I made sandwiches."

Jay kissed the side of my face and murmured, "Told you he was good for something."

"I heard that!" Rhett called as he disappeared again.

But their laughter didn't quite cut the tension. It just *danced* over it. The air still buzzed faintly—thick with their scents, with mine. With the lingering threads of bondless claim, with all the pressure we'd kept carefully at bay. There was no regret. But there *was* something else.

A quiet knowing.

Like they could feel me differently now. Like I could feel *them*. Not just physically, not even chemically—but on a level so deep it didn't have words.

The heat might have passed, but the burn hadn't gone out.

I was still curled against Jay's chest when Roan stepped into the doorway, steam curling around him like smoke.

His skin glowed a deep, sun-warmed gold, ruddy from the punishing heat of the shower, like he'd needed the scalding water to rinse off the last of the frenzy. It hadn't worked—*nothing* could rinse away what we'd done. The proof was still etched on his body with long, raised marks down his arms and shoulders, angry red where I'd clawed him in the thick of it.

My face flushed. The bite he'd made on my neck throbbed. Like my body *knew* the mark it bore, and recognized the one who left it. Roan's gaze flicked to it the second he stepped inside. His jaw ticked—just once. But when his eyes met mine, they were softer than they had any right to be.

"You ready to eat?" he asked.

The words were simple. But his tone wasn't.

There was that quiet thread of command again, woven into his voice like steel wrapped in velvet. He didn't need to raise his voice to be obeyed. He *wore* authority like a second skin, even with his hair still wet and water dripping down his chest.

Still, there was a gentleness there too—beneath the dominant aura cloaking him. It calmed me, loosening something tight in my chest.

I sat up slowly, pressing a hand to Jay's thigh under the water. "We probably need to talk."

Roan didn't even blink. "We can wait." There was no hesitation. No anxiety about what might come next. Just complete, unshakable calm. "Right now, you need food. Water. Rest. Talk can wait until you're whole again."

"He's right." Jay nodded behind me, fingers brushing along the inside of my arm. "We'll still be here when you're ready."

Even from the other room, Rhett chimed in—his voice lighter, but his words still firm. "Yeah, no deep thoughts until you eat at least two sandwiches. Non-negotiable."

I laughed softly, but it caught in my throat. They were giving me space—gentle, deliberate generosity in the wake of everything I'd given them.

But I could feel the clock ticking, even in this snow-wrapped hideaway. Outside, the world hadn't stopped turning.

The playoffs were coming. The team would need them back for drills. I'd need to return to the city, to the office, to the PR cleanup and the mess I'd left on pause.

Real life was waiting.

And whatever this thing was between us—this fire, this bondless ache—still didn't have a name.

Yet, in this moment, with Jay holding me steady, Roan's presence filling the room, and Rhett being irreverent and loud just to make me smile...

For just a little longer, I let it all wait.

THE NEW BED felt like a dream—fresh sheets, clean blankets, soft pillows that hadn't been tangled and soaked in the heat of bodies and scent. Someone had aired the room out, wiped down the surfaces. There were even bottles of water on the nightstand and snacks within reach.

They were taking care of me. *Still.*

I hadn't realized how much I needed that until I was curled under the blankets, muscles aching in ways I didn't want to admit, belly full for the first time in days.

Rhett lay stretched beside me, loose-limbed and lazy like a lion in the sun. One arm was tucked under his head, and the other played idly with my hair—soft strokes from crown to nape, slow and soothing. Over and over again.

It felt so good I nearly purred.

He must've felt it, too—some subtle change in my breathing, a little hum in my throat—because his mouth curved in a smirk I could feel without even looking.

"You're enjoying this a little too much," I said, trying for dry, but it came out softer.

His fingers slid down, just behind my ear, making me shiver. "Only because *you're* letting me."

I arched a brow, glancing up at him. "And you think that's about *you*, not me?"

Rhett's grin deepened, but when his eyes met mine, something else flickered beneath the surface.

The playfulness was still there—he wore it like armor, like instinct—but I saw the edge of something rawer behind it. A kind of focused intensity. A *need* he didn't know how to ask for without dressing it in jokes and charm.

And for all his alpha swagger, I could see it clearly now —he didn't want to be brushed off. Not by me. Not after what we'd shared.

I reached up and brushed his cheek with the backs of my fingers. His stubble rasped against my skin, and his hand went still in my hair.

"Will you keep petting me?" I asked quietly.

It wasn't a question, not really. It was my answer. My way of saying *yes*. I liked it. I wanted it. I *wanted him*.

Rhett made a low sound in his throat, almost a grunt— satisfied, like something in him had unclenched—and his hand resumed its slow strokes through my hair.

I smiled to myself and rolled back to my side, facing the doorway. He shifted with me, settling in again with his chest warm against my back, his breath ghosting over my shoulder.

And that was when I saw them.

Roan stood in the doorway, bare-chested, arms crossed over his chest. Watching. Always watching. Jay was just behind him, leaning in the frame, expression unreadable but warm.

They weren't interrupting.

They weren't assuming.

They were *waiting*.

And that was what did me in.

Not the heat. Not the knots. Not even the claiming.

This. The restraint. The careful, patient way they were holding back now, like I was breakable. Like I needed space to breathe.

Maybe I did.

But I didn't want the *distance*.

My throat tightened, something sharp blooming behind my ribs. I reached out under the blankets, fingers stretching toward the door.

Not a command.

Just an invitation.

Roan's gaze dropped to my hand. His whole body shifted—so subtle I might've missed it if I hadn't been watching him so closely. The tension across his shoulders eased, his eyes gentled.

Jay didn't say a word, but I could feel the change in him too. Like maybe they'd all been holding their breath since the heat broke.

Maybe now... we could exhale.

I let my hand rest where it was, fingers lightly curled, reaching out into the quiet. The warmth from Rhett behind me and the soft shifting of the bed beneath us was a balm, but then I felt something else—movement, steady and deliberate.

Jay eased onto the bed beside us, settling in close, his body warm against mine in a way that sent a fresh pulse of calm through me. I felt the steady beat of his breath, his hand finding mine, fingers intertwining like a silent promise.

Then Roan joined us, his presence filling the space with that familiar weight of power and protection. He settled at the head of the bed, careful not to crowd, but close enough that I could feel the heat radiating off him in waves. His hand lifted, gentle as a whisper, to cradle my cheek.

Slowly, the tension in my chest began to ease, the sharp ache of uncertainty dulling to something softer—something I hadn't been ready to admit before now.

As the minutes stretched, the quiet breathing around me slowed. One by one, the men drifted off to sleep—Rhett still tracing lazy patterns in my hair, his hand heavy but gentle on my side. Jay's fingers laced with mine, warm and grounding. And Roan's touch, featherlight against my cheek, kept me tethered to the moment.

There was something in that—something utterly captivating.

Not the wild ferocity that had pulled me into them before.

No. This was different.

This was care.

Deep, steady, unyielding care.

As my eyelids fluttered shut, I realized I craved it even more than the heat, more than the storm of passion and claim. Still, sleep remained elusive and I kept looking, checking to make sure they were still there.

The soft light in the room caught the faint shimmer around Roan's eyes—the tired gold of a man who had given everything and wasn't finished giving.

His fingers brushed against my skin, featherlight, and his voice was just a breath, a murmur meant for me alone.

"Sleep, Wren. We have time." It wasn't just words. It was a promise. One that settled inside me, quiet but fierce, from his soul to mine.

When I reached for his hand, he linked our fingers and everything inside of me settled. This time when I let my eyes close, sleep wrapped me up and I drifted off, safely cradled by all three.

TWENTY-SIX

WREN

I woke to the smell of coffee and the low murmur of voices, warm and familiar.

The bed was mostly empty—just the lingering indentation of where bodies had been, sheets rumpled and still holding the scent of skin and salt and something softer that hadn't quite faded. My muscles protested as I sat up, not sharply, but enough to remind me just how thoroughly I'd been... *handled.*

I stretched slowly, feeling the pleasant ache in my thighs, the tender pull across my hips. Even my scalp was sensitive where Rhett had threaded his fingers through my hair half the night.

Despite the way I moved like I was made of half-cooled wax, I felt... good.

Whole.

Wrecked, maybe. But good.

The soreness was just another echo of what we'd done. What we'd been. I caught Jay watching me from across the room as I padded in, still in one of their long shirts, his mouth twitching at the corners.

"You okay?" he asked, though his tone already said *yes, obviously*, because he'd been cataloging every blink and breath of mine since dawn.

"Bit stiff," I said, stretching again with a wince.

Rhett, naturally, leaned in from the kitchen with a wicked grin. "You're welcome."

I groaned and threw a clean towel at him. "I hate you."

"No, you *love* me," he called after me as I wandered toward the coffee pot.

"I tolerate you," I corrected.

Roan glanced over his shoulder from where he was zipping up a duffel. "You're moving like you got tackled by a pack of wild animals."

"Gee, I wonder why," I muttered into my mug, cheeks heating even though they were all being—almost annoy-ingly—affectionate about it.

After breakfast, they packed efficiently. Roan's SUV was already warming up outside, snow dusted across the wind-shield. Rhett and Jay drove off to the other cabin to grab my car and the rest of my things. I took my time cleaning up—brushing my teeth, putting on something clean, trying to pull myself back together for the world outside this snowy cocoon.

But the closer we got to leaving, the heavier something settled in my chest.

It wasn't dread. Not quite.

Just... reluctance.

When the cars were packed, we stood in a loose little cluster by the vehicles. My car sat in the driveway beside Roan's, looking much smaller now—like it didn't belong to the same story.

No one really wanted to break the moment, but logistics eventually forced the issue.

Roan jerked his chin toward his SUV. "She drives her own. We're three deep in mine."

Jay raised an eyebrow, then looked at Rhett.

Rhett mirrored the look. "Oh no. You're not gonna Jedi mind-trick me out of this one."

"You two figure it out," Roan said dryly as he climbed into the driver's seat.

Jay and Rhett stared each other down in mock seriousness. Then, wordlessly, they began:

One. Two. Three. Shoot.

Rhett's grin was immediate. "Scissors beats paper, baby."

Jay sighed, dramatic, but there was amusement tugging at his mouth as he turned toward Roan's passenger side. "Unbelievable."

I watched the whole thing with this strange, warm pull in my chest. It was almost gooey, but not in a way I hated. It was a kind of affection that didn't feel fragile or forced. No one was trying to control me, not now. Not with choices or cars or touches.

This wasn't about power.

It was about *being allowed to enjoy* each other.

That was... new.

The fun part? I didn't mind it. Not even a little.

I was still smiling as Rhett loaded himself into my passenger seat, long legs stretched out and already fiddling with the music settings like he owned the space.

I glanced sideways at him as I buckled in. "You gonna survive not being the driver?"

Rhett didn't hesitate. "Baby, I'll be your passenger penis anytime you want."

I choked on a laugh, half startled, half delighted. It

burst out of me before I could stop it—loud, unguarded, and real.

He grinned like he'd just won the lottery.

"You're the worst," I said, still laughing.

"Only the best parts," he said with a wink, leaning back, completely at ease.

And as I pulled onto the snowy road, my car full of warmth and inappropriate charm and something I wasn't quite ready to name—I didn't feel alone.

Not anymore.

The roads were clear enough, the snow compacted into neat lanes bordered by trees still flocked in white. The whole world looked soft around the edges, like it hadn't quite woken up yet.

Rhett, however, had *no* such delay.

He leaned back in the passenger seat, one arm slung across the console like he belonged there permanently. The music he'd queued up was a ridiculous mix of upbeat funk and indie covers, and he was drumming on his thighs with more rhythm than I wanted to admit was impressive.

"Do you do this in every car you ride in?" I asked as we turned onto the main road out of the forest.

"Only the ones with hot drivers," he said, flashing a grin. "Also, ones with working speakers. I have standards."

I shook my head, but I couldn't help smiling. His energy was infectious—big, bright, and impossible to ignore. He was like a campfire, warm and a little wild, always drawing you closer whether you meant to come or not.

Somewhere around the thirty-minute mark, the music mellowed and so did he. His fingers moved lazily against the console, more a comfort than a beat now.

"So," I said, "fifteen cousins? Was that an exaggeration or real numbers?"

Rhett huffed a laugh. "*That* was just the ones I see regularly. If we're counting *all* of them, it's more like thirty-something. Both of my parents come from huge families—five siblings on one side, six on the other. And everyone bred like they were trying to start their own colony."

"God," I said, wide-eyed, "that's not a family tree. That's a forest."

He grinned. "Exactly. We've got this... *compound* at home. My mom's parents and my dad's parents both live there—opposite ends of the land. Bunch of little cottages scattered around, one big main house where everyone eats and drinks and yells at football games."

I blinked. "Wait, like a literal family compound?"

"Oh yeah. We've got bunk rooms, guest suites, one of those industrial kitchens that could feed an army. There's a pool, a pond, an old converted barn that we turn into a party hall during the holidays. If you bring someone home for Christmas, they basically need a map and a buddy system."

"Is that... normal?" I asked, enchanted despite myself.

"God, no," Rhett said, grinning. "But it's ours. Loud as hell, kind of chaotic, but it's home."

I glanced over at him. He looked so *easy* in that moment—no posing, no playacting. Just Rhett, warm and open, talking about his clan like it was the most natural thing in the world.

"I can't even imagine what that's like," I said quietly.

He glanced at me, sensing the shift. "Yeah?"

"My family's... not exactly like that."

He didn't push, just let the silence stretch until I found my words.

"My mom left when I was little," I said finally, eyes still on the road. "My parents tried, I think. But they were never really… a match. My mom was post-heat wildness, and my dad—he wanted something stable. I think I was the moment they tried to get serious, but it didn't work."

There was no bitterness in my voice, not anymore. Just the truth.

"I was a heat accident," I added, the words coming out more easily than I expected. "Used to hate saying that out loud. Like it made me a mistake."

Rhett was quiet for a moment. Then he said, "Doesn't sound like a mistake to me."

My throat tightened.

I risked a glance over. His gaze was steady—no jokes, no smirk. Just listening. Just *seeing me*.

"I think," I said slowly, "part of why I was so reluctant when my designation came in was… I didn't want to turn out like her. To lose control. To *leave* people behind."

He didn't speak right away. His hand slid across the console and rested palm up, open, between us.

Not reaching for me. Just there if I wanted it.

I let my fingers slip into his.

"Wren," he said, voice low and sincere, "you are *nothing* like her."

"How do you know?"

"Because I've seen the way you hold yourself back. The way you *fight* for control. That's not weakness. It's strength. You didn't run. You stayed. And if you hadn't, we never would've had this."

My chest ached in a different way now. "You really are good at this, you know," I said quietly.

"At what?"

"Seeing people."

He gave me a smile that was half-shy, half-devastating. "I like seeing you."

The silence after that wasn't awkward. It was full of breath, feeling, and something deep that didn't need to be named out loud.

I squeezed his hand once and let go, easing the car into the slow curve of the freeway ramp. He didn't protest. He just leaned back again, one leg stretched long, one hand behind his head.

"By the way," he said after a moment, the grin returning like sunlight through clouds, "passenger penis offer still stands. Long drive? Road trip? Stop-and-go traffic? I'm your guy."

I barked a laugh so hard it shook me.

"Jesus, Rhett," I wheezed, wiping my eyes.

"Hey, you get snacks and entertainment," he said, smug. "It's a *package deal.*"

"Oh my god," I groaned, but I couldn't stop smiling. Not even a little.

Somewhere in the back of my mind, I realized that the ache in my chest was starting to feel a lot like *hope.*

We stopped about an hour outside the city at a little gas station with a drive-thru coffee hut and a convenience store that promised *hot snacks* in flickering neon.

Everyone stretched their legs, and I took my time inside, grabbing two iced coffees, one hot, and a pile of snacks that looked like they'd been fried yesterday and kept under a heat lamp out of spite. Rhett made a delighted noise like I'd brought him a bouquet of chicken tenders when I handed him his coffee and a greasy paper bag.

Roan was finishing up at the pump when I walked over, the wind lifting strands of my hair across my cheeks. He glanced at me over the top of the SUV.

"If you want a break," he said casually, "I'll take Rhett the rest of the way. No problem."

I blinked, then shook my head, a smile tugging at my mouth. "I don't mind dropping him off."

Roan nodded once, like he expected that answer, but something flickered in his expression when I didn't immediately turn to go.

And before I could second-guess it, I said, "Hey... would you guys want to come over later? For dinner or something. I have no idea what's actually in my fridge, but we could eat. Talk."

The words tumbled out too naturally. No big drama. Just a soft, open offer. But a part of me held still after saying them, braced without meaning to.

Because the truth was, letting someone into your bed was easy.

Letting them into your *home*—into the *quiet*—that was harder.

Roan's eyes softened instantly.

"I'd love to come over," he said simply. "If you'll let us bring dinner. Keep it easy."

I let out a breath I hadn't realized I was holding. "Yeah. That sounds perfect."

Something flickered between us then—unspoken but grounding. And I didn't think. I just stepped forward and wrapped my arms around him.

He didn't hesitate.

He folded me in like I belonged there, big arms wrapping tight around my back, the solid wall of his chest pressed to mine, anchoring me to the ground and holding me up at the same time.

We didn't say anything else. We didn't need to.

When I finally stepped back, a little steadier, I turned to head toward my car—but paused beside Jay, who was leaning against the back of Roan's SUV sipping his coffee like the world was no big deal.

"Hey," I said softly.

He looked up, curious.

I stepped in and gave him a hug too.

He made a surprised little sound in the back of his throat, but his arms came around me easily, warm and secure, and his chin brushed the top of my head for just a second.

"Anytime," he murmured, low enough that only I could hear. "You ever need me, I'm there."

Then, with a hint of mischief, he added under his breath, "Cough twice if you want me to stash Rhett in Roan's truck."

I snorted against his chest. "Tempting."

He leaned back, one brow arched. "The offer stands."

I shook my head, grinning, then turned to head back to my car where Rhett was already sprawled in the passenger seat like he owned it—again—chicken tenders in one hand and his sunglasses on, despite the fact that it was cloudy as hell.

I slid in behind the wheel, heart feeling full in a way I wasn't used to.

My phone vibrated on the charging plate as I buckled in. I picked it up, eyed Marchand's name on the caller ID. There was an ungodly number of missed calls, voicemail messages, and texts. I hadn't paid attention to a single one so far. They were all tomorrow's problems.

And so was Marchand. I put the phone back down and let it roll over so he could leave a message too. Rhett didn't comment, but I caught the way the corner of his mouth kicked up into a smile.

"Rhett?"

He cocked his head toward me.

"Crank it up."

His grin grew. "Yes, ma'am."

Then we were pulling out and I followed right behind Roan's vehicle, head beginning to nod to the music. Tomorrow could also wait.

CHAPTER

TWENTY-SEVEN

WREN

By the time the doorbell rang, I'd changed clothes three times, wiped down the already-clean counter twice, and made the monumental decision to let my kitchen exist in its natural state of organized chaos.

I wasn't hosting a PR event. I wasn't meeting someone's parents.

Still, my stomach flipped as I crossed the room and opened the door.

Roan stood there, big and warm and so familiar now it almost startled me. No armor, no uniform, no scent of woodsmoke and snow. Just him. His eyes landed on mine, and for a second, we didn't speak.

Then he held up a six-pack of ginger beer and said, "Told the others to come later."

I stepped back to let him in, heart skipping a little. "Did you tell them why?"

He glanced at me sideways, his mouth curving. "Told them to grab something decent for dinner and give us space. They got the message."

I liked that. Not the part where he took control, but that he *made space* for this. For me. For us.

He moved into the kitchen like he'd been there before, setting the drinks on the counter and turning back to face me, easy in his body but alert under the surface, like he'd been turning this conversation over in his head for hours.

And then, without preamble, he said, "I wanted to talk to you. About how you want to handle... this."

There it was.

This.

The unsaid, unclaimed territory between heat and real life. The thing that lingered after the mating haze cleared and you had to figure out if anything was still left standing.

I leaned against the counter, arms loose at my sides, heart ticking faster. "Handle it how?"

His gaze was steady. "You tell me."

I hesitated, then asked the only question that mattered. "Do we have a relationship?"

His eyes flared faintly. Not startled. Just *fierce*. Then, very calmly, he said, "Yes."

Before I could react or respond to that, a low growl slipped from somewhere in his chest. It wasn't threatening. If anything it was almost... reluctant. Like it had broken free without his permission.

Roan paused, took a breath, and visibly dialed himself back.

"Yes," he said again, quieter now. "We do. And if you need more convincing..." He stepped closer, not crowding but *present*, his voice dropping an octave, "I'm on board."

There was no teasing in his tone. No manipulation. Just Roan being absolutely clear. He wasn't asking if I wanted him to claim me. He was *offering* to stay. To be mine, if I'd have him.

I felt the corners of my mouth lift. Whatever awkwardness I'd braced for... it just wasn't here. He didn't leave room for it.

It wasn't pressure. It was him being here, with me, in this moment—together. I should have known he would do this, that he would sand the edges off and make this about us as a team. This was him saying, *I'm here. What do you want?*

I took a breath, giving myself a moment in the quiet humming between us.

"I think I'm still figuring out what that looks like," I admitted. "For you. For Rhett. For Jay. For me. For all of us."

While I may not know everything, I did know that there was an *us*. It had been there before they'd come for me and it was definitely present the morning after, the day after, and tonight now that we were home.

"No matter what or how we decide, I know I want something real."

Roan's nod was slow. "Then we'll build it. On your terms. But *ours*, too." The fact he added that last bit settled some of the unease in my system. He'd given me a lot of power while I'd been in the throes of heat and I adored him for it. But...

"Good," I said, answering what felt like a promise from him with one of my own. "If you didn't include your thoughts and feelings in this, I'd have more objections."

"Oh, really?" A hint of challenge gleamed in his eyes. "Is that so?"

"Yes," I said, matching the glint in his eyes. "If you think you're just going to agree to whatever I want, you've clearly forgotten who you're dealing with."

Roan's smile was slow, dangerous only because of how soft it was. "Oh, I remember exactly who I'm dealing with."

He took a step closer, deliberate but unhurried, the air between us thickening with awareness. His hand came up, rough fingers brushing the side of my jaw as though asking permission.

I didn't move away. If anything, I leaned into his touch.

"Wren," he said, voice lower now, quieter as if my name was something sacred and heavy in his mouth. "You know I meant what I said, right? That this isn't about what happened in the cabin. It's about what happens *now*."

"I know," I whispered. I understood exactly what he was saying and it made me even more eager to explore what we could be.

The pulse of heat that sat like a live wire under my skin for the past several days was gone, replaced by something far steadier, and deeper.

Roan's thumb stroked along my cheekbone, tracing the faintest path. "Good. Because I'm not going anywhere."

Then he kissed me.

It wasn't a claiming. It wasn't about control or chemistry or dominance. It was simply *him*—warm, sure, and unhurried. God, the man's charm was as much a part of him as his talent on the ice. The way his lips moved against mine said so much without saying a word.

It was slow enough that I could taste the breath between us. His other hand came up to cradle the back of my neck, and he exhaled against my mouth, the sound turning into a soft hum that vibrated right through me.

When I parted my lips, it wasn't because I had to, it was because I *wanted* to.

It was all the invitation he needed to deepen the kiss, just slightly, enough to draw a small sound from my throat that he swallowed with a satisfied sigh. My fingers found their way to his shirt, gripping the fabric, not to pull him closer but to steady myself.

He smiled against my lips. I felt it.

Felt the tease before he even pulled back to say it.

"Still figuring it out, huh?" he murmured, voice roughened at the edges.

"Apparently," I said, a little breathless. "Though I think we're making progress."

His answering grin was pure delight, chased quickly by something quieter, something that sat deep in his eyes. He brushed his thumb across my bottom lip once more, then dropped his hand, letting the touch linger in absence.

"I'll take progress," he said softly. "One step at a time."

"Even if I trip sometimes?"

"I'll be right there to catch you," he said, simple and sure.

"What happens if you trip?" As unlikely as that case might be, Roan was by far the steadiest of us all, it still needed to be asked.

He chuckled. "You'll have my back, little flame. You always do."

The warmth present in that declaration of trust dazzled me. Roan Whittaker was not known for taking prisoners, but I had a feeling that between us—we might just change that.

The pleasure in his voice lingered long after he stepped back. It felt like sunlight spreading beneath my skin, quiet but alive. I was still holding that feeling when the doorbell rang again.

Roan gave me a faint, amused look. "Timing."

"Apparently, they're incapable of being fashionably late," I murmured, smoothing my hair as I went to answer.

Jay and Rhett stood on my front step, the winter air

curling around them, both holding brown paper takeout bags that smelled absolutely sinful. Rhett's grin was wolfish. Jay's was smug.

"Dinner delivery," Rhett announced, holding one up like a trophy. "Your favorites."

I blinked, then laughed outright as the scent hit me. "Is that—oh my God—Ethiopian? You actually remembered?"

Jay's mouth quirked. "Of course we remembered. You nearly bit Rhett's hand off last time he tried to steal your tibs."

"Nearly?" Rhett said, scandalized. "That was a *real* bite."

"You deserved it," I said sweetly, stepping back so they could come inside.

Roan had already pulled plates from the cupboard and was setting out the ginger beers he'd brought, the glass bottles clicking softly against the counter. The whole thing unfolded so naturally that I had to take a beat just to absorb it.

Four people in my kitchen, unpacking food, laughing over dumb jokes, the kind of easy chaos that felt like family.

Dinner was messy and delicious. Rhett tried to pretend he didn't like injera until I caught him sneaking another piece. Jay added his usual quiet wit to the mix, throwing in small, dry observations that had me laughing until I nearly choked on my drink. Roan mostly watched, amused, adding a comment here and there, that golden calm in his eyes like an anchor holding us all steady.

At some point, the food gave way to cards—Rhett insisting on teaching me a game that made absolutely no sense, Roan cleaning up the table, and Jay calling him a shark under his breath when Roan won three hands in a row. The ginger beers disappeared, replaced by sparkling water and half a bowl of chocolate-covered almonds that Rhett guarded like treasure.

For a few blissful hours, everything was easy. No heat. No tension. No complicated questions waiting just outside the light.

Just *us*—real, relaxed, laughing so much my cheeks hurt.

Eventually, Roan stretched, checked his watch, and sighed. "All right. Drill at eight tomorrow."

The groans were immediate.

Jay tossed down his cards. "You're the devil."

Slouching dramatically in his chair, Rhett shot Roan a droll look. "Can't we just—stay? She's got couches. Blankets. Snacks."

I laughed. "I'll even let you have the rest of the almonds if you go quietly."

He brightened. "Done."

They helped me clean up in their normal modes with Roan's efficiency, Jay's attention to detail, and Rhett causing good-natured chaos. When it came time to leave, the goodbyes came naturally, too.

Roan kissed me first. It was softer than before, a brush of promise that left my pulse skipping.

Then Rhett caught me up in a bear hug that lifted me clean off the ground. "You're amazing," he said into my hair, voice rougher than I expected. "Don't forget that."

"I won't," I managed, breathless and smiling.

Jay was last. He didn't say anything at first, just pulled me into a quiet, lingering hug that felt like calm itself. When he finally leaned back, his gaze was steady and fond.

"I'll bring you coffee tomorrow morning," he said.

"Jay—"

"Don't argue." A small smirk curved his mouth. "Croissants still your favorite, or have you switched to danishes?"

My throat tightened unexpectedly. "Croissants," I said softly. "Always."

He nodded, satisfied, brushing his thumb briefly along my knuckles before stepping back.

"Then I'll see you in the morning."

The space was too quiet once the door shut behind them. Not in a bad way, just in the way silence always seemed to follow something good. The echo of laughter still lingered, faint and sweet, like the warmth on my lips where Roan had kissed me, or the low brush of Jay's voice in my ear.

I let myself stand there for another beat, toes curling into the rug, one arm crossed over my waist like I could hold the feeling a little longer.

Sadly, reality didn't wait no matter how much we might want it to.

So I padded into my bedroom, grabbed my laptop and my phone from where they'd been haphazardly abandoned when I got home, then carried them out to the living room. After I made a cup of tea, I curled up on the couch, a fresh blanket over my lap and then I opened the floodgates.

First up: the *news*.

The front page of two major league sports networks had the Vultures front and center, head coach in the middle of a press conference and a banner headline screaming:

PLAYOFF SPOT AWARDED: VULTURES WIN LOTTERY SLOT IN UPSET SHAKE-UP

Which would've been a whole *thing* by itself... except the subheader made my stomach tighten.

Accusations of Poaching: Are the Howlers Trying to Lure Talent Ahead of Time?

I clicked the link.

The article wasn't subtle.

In fact, it was practically a manifesto. One that accused the Howlers' management of "inappropriate communications," "unprofessional overtures," and "targeted tampering." There was even a vague allusion to *specific players* being approached—though no names were listed.

The article had quotes from Vultures PR. And none of them were friendly. I rubbed a hand down my face and opened my email.

And there it was. A subject line that lit up my stomach with dread:

RE: DAMAGE CONTROL — WE NEED TO TALK IMMEDIATELY

From: Marchand

I opened it.

And winced.

Wren,

I don't know what the hell kind of vacation you thought you were on, but it's time to show up. The Vultures are spinning this like a full-scale PR war, and we're bleeding goodwill by the hour.

You *told me* nothing would get out of control.

Fix it.

We're meeting first thing tomorrow. No excuses.

I stared at it for a second, chest tight with frustration. No "hope you're well." No acknowledgment that I'd taken leave with full sign-off. No consideration. Just accusation. Just pressure.

But he wasn't the only name in my inbox.

I had five new emails from Rylan, all variations on *"we need to finalize my terms before the offer window closes"* and

"I've got three agents sniffing around now that the Vultures are playoff-bound."

Because, of course he did.

I sat back, scrolled through the avalanche, and watched the shape of the world reassert itself—loud, fast, and sharp-edged. My heat was over, but the aftermath was just beginning.

The playoff bracket updates were flooding in. League PR was scrambling to spin the sudden wildcard spot the Vultures had landed. Every agency with a decent roster was eyeing the chaos, waiting to make a move.

This was my world.

One I was damn good at navigating.

Something in me resisted the rhythm of it now as if I'd stepped off a moving sidewalk and needed a second to reorient. My instincts still worked, but the *urgency* that used to drive me felt dulled by something else.

Maybe because I wasn't just thinking about press angles and spin cycles anymore. I was thinking about Roan's hands on my cheeks. About Jay asking what kind of pastry I wanted in the morning. About Rhett's voice when he said I was amazing.

About how, when the chaos ended, they'd be waiting.

I exhaled, steadying myself.

Right now, I needed to keep the Howlers' playoff rep from bursting into flames. I'd figure out the rest—Jay's coffee, the fallout from Marchand, my role with the team— all of it.

One step at a time.

Just like Roan said.

First up...

TWENTY-EIGHT

WREN

I wore war paint in the form of lipstick and a pantsuit. White blazer, tailored within a breath of my skin, paired with a silk blue blouse and tapered navy slacks that showed off the heels I'd already been walking in for an hour. Not a wrinkle on me. Not a hair out of place.

Blue and white. Howlers' colors. Message received.

Jay walked beside me through the main arena entrance, gear bag slung over one shoulder, his hair still slightly damp from his shower, a navy hoodie unzipped over a gray training shirt. He looked relaxed. At ease. A solid wall of calm at my side.

I sipped my coffee slowly as we walked, feeling the caffeine coil into my bloodstream like a silent threat to the people who were about to test my patience. The croissants he brought that morning were already gone, thank you very much, and I'd been up since before sunrise triaging inbox fires and organizing my talking points like I was prepping for a press briefing at the UN.

Jay didn't say much, but he didn't need to. We moved through the halls of the Howlers' arena like we both belonged there—him headed to the locker room, me toward the war upstairs.

When we reached the hallway where we'd split, we paused.

He didn't kiss me.

But his eyes lingered on mine, the moment thick with all the things we weren't saying in front of a dozen security cameras and early-morning staffers. Respect. Want. Solidarity.

"I'm looking forward to drills," I said, giving him a slow smile. "Think I'll watch today."

His eyes gleamed. "I'll be sure to tell Rhett. He'll want to give you a little something-something to keep you entertained."

I laughed under my breath and gave an exaggerated eye roll as I pivoted toward the elevator. "You boys and your 'something-something.'"

He said nothing else, just lifted his chin slightly, then turned toward the locker rooms, disappearing around the corner with quiet confidence.

My amusement faded as soon as the elevator doors slid shut. By the time they opened on the executive floor, I'd already shifted back into full PR director mode—shoulders straight, spine steel.

Marchand's assistant barely looked up as I passed. She didn't need to. He was expecting me. Of course he was.

The door to his office was open. And it wasn't just him waiting.

Rylan was already seated, slouched into the chair like he'd been holding court for a while. His agent, a sleek, smug little man named Devin Hart, perched on the arm beside him, tablet in hand. And across the room, legs crossed like she belonged here, sat *Carrie Hall*, the Vultures' head of public relations.

Unsurprisingly, no one was smiling.

Marchand looked up. "You're late."

"I'm exactly on time," I said, breezing into the room like I owned it. "You want to split hairs, I can start quoting timestamps."

Rylan gave me a lazy once-over, his eyes catching on the sharp white lines of my blazer before flicking away, unimpressed. "Well, damn. Thought maybe you were here to talk us off the ledge. Guess it's a firing squad instead."

"If you're guilty," I said mildly, "maybe you should be worried."

Devin cleared his throat. "Let's not turn this into a scene—"

"Too late," Carrie interrupted, crossing one leg over the other. "It's already a headline. Our phones haven't stopped ringing. Media wants to know if the Howlers are officially courting playoff sabotage."

"And I'd like to know," I said crisply, turning to Marchand, "why we're allowing an *opposing team's PR rep* to sit in on an internal meeting."

Marchand exhaled through his nose, clearly annoyed that I hadn't come in apologizing.

"She's here because it's her player being poached."

"There's been no poaching," I said, unflinching. "Unless you're admitting that Carrie's client made an offer to ours while still under contract."

That landed.

Even Carrie sat up a little straighter.

"Rylan," I added, voice cool, "you still want to play for this team?"

His eyes narrowed, just slightly. "I want to play. Period."

"That's not an answer."

"It's the only one you're getting until I see a contract."

"Then sit tight," I said. "And if your agent can't keep you from leaking sensitive conversations to our rivals, maybe it's time we reevaluate who should be in this room."

The temperature dropped by ten degrees.

Marchand looked at me like he couldn't decide whether to strangle me or thank me. I didn't care which. I wasn't here to please him. One thing he should remember was what he hired me to do. I was here to protect this team, and I'd be damned if I let it fall apart now.

Carrie recovered first. Smooth, confident, a smug little smile that had probably shaken less seasoned PR directors than me.

"You can't keep him," she said lightly. "Rylan's already in breach by holding those conversations. If you were smart, you'd be more worried about damage control than holding him hostage."

"Hostage?" I tilted my head. "That's a bold word for a player with a signed, legal contract that runs through the end of playoffs."

She smiled wider. "Contracts are negotiable. Especially when they're compromised."

"Compromised?" I echoed. "Interesting. Since that would require you to admit your player broke protocol first. Are you really planning to go on the record confirming that?"

That shut her up. The room tightened like a rope winding around a throat.

I didn't stop there.

"Even if the Vultures wanted to terminate his contract today, and I'm not suggesting that's even on the table," I added, glancing briefly at Rylan, "league rules clearly state no *new* team agreement can take effect until after the season concludes. No matter how you spin it, he's yours until then."

The silence crackled.

It didn't just cut Carrie off at the knees—it took the legs out from under Rylan, too.

His agent, Devin, let out a bitter scoff. "Unbelievable. *You're* the one who made the approach, Marchand. Don't act like we started this dance."

All eyes turned toward Marchand.

His jaw worked, fury creeping into his expression. "Watch your mouth, Hart."

"You told me there was interest," Devin snapped, "you brought Rylan into it—"

"I said there was a conversation," Marchand growled. "And it was *your* client who showed up in my office ready to jump ship the moment the Vultures hit the bracket."

Carrie shifted, glancing at Rylan now with less PR-polish and more calculation. Devin started to say something else, but Marchand leveled him with a look that dared him to continue.

I stayed quiet. Let them spiral. Sometimes silence was the sharpest knife.

Then, slowly, *finally*, Rylan moved.

He rose from the chair in one smooth, quiet motion, the lazy slouch gone, replaced with something leaner and far more alert. I felt his eyes on me before I saw him move— *really* felt them. A prickle at the base of my spine. The hair on my arms rising.

I turned. Met his gaze directly.

Something in his expression had changed. His nostrils flared faintly, his eyes narrowing. His attention sharpened —not just on the conversation, but on *me*.

He was picking something up.

Not the scent of the others—I'd scrubbed thoroughly, dressed clean, even used scent-neutralizing balm. But his instincts were too well-honed. It wasn't what I wore. It was what lingered beneath. My *altered* body chemistry. A trace of something... shifted.

Rylan didn't speak.

But his focus had changed from disinterest to laser-fine intensity.

I held his gaze without flinching.

"You're costing yourself more than leverage," I said calmly. "You've handed the Vultures doubt about your loyalty, your judgment, and your discretion. Even if you were released, what makes you think any team would still want you after this mess?"

Carrie frowned.

Rylan said nothing. But I saw it—the flicker of emotion behind his stillness. Disdain. Irritation. Frustration.

But also... curiosity.

It simmered in the way he looked at me, now. The kind of look predators give just before they lunge. Only this time, I was the one holding the leash.

"How sad for you," I said softly, gaze still on Rylan. "You could've used the wildcard to show strength. Stability. Instead, you've turned yourself into a liability."

That landed. Hard.

His mouth curled, just slightly. But there was no humor in it.

Marchand shifted behind the desk, clearly aware that the dynamic had changed. His voice was short, clipped. "Wren. Stay behind. Everyone else—out."

Devin bristled. "She doesn't have the right—"

"I said *out*," Marchand barked.

Carrie stood, eyes still flicking back to me like she was trying to decide if I'd just outmaneuvered or humiliated her. I leaned into both, but I wasn't the one keeping score. Devin huffed and muttered something under his breath. But it was Rylan who lingered last.

He stepped close enough that I had to lift my chin to meet his eyes.

"You're not who I thought you were," he said softly. "I should've paid more attention."

"You still can," I replied, voice just as quiet. "But next time, don't wait until the house is on fire to ask who's holding the extinguisher."

His nostrils flared again. Then, without another word, he turned and followed the others out.

The door had barely clicked shut before Marchand shoved himself out of his chair and crossed to the bar cart. No offer of a drink for me. Not that I wanted one. It was barely nine in the morning.

He poured two fingers of something amber into a crystal glass and downed half of it before turning toward me.

"What the hell was that?"

"Control," I said simply, "of a narrative that was about to spiral into freefall."

"You humiliated me."

"No," I said, calm but firm. "*You* humiliated you when you started this little game. I stopped the bleeding."

He glared at me, glass still in hand. "You could've given me a heads-up. You didn't even loop me in this morning."

"You told me to fix it," I reminded him. "It's fixed."

His eyes blazed and his jaw tightened. Power punched the air around him, and ballooned outward like he wanted to choke me with it. "Have you forgotten who you work for?"

Surprisingly, I remained unmoved. Then, I'd never let him bully me. Normally, I'd take a gentler tack first, but that ship sank when he kept escalating in my absence.

"Have you forgotten what my job is?" Because both of us could play this game. "I'm not here to cater to your ego or your pride. I'm here to protect this team from all threats—even those that start at the top."

"Why didn't you call me on your way in? Why didn't you brief me?" He rapped his knuckles against the tabletop, the sound echoing in the hush.

I could have pointed out that he was already in a meeting with them when I arrived. I could have told him that I came straight up here to do exactly that and *found* him in the middle of that meeting. Instead, I just went for his jugular. "Because I knew you'd be too busy trying to save face to think strategically." I arched a brow. "Which is exactly how we got here in the first place."

Nostrils flared and eyes blazing, he *glared* at me.

"I warned you about Rylan," I went on. "When he was on the team before, when he was cut, and when his agent approached us two years ago in the off season. You didn't want to hear it then and based on your ambushing tactics with him last week, you didn't want to hear it now. Then you let him think he had negotiating power in the middle of a playoff push and dangled me as the bait."

"You're accusing *me* of blowing this up?"

"I'm accusing you of not knowing how to pick your battles. You're trying to strong-arm a player you never had a handle on, and you let your ego write checks your strategy can't cash."

Marchand's mouth twisted in an ugly scowl. "Don't

give me that tone, Wren. I brought you in to manage PR, not run this team."

"You brought me in to clean up your messes," I snapped. "That's exactly what I'm doing. But let me be perfectly clear—if you keep treating me like your secretary instead of your Director of Public Relations, this team won't just lose face. We'll lose the locker room. The sponsors. The playoff momentum. All of it."

He slammed the glass down on the edge of the bar cart hard enough that I thought it might crack.

But he didn't argue.

I folded my arms, letting the silence stretch.

"You're rattled," I said finally, voice softer but no less steady. "The Howlers are in the playoffs and instead of celebrating that, you're trying to maneuver new players into position, but *you* don't control the pieces on the board."

His eyes snapped to mine.

"You thought Rylan was leverage. You thought a power play would win this. But it's not about chess anymore. It's poker. And you just showed your whole damn hand."

A muscle ticked in his jaw.

"Do you want to win, Marchand?"

He didn't answer right away. But his chest rose and fell once, then again, and his gaze dropped to the drink he hadn't finished.

"Yes," he said. Gritted out like he hated that it was me asking the question.

"Then stop making it personal," I said. "Use what I gave you. Get control back. Let me do what I *do*."

He looked up at me again, and this time, there was no anger. Just a resigned kind of awareness. I'd won this round —and he knew it.

"Make sure it doesn't happen again," he said.

"Then don't put me in a position where it can."

"Wren," he said slowly as he straightened. "You better hope they win, because if we lose the playoffs—someone's head will need to roll." The implication being it would be mine.

We stared at each other for another long moment before I turned and walked out, my heels clicking sharply against the polished floor.

It wasn't until the elevator doors closed behind me that I let my shoulders drop and exhaled slowly. One crisis handled.

And somehow, I was still thinking about Rylan's eyes on me—too aware, too intent.

I wasn't wearing Roan's scent. Or Jay's. Or Rhett's.

But that didn't mean something in me hadn't changed. Something that could be detected by another alpha. Predators like Rylan always knew when blood was in the water.

Let Marchand stew.

I had what I needed from that meeting—leverage, position, and a clear path forward. The fallout would still come. There were calls to make, headlines to manage, and somewhere in my inbox, a growing PR storm over whether or not the Howlers were "poaching talent" during the most critical part of the season.

But none of that mattered more than seeing my team.

Not the management. Not the league. Not the press.

My team.

I took the long corridor down toward the rink-level suites, the distant echo of whistles and shouts growing louder as I got closer. I could hear Jay's voice before I saw him—cutting through the air in a bark of laughter, followed by Rhett's unmistakable heckling.

The moment I stepped into the viewing box overlooking the practice rink, the cold glass against my palms grounded me. The ice gleamed below, sun filtering through the narrow upper windows in bright white bars. The Howlers were in full motion—sharp, fast, fluid.

Jay was running a tight drill on one end. Rhett had a cluster of players lined up along the boards for individual shots, barking out quick notes in that deceptively lazy drawl that always carried a deeper edge of discipline.

And Roan... Roan was everywhere.

Watching. Managing. Tracking flow, placement, tension.

He skated like a machine—smooth, powerful, and *aware*. The alpha in him wasn't just dominant on the ice, it was gravitational. Yet there was *ease* in him today, too. His movements less tight, less coiled. As if something in him had settled.

I wondered, for a breathless second, if that had anything to do with *me*.

A knock came at the suite door. I turned just as Coach stepped inside with a clipboard under one arm and a thermos in the other.

He offered it to me with a dry look. "Thought you might need something stronger than arena coffee."

I took the thermos, amused. "Tell me it's not bourbon, still too early for that."

"It's dark roast," he said. "Don't insult my taste."

That earned a soft laugh. I sipped gratefully, the fresh brew hitting my throat like armor.

"Word's already out?" I asked.

He nodded grimly. "The Vultures just posted a vague denial. Rylan's trending. And Marchand's breathing fire."

"Good," I said. "Let him."

Coach studied me for a beat, then tilted his head toward the glass. "They're glad you're here."

I blinked. "What?"

"Down there," he said, with the kind of weight that made me still. "Jay. Rhett. Roan. Hell, the whole damn locker room. You walk in, and things shift. They settle."

I didn't know what to say to that. So I didn't. Still, something in my chest pulled tight.

"Watch drills," he said, turning for the door. "And maybe let yourself enjoy what we've built."

Then he was gone, leaving me with nothing but the sound of skates cutting ice and the quiet, irrevocable feeling that he might be right.

No matter what waited in my inbox... or what trouble Rylan was brewing next... this—*this*—was the reason I loved this job. Not just to manage reputations. But to *belong*.

Roan cut a look up at the suite just then, like he'd heard my thought and I raised the thermos toward him in a silent toast. I didn't have to see his face to *feel* his smile. Then his attention was back on the ice, on the drills, on the game.

TWENTY-NINE

RHETT

First day back and my thighs were already screaming like we owed them rent.

The drills were brutal. No easing in, no "shake it off, boys." Just sharp, crisp execution and Roan barking out directions like he was training wolves to chase blood in snow.

And still—I was having a hell of a time.

Maybe it was the playoff buzz under my skin. Maybe it was the clean-cut pace of Jay slinging the puck like a surgeon on the left wing or the way Roan cut across the ice, every movement lean and merciless. Or maybe, it was that I could *feel* her here.

Wren.

Even when I didn't see her, I *felt* her. Like static building in the background, threading through every player in the rink. Half of them kept darting looks toward the upper suite where she'd been earlier. Some pretended not to glance. Some didn't even bother.

Yeah. Everyone was wondering what the hell had gone down with Rylan.

No one was dumb enough to ask outright. But between drills, the whispers started like they always did. Harmless stuff at first—speculation, what-if scenarios, locker room banter. Until it started to drift toward real talk. Subtle jabs. "I always thought Rylan was a dick" kind of energy.

Roan shut it down fast.

"Focus," he barked during a break, loud enough that even the guys trying to look casual flinched. "Playoffs are coming, and if you're spending more time dissecting gossip than your coverage zone, you won't be on the goddamn ice."

Silence fell fast. Heads snapped forward. Sticks hit the ice.

He wasn't wrong.

Still, that didn't mean I couldn't offer a little *levity* to the mood.

After all, Roan had the intimidation game locked down. Jay, meanwhile, brought the calm—he kept pace with the rookies during the more punishing drills, quietly correcting footwork or body alignment when needed. Guys respected him. More than that, they *listened*.

Me? I was the jackass with the grin and the fastest one-liners. The guy who called out a perfect saucer pass and followed it with, "You miss that net again, I swear I'll tie your gloves together and let you fight your way out like a raccoon in a trash can."

At the same time, I knew *exactly* when to step back and let Roan's authority hold the line.

We each had our roles. And right now? Mine was keeping the guys from burning out *before* Roan could push them into something sharper.

Still, every time I caught sight of her across the rink—dark hair, pristine pantsuit swapped now for a sleek branded jacket, tablet in hand and phone pressed to her ear —I wanted to *do something.*

Something dumb, probably. Flash her a grin. Tap the glass. Make her look at *me* and not the chaos she was juggling.

Because Wren wasn't just handling fallout. She was *orchestrating* the press like it was her own damn symphony. Interviews were flowing. Talking points distributed. Reporters were quoting team values and brushing off poaching rumors like the Vultures were just throwing a tantrum.

And the team? They were watching. The rookies who'd dared to look at her sideways a week ago were back to nodding with respect.

She wasn't the scandal.

She was the one putting the fire out.

Hell. *She was the fire department.*

And me? I was skating harder. Faster. Sharper.

Because for the first time in my entire career, it felt like I had more than a team to play for.

I had her watching.

SHE HADN'T COME DOWN after drills.

Not that I blamed her, between the Rylan mess and the playoff push, her day had probably turned into a twelve-alarm fire by noon. However, once I'd showered, I couldn't help myself.

I ducked out, grabbed a bag of snacks—real food, not vending machine garbage—and circled back to the office tower attached to the arena. I knew the code to the PR suite.

She'd given it to us the night before like it hadn't meant anything, but I'd kind of had it before.

It meant everything now.

The hallway outside her office was quiet. Too quiet, considering the chaos behind the headlines. Her door was cracked, and I could hear her voice—low, steady, razor-sharp.

"...you can quote that, but only if you include the statement about league policy. I'm not interested in speculation —only facts. If your editor needs more, I'll issue a release. Otherwise, we're done here."

Click.

I leaned on the frame, just outside the line of her vision.

Wren was at her desk, still in that branded black jacket with the Howlers crest, her hair swept back, tablet on one side, laptop on the other, a half-drained bottle of sparkling water beside it all. Her phone buzzed again and she picked it up without missing a beat.

"Amber, I said no comments from players. If we let anyone speak on the Rylan situation, it turns into a gossip war. He's not worth the airtime." A pause. "Yes, I said that on the record."

I *loved* watching her work.

It wasn't just the way she handled pressure, it was how she *wielded* it. Like every fire she walked into just gave her another excuse to pull off something impossible.

When she finally ended the call and leaned back in her chair, rubbing at the bridge of her nose, I took that as my cue.

"You ever stop to breathe, or is that only an end-of-season perk?" I asked, stepping inside and holding up the bag.

She jumped. "How long have you been standing there?"

"Long enough to hear you verbally neuter three reporters and a network flunky. Impressive. I brought bribes."

Her expression warmed instantly, even if her posture stayed tense. "Snacks?"

"Snack *offering*," I said, tossing the bag onto her desk. "Protein bars, chocolate-covered almonds, and trail mix. Grown-up gas station cuisine."

She cracked a smile. "You really do know how to charm a girl."

I stepped closer, pretending to study the headlines still pulled up on her monitor. Most were some flavor of *Vultures deny tampering* or *Rylan frozen out in scandal storm*. But one caught my eye.

"PR Director Wren Foster Fans the Flames with Silent Strategy"

I let out a low whistle. "You're getting your own coverage now?"

"Yeah," she muttered, turning the screen away like I might read too much into it. "Because being competent apparently means I'm secretly negotiating all backroom deals."

"Hey," I said, nudging the screen gently back. "They're not calling you *the problem*. They're calling you the one with teeth."

Wren gave me a look. "You think that's a good thing?"

"Oh, honey," I said, grinning, "I think that's the *sexiest* thing."

She laughed, but the sound was short-lived, cut off by a sharp knock at the door.

"Someone's popular," I murmured.

Wren called, "Come in," already distracted again, glancing at her phone. But it wasn't a player or another member of staff at the door, it was a delivery guy with a slim black box and an apologetic expression.

"Uh... these are for Wren Foster?"

She frowned. "That's me."

He held the box out like it might bite him. "They're from... a Rylan?"

Her whole body stilled.

I took the box from the guy, who looked *very* ready to leave, and dropped a tip into his hand without breaking eye contact. When the door shut behind him, I looked down at the box, then back at her.

"You want me to toss it?"

Her lips parted, but nothing came out.

I opened it slowly. Long-stemmed, blood-red roses. Twelve of them. No card.

I didn't speak.

Not for a long moment.

But *something* dark and cold unspooled in my chest, threading through the edges of my calm. I wasn't angry that she got flowers. I wasn't jealous. I was *aware*.

The timing wasn't romantic, because as Wren herself would say, it was *strategic*.

That prick knew exactly what kind of message roses from him would send to her, to anyone else who might scent them.

She reached for the box, but I stopped her with a hand on her wrist. Gently. No pressure. Just a question.

"You want these?" I asked softly.

She hesitated. Then shook her head. "No."

I nodded. Closed the lid. Set it aside—nowhere near her desk.

When she finally looked at me again, something uncertain flashed in her eyes. And that was enough of that. I didn't give her time to feed her doubts or her worries. I crossed the space between us, leaned in, and brushed a kiss against her temple, then her lips.

"If he thinks he's still in this game," I murmured, "he's an even bigger idiot than we thought."

Her breath hitched—just slightly.

When I pulled back, she was smiling again. This time, for real. I brushed my knuckles down her cheek. "I'll take care of these. You eat and take at least ten minutes for yourself." I didn't make it an order because our girl did not do orders well. "You need a ride home after work?"

"I don't know when I'm getting out of here," she admitted and I smoothed away my frown even as it formed. This was her job, her work, what she did and respecting that was important. Even when I wanted her to look after herself more.

"Tell you what," I said, leaning my hip against her desk. "If you're still here at five and it's not looking like you're getting out of here anytime soon, send me a message? I'll grab dinner and deliver it."

Lips pursed, she studied me for a moment. "Only if you promise to eat with me."

"Deal." I grinned, then pushed away from the desk before I gave into the urge to kiss all her worries away. Her door locked and her desk was really solid. My hard dick was not on board with my thoughtfulness though, it really liked the idea of just messing her up and letting us both get lost in the moment.

Tucking the flower box under my arm, I gave her a little salute as her phone buzzed and she already had it at her ear. "No, I said there will be no interviews until after the first couple of games. The players need to focus..."

She curled her index finger in a wave to me and I let

myself out. The moment the door closed, my smile fell away.

I carried the box of roses like it was a live grenade. The kind of thing that didn't explode on contact, but poisoned slowly, with intention.

Roan and Jay were already down in the trainers' office, getting iced and stretched after drills. I skipped the hallway greetings and dropped the black box onto the counter between them. Jay raised an eyebrow. Roan didn't blink.

"Rylan sent them," I said flatly. "No card. Just twelve red roses. Showed up in Wren's office like a little present."

Jay's face darkened instantly.

Roan leaned back slowly, his eyes never leaving the box. "You opened it?"

"Yeah. She didn't want them."

Jay stood and crossed the room to open the box fully, gaze flicking down over the flowers. "Not just roses. These are scent-bombed," he muttered. "There's no way this was a simple gesture. They're designed to trigger attention."

"Exactly," I said. "That asshole wants everyone who walks in her office to think she's still on the table. He wants *us* to smell it on her."

Jay's hands curled into fists before he shoved them deep into his pockets.

Roan still hadn't moved. "She okay?"

"She didn't flinch," I said. "Told me no. I handled it."

Jay exhaled sharply, pacing once before he stopped, then looked at Roan. "We should go to Marchand. This is deliberate. This is league line–adjacent and—"

"No," Roan said quietly, but with that steel that made people shut up.

"You don't think we should do something?" Jay frowned.

"I *do*," Roan replied. "But we're not going to handle it like a couple of pissed-off rookies swinging sticks behind the bench." He pushed off the wall, finally stepping toward the flowers, his expression unreadable. "Rylan wants to rattle us. Wants to make a play that forces our hand, makes us look like we're unstable."

"Because he *knows* we're not," I muttered.

Roan met my gaze. "Exactly. That's why we don't take the bait."

"So what do we do?" Jay asked, voice low, simmering.

"We make a plan," Roan said. "We protect Wren without turning it into a pissing contest. We keep her name clean, her scent clear, and we make sure Rylan never gets within arm's length of her again." His gaze moved to me. "That starts with staying steady. No fights. No outbursts."

"I didn't say I was gonna deck him," I muttered.

"You didn't have to." Roan's mouth curled faintly. "I know that look, Rhett."

Jay chuckled dryly. "Yeah, it's the same one he had during the Rivets game last season. Right before he put Torres through the boards."

I held up both hands. "*That* was provoked."

Roan crossed his arms. "So is this. But we're not on the ice yet."

That calmed something inside me. *Yet.* As in—we *would* be. When we were, Rylan was going to feel every ounce of what we'd been holding back.

Roan turned to Jay. "She still good for morning coffee?"

Jay nodded. "She didn't say otherwise."

"Then you bring it. Sit with her if she has time. Not because she *needs* a babysitter, but because she's running point on a storm none of us can help with right now."

"I'm on it." Jay glared at the flowers then at us. "What about tonight?"

"I'm bringing her dinner here, if she's still at work. Probably take it to her place if she gets out of here on time." Not leaving her exposed was a good plan. The fact neither Roan nor Jay amended my idea said it was.

Roan glanced back at the roses. "We'll get rid of these. Quietly. No drama. No firestorm."

"Understood," Jay said.

But me? I looked down at that box one more time and imagined Rylan's smug face behind every petal.

Yeah.

I'd be calm. I'd be patient.

But when the time came to settle the score?

I'd make damn sure he learned exactly how we played.

THIRTY

The call had already been going for twenty minutes by the time my doorbell rang.

I hadn't expected anyone. I'd barely remembered to toss on soft joggers and an old Howlers tee after peeling off the suit I'd worn to the arena. My hair was in a clip. No makeup. Barefoot.

Hardly the image of professional composure, and yet here I was—one earbud in, phone wedged between shoulder and cheek as I padded to the door, laptop still open on the kitchen island behind me.

"Yes, I understand your frustration, but you don't get to reframe league violations as 'misunderstandings' because the narrative doesn't suit you," I snapped, one hand on the deadbolt.

Carrie's voice, haughty and sharp, fired back in my ear as I pulled the door open—and nearly lost my grip on the phone.

Rhett stood there, a brown paper bag cradled in one arm and a bottle of wine peeking out of the other. His hair was damp from a shower, his cheeks pink from the wind, and he had that same smug, devastating smile he always wore when he knew he'd just made your day better.

And damn him, he *had*.

"Shhh," I whispered with a smile, pointing to my ear.

He winked, stepped inside, and silently brushed a kiss to my temple as he passed. The scent of roasted chicken, lemon, and rosemary followed him. He headed for the kitchen without a word.

"—and furthermore, Wren, if your team hadn't actively courted Rylan—"

"Oh, for God's sake, Carrie," I bit out, reclaiming the conversation. "No one courted Rylan. He showed up uninvited and overstepped from day one. If the Vultures were so interested in controlling their narrative, maybe they should try actually controlling *their players*."

The owner of the Vultures made a sound like a strangled cough. Marchand didn't say a word, which usually meant he was suppressing a smile. The league rep—Hollis —sighed into his mic, sounding like a man juggling nitroglycerin.

"Let's redirect," Hollis said in the smooth, overly patient tone of someone who'd been through one too many of these calls. "This post-season tension is exactly what we want to avoid. Now, perhaps a solution that gives both parties a way to save face... such as a trade, post-playoffs, might offer a—"

"No," I said sharply. "Absolutely not."

A beat of silence.

Then Marchand's voice, measured and amused: "Wren—"

"No, Adrien." I cut in before he could *consider* it. "I'm going to be very clear here. Even suggesting a trade opens the door for speculation we can't shut down. We're already dealing with the fallout of a tampering scandal and a public breakdown of negotiations between the league's two most contentious teams. A trade? That's blood in the water. You'll tank morale, enrage the fan base, and set both teams up for months of press nightmares."

The quiet wasn't shocked, it was calculating. Because everyone on the call knew what a trade could *actually* mean.

Roan.

It would be Roan they asked for.

Not just because he was the cornerstone of our team, but because taking him would gut the Howlers from the inside out.

My heart clenched, but my voice didn't waver.

"We're not losing a single player. Not now. Not later. Not to fix *their* mistake."

Marchand exhaled. "She's not wrong."

Thank *God* he backed me up. He didn't always, but when he did... he didn't flinch.

Hollis tried again. "I'm not suggesting it's a formal trade offer, only that—"

"Then stop suggesting it," I said crisply. "Let us handle our teams. The playoffs are already selling themselves. Let the games speak."

Rhett moved in my peripheral vision, unpacking containers with practiced hands. He'd set the table. He'd poured water. He'd even dimmed the overheads and lit the candle I didn't remember buying that sat in the center of the table.

He disappeared for a second, then returned with the bottle of wine and two glasses, setting them beside me as I paced back and forth in front of the island. When he raised his brows in silent offering, I nodded, nearly limp with gratitude.

The cork popped cleanly, the softest *shhfff*, and he poured the wine like it was an ordinary Tuesday and not the middle of a PR war.

His glass remained untouched. Mine, however—he lifted and held out gently. Like a gift.

I took it.

With the call still running in my ear, I sipped. And *melted*.

Roasted garlic and lemon teased my nose, warm and rich and mouthwatering. He'd brought the rosemary chicken from that place downtown, the one I'd once raved about during an early morning carpool on our way to an out-of-town pre-season game.

He'd remembered.

He didn't interrupt. He didn't hover. He just *was*. A steady, grounding presence who knew exactly how to walk into a hurricane and not get blown off course.

I sank into the moment, just enough to breathe.

Enough to remind myself that no matter what flaming chaos waited on the other end of the line, I wasn't alone in this anymore.

I sipped the wine Rhett had poured me, more for the effect than the flavor—although the citrusy white was crisp and exactly what I needed. I didn't have the mental band-width to ask how he knew that too.

Because the Vultures' owner wasn't done pushing.

"We all want this to go away," he said smoothly, that faux-genteel tone of a man used to buying his way out of a mess. "But the longer this drags on, the more damage it does. Perhaps if you'd taken the approach seriously, Marchand, we wouldn't be having this conversation."

"Seriously?" I muttered under my breath.

Carrie, like the *vulture* she was, swooped in to double

down. "We made a genuine offer. You responded with stonewalling and now the league is left with a situation escalating in the press."

"Because *you* leaked it," I said, tone cool.

Marchand's chuckle cut through the line, dry and without humor. "You want to talk about escalation? You sent Rylan to us without formal process. You broke protocol. And now you're trying to weaponize the fallout as if we're the ones throwing punches."

"The league has rules," the Vultures' owner snapped. "If you won't trade, we'll go to arbitration."

"You can't arbitrate what never existed," Marchand said, suddenly sounding a little too much like *me*. "We didn't sign a contract. We didn't even agree to talks. My head of PR said no. I said no. My captain said *hell no*. There's no case."

It was almost funny—listening to him mimic my exact arguments. Almost.

Carrie started to speak again but Hollis cut in, his voice tight with irritation. "Enough. This isn't a free-for-all. If this continues, both teams may face fines. Possibly even penalties."

That snapped my head up.

"For what?" I said, sitting up straighter. "What exactly are we being punished for? Saying *no*? For refusing to participate in a contract violation? For keeping our players focused when someone else is leaking and spinning false narratives to distract from their own failures?"

Rhett raised an eyebrow and tipped the bottle toward me in silent question. I nodded—sharply—and drained the rest of my glass before he even got the pour going. He refilled it without a word.

"You tell me," I continued, calm and clipped even as my

stomach twisted. "What precedent does this set, Hollis? That we're responsible for the circus because we chose not to perform in it?"

There was silence. Glorious, telling silence.

Rhett leaned against the kitchen counter, his arms crossed, eyes on me. His support was silent but fierce. I could feel it like gravity, steadying me.

"Fine," the Vultures' owner snapped. "Clearly, we're not going to reach an agreement. Let the public decide."

Oh, they would. And I knew exactly which team had more loyalty, more heart, and *less bullshit* to explain.

"I'll be issuing a public statement shortly," Carrie added. "I trust you'll all do the same."

Then—mercifully—there was a tone that indicated she'd rung off. The Vultures' owner wasn't far behind. Which left me, Marchand, and Hollis.

And wine. Thank god for the wine.

Thank god for Rhett too. When I raised the glass to him before I took another long swallow, his lips twitched into a small smile. His concern remained though, concern and support.

"I hope you both understand," Hollis said, with a very long sigh, "I'm not trying to play favorites. But I've got a complaint on my desk, I've got media hounding every angle, and now I've got two teams breathing fire. What the hell else am I supposed to do?"

Marchand spoke before I could. "You could start by recognizing this isn't on us. Wren is right. We were the ones approached. We didn't solicit the player, we didn't initiate contact, and we *sure as hell* didn't agree to a trade."

I blinked. Okay, *damn*. He was really going for it.

Marchand continued, calm but pointed. "Now they're the ones leaking everything. And the timing? Right before playoff brackets get announced? Seems awfully convenient. Especially with the Vultures squeaking in on a wild card slot and the Howlers locked in as top seed."

Hollis didn't speak, but I could hear him listening.

So I went in for the final blow.

"How better to psych out a team and their fans than to sow discord right before round one?" I said quietly. "You don't need a rulebook to know what this is. This is strategy. Off-ice warfare. And you don't punish the team holding the line because someone else decided to light a match."

Marchand exhaled through his nose. "She's not wrong."

I leaned my head back, rubbing the back of my neck with one hand. Then Rhett was there, replacing my hand with his own strong grip and I damn near moaned as he worked the tension loose.

Hollis sighed. "Send me a copy of your internal timeline, Wren. And make sure there's documentation for every time you said no. I'll handle the rest."

"Done." With that, the line disconnected.

I let the phone slide to the counter and reached for my glass. My hands were shaking a little—just enough that Rhett noticed. He slid his hand around to cup my throat in a grip that was as much collar as it was support before he pressed a kiss to my temple. "You're a goddamn force."

"I need carbs," I mumbled.

"I brought potatoes," he murmured, teasing kisses along my cheek to my ear and a shudder went through me as my nipples went taut.

"I could kiss you."

"You could," he said with a low chuckle. "And later, you *will*."

"Later?" It came out more a whine than I meant for it

too, but he scraped his teeth over my earlobe before he sucked on it and I went up on my toes.

One moment I had a wine glass in my hand, the next it was on the counter and Rhett had me up and on it as well. He stripped my sweats down in a movement so smooth, I barely saw it happen. Then he had my knees apart and his hands cupping my ass as he lifted me, his touch firm and demanding.

"Yes," he said in a husky voice as he took a deep breath. "I'm starving and I haven't eaten you in three days..."

"Oh." The single syllable fell out of me. "Fuck."

"Oh, we will," he promised before he buried his face against my cunt and began to devour me like it was his personal mission in life. His tongue, teeth, and lips alternated between stroking, licking, sucking, and biting, each movement sending jolts of pleasure straight to my core. The smoothness of his freshly shaven face added another layer of delectable sensation. The heat built inside of me, the pressure coiling tighter and tighter.

I was close, so goddamn close and he kept edging me right there and then lapping with these stroking licks that refused to push me over. Just when I thought I couldn't take it anymore, he sucked my clit into his mouth, his tongue flicking over the sensitive nub with a ruthless intensity, and I came.

Hard.

My body convulsed as I squirted, the release so intense that it left me breathless and shaking. But he didn't stop there. He continued to feast on me, his touch relentless, his hunger insatiable, and I found myself spiraling into another orgasm, my cries of pleasure echoing through the room.

As I came down from my second peak, my legs shaking

so badly that I didn't think I could stand, I was already half begging, "Rhett," I whispered almost hoarsely. "I need..."

"Shh," he said, his face glistening as he grinned and undid his belt buckle. "You never have to beg me, Wren. Ever..."

With ease, he lifted me off the counter and set me on my feet, then braced me there, and placed my palms flat.

"Hold on," then he bent me over and slammed into me in one hard push that made me see stars. The angle seemed to increase how deep he could go and how thick he felt. It was overwhelming, a perfect blend of pleasure and pain, and I met his every thrust with equal fervor, my body arching to meet his.

The orgasm seemed to start at my toes and rocket through my system. I pounded my fists as I came, slamming back against him even as he controlled the pace, but he was swift to follow me. The feel of his cum inside me as decadent as it had been in my heat, only now I could savor the way it filled me.

We lingered there, shaking and spent, our bodies slick with sweat.

His breathy chuckle made me smile. "What's so funny?"

"We both really need more carbs for this," he said and I started laughing with him. Satisfaction spiraled through me.

"Hmm, does this mean a repeat performance later?"

At my husky inquiry, he nipped my ear. "Am I invited to stay the night?"

"Oh," I said with a shudder as he scraped his teeth over my earlobe before he sucked on it. I went up on my toes, the feel of his cock still buried inside of me and getting thicker again a temptation to layer upon temptation. "If you do... we might even make it to my bed."

"Challenge accepted," he whispered.

We ate—eventually—but we didn't make it to bed until sometime around two in the morning when he carried my limp body up the stairs and sprawled out with me.

Sex with Rhett during heat had been amazing.

Sex without it?

Addictive as hell—especially when he woke me up the next morning with his face buried between my thighs again.

THIRTY-ONE

JAY

I brought two coffees in addition to mine. Just in case.

One of them was her go-to—hazelnut, with just a hint of oat milk and half a raw sugar packet stirred in before the lid went on. The second was a flat white with an extra shot of espresso, also oat milk. The last was for me, triple espresso light on the latte, because I had a feeling today was going to *need* it.

Tucked under my arm was a little brown bag from the French café she liked, the one with the actual pastry chef who knew how to make kouign-amann that didn't just taste like sugar bricks.

I'd barely made it to the porch when the door opened and Rhett leaned casually in the frame, barefoot, t-shirt wrinkled, hair even worse.

He grinned like a man who had absolutely *no shame*. "Morning, lover boy."

I stared at him for one long second, then handed him the second coffee—the one without the hazelnut. "Didn't realize I had competition for the last kouign-amann."

He looked at the bag like it was holy, then stepped

aside. "That's why I *like* you, Jay. You come bearing gifts even when I beat you to the prize."

I rolled my eyes and stepped inside, seriously, the guy never quit. It made him damn successful on and off the ice, even if there were days when I got why he inspired the urge to punch him. She was seated at the kitchen island in a loose sleep tee and shorts, barefoot, hair up, one leg tucked under her while she worked at her laptop.

Her eyes lit up when she saw me. "Jay."

Yeah, okay. That helped.

"Good morning." I walked over and set the coffee and the treat down beside her. "Brought you breakfast. I wasn't sure if you'd already eaten."

She gave a soft, delighted sound and reached for the coffee first, eyes fluttering closed when she took a sip. "This might be love."

"Better not be," Rhett muttered from behind me. "Or I'm gonna have to start sleeping with the guy who owns that café."

Wren snorted, then caught my gaze and—God—it did something to me. There was warmth there. Openness. *Want.*

I'd never considered myself someone who needed reassurance. But that look? That was my oxygen.

"I'd like to take you on a date," she said, voice soft but sure.

That startled me a little. "A date?"

She nodded. "A real one. With food and...whatever you like."

"Wait—*you're* asking *him* out?" Rhett asked, grabbing an apple from the bowl and tossing it in the air. "I mean, I get it, the hair, the cheekbones, the intense brooding—"

Wren reached out, placed a hand firmly over his mouth, and arched an eyebrow. "You're not helping."

His muffled laughter vibrated against her palm. But when she pulled her hand back, Rhett winked at both of us. "I fully support being romanced. Just saying. You want to seduce me with a charcuterie board and a night of bad decisions, I'm in."

"Duly noted," she said dryly, then turned her attention back to me. "But yes. If you want to, I'd like to take you out."

A slow smile curved my mouth. "I would enjoy that." Under-fucking-statement of the year, but I was definitely in.

She let out a breath like she hadn't realized she'd been holding it. "Only problem is... I don't want to be a distraction."

That seemed fair. We had a *lot* going on right now. Though, I didn't think she wanted me to tell her that she was as far from a distraction as you could get. The games were a distraction, not her.

"The playoffs," I said.

"The brackets drop today," she confirmed. "Everything's about to get louder and messier. I don't want to pull you away from the focus."

"I think you're the one who's been *helping* me stay focused," I told her. She needed to know that, if nothing else. Particularly with all the shit she was wading through to protect us—and the team. "But I get it. We've got a job to do."

Rhett crunched through a couple more bites, his mood bright enough to light up a neon sign. "So serious. We'll get through this, then we can take turns dating you while Jay files spreadsheets about my greatness."

"I'm not putting that in a spreadsheet," I said, not even having to put effort into my dry tone.

"Oh, but you'd *read* it." The man never shut up. At the same time, there was a happiness radiating off of both of them. A kind of joy I was more than happy to see.

Wren shook her head, laughing softly, and picked out a pastry from the bag, before breaking off a buttery corner. "I don't know precisely who we're facing yet," she said after a beat. "But I have ideas."

"So do I." I sipped my coffee. "We'll be ready."

Her smile was there again, subtle but genuine. When she offered me a piece of the pastry, I opened my mouth to let her feed me. It was a little sweeter than I liked but no way in hell would I tell her no.

Leaning against the counter, I soaked in her good mood. Rhett finished his apple before he took another drink of his coffee and gave her little mournful eyes until she fed him some pastry too in between skimming her emails.

She shared more with me, but I was sure that was as much because I brought it as it was to give Rhett shit. Not that it mattered, I enjoyed her simple pleasure in the activity. Enjoyed even more that we just were, the three of us in her quiet kitchen before we had to hit the ice and the press.

Eventually, time did what it always had, and we needed to get out of there. She slipped off her stool and headed upstairs to change while Rhett and I made short work of cleaning the kitchen up. After, we walked out together.

We piled into our respective vehicles—Rhett still smug in his—and by the time we rolled into the arena, the whole day had shifted gears.

Wren peeled off toward her office, phone already in hand, heels clicking with purpose.

And I wasn't surprised when I pushed into the locker

room to find Roan already there—changed, stretching, focused.

He looked up as Rhett and I came in, his eyes narrowed as he focused on Rhett and I didn't miss the way his nostrils flared. Faint amusement touched his expression before he went all business.

"Let's do this," he ordered.

The ice had bite that morning.

Not just the usual crisp cut beneath our blades or the sharp sting in the air. No—this was *mental* tension. Static coiled tight and humming under the surface. The brackets were coming. Every player knew it, and no matter how long they'd been in the league, this time felt *different*.

Because we weren't just fighting for position.

We were the team to beat.

Roan skated tight circles near the blue line, barking corrections at Nate and Lewis, his voice cutting through the ambient echo of puck strikes and blade turns like a whip.

"You drop that left shoulder again, you're going to hand them the puck gift-wrapped. *Again*, Lewis!"

I didn't even flinch. That tone wasn't new. Roan didn't yell for the sake of yelling—he *corrected*. Pinpointed flaws like a surgeon and expected you to fix them like your job depended on it. Because right now, it did.

But guys tightened up when he got like that. Lewis started skating more mechanically. Nate's shoulders hunched. Focus wavered. Tension crept in.

So I adjusted.

"Lewis," I called, tone calm, voice lower but firm. "Eyes on the outside edge. Don't worry about Roan, worry about the lane. Again. Let's go."

He nodded. Just that small reminder pulled him back into the present.

That was how it worked between the three of us. Roan demanded precision. Rhett fired them up. I pulled them steady.

It was a rhythm. A pulse. An ecosystem.

And on mornings like this, it *mattered*.

Across the ice, Rhett flung himself into a drill, full sprint toward the crease, burning hot as ever. He weaved with sharp, reckless agility, passed off to Anders, doubled back for the puck—and damn near collided with Paxton when the defenseman cut the angle wrong.

The sound of their sticks clashing echoed hard. Rhett spun out of it with that grin he always wore when shit almost went sideways, and clapped Paxton on the shoulder.

"Dude," Pax snapped. "Warn me before you come in hot like that."

"Wouldn't be a surprise play if I warned you." Rhett winked and skated backward, but I caught the slight flicker of heat under the humor.

Pax wasn't alpha, but he was close enough on the spectrum to bristle when Rhett got like that.

Before Roan could snap at both of them, I coasted in between, cutting the tension like a scalpel.

"Save the full-contact chaos for game day," I told Rhett, firm but light. Then to Pax, "His fault, yeah. But that's why we drill it. You're both better than that."

Roan's eyes flicked over to me. A flicker of acknowledgment passed between us.

He saw it. I'd taken the edge off before it spiked too far.

He turned back to his line. "Again! Top line reset!"

Another horn blared. New drills loaded in. Passing, breakaways, blue-line coverage. Over and over until sweat burned through pads and lungs heaved.

Rhett was still riding hot, pushing himself hard and

calling out encouragements even while he worked, and the guys followed. They always did. Roan drove the structure. Rhett lit the fire.

Me?

I kept the goddamn thing from burning down the whole building.

Even with all of that humming beneath the surface—everyone skating harder, tighter, smarter—you could *feel* it. The noise outside the rink.

The bracket announcement was imminent.

Everyone knew the Vultures were gunning for us. Not just on the ice, but off it too. They were trying to rattle cages. Leak drama. Stir the pot and keep us off balance. I'd seen it a dozen times before from other teams. It always came down to psychological warfare this close to playoffs.

But the Howlers?

We didn't break.

I skated up alongside Roan during water break. He was frowning at the corner of the rink, running something mental in his head. Maybe lines, maybe plays, maybe how to keep the newer guys from crumbling under the weight of *expectation*.

He didn't say anything at first, just handed me a water bottle.

"You good?" I asked.

He gave a grunt of assent. "They're pushing harder today. It's good. We need that."

"But?"

He glanced at the far bench, where half the team was crowding around someone's phone.

"Distraction's bleeding in," he muttered. "I'd rather they get it over with."

"They will," I said. "Soon."

Roan's jaw flexed once. "When it drops, they'll want to talk. To speculate. We shut it down."

I nodded. "Rhett'll keep the mood light. I'll keep the tempo."

His eyes met mine.

"I'll handle the noise," I added.

A breath passed between us.

"I know," he said, quiet. Then he looked back at the rink. "Let's make them *earn* their spot."

I grinned. "They don't stand a chance."

Roan skated off without another word.

The horn blew again and we dove back in.

THE BRACKETS DROPPED right about lunchtime, exactly when I expected. Coach walked into the locker room like he already knew the temperature and intended to reset it.

He didn't bark. Didn't raise a hand or his voice. Just let the weight of his presence carry the room as every player stilled mid-grumble or glance at their screens. Word spread fast. We weren't facing the Vultures in round one.

"No Vultures first," he confirmed, dropping his clipboard onto the bench like a gavel.

Disappointment flared across a few faces. I felt it, too. It wasn't just about rivalry, it was about momentum. About shutting that kind of noise down early. Sure, part of me had wanted to be the one to take Rylan out personally. I wasn't proud of it. But I wasn't lying to myself either.

Roan stood with his arms crossed, posture tight, but still. He didn't react with anger or annoyance, not outwardly. But I'd known Roan a long time. That stillness? That was steel being drawn. The rest of the team saw his command, his rock steadiness. Me? I saw the core. Rylan was so much meat when we got him in the grinder.

Rhett, predictably, was the first to break the silence. "You've got to be kidding me," he muttered to no one in particular.

A couple of guys echoed the same sentiment. Younger players, mostly. We'd been so locked in this week, preparing for blood. The Vultures were the kind of distraction that stuck like a burr.

Coach didn't flinch. Just gave the room one of his slow, deliberate scans.

"They've got three games to play before they even get a chance at you," he said. "Three. That's a climb. Meanwhile, you have your own path. Make no mistakes, we're going to treat every game like it's the damn championship."

That quieted them. Even Roan gave a faint nod. It made sense. Make them work. Make them *sweat* for the privilege of standing across from us.

Coach turned toward us again. His eyes swept from Roan, to Rhett, to me. "You think you've earned a break?" His tone sharpened just a touch. "You haven't earned shit yet."

He let that sink in.

"The bracket isn't the reward. The finals are. Make them fight for it. Every damn minute. You play hard. You play smart. You protect each other. You keep your heads."

I could almost feel Wren's name echo in that last part.

Coach pointed a finger, steady and grounded. "Let the Vultures make fools of themselves in the media. We'll handle our business on the ice."

The team settled like a tide rolling back. Energy redirected. Focus restored.

Roan caught my gaze across the room and gave a slight tilt of his head. *They're not getting through.*

I nodded back. *Not if we can help it.*

Rhett bumped my shoulder as we headed back toward the tunnel. "Still wish I could've decked Rylan first."

"You'll get your chance," I said with a grin. "Let them climb the ladder. We'll be at the top, waiting."

We hit the ice again like a unit forged in fire, sharper, harder, and totally dialed in. Roan snapped through corrections like a man possessed, but the team didn't flinch, not now. They absorbed the critique and adjusted. Rhett kept the energy high, his taunts just light enough to keep things competitive without sending the younger guys into ego overdrive.

And me?

I did what I always did. Kept us steady. Leveled the emotional pitch, bridged the space between Roan's intensity and Rhett's fire. Adjusted the tone when the tension got too thick, talked rookies through a failed play, gave pointers, tapped shoulders.

We were balancing each other without even thinking about it. Practiced. Trusted.

The bracket was just the start.

If the Vultures made it to the finals, they'd be crawling by the time they got there.

We'd be ready.

Waiting.

Hungry.

Ready to deliver the final blow. They picked the wrong damn team to start this fight with, and we had zero problems with ending it.

THIRTY-TWO

By the time I pulled into my driveway, the clock on my dash had just ticked past 11:42 p.m.

Every inch of my body ached—from the tops of my feet to the muscles behind my eyes—and I was pretty sure I'd drunk enough coffee today to single-handedly keep my favorite café in business for the next quarter. My throat was dry from too many press calls, and I had a half-dozen unread texts waiting for me about game-day coverage tomorrow.

But I still felt good. Tired, yes—but not defeated. The strategy was solid, the messaging tight. The league couldn't twist our words if we gave them none to twist.

Still, I'd barely seen the guys. Not since this morning, when Jay brought coffee and Rhett teased me into laughing despite everything. And Roan—Roan had been laser-focused. The kind of locked-in that made everyone else step in line without question.

So when the dark silhouette of his SUV pulled to the curb just as I stepped onto the porch, my heart leapt before my brain could catch up.

I turned toward the sound of the engine shutting off. A moment later, his door opened.

Roan.

He stood there a beat, backlit by the streetlamp. His shoulders tense, his jaw shadowed with stubble. Then he started walking, slow, deliberate strides that made something flutter in my stomach.

"You're supposed to be sleeping," I called, voice lower than I meant.

"So are you," he answered, and the corner of his mouth curved, just slightly.

"You okay?"

"I just needed to see you," he said simply.

That was it. No dramatic reason. No fire to put out. Just... me.

I didn't hesitate. "Come in."

Inside, the house was dim and quiet, the soft click of the door shutting behind us the only sound. I toed off my shoes and set my bag aside, watching as he followed me through the front hall like it was the most natural thing in the world.

Maybe it was. Maybe we'd already passed the point of pretending otherwise.

Upstairs, I guided him toward my room with a touch to his wrist. My fingers barely grazed his skin, but the reaction was immediate. His breath shifted, his eyes dropped to where I touched him, then lifted back to mine. He let me lead.

In the bathroom, he shed his shirt first as I stripped out of my suit. I didn't mean to grab it—but once he took it off, my hands just... moved. The fabric was soft and still warm from his body. I tugged it over my head without thinking.

Roan caught the motion in the mirror, just as he rinsed

his hands and braced them on the edge of the sink. His eyes met mine through the reflection.

And lingered.

That same shirt hung loose on me, hem brushing the tops of my thighs. He didn't speak, but the heat in his gaze said enough.

He looked... undone in a quiet way. Not tired, exactly. Just stripped down, like the armor he wore all day was left somewhere out on the ice.

His gaze drifted to the bathroom counter, just for a second.

The bottle of suppressants sat there.

Unopened.

He didn't ask. Didn't comment. But I caught the faint tension in his jaw. Saw the question forming behind his eyes, even if he bit it back.

I didn't offer an explanation. When I held out my hand, though, he closed his fingers around mine instantly, tight, warm and solid.

"You were there when I needed you," I said softly, pulling him closer. "I'm here for you now."

He didn't move for a long beat. Then his forehead dropped to mine, his breath catching on the exhale.

"You have no idea how much I needed to hear that."

"I think I do."

He wrapped an arm around my waist, just holding me there in the soft, still air between us. Neither of us said another word as we turned out the lights, moved toward the bed, and climbed under the covers. It wasn't about sex. Not tonight. It was something quieter. Stronger. A tether instead of a fire.

As I lay curled against him, his arm draped heavy and protective over my waist, I realized something:

We were building something. I couldn't wait to see what we became.

❧

THE SOUND HIT ME FIRST.

Even from behind the thick glass of the owner's suite, the roar of the crowd rolled over my skin like a wave—electric, pulsing, alive. The stadium was packed, fans screaming, faces painted, jerseys in team colors flooding the stands like a crimson-and-blue tide.

Playoff energy wasn't just different. It was primal.

And we were home.

I stood just behind the front row of the suite, arms crossed loosely as I scanned the rink, already tracking the players on the ice as they flew through warmups. Every sharp turn, every stop, every slap of blade to puck sent a shiver through the arena, and somewhere deep in my chest, it echoed.

I should have been exhausted. Two hours of sleep, max. A single cup of coffee on the way in. A to-do list longer than my arm. The press briefing I gave this morning already felt like it happened last week.

None of what happened before tonight mattered. This was the first game of the playoffs.

Everything from this moment mattered now.

"Nice turnout," Marchand murmured beside me, holding a tumbler of something probably older than I was. His suit was sharp, and his tie in team colors, of course, was bold. I'd nearly smiled when I noticed.

"We sold out in under four hours," I said, cool and measured. "Merch sales spiked, too. Ticket bundles for rounds two and three already pushed capacity limits. If we advance, we're golden."

"When," he said, not bothering to hide the pride in his voice. "Not if."

A quiet laugh escaped me, despite myself. "You'd better knock on wood."

He did—with one knuckle, against the edge of the bar behind us.

The suite was crowded tonight, and I knew nearly every person in it. Press, sponsors, a couple of league executives who made polite conversation but were clearly more interested in whether the Howlers could keep up the performance we'd delivered all season long. There was pressure in the air, disguised as small talk. I kept my posture open, my tone smooth, my game face firmly on.

The puck dropped five minutes later, and the temperature in the building spiked like someone had lit a match.

Roan dominated the first shift. Not flashy, he never played that way. He was always controlled, like he was the hinge the entire game swung on. Jay was pure speed, weaving through the defense with balletic precision. And Rhett... God. Rhett was fire.

He sprawled across the crease like a menace, pads slamming, crowd roaring.

Marchand took a slow sip of his drink. "That man is going to get fined."

I didn't bother to argue.

Because two minutes later, Rhett stacked the pads on a two-on-one, popped back up grinning, and launched the puck down the ice in a pass so filthy it set up Jay for a clean, effortless goal.

Just like that, we were up by one.

The crowd *exploded*. Fans jumped to their feet, the chant

rolling through the arena like thunder—*Howlers, Howlers, Howlers.*

I didn't sit. Couldn't. My pulse was high and steady, my palms tingling. My gaze never left the ice.

It wasn't just a game.

It was a *declaration.*

This wasn't about Rylan, or the Vultures, or whatever narrative the league thought it could spin. It wasn't about gossip or scandal or smear tactics.

It was about the ice. The team. *Us.*

My phone buzzed once in my pocket.

JAY:

You standing up? Thought I felt it. ;)

I bit back a laugh and sent a quick reply:

Maybe. Play harder and I'll scream.

Another buzz.

JAY:

God, please. Roan will check me into the glass.

My smile faded only slightly as I tucked the phone away and focused back on the game.

Because the other team came to play, too.

And this? This was just the beginning.

THE SECOND GAME was blood and blades.

If the first had been a show of dominance, the second was a straight-up brawl with a puck in the middle.

From the opening shift, I knew it was going to be ugly. The air in the arena was charged, the noise sharper, more frantic. Fans were louder, more rabid. Every slap of the puck, every scrape of a blade on the ice sounded like a challenge. And the opposing team had clearly watched film and come in swinging.

They wanted to rattle us. They wanted to slow us down.

They wanted Roan.

I knew it the moment he took his first shift. He skated clean, precise, measured, but I didn't miss the faint stiffness in his shoulder, the way his right arm didn't extend quite as far when he checked another player. Most people wouldn't notice. But I did.

I *felt* it.

And it made my pulse pound.

Roan didn't show pain, not even in the locker room last night after the win. He let the team doc look at the hit he took in the third, kept it light, let Jay and Rhett rib him a little, even smirked when I arched an eyebrow at him. But I'd seen the way his jaw clenched. The way he rotated the shoulder when he thought no one was watching.

He could play through it.

But I hated that he had to.

Even now, watching from the owner's suite again, surrounded by sponsors and execs and media handlers pretending not to sweat, I had to fight the urge to bolt downstairs, grab a stick, and start knocking heads myself. My skin buzzed under my blazer, nerves stretched taut and tuned to my guys on the ice below.

Marchand didn't hover, but he lingered nearby. "They're targeting him."

"They're trying to find a weak point," I agreed, keeping my voice even. "They think if they get Roan off the ice, the rest will unravel."

"They'd be wrong," he said after a beat. "But not *completely*."

No. They wouldn't unravel. But Roan was more than our captain. He was gravity. Rhythm. Pulse. Without him… things would fracture.

Jay was working overtime to keep the plays flowing, and Rhett—my beautiful, reckless, wild thing—was putting on a show in the net. He'd already stolen three sure goals and earned a penalty for taunting a forward who tried to crowd his crease.

The doc had eyes on the bench, just off the tunnel. I caught his expression once through my binoculars — calm, focused, calculating. He'd check every player post-game, just like he had the night before. But if Roan couldn't keep his range, I knew the choice might be taken out of his hands.

And I didn't know what that would do to us. Or to *me*.

Because I was running hot tonight.

Overclocked. Wired.

The tight bun I'd worn to keep things professional was already coming loose. My blazer had come off after the second period when the temperature in the suite climbed with the energy of the crowd. There was a crackle in my blood, like static, and every breath I took had to be slow and deliberate. I wasn't in heat, not even close, but I wasn't *not* feeling something.

I caught one of the league execs watching me out of the corner of his eye.

Not the time, buddy.

A hard whistle pulled my focus back to the ice just in

time to see Rhett stop a breakaway cold and kick the rebound to Jay, who swung it to Roan. He shot across the blue line like a missile. The goal was dirty — scrappy and wild, with two defenders on him and one clinging to his jersey — but it counted.

2–1, Howlers.

The crowd lost its mind.

I didn't cheer.

I *breathed.*

They were back on the ice less than a minute later.

Still fighting. Still leading.

And I couldn't stop watching the way his shoulder moved.

When the buzzer finally blared and the game ended with a narrow win, my heart was hammering. We had the victory — barely — and as the team moved toward the handshake line, I pulled out my phone.

Texted one word to the group thread that had become a quiet lifeline:

> Status?

Roan responded first.

ROAN:

> Functional. Mostly pissed.

JAY:

> No dislocations. No new bruises. No sense of self-preservation. So, same.

RHETT:

> Can confirm. Would still hit.

My snort surprised the people near me.

I smiled anyway. Let them wonder.

Because my boys weren't broken.

Tomorrow, we'd fight again.

I'D THOUGHT I knew what tension felt like.

I'd walked through scandal, through the storm of Rylan's bullshit, fielded reporters like landmines, turned press releases into weapons, and spun narratives with a smile. I'd held my own in boardrooms full of alphas and billionaires. I'd even walked into heat with three of the most powerful men I'd ever known and come out the other side still standing.

But this?

This was different.

This was *war*.

From the moment the puck dropped in the third game, the ice was a battlefield. Not a game. Not a match. A *grudge*. Our lead in the series had the other team frothing, and the strategy was clear: hit hard, hit fast, hit dirty.

Roan knew it. He read it in the first thirty seconds and adjusted accordingly, but there was only so much a captain could do. Jay played smart. He was fast, fluid, always one step ahead. And Rhett, god help him, was the chaos we needed when the tempo threatened to stall. But the danger was pulsing under the surface, waiting.

From the box, I could feel it coming. The way the crowd leaned forward. The shift in the rhythm of the plays. The brutal hit Roan took in the corner that didn't even draw a whistle.

The look on Jay's face when he snapped something low to one of the refs under his breath, and the way the ref *didn't* respond.

Something was off.

And then... it happened.

Jay had the puck on the rush, slicing through neutral ice like he was born there. Roan was wide, ready. And even from across the rink, I could feel Rhett's focus in the crease, locked on the play like he was already bracing for fallout. The play was fluid, beautiful—until it wasn't.

From the blind side, a defender launched.

Full body. High elbow.

Time slowed.

I couldn't even scream. The sound caught in my throat as Jay's head snapped back, his body went limp mid-air, and he crashed to the ice like a broken marionette.

The crowd sucked in a breath.

Then silence.

Then chaos.

Rhett was out of the crease and on the guy who hit him before the whistle even blew. Roan was there a second later, fists clenched, fury barely contained. The other player was dragged back by two teammates and a ref, but Rhett wasn't backing off — not until Roan shoved him hard and pointed to Jay.

Jay.

He hadn't moved.

I didn't remember standing. Didn't remember the way I must've shoved past someone in the box—a sponsor, maybe one of the owners—didn't hear Marchand bark my name. All I knew was that I had to get *down there*. My body was moving before my brain caught up.

But the med team was already on the ice.

One checking Jay's vitals. Another stabilizing his neck.

I stopped just short of the glass, my palm flat against the cold as they lifted him onto the stretcher. The whole arena was a vacuum. Thirty thousand people and not one of them made a sound.

Except for Rhett.

He stood frozen in the crease, chest heaving, like the net was the only thing keeping him from going feral all over again.

Roan stood near the bench, his knuckles white where they curled over the top of the boards.

Jay disappeared down the tunnel taking what felt like half of my lungs with him. When I finally turned back, Marchand had stepped beside me. His mouth was tight, his jaw clenched, and for once, the CEO mask had cracked.

"Medical team's on it," he said. "We'll get you updates the second they know."

I nodded, even if the motion didn't feel real. I was aware of too many things at once — the hush in the box behind me, the murmur of the crowd, the buzz of my phone in my coat pocket.

The referee skated to center ice. Five-minute major for the hit. Ejection.

Not enough.

Nothing would be enough.

Roan skated back into position. Rhett didn't move, not even when the ref waved him back into the crease. He just stood there, shaking with restrained violence, like the net itself was the only thing keeping him from tearing someone apart.

The game resumed, but it wasn't a game anymore. No,

it was a reckoning, and they'd united the whole team in wanting to take them down.

If the league didn't do something after this, I'd burn the whole damn system down myself.

THIRTY-THREE

ROAN

The final buzzer didn't sound so much as it cracked through the tension like a hammer on ice.

We won the game, even though it didn't feel like it.

I didn't skate the handshake line. Neither did Rhett. We left that to the rest of the guys while we headed straight for the tunnel, our gear still on, helmets in hand, every muscle tight enough to snap.

Jay should've been here.

That hit had been dirty as sin. The player aimed high, adjusted his timing and went specifically for Jay. The kind of move that was supposed to have been outlawed a decade ago. I'd watched it play out in real time and I *still* couldn't wrap my head around the angle. Jay hadn't even seen the bastard coming.

I had.

Too late.

My jaw hurt from clenching. My gloves had blood in the lining. It wasn't Jay's, thankfully, but mine, from punching the wall of the locker room tunnel when they'd taken him off the ice.

The moment I stepped into the medical wing, I found him in the exam room, hooked up to the monitors, his eyes open now but glassy. Pupils still sluggish. Doc was with him. One of the trainers. The lights were dimmed.

"You're fine," I muttered under my breath, a prayer to the universe as much as a report to myself. "You're gonna be fine."

"You here to babysit me?" Jay's voice was hoarse, but there was a thread of life in it.

I moved to the side of the bed, planting one hand on the rail. "No. I'm here to break both your kneecaps if you try to put skates back on too soon."

Jay grinned. It didn't last long. The wince that followed twisted something in my gut.

"He's lucky," the doc said, stepping back. "Concussion, yes. But it could've been a lot worse. He's already more alert. We'll keep him monitored for the next twelve, twenty-four hours. But he's off the ice until I clear him."

"No arguments," I said.

Jay raised a hand in surrender. "I'm concussed, not stupid."

I was going to kill someone for this.

"Coach is in the locker room." Rhett's voice came from the hallway. "Livid."

"He mad about the hit?" I asked.

Rhett snorted. "He's mad I nearly threw hands in the middle of the third period. Gave me the whole 'play smarter, not hotter' speech."

I stepped out into the hall and found the other alpha, shirt off with a bag of ice pressed against his jaw. His knuckles were raw, still smeared with the evidence of his restraint.

"He thinks I cost us momentum," Rhett said, tone sharp enough to cut. "Even though we won. Even though they tried to fucking *murder* Jay out there—"

"Hey." I stepped in front of him, blocking the nearest bench he looked one second away from launching across. "We don't waste energy chewing glass. You want to kill someone, wait until the league review drops."

Rhett's nostrils flared, his jaw ticking.

Then—a very decisive click of heels.

She was there.

Wren.

Hair pulled back, coat still on — and a look in her eyes like she'd just walked through fire and hadn't noticed. The moment her gaze hit Rhett, he stilled. That wildness in him pulled back like the tide retreating from the shore.

When she shifted that look on me, it was all I could do not to wrap her in my arms and bury my face in her neck.

"You okay?" she asked. It wasn't just her words, but how her voice was low, soft, and checking on me, even as she held herself under the firm grip of control.

I nodded. "You?"

She didn't answer. Just moved past me and into the medical room, crouching next to Jay's bed like she belonged there.

Jay blinked at her. "Hey, boss lady."

She smiled. Then curled her hand around his, brushing her thumb gently over his knuckles.

I stepped back, gave her space. Rhett did too, watching the quiet scene from the hallway.

It hit me then what just happened. Not the win or the rage bubbling beneath my ribs or the violence of what happened and needed to be repaid in kind. It was *Wren*. The three of us and *her*.

The way she'd come in and calmed Rhett with a look. The way Jay lit up when he saw her. The way my heartbeat evened out knowing she was with us now.

She had become our gravity.

Despite everything I promised her about not using her heat to bind her to us, every damn one of us was already caught in her orbit. I couldn't be mad about it. It was *her*.

Jay's eyelids fluttered again, half-lidded and heavy. He was fighting the fog, but not well.

"His pupils are better, but I don't like the way he's still drifting," Doc said with a frown that didn't ease even as he pulled back from the bed. "I'd prefer he get a CT and full evaluation. I want to transport him to the hospital, rule out anything more serious before I even think about letting him out of my sight."

Jay groaned. "Doc..."

Wren didn't flinch.

"That's fine," she said, already rising from the chair beside him. "I'll follow you. As soon as I handle the press, I'll meet you there."

Jay shifted, brow furrowing. "You don't have to—"

"Yes, I do," she said simply, smoothing her hand down his arm. "So try not to fight me about it. You're staying with me tonight once we get the all clear."

There was no anger in her words. No push. Just certainty and it worked.

Jay blinked up at her again, like she'd hung the moon. "Okay."

My shoulders loosened a fraction. That right there— that's what he needed. Not orders. Not pressure. Just her, steady as hell, making it all make sense.

"I'll ride with him," Rhett said, stepping up beside the bed, and I knew without him saying it—he was making sure *I* didn't have to go. He was covering Jay. And leaving me to cover Wren.

I caught his eye and gave him the smallest nod. *Got it.*

Doc still didn't look thrilled. "You're not family," he pointed out, directing that at Wren.

She gave him a cool smile. "According to team documentation, I'm listed on every one of their emergency contact forms. Including Jay's."

Jay hummed, clearly trying not to grin. "She made me do it."

"That may be." Doc crossed his arms. "Still doesn't make it protocol."

"I'll sign whatever release you want," Wren replied. "You're taking him to St. Luke's?"

Doc hesitated, then nodded. "I'll allow it. But I'll be the one clearing him for release. Not hospital staff."

"Understood." She was already reaching for her phone.

Jay glanced at Rhett. "You okay driving?"

"I'm better than you," Rhett said dryly. "And I don't have a head injury."

Doc muttered something about alphas being terrible patients as he turned to prep for transport.

"Not an alpha, Doc," Jay mumbled, but that didn't seem to help his case. It was my turn to hide a smile.

I stayed where I was, still braced in the doorway, watching as the pieces clicked into place around her. Wren didn't raise her voice, didn't bark commands, didn't posture. Yet everything shifted as soon as she took control. Rhett backed her play. Jay relaxed. Even Doc fell in line.

Then the door opened again.

Marchand.

Of course.

He didn't speak right away, but I didn't miss the way his gaze cut from Wren to Jay to Rhett before landing on me. Assessing. Calculating. He didn't miss much, but I knew that look. He wasn't thrilled with what he'd heard.

Still, to his credit, he didn't interrupt the medical decisions being made. Not until Doc and Rhett wheeled Jay out ahead of them, headed for the back entrance and the waiting transport van.

Only then did Marchand speak.

"You've got the press wrangled?" he asked Wren, voice low and careful.

She didn't turn around. "I will. Give me ten minutes. Then I'll be at the podium."

"You're really taking him home?" There was a sharpness to the question, one he tried to temper but didn't quite manage.

Turning slowly, Wren arched one eyebrow. "Do you have an issue with your head of PR ensuring a key player gets medical clearance and support in a stable environment?"

"I have an issue with optics." Marchand exhaled slowly. "And unnecessary exposure."

I stepped forward. "He's already exposed. The hit was in front of a stadium full of fans. You think the press aren't already all over it?"

His jaw tightened.

Wren, cool as ever, didn't take the bait. "I've already drafted the statement. We're controlling the narrative. But I won't pretend that Jay's going to be sitting home alone with a bell to ring if he needs help. That's not who we are."

Marchand's gaze slid between us again. Measuring. Finally, he just gave a clipped nod. "Handle it."

"Always do," Already tucking her phone into her blazer, she just gave him a return nod.

I watched him go, jaw tight. Distrust swarmed through me. I had no idea what he was up to, but I wanted to be ready to intercept.

"You okay?" I asked once we were alone again.

She turned to look at me, that calm exterior finally cracking just enough to show the wear underneath.

"No," she admitted. "But I will be."

Closing the distance, I pressed my forehead to hers. "We're right behind you."

Her hands curled in my shirt, just for a second. Just long enough.

"I know," she whispered. Then, just like always, she pulled herself together. Straightened her spine. Smoothed her expression. Composed, she headed out of the medwing on a direct course for the press room like she was going to war.

Because she was.

And damn if I didn't love her for it.

The thought hit with the weight of a freight train and the gentleness of a whisper. No fanfare. No dramatic revelation. Just truth—solid and steady in my chest like it had always been there, just waiting for me to stop trying to explain it away.

I *loved* her.

Not the idea of her. Not just the fierce firebrand who could command a room, or the woman who'd tangled herself in my sheets and scent.

I loved the way she carried the weight of the team without complaint. The way she reached for Jay's hand when she thought no one was looking. The way she spoke

Rhett's language in jokes and sideways glances and never tried to rein him in, only anchored him.

The way she looked at me like I was both her shield and her soft place to fall.

And yeah, I realized I'd been in love with her for a long damn time. Maybe since before she even knew what she meant to us.

Maybe since before *I* did.

So I stood there in the quiet left behind, watching her disappear down the corridor, heels sharp on concrete, hair catching in the harsh light, already halfway into her next battle—and I knew with unshakable certainty, whatever came next, however far this went...

She was *it* for me. Always had been. Absorbing that knowledge, I blew out a breath then stopped wasting time.

Threw on a clean team polo, tugged off the pads and gear with the kind of speed I usually saved for third period tie-breakers. Barely took a second to wipe the sweat off my face, and splash water on the back of my neck.

There wasn't a bruise on my body that mattered more than being close enough to see her hold that line.

Because Wren was out there, already fielding questions, already shielding Jay from rumors and controlling the narrative with that deceptively calm voice and those razor-sharp eyes. Even if she didn't need backup, and she never looked toward the wings once—*I* needed to be there.

Not as a captain. Not for the team. For her.

So I slipped into the media gallery, off to the side where the spotlight didn't quite hit. Arms crossed. Jaw tight. Watching.

God, she was already in motion and absolutely stunning. Standing at the podium, headset on, crisp blouse under her jacket, a Howlers pin gleaming silver at her collarbone. That cool, clear voice projected across the room like she was commanding an entire battalion.

"Jay Kim's condition is stable," she said evenly, eyes scanning the sea of reporters. "He was evaluated on-site, and our medical staff, under Doctor Halvorsen's direction, made the call to transfer him for further observation. No official statement on his return will be made until that evaluation is complete."

A hand went up from someone in local press—Salazar. Always fishing. "Is it true he was unconscious for over a minute? Is this a potential season-ending injury?"

Her eyes narrowed by a degree. "I won't speculate on a player's health when the final call belongs to a physician. But I will say this: Jay Kim is one of the strongest athletes I've ever had the privilege of working with. If there's a way for him to come back this season, he'll find it."

Clean. Calm. But there was steel under every word. The room knew it too, because the usual murmurs were replaced by scribbling pens and the sharp click of keyboards.

Another voice cut in, this one was national press, maybe even league-affiliated. "There's speculation the injury was avoidable. That it stemmed from the Howlers' aggressive formations this series. Is the team playing too recklessly?"

My jaw ticked, and my arms tensed, but Wren didn't so much as blink.

"Physical play is a part of the sport," she said, "and if anyone is suggesting that players should hold back in the playoffs, then I'd question whether they've ever actually *watched* a game. The Howlers are aggressive. But we are not reckless. We are trained. Tactical. Committed."

She paused, then added, "If there's concern about reck-lessness, I'd suggest reviewing the tape of the hit that took

Jay down. Because my concern isn't our style, it's that a deliberate charge like that wasn't flagged."

A ripple moved through the room. She'd done it. Turned the question inside out without even breaking stride.

That was the moment she glanced up, just for a second. She didn't say my name or nod, but my awareness of her hummed and climbed up a notch as she found me in the shadows and stayed on me.

That look grounded me. Hit deep and true like my knot when I'd taken her. I was exactly where I wanted to be— here for her.

THIRTY-FOUR

WREN

It was late—so late the streets felt half-dreamed—when Roan pulled the SUV up in front of my house. The hum of the engine died, leaving only the faint tick of cooling metal and the low hiss of the wind. Jay had been quiet most of the drive, slouched against the window, the soft rhythm of his breathing just uneven enough to keep me glancing over at him.

The doctors had said his concussion was serious but not dangerous. Clean scans, steady vitals. They'd kept him longer than he liked, of course, poking and shining lights in his eyes, asking the same questions over and over. He'd answered them with that same lazy charm that fooled no one, least of all me. He was hurting, but trying not to show it.

Rhett followed behind us in my car, headlights a steady presence in the mirror. We'd all agreed it made more sense that way—Roan and I had driven separately, but there was no way I wasn't riding home with Jay. After everything that night, I needed to see him safely through my front door, into my house, into a bed that wasn't sterile and white and humming with machines.

We'd won the third game. The Howlers were advancing. The finals were close enough to taste. But none of that mattered with Jay having gone down. The arena seemed almost preternaturally too quiet, when his body had gone limp on the ice. Even now, hours later, the image made my stomach twist.

As Roan slowed to park at the curb, I caught the flicker of flashbulbs—brief, sharp bursts that turned the night electric. My pulse spiked. "You've got to be kidding me," I muttered. "Who the hell—"

"Press," Roan said flatly. His jaw was already tightening. "They must've been waiting since the hospital release."

"Roan, I've got it." I reached for the door handle, but he shot me a look—alpha calm over alpha fury.

"Your job is to protect the team," he said, voice low and even. "My job is to protect *you*."

Before I could argue, he was out of the car, shutting the door behind him and cutting across the street like a wall of intent. Cameras flared, voices rose—sharp, fast questions about Jay's condition, the team's odds, my supposed *relationship status*. Roan didn't raise his voice, didn't even have to. His presence alone was enough to make most of them backpedal.

From inside the car, the world out there looked almost cinematic—Roan standing there, broad shoulders blocking the glare, the press retreating with muttered complaints. Rhett pulling my car in behind us, lights going off, and I could already picture his expression when he saw the scene. Roan was right to get out first. He'd have words otherwise, and none of them gentle.

Jay stirred beside me, blinking awake. The movement was slow, like surfacing from deep water.

"Hey," I said softly. "Home."

He looked around, then smiled—a hint of teasing in his warmth despite the pain visible around the corners of his eyes, and so *him*. "Home," he echoed. "Good word."

I wanted to reach for him, but I didn't. Not yet. He was still pale, and his pupils—though finally even—made me ache to check again.

Jay exhaled, shoulders sinking. "You know, I could've handled a little press. Given them my good side."

I gave him a sidelong look. "You don't *have* a good side right now. You look like you wrestled a brick wall."

"Won, though," he murmured, smiling again.

I shook my head but couldn't help returning it. "Barely."

He was still grinning when he said, voice quiet but sure, "At least this story has a fun ending."

I arched a brow. "Does it?"

His grin widened, dimple flashing even through the exhaustion. "Yeah. I get to sleep with you tonight."

I rolled my eyes, heat creeping up my neck despite myself. "You're concussed."

"Still true."

He leaned back, eyes closing again, a small, satisfied smile on his lips. Blowing out a breath, it felt like I was releasing my first real exhale in hours.

Outside, the flashes stopped. Roan had sent them off, likely with a warning look designed to keep them away. No matter what, we'd be the story. And I'd deal with it when I had to. The press wasn't the important one right now.

When the last car pulled away, Roan came to open the back door to help Jay. The fact Jay didn't argue was all the confirmation I needed that he was hurting way more than he was saying.

I hurried ahead to the front door, keys trembling a little in my hand as I fumbled with the lock. Behind me, I could hear Roan murmuring to Jay, steady and patient, while Rhett's footsteps crunched up the walkway.

The door finally gave, swinging open on the soft scent of home—cedar, laundry detergent, something faintly floral from the unlit scented candles in the living room. I flipped on the entry light just as Roan and Rhett came in, Jay's arms slung over their shoulders, his feet dragging a little.

"Upstairs," I said quietly. "My room."

They nodded without question, the three of them moving in practiced sync, like they'd done this a hundred times before—though never quite like this. I led the way, every creak of the staircase feeling amplified in the stillness of the hour.

When we reached my room, I turned down the covers and helped guide Jay to the edge of the bed. Rhett set his hand briefly on Jay's shoulder, eyes scanning him with quiet worry.

"I'll grab water," he said. "And the pain meds."

"Thanks," I said, and he disappeared down the hall.

Jay groaned softly as I knelt in front of him, fingers working at the buttons of his shirt. "There are easier ways to get me in bed, you know," he murmured, that crooked half-grin tugging at the corner of his mouth.

I couldn't help the answering smile that curved mine. "Who asked for easy?"

He laughed, low, rough, and a little pained. The sound hit me straight in the chest. When I helped him out of his shirt, then eased him down to his boxers, he didn't protest.

He just looked at me, eyes soft, dark, and full of that quiet affection that always seemed to undo me.

"Don't get any ideas," I said, cupping his cheek with one hand. His skin was warm beneath my palm, his lashes heavy with exhaustion. "You need to get better first."

He turned his face slightly into my hand, that faint, dizzy smile still there. "I already am better," he whispered. "'Cause I'm here."

Before I could respond, Rhett came back in carrying a glass of water and a couple of pills. "Doctor-approved," he said, handing them over.

Jay managed to take them without complaint, then sank back against the pillow, out cold almost before I'd pulled the blanket up over him. I brushed a hand through his hair once, gently, before stepping back.

Roan and Rhett both lingered near the doorway, their postures saying what their words didn't. Neither of them wanted to leave.

I sighed softly. "The bed's not big enough for all of us."

"I'll take the couch," Rhett offered immediately, already halfway to the hall.

"You could use the guest room," I pointed out. "It's more comfortable."

"Yeah," he said with a small smile. "Alright."

Roan didn't move, though. His gaze stayed on me, steady, assessing. "I'm staying in here," he said simply.

"I figured," I murmured.

Before the silence could thicken, I stepped forward and wrapped an arm around each of them. "Congratulations, by the way," I said, my voice roughening with emotion I'd been holding back since the rink. "You guys played your hearts out tonight."

Rhett gave a soft huff of laughter, squeezing me back. "Wouldn't have it any other way."

When I started to shake, it took me a second to realize it was happening. The adrenaline, the fear, the relief—it all hit at once, leaving me trembling in their arms. Roan pulled me tighter against his chest, solid and grounding, while Rhett closed in behind me, his chest blanketing me in warmth from the contact.

I was caught between them, surrounded by strength and safety, and for the first time since Jay went down, I let myself cry.

The tears came hot and quiet, hidden against Roan's shirt. Neither of them said anything, and they didn't need to. The only sounds were the slow rhythm of their breathing and the faint, steady heartbeat pressed against my ear.

For a few minutes, that was enough.

The house had gone still after Rhett settled across the hall. I could hear the faint creak of the floorboards, the distant rush of water from the guest bathroom's sink, and then nothing but the soft sound of Jay's breathing.

Roan stood near the door a moment longer, watching Jay with that steady, protective focus of his. Then, when he seemed satisfied that our beta was truly asleep, he returned his attention to me.

"Go get ready," he said quietly. "I'll stay with him."

There was no arguing with that tone. There rarely was.

I nodded, slipping into the bathroom for a fast shower to wash away the last of the night from the scent of the hospital to the sting of fear I'd been carrying. By the time I came out, face damp, hair loose and brushed, Roan was at the edge of the bed, kicking off his boots and pulling his shirt over his head.

The sight of him, all solid lines and quiet restraint, did something to the remaining tremor in me. He didn't say anything—just folded his clothes neatly, the motion unhurried, grounded, like he was doing it as much for me as for himself.

"Get in," he said softly, once I hesitated near the bed.

I did. The mattress dipped beneath my weight, the warmth of Jay's sleeping form nearby comforting in its own right.

"I'll be right back," Roan said, pressing a kiss to my head. Then he vanished into the bathroom. One fast shower later, he was back, sliding in behind me, his bare skin brushing mine as he settled. The contact made me inhale sharply, not out of surprise, but because it felt *safe*. Like my body finally believed we were home.

He rested a hand at my waist, not possessive—grounding. My faint trembling hadn't stopped completely, but the steady rise and fall of his chest against my back helped slow it.

"Talk to me," he murmured after a long silence.

"I'm okay," I whispered. "Mostly."

"That's not what I asked."

I smiled faintly. "You never actually asked anything."

He huffed out something close to a laugh. "Fair. Then let me try again." His thumb traced a slow, absent line over my hip. "You dazzled me tonight, cool, competent, in control as always and you stepped in front of the press in their feeding frenzy like the damn champ you are."

A smile tugged at my lips. "That's the job." My smile faded as a small shudder rippled over me. "Jay scared the hell out of me."

He didn't deny it. Just breathed out and pressed his forehead briefly to the back of my shoulder. "Yeah."

The warmth in my throat caught for a second. "I'm tougher than I look."

"I know that," he said, voice low, almost reverent. "That's half the problem."

For a while, we just listened to Jay's soft breathing and the wind brushing the windowpanes. The world outside felt far away—the arena lights, the noise, the cameras.

"We've got a day," I said after a while. "Before we know who we're facing next."

"Then we rest," Roan murmured. "When the time comes, we fight like hell again."

"That's the plan."

He was quiet, long enough that I thought maybe he'd fallen asleep. But then his hand tightened gently at my waist, grounding me again.

"Wren," he said, and I could hear the shift in his tone— the careful edge that meant he was thinking too much, weighing his words. "After all this—after the playoffs are done, win or lose—can we talk?"

"Talk," I echoed softly.

"About this." His breath brushed the back of my neck. "You and me. The guys. Figure it out."

The words wanted to be a request, but the way they came out—steady, certain, laced with command—made it something else entirely. Typical Roan. Trying to ask, and still leading.

The funny thing was, I didn't mind. Not even a little. Because Roan *was* doing his best for me. For us.

"Yeah," I whispered, turning my head enough to catch his gaze over my shoulder. "We can talk."

His eyes softened, something like relief passing through them. "Good," he said quietly. Then, almost under his breath, "I just need to know we're not losing this too."

I reached down, finding his hand and threading my fingers through his. "You're not," I told him. "We'll figure it out."

He pressed a kiss to the curve of my shoulder, simple and sure, before his hold on me eased just enough to let me breathe again.

Within minutes, Roan's breathing evened out completely, following Jay into sleep. As tired as I was, I stayed awake a little longer, feeling the steady weight of them both there—one beside me, one behind me—three hearts still beating after everything that night had thrown at us.

We were going to be okay. Jay would get better. We'd kick the crap out of the next team, then the guys would take home a championship and the title.

I refused to entertain any other result. Roan shifted against me, the weight of his hand against my abdomen tightening as he pulled me more firmly into him. He didn't wake. I put a hand on Jay, wanting to feel him breathing, him *there*, and I swore he sighed in his sleep. His relief seemed to flow right through me. I lingered there for a while and then finally my eyes drifted close, and sleep swept me away.

THIRTY-FIVE

WREN

I woke to warmth and quiet. For a few long, drifting seconds, I didn't open my eyes. The world was all soft around the edges with weak sunlight filtering between the mini-blinds, the hum of the wind outside, and the slow rhythm of breathing that wasn't mine.

Jay's breathing registered first because I had my hand on his chest. It rose and fell steadily. Then the soft caress of Roan's breathing teased my nape. He was awake. I could feel it before I heard him shift, the subtle change in the air between us, the careful way his hand moved against my hip.

"Morning," he murmured, voice low, still rough with sleep.

I made a small sound that might've been a reply, or just the start of one. My body didn't want to move yet. To be fair, my brain didn't want to move either. The exhaustion had sunk deep, the kind built on a house of cards staged on a foundation of stress, overcommitment, and emotional duress.

"Hey," he said again, softer this time, closer. His nose

brushed the back of my neck, and then the faintest press of his lips followed—barely a kiss, more like a promise of one.

That was enough to nudge me fully awake.

I twisted slowly, easing my hand off of Jay carefully so I wouldn't jostle the bed too much or disturb him. The light caught Roan's face just right from messy hair that was adorably scruffy, the stubble shadowing his jaw that added a grittier, bad boy vibe to his look and stunning eyes, the clearest I'd ever seen them.

"Morning," I managed, voice scratchy, small. "How long have you been awake?"

"A while." He smiled a little. "Didn't want to wake you. You looked... peaceful."

I snorted softly. "I don't think I've felt peaceful in weeks." I almost said *ever*, but that seemed a bit hyperbolic. The past few weeks, on the other hand, had been rough.

"Then maybe it's about time." He curled his arm around my neck, rolling me over so we were face to face. The gentle brush of his calloused thumb against my cheek, captivated me, My body reacted before my brain fully processed his action, leaning in toward him as I tilted my chin a little higher to give him better access.

The space between us shrank until there wasn't any at all. The first touch of his lips to mine was a slow, almost tentative kiss. He tested if I would welcome the contact while not demanding. The man undid me utterly with how thoughtful he was even in passion. There was definitely passion. When I sighed against his mouth aware of the softest pressure, he deepened the kiss with a sweep of his tongue.

The world around us stayed quiet as he teased his tongue against mine and began to sweep his tongue in and out, The gentle thrusts echoed the way his hips pressed against mine. The thin barrier of his briefs were nothing to the weight of his erection as it seemed to pulse against my belly.

Behind me, Jay's soft breathing hadn't changed though the light seemed to dim, then grow stronger before it dimmed again. A storm front moving in, maybe. That thought drifted past the inferno Roan stoked and became so much ash as he shifted his grip to wrap his hand around my throat.

My pulse tripped, dashing down a flight of stairs until it was racing. The massage of his lips against mine demanded even as it coaxed. The trembling that haunted me the night before hadn't fully disappeared, yet it seemed to shift and change as he explored my mouth.

His kiss was so thorough, I forgot where his mouth ended and mine began. We breathed together, a dance of lips, teeth, and tongues. Every deliberate movement took us deeper, then it was just us communicating.

He traced the shape of my lower lip with his before daring me with teasing little licks that I had to answer. It was like we communicated in some unspoken language and it rolled through my body like a building storm. The weight of his cock, thick and ridged and right there had me writhing against him.

The necklace he formed with his hand flexed against my throat as I rotated my hips, seeking to add another layer of tension to this dance between us. I dug my nails into his bare shoulders as he slid a finger under the gusset of my panties, then he was delving deeper against the liquid softness.

A rush of heat spilled into my system and he bit down on my lower lip, the sting riveting me in place as he thrust one, then two fingers into me and traced his thumb against my clit. I obeyed and began to rock my hips, riding his hand as he laved his tongue over the bite before he deepened the kiss once more.

I was all but purring into his mouth as he bumped his hips up once and I slid a hand down to wrap around his cock. It poked upwards from his waistband, all hot and silken and utterly hard. Alternating between squeezing and stroking, I answered the motion of his fingers with my own.

Groaning, he pushed three fingers into me, stretching me even as I caressed a thumb over the blunt tip of his cock where beads of pre-cum leaked. The moisture added to the ease of my strokes and it was my turn to bite at Roan's tongue. The lightest scrape of my teeth and there was a rip as my panties tore and then he replaced his fingers with his cock.

He urged me upwards as he pushed just the tip in. Hiking my leg higher, he eased his access and then I groaned as I surged toward him. The first rush of him filling me, stretching me, coiled the tension in my belly even tighter.

Still, he didn't release my mouth. Instead, he mirrored the thrusts of his cock with his tongue. He had one hand on my hip while the other stayed firmly around my throat. It should feel controlling, dominating, and overwhelming— but all I experienced was adoration, desire, and fuck— pleasure.

Guiding the movement of my hips, he sank in deeper with every thrust. There was no hurry to this sex, no rush, he seemed intent on making me feel every exquisite inch of him. I fisted his hair, rocking with him in the deliberate rhythm he set, and glorying each time he ground against me.

The lazy coils of pleasure tightened inextricably with

every hard push of his cock inside and the teasing pressure of his weight and friction against my clit. When he sucked on my tongue, squeezed his hand, and rolled me onto my back to begin to pound into me, I saw stars.

The motion stretched me as he pushed into me deeper and deeper with each stroke. The angle added another layer of intensity to his taking and then all I could feel was him. The trembling translated to a full body quiver as the tension pulled so taut, I was ready to burst.

I wrapped my legs around his hips, helping with the angle and arching my body to meet his thrusts. He played my body as masterfully as he pursued a puck on the ice. Then like a string of bombs detonating slowly but gaining in intensity, my orgasm struck.

One rolled into another, then another until sobs tore at my chest and Roan licked the screams from my throat. Not once did he let up on the rhythm, slamming me forward from release to release until the world blurred utterly. I was nothing but sensation and motion, obeying his body as he plowed into me and when he let out a shout, I held on as the tremors ripped through him.

The feel of his knot engorging stole my breath, because he filled me to bursting and still stretched me further. I clung to him, dragging him back in for a kiss, so intimately aware of every single inch of him touching me and how.

I had no idea an alpha could knot when I wasn't in heat, but I cherished the feeling of it, the heavy weight and how utterly my body melded to his. The feeling was transcendental. I hung in the space where bliss and desire collided, splintering me utterly and leaving me marked.

Tears slid out of my eyes, hot and wet, and utterly unexpected. He rained kisses down on me, lapping up the salt before kissing me again. The pressure of his grip on my throat eased and he stroked and petted me as I shook, yet his knot remained so firmly entrenched, we were one.

Roan didn't end and he seemed to pound himself into my soul, his breath was mine, his heart pumping the blood in my veins, and his scorching presence etched into my bones. How long we lingered there, I had no idea.

He buried his face against my throat, his body a hot blanket over mine. We clung together, floating on the lazy river of pleasure until bit by bit, his knot began to deflate. But the rush of cum filling me threatened to leave me drunk on him. The mess was utter decadence and I treasured the connection.

A shift on the bed registered and I turned my head to find Jay staring at us, pupils blown and his lips curved into the sexiest smile. "Good morning," he said in a voice thick with need and still a little rough from sleep.

"Did we wake you?" I whispered, not the least embarrassed for having been caught utterly destroyed in Roan's arms. Hell, my inner muscles kept fluttering around his cock and it was semi-hard again already.

"Worth it," Jay whispered before he stroked a hand over my hair. "Can I kiss you?"

"Yes."

No hesitation, not even a single drop of it. When he leaned in to kiss me, Roan stayed where he was. The stroke of Jay's tongue against mine tasted like sweetness and hope. It was a balm to the scrapes his injury left on my soul. His kiss was full of heat and hope and—happiness. The bubbles of it seemed to float through me.

Roan nibbled kisses to my throat before he raised his head. Jay lifted his at the same time and the two men locked eyes.

"How are you feeling?" Roan was all captain, all alpha, measuring and testing.

"Hard," Jay admitted without an ounce of shame. "Hungry." Then he dipped his gaze back to me. "Horny as fuck. Waking up to the two of you is the best goddamn thing all week."

A shiver raced through me and my nipples went taut. Roan studied Jay for another moment, then glanced down at me. "Do all the work for him, Wren…"

I grinned, fresh passion bursting through me in a flashfire. I wanted Jay and I wanted him now. Roan's command just seemed to intensify that desire to utter desperation.

"I can—" Jay started, but Roan was already pulling out of me as I sat up and between us, we pushed Jay onto his back. I peeled his boxers down and he hadn't been lying. His cock was thick, the veins bulged out on the underside and the tip was a mottled color, his need so damn apparent it had to be pain.

"Do you have a hole you want most?" I asked Jay, eying his engorged cock. I could swallow him, if Roan helped, we could lube my ass or…

"Cunt," Jay said on a gasp as I wrapped my fingers around him and gave him a firm pump. "I want to fuck you through Roan's mess. Mark you up and—" The rest ended on a gasp as Roan lifted me and I angled Jay's cock, and between us, I had Jay mounted and inside of me.

Roan pulled my shirt upward and off, baring my tits and Jay stared up at me, dazed as I began to ride him. Behind me, Roan stroked my ass. "Harder, Wren. He can take it. He wants to feel every inch of you and you have to pound to let him go deep."

It was like being utterly drunk on them and yet hyper aware at the same time. Unlike heat, I wasn't mad with the desperation to just be fucked. Yet, I wanted to fuck them until they were the ones weeping with it. Jay covered my breasts with his palms, massaging them and then tugging, first gently, then with more of a hard twist.

Hand on my back, Roan pushed me forward until my breasts were at Jay's face.

"Suck her sweet tits," Roan told him. "She likes it when you give her a little pain."

Jay needed no other encouragement, he sucked a nipple against his teeth even as he twisted the other with just a little more force. It was my turn to gasp as I flexed and gripped at his cock even as I slid up and down. The squelch of wetness as he pushed up into me was almost an aphrodisiac and then Roan speared his fingers into my ass, and the pressure filled me to bursting.

Over and over, I rocked on Jay until he let out a hard grunt, his whole body stuttering and then Roan slapped my ass. The sharpness of the pain coupled with Jay's shudders sent me over the edge and I came again. The combination of their cum filled me and I let out an almost keening scream before the world seemed to spiral into shatters of light.

When I floated back to earth, Jay and Roan were taking turns petting me and Roan's cock was nestled against my cunt and Jay was already stiff again.

I blinked slowly as Roan fisted my hair and tugged my head back. The nudge of his blunt head pushing into me alongside Jay's cock where he was still buried in my cunt sent another shock to my system.

"Yes?" Roan asked—no, Roan demanded. The heat in his eyes had gone from a gentle fire to a raging inferno. I couldn't have said no even if I'd wanted too. I flicked a quick look to Jay who squeezed my hip to let me know he was on board.

"Ye—" I didn't even finish the word before Roan pushed in and Jay and I were both gasping at the intensity of it. What came next was a series of hard, swift pumps as they stretched me past pain into a world where I writhed on pleasure. They were so damn hot and I was fuller than I'd ever been and yet they didn't relent.

I heard their sharp shouts as they came, the brutal force so intense, I screamed. I was pretty sure I came twice in those moments before I blacked out utterly.

Fuck, we might need to burn this bed too.

CHAPTER

THIRTY-SIX

WREN

Jay looked better. Still pale, still moving gingerly, but the shadow that had haunted his face last night was gone. It was replaced by something softer, and—if I was being honest—by the smug curl of a man who'd woken up in the middle of a very pleasant tangle.

Not that I was complaining.

My body ached in all the ways that made me want to smirk into my coffee instead of limp to the shower. Roan's handprint was still faint on my hip, a ghost of possession that somehow didn't make me bristle the way it once might have. And Jay—damn him—had managed to make being injured look rakish, half-lidded and dangerous when he'd leaned in between us earlier that morning.

It was ridiculous how easily they both unraveled me. Worse, how easily I'd let them.

The kitchen smelled like coffee and something buttery, sunlight pooling across the counter where Rhett stood barefoot, shirt unbuttoned, looking every inch the chaos he was. His grin split wide when he caught sight of us.

"You could at least pretend," he said, voice low and teasing, "that you didn't enjoy yourselves without me there."

Jay made a sound that might have been a laugh, though it came out rough. Roan only shook his head, calm as ever, reaching for a mug like Rhett hadn't just accused us of debauchery.

I would've rolled my eyes if my legs didn't still feel like jelly. "Maybe if you'd been in there, you'd be suffering too instead of ready to go for later." The last slipped out of me, far dirtier than I intended but I found I didn't mind it that much.

Rhett's dimples flashed, wolfish. He was such a bad boy and so damn over the top with his comments. Not that I was complaining. Nope, not even a little.

"Suffer?" he scoffed on a laugh. "Sweetheart, that's not what it sounded like, but I promise to be up to any other pleasuring you might need later."

My face heated, traitorous thing that it was, but I refused to give him the satisfaction of a blush. "Keep talking and I'll make sure later *is* a *lot* later."

Roan's quiet chuckle from behind me was almost worse than Rhett's grin. It slid under my skin, steady and sure, like it always did, like he *knew* how to disarm me without saying much at all.

Jay leaned his hip against the counter, eyes half-lidded, that faint, sharp smile tugging at his mouth. "Play nice, Wren. He's just jealous."

"Damn right I am," Rhett said. "You all look far too pleased for my liking."

"Maybe we're just happy you're awake before noon for once," I shot back, reaching for the coffee pot. My hands were steady, my voice light, but under it all, something quiet and full had settled in me.

Peace.

It was strange, that word. Foreign. But I could feel it all the same, threading through the soreness, the laughter, the way they looked at me like I wasn't just an omega to be managed, but a person they wanted to *know*.

Rhett swept a hand toward the counter, where takeout containers were lined up like a feast. "Before anyone complains, yes, I went out. Got the good stuff—croissants, eggs, fruit. Don't say I never do anything for this pack."

This pack. That phrase hit hard. Were we becoming a pack? Was that what we were building? Even as I tried to process the words, I tucked them away. If I focused on them too hard, it could disrupt the warm serenity of the moment. I wasn't ready for that.

Not yet.

Jay eyed the spread, then reached for his mug.

"No coffee," I said quickly, catching his wrist before he could take a sip.

He made a sound somewhere between a grunt and a growl, glaring at me through a strand of black hair. "You can't be serious."

"Head injury," I reminded him. "Caffeine's a no-go for at least another few hours."

Roan was already circling around him, calm and methodical. "Look at me, Jay." He tilted Jay's chin up gently, checking his pupils in the morning light. Jay tolerated it, barely.

"Still reactive," Roan murmured.

"Still in pain," Jay countered, voice rough.

Leaning against the counter, Rhett folded his arms and

watched them both with a faint smirk. "Could probably take another pain med now. Or—" his grin went wicked, "you know, science says orgasms help with pain management."

This time Jay didn't measure his reaction, he half-groaned, half-growled even as he rubbed a hand over his sweet face. "You're insufferable."

"You're welcome," Rhett said with a wicked grin warming his expression. His honey brown skin held a glow in the morning sun, but nowhere near as much as the glee shining in his brown eyes.

Roan's shoulders shifted like he was trying not to laugh. It didn't work. He turned away, the corner of his mouth betraying him.

Without missing a beat, I smiled sweetly as Rhett took a deep drink of his coffee, probably as much to taunt Jay as to enjoy the caffeine himself, then said, "Thank you for volunteering our time later for Jay. I want him to orgasm as much as he needs."

Rhett sputtered coffee so violently it almost came out his nose. Roan outright laughed this time—low and rich—and my poor Jay looked like he was regretting every decision that had led to this conversation.

"Guess I walked into that one," Rhett said, wiping his chin with a napkin, still grinning.

"Walked? You strutted," I shot back.

"Alright, fine." He held up his hands in mock surrender. "I'll be good."

"Doubtful," Jay muttered, taking his pills with a swallow of water.

We made quick work of unpacking the food, the clatter of dishes and easy ribbing filling the quiet corners of the kitchen. It felt... good. Comfortable, like something we'd all been pretending we didn't need until it was right here in front of us.

When we finally sat down, Roan caught my hand before I could take a seat. With a single tug, he pulled me down onto his lap instead. His arm settled around my waist, heavy and warm, his nose brushing just beneath my jaw in a lazy kiss that sent a shiver down my spine.

His eyes—steel-gray and intent—held mine. "Mind if we share you this morning," he asked softly, "or would you rather sit on a hard chair?"

I snorted. "As opposed to your hard thighs?"

It was Jay who nearly choked this time, on his orange juice. Rhett thumped the table, laughing outright.

Mouth curving, Roan met my gaze entirely unrepentant. "Hard muscle and hard wood are totally different things."

"Lucky for you," I said, leaning back against him with a smirk, "I've got experience with both."

Rhett let out a low whistle. Jay groaned again—but this time, there was laughter under it.

Just like that, the morning light turned a little warmer. The pain and chaos of the night before faded beneath the hum of connection, messy, imperfect, but real.

I rotated from Roan's lap to Jay's side mid-bite, teasing Rhett with a wink as I balanced a forkful of scrambled eggs. The coffee steamed between my fingers, the rich smell mingling with the buttery scent of croissants and the faint tang of orange juice.

"Careful," Rhett said, leaning forward to snag a bite from my plate. "You're making me hungry *and* distracted."

"Good," I said, sliding onto Roan's lap again. "That's the point."

Jay snorted beside me, reaching for his glass, while

Roan kept his arm snug around my waist. We laughed, joked, rotated seating, passed food back and forth. It was lazy, easy, and for a brief time, completely ours.

Then my phone buzzed on the counter and I popped up to grab it. The screen flashed Marchand's name.

"Oh, hell," I muttered.

Roan's gaze flicked to me, steel-gray eyes unreadable, while Rhett leaned back, eyebrows lifting. Jay's dark gaze narrowed in a mix of curiosity and anticipation.

"Marchand?" I answered, lifting the phone.

"Wren!" His voice was sharp, electric, laced with anger —but also that gleeful undertone that always made my teeth grit with excitement. "I don't even know *how* the game went into overtime! And now the league decides after the fact?"

I could practically see him pacing. "It's gone all the way to the Vultures. Can you believe it? The audacity."

And then that undertone, that almost feral thrill he always had when there was a chance to annihilate a rival team—well, it slithered through the phone line like liquid fire. "I want the fans whipped into a frenzy. I want the Howlers *howling* while I'm speaking. You're on press duty— *now.*"

I inhaled, steadying my voice as my fingers tapped out notes in the air. "Understood. I'll get the messaging out."

Marchand let out a bark of approval. "Good. Don't waste a second. The next ten days are going to be vicious unless the Howlers lock down four wins immediately— best of seven. I don't want excuses, Wren."

I exhaled into the phone. "No excuses here."

As I spoke, I felt their eyes on me, the three men in my dining room. Every so often, one of their phones buzzed.

Likely Coach. Jay's lips pressed into a thin line as he read whatever popped up. Rhett's dimples flickered with restrained amusement at a text, and Roan's calm demeanor didn't falter, but I knew he had already scanned the alert before I even noticed.

The air was charged already from the warmth of breakfast, the sunlight, and the feel of their bodies pressing into mine. But that same air now went electric as it pulsed with strategy, stakes, and the knowledge that the next ten days weren't going to be gentle.

"Alright, Marchand," I said, my tone tight and professional now, though my body hummed from breakfast and the morning's playfulness. "Fans are about to get *very* excited. And you'll have the Howlers behind you all the way."

"Good," he growled, and the line went dead.

I set my phone down, letting out a slow breath. The playful chaos of our morning hadn't vanished, just... shifted. Now the work was about to hit, full force. I had three very patient, very aware men here to keep me grounded, entertained, and maybe a little dangerously distracted.

I set my coffee down, finally letting myself acknowledge the truth I'd been skirting all morning. They couldn't be a distraction for me, and I didn't need to be one for them. Not now. Not with the Vultures breathing down our necks. Especially Rylan. That bastard had an axe to grind, and the rest of his team wasn't far behind.

Roan sighed softly, just once, but it was enough to make me glance at him. He wasn't tense, at least not outwardly. Yet the quiet weight in his shoulders told me he had already begun bracing himself. Rhett scowled at my words, muttering creatively about every slight Rylan had ever inflicted, and even Jay, usually sharp with his humor, gave a slow, deliberate nod. The pain around his eyes had eased, but he was still fragile. I knew him well enough to recognize the subtle twitch of restraint he used to keep from moving too soon. But if he sensed even a hint of weakness in the team, he'd be on the ice.

And they needed Roan focused. I could see him already steeling himself, setting aside his personal wants, his desires. The captain the Howlers needed, not the man I wanted to press against in moments like these. That ability to hold himself apart from his own urges. It was one of the things I loved most about him. Despite Rhett's bitching, which was relentless, loud, and increasingly creative about Rylan and the rest of the Vultures, no doubt existed within me that he would back Roan's plays every step of the way.

Jay's voice broke through my thoughts, quiet but firm. "Your work starts now."

I offered him a small smile, the warmth softening the tension. "Yes," I said, "but you can still stay here..."

Both Roan and Rhett raised their brows, amused, incredulous, maybe even slightly scandalized. I grinned. "All of you can."

They knew, though. Once the finals started, this cozy, messy, sunlight-filled breakfast, this teasing and laughing and leaning on each other, would have to be put on hold. Their focus would need to be absolute. I wouldn't pressure them, wouldn't pull at them. I'd be there to support however I could, quiet and steadfast, from wherever they needed me to be.

Roan's clear steel gray-eyed gaze found mine, unwavering and serious. "When the finals are done—we talk."

There was no question in that statement. None of the

others intervened. I didn't fight it, didn't push. None of them had asked about the suppressants, and I hadn't volunteered a word.

"Yes." My voice was simple. Clear. Certain.

Win or lose, when the finals were done, we would figure out our pack.

CHAPTER

THIRTY-SEVEN

ROAN

PRE-GAME

The locker room smelled like sweat, leather, and raw adrenaline, and I thrived in it. The Howlers were fired up, bouncing on the balls of their feet, sticks tapping against benches and floors like they were trying to drum the arena itself awake. I moved down the line, clapping hands, bumping shoulders, letting my voice cut over the roar before the game even started.

"Listen up!" I said, forcing calm over the surge of energy. "This isn't just any series. This is ours. The Vultures think they can push us around. They think Rylan's antics intimidate anyone here. They're wrong. Every hit, every check, every shot—we take it to them."

The guys leaned in, eyes sharp, voices low but buzzing. They wanted this. They *needed* this.

Jay's bench was quiet, at least compared to the rest of us. Doc had just finished a final check, nodding slowly. Jay flexed his fingers, tested his knees, then gave me a look that said: "I'm cleared, but don't expect me to go easy." I didn't.

397

Rhett was pacing near the lockers, spinning a puck with his stick, half-grin on his face, half-serious, fully dangerous. "They won't know what hit them," he said. "If Rylan opens his mouth, I'm gonna—" He let the sentence trail off in the way that made everyone in the room imagine exactly what would happen, and it made them laugh. Tension broken, energy higher.

I turned my attention to the screen above the benches. Wren's face appeared on the close-circuit feed, crisp and commanding, smiling like a challenge as much as encouragement. Her voice was calm, measured, but every word struck like lightning. She was speaking directly to the team and the fans simultaneously, building fever pitch in the arena. They'd been streaming in for an hour already, the crowd growing louder with every second, chanting our name.

For a beat, I swore it felt like her sharp whiskey-colored eyes met mine, and I felt that grounding pull—the same one she always gave me. Then she was off again, voice cutting through the roar: *This is your time, Howlers. Own it. Play hard. Play smart. Play for each other.*

I let the words sink in for the guys. They didn't need me to translate. She didn't just hype us up, she reminded us who we were.

Rhett leaned closer, voice low. "She's terrifying and perfect at the same time."

I didn't answer. I only nodded, letting the focus settle. The adrenaline, the fire, and the noise were all fuel. Jay's eyes flicked to me, a subtle smirk breaking through the tension. He was ready. So were we.

The arena was coming alive outside, and inside, our pack tightened. One heartbeat. One purpose. The finals were here.

The locker room emptied faster than I expected, the team moving toward the ice like predators on instinct. I followed last, giving a final glance to Jay, who was stretching deliberately, testing each muscle, each joint. His black hair fell into his eyes, but I didn't need to see his face to know he was ready. Doc had cleared him, but the fire in those narrow eyes told me he'd push himself to the edge anyway.

Rhett was already at the far end of the rink, gliding lazy circles through his crease, stick flashing as he played keep-away with a couple of overconfident forwards who thought they could sneak one past him during warm-ups. He exaggerated every save—dramatic glove flashes, sprawling pad slides, even a mock slapshot clear that sent the puck ringing off the boards.

Even in warm-ups, he demanded attention.

His grin was wide, dimples flashing, but there was precision beneath the chaos. Every movement was deliberate. He knew exactly how to hype the team without breaking their focus.

"Come on, rookies!" Rhett called from the crease. "If you can't beat me in warm-ups, you're not scoring all night!"

It drew laughter and groans, but also sharpened something in the younger players. They started skating harder, shooting faster.

I stepped onto the ice, keeping my pace steady, deliberate. My eyes swept the rink, tracking lines, posture, tension. I spoke sparingly, correcting positioning with a tap of my stick or a shift of my shoulder. Leadership wasn't loud—it was controlled, measured, and earned.

"Head up, Carter! Eyes wide! Don't let them dictate the tempo!" I barked, and the forward adjusted instantly.

Rhett skated up to the edge of his crease as I passed, knocking his mask up with a laugh. "Steely glare, huh, Captain? Relax a little. You'll scare the Vultures before they even make it to my net."

I shot him a glance, flat and sharp. "They already think we're weak if we laugh too much. Don't give them reason to change their minds."

He raised his hands, still grinning, but let it drop into the rhythm of the warm-up. That's what made him invaluable. He could lift spirits without ever breaking the focus we needed.

I caught Jay weaving through drills, movements clean, careful, measured—but with that edge in his stride that said, *don't get in my way today.* My shoulders relaxed just a fraction; the team was ready.

The Vultures' presence was a weight even on the ice. I could feel the tension in every pass, every fake, every slapshot bouncing off the boards. The crowd's energy had started to seep in, the chants and roars through the arena creating a pulse that mirrored ours. Every player was keyed in, but they fed off the electricity rather than letting it control them.

I took a deep breath, feeling Rhett's easy confidence brushing against the edge of my focus, Jay's steady intensity, the way our lines flowed together. Our team was cohesive. Fierce. Dangerous. That mattered more than anything the Vultures could throw at us.

RHETT

GAME 1

The Vultures skated onto the ice like they owned the place. Their lines were tight, their hits sharp, their eyes full of challenge. The adrenaline hit me like a punch, muscles coiling, heart thundering. This wasn't a warm-up. This was war on ice, and I was the last line of defense.

The arena was alive, the fans already howling, the energy rolling over the boards and into the crease like electricity. I caught a flicker of Wren's face on the overhead screens—calm, commanding, setting the crowd on fire—and instinctively scanned the stands toward where she'd be. That grounding pull, that tether to something beyond the rink, steadied me just enough to lock in harder.

Rylan was first. Of course it was Rylan. Former Howler, now Vulture, jaw set, eyes cold and sharp, a constant physical and mental threat. He crashed our zone with a sneer, throwing cheap shots, slashing sticks, crowding the net every chance he got. Every time he drifted into my crease, my blood boiled. He wasn't just a rival—he was a problem I fully intended to shut down.

The puck dropped, and I went feral.

Every shot, every deflection, every ugly bounce across the blue paint was met with ruthless focus. My glove snapped up, my pads flared wide, my stick cutting angles before they even opened. I felt the ice under my skates, the thrum of the crowd behind me, the roar vibrating through my ribs. I was locked in. Nothing existed except puck, posts, and the relentless pressure of the Vultures.

Rylan tried again, barreling into one of our defensemen, then drifting too close to my crease like he wanted a reaction. I didn't even blink—dropped low, smothered the puck, and let my pads shove him back just enough to make the point. He spat something sharp at me as he peeled away, and my gloves tightened around my stick.

Oh, it was personal now.

Roan was everywhere, controlling lanes, directing traffic, blocking shots like a man built for war. I tracked him mid-pass to Jay, their timing perfect, rehearsed, lethal. My focus snapped back to the slot just as Rylan charged again—I cut the angle and swallowed the shot before it even had a chance.

No goals today. Not on my watch.

Late in the third, tied 2–2, the tension was a living thing. Every save I made punched through the crowd, the chants feeding straight into my bloodstream. Then Roan threaded a perfect pass to Jay, and he buried it.

The bench exploded.

I slammed my glove into the post and pumped a fist, letting the roar wash over me. Controlled chaos. Statement made.

Final: Howlers 3 – Vultures 2.

Series: Howlers lead 1–0.

As I skated toward the bench, still breathing like I'd just survived something feral, my eyes flicked back to the over-heads—Wren's calm, commanding face still there, still fueling the crowd. Roan gave me a quiet nod. Jay was grinning, shaking his head at my running commentary and muttered threats about Rylan.

And me?

I leaned on my stick and muttered, just loud enough for the nearest forwards to hear,

"Come at me, Rylan. You're not getting past this crease again."

Home ice.

Team intact.

Net locked down.

We were going to slaughter them.

JAY

Game 2

The roar of the crowd was different today—edgier, louder, as if they knew we were walking into a storm. Coming off last night's win, the energy should have been electric, but Roan's focus kept it tethered, grounded. He moved among us like a lighthouse, quiet but unyielding, making sure we didn't ride the high too far. I leaned into it, inhaled the rhythm of the locker room, letting my beta nature keep the guys centered. Calm, composed—ruthless when the puck dropped. That was me today.

Warmups were charged. I skated through the drills, eyes forward, hands tight on my stick. Then I saw him. Beckett Rylan. Circling where Wren stood talking to the press near the ice, during the warmups, visor down, smirk sharp, a predator marking territory. My jaw tightened. I felt more than saw Roan's gaze flare across the ice before it settled back into his composed stare. I needed no warning. Rylan wanted to get a rise out of Roan. This was going to be brutal.

All too soon, the puck dropped. Game on.

Rhett owned the crease. He was a wall—unshakable. Every shot found him, every rebound he controlled. Thirty-nine saves, each one keeping our lead alive. I was moving like a shadow, threading passes, driving the net, staying deadly calm in the middle of chaos. I could feel Roan's temper simmering under the surface, could see the mental calculation behind every movement, every check.

Then, it broke.

A sloppy rebound snuck past Rhett late in the game. One. Two. The Vultures pounced, exploiting every turnover, shutting down our top line. I kept my cool, let the frustration roll through me, tucked it into the cold efficiency of my skating. Stay composed. Stay lethal. That was the only way forward.

Midway through the second, the inevitable happened. Roan and Rylan dropped gloves in center ice. Savage. Personal. Primal. It was so beyond Roan's normal behavior, the feral buzz set the arena on *fire* as well as the team. Every swing, every shove, every collision carried old grudges, unspoken history and just *raw* fury. I stayed low, watching, ready to move, letting the fight unfold as it had to.

Rhett faced forty shots by the final buzzer. Forty. He kept us in the game longer than we deserved at times, but the relentless pressure finally cracked the wall.

Final: Vultures 4 – Howlers 1. Series tied 1–1. Roan got a game misconduct and a fine. We left the ice simmering, the sting of defeat raw. The Vultures had come out with intent and executed, exploiting every weakness. But I didn't panic. Calm. Composed. Determined.

We'd bounce back.

We always did.

WREN

Game 3

The desert sun hammered down outside the arena, a dry heat that pressed against the glass and seemed to seep into the stands, carrying the same hostility we'd feel the second they stepped on the ice. I tightened my grip on the tablet, scrolling through stats, updates, and last-minute adjustments while the crowd built into a roar, the air thick with anticipation. The Vultures had a chip on their shoulder, and we needed to feed it right back to them.

From the moment the puck dropped, it was clear that the brutality from the first two games was about to be amped up considerably. Every pass, every shot, every check carried the weight of revenge, and I could feel the Howlers responding in kind. Jay was everywhere, moving with the precision and composure that made him a cornerstone, threading plays, setting up shots.

Then it happened. A blindside hit from Rylan, like he'd been waiting for the exact moment, sent Jay sprawling into the boards. My stomach dropped.

The bench erupted immediately. Rhett shot halfway up the ice before he had to be physically restrained, growling like a predator. Roan's hand on his shoulder brought him back, the calm authority cutting through the surge of anger. I took a deep breath, forcing my own pulse to steady. Focus. The team needed me right here, right now, not lost in worry.

Jay was grimacing, but the doc had cleared him as day-to-day, no complications from the previous concussion. He'd shake it off. I kept my eyes on him anyway, tracking every shift, every touch of the puck. I could see the fire in his dark eyes whenever he got close, the controlled beta energy keeping him in the game despite the pain.

Late in the third, everything came together. Roan exploded into Rylan with a hit that shook the ice. Thunderous. Primal. Pure captain energy. The arena went wild— Howlers fans were in the house—and the energy surged down the bench as the puck slid to Jay, who buried the go-ahead goal with effortless precision.

The final buzzer sounded, and we had it. Howlers 5 – Vultures 3.

Relief and adrenaline mixed into a potent rush, but I stayed sharp. Jay's injury had me on edge the whole game, but the doc confirmed, again, post game that it remained minor. I exhaled, letting my shoulders relax just a fraction, eyes still tracking the team as they celebrated on the ice.

The win felt hard-earned. The Vultures had come at us with everything, and we'd responded, not just with skill, but with focus, composure, and the pack mentality that bound us together. I smiled briefly, quietly, letting the sense of control and connection settle over me.

This wasn't just about the wins. It was about keeping them safe, keeping them steady, and making sure we were ready for whatever came next.

In the series, we led two to one.

CHAPTER

THIRTY-EIGHT

WREN

TWO-DAY BREAK – SATURDAY & SUNDAY

The hotel room felt like a furnace. I could feel my body gradually descending into heat again, a slow, insistent tide beneath the scent blockers. Every breath, every movement of Roan, Rhett, or Jay amplified the pull. Even in the empty hotel corridor, I sensed Rylan's presence like a predator's ghost, teasing the edges of my restraint.

I layered blockers constantly, drank cold water obsessively, and excused myself often from communal areas. Roan noticed. The subtle brush of his hand when I shifted, the barely-there check-in across the room. It helped. Jay stayed professional but close, a quiet anchor. Rhett, seemingly oblivious in his cheerful stubbornness, occasionally bumped me in passing, and I suppressed a shiver that had nothing to do with the temperature.

Alone in my room, journal open, I wrote:

This heat will be as brutal as the last. I will

407

make it through the Finals. I will survive. I will support them. I am not prey.

❦

GAME 4 – TUESDAY (HOME)

Home again. The arena smelled of ice polish and primal tension. My blockers were holding, barely, and every goal, every hard hit, every surge of alpha aggression made me acutely aware of my own body's state.

I stayed near the bench, clipboard in hand, scanning. I was ready to intercept the press and to answer any questions.

"Wren," Roan said, leaning slightly toward me, jaw tight, protective. "Keep eyes on the lines. Watch Rylan on the first shift, he's circling."

"Already on it," I murmured, masking the faint tremor of my pulse in my voice.

Rylan's gaze found me repeatedly. I could feel it, slicing through the blockers, a silent challenge. Every time he came near during pregame media scrums, Roan's shoulder brushed mine, subtle, protective.

The game itself was brutal. Rhett was outstanding, but Rylan capitalized on a defensive lapse, scoring twice. My body screamed beneath the layers of control, but I stayed grounded, focused on the team, not on the pull I felt toward either Alpha.

Final Score: Vultures 3 – Howlers 0. Series tied at 2–2.

I left the arena exhausted, the pre-heat gnawing at my muscles, my mind still racing from Rylan's provocations and the intensity of the physical play.

GAME 5 – THURSDAY (HOME)

Morning brought a dull ache and sharp awareness. My pre-heat had peaked overnight. I knew my blockers wouldn't fully mask me this time. Every breath carried a tremor of scent, but I forced calm.

"Good morning, Wren," Jay said, bumping into me in the hallway. His shoulder taped tight, he smiled.

"Hey Jay," I said, forcing a neutral smile and not letting myself react. I wanted their focus on the ice and not on me. I could do this for them.

The arena roared. I stayed near the press area, clipboard always at the ready. Roan's eyes flicked toward me occasionally—vigilant, silent—but I met none of his glances directly, keeping professional distance. Rhett and Jay were visibly fatigued, and Jay's movements were careful. He protected his shoulder.

Rylan prowled near the press area, smirk curling. I felt the predator scent brush past me despite blockers, heart jumping.

The Howlers played brutally smart. Roan blocked Rylan's attempts at disruption; Rhett's saves were flawless. Jay pushed through pain, assisting the game-winning goal late in the third. I exhaled quietly, coating myself in blockers mid-game, muttering under my breath: *Stay in control. This is not about you.*

Final: Howlers 2 – Vultures 0. Series: Howlers lead 3–2.

GAME 6 – SATURDAY (AWAY, ELIMINATION GAME)

The hotel room was stifling. Every sound, every shift in the locker room made my senses flare. My heat was fully active now, subtle but undeniable. Roan, Rhett, and Jay moved around me with silent awareness, protective but respectful, anchors against the storm inside me.

Rylan arrived early, lingering near the press entrance. His Alpha scent teased me, testing the limits of my restraint. I layered blockers, paced, sipped cold water, and journaled quietly: *You will survive. You will support them.*

The game was a physical war. Rylan was everywhere, aggressive, taking every opportunity to test Jay's shoulder and Roan's patience. Rhett's saves were miraculous, holding them in the game. Jay endured punishing hits but still contributed. I hovered near the bench, using every ounce of willpower to suppress instinctive reactions to both Rylan's presence and the draw I felt toward my pack.

Final buzzer had the series at Howlers 3 – Vultures 3 (forcing Game 7). My knees weakened slightly with relief and exhaustion, but I stayed upright, masking every tremor.

～

GAME 7 – MONDAY (HOME, CHAMPIONSHIP DECIDER)

The arena vibrated with tension, scent of ice and competition thick in the air. My blockers barely held. Rylan prowled, leaning subtly in my direction, calculating, Alpha instincts teasing me. My pulse raced.

The game was a brutal chess match. Roan and Rylan collided repeatedly, hits echoing across the ice. Rhett made incredible saves, Jay pushed past shoulder pain, and Jay moved with careful precision.

Every time Roan took a hit, my instincts flared, protective and primal. I caught his eye across the ice. An unspoken understanding passed between us: we would survive this, together.

Late in the third period, the Howlers executed a perfect play. Roan's defensive block led to a rebound, Jay tapped it in. The crowd erupted. I clamped my hand over my mouth, suppressing a gasp as my blockers nearly failed from the intensity of the moment and the surge of my heat.

Final: Howlers 3 – Vultures 2. Series: Howlers win 4–3. *Champions.*

~

POST-GAME / LOCKER ROOM & PRESS

The locker room reeked of sweat, blood, and celebration. Roan immediately came to me, brushing a strand of hair from my face.

"You did great," I told him, then swept my gaze to each of them. "All of you did. It was—amazing." I was so damn proud of them. Beating the Vultures had been as much about the team as it had been personal. If nothing else, they'd served Beckett Rylan his ass and giving Marchand a reason to *never* let that prick back on our team.

All I had to do was make sure that remained the case. I left the locker room before I could be persuaded to stay even a second longer. Even with blockers on my scent, close quarters with them were going to reveal the need.

I stepped up to the podium, the weight of the Apex Trophy Finals finally behind us, though the temperature in the room reminded me how close we had come to losing it all. The press had already begun their questions, cameras flashing, recorders buzzing.

My pulse was steady, but my mind wandered to the last moments of Game 7 — to Roan limping off the ice, the rookie forward who had buried the winning rebound, and Jay smiling through pain, his taped shoulder a testament to sheer determination.

"Wren, congratulations," one reporter began. "How does it feel to see the Howlers lift the Cup?"

I cleared my throat. "It's surreal. Every single player left everything on the ice. Whittaker led with heart, Rhett Navarro was incredible in net, and even the guys like Jay Kim fighting through their injuries showed why this team is special."

Another hand shot up. "There were some particularly heated moments between Roan Whittaker and Beckett Rylan this series. How did that affect the team?"

I paused, letting my gaze sweep the room before landing on a shadow near the back. Beckett Rylan sat there, arms crossed, expression unreadable. My stomach clenched. I hadn't expected him to attend, maybe I should have. Still, I refused to give him the privilege of my reaction and kept my voice steady.

"Their rivalry is... part of the narrative of this series," I said carefully. "But the Howlers stayed focused on the game. It was about the team, not any personal vendettas."

A reporter leaned forward. "What about your own role?

There was a lot of tension off the ice — some say you were a target."

I swallowed. "My job is to support the team. Behind the scenes, in the locker room and on the bench, I handle communications, strategy, and coordination. Yes, there's pressure. Come on, it's hockey. There's *always* pressure. But it's the same for every team staffer in a finals series."

A murmur ran through the crowd when Rylan shifted in his seat. I felt the subtle, familiar pull. His scent, alpha-strong and teasingly provocative, brushing against my awareness despite the distance. My throat tightened, but I forced a smile.

"And just to clarify," I added, "any distractions off the ice did not change our focus on winning. As you can clearly see by who won the finals."

Was that a dig at Rylan? Yes. I wasn't even ashamed of it.

Questions came faster after that, about the injuries, the future of the roster, and the team's next steps. I answered each with a professional tone, careful to stay neutral, to stay safe. But all the while, I felt him watching, a silent echo of the chaos on the ice, the tension that Roan had carried and that now, somehow, rested in the room with me.

When the conference finally ended, I walked away from the podium with my hands pressed together, exhaling slowly. The flash of cameras followed me, but my mind lingered on the look Rylan had given me from the back row, as if I needed a reminder that the war on the ice wasn't quite over.

The hallway outside the press room smelled faintly of bleach and stale coffee, but beneath it all, I could sense him —Rylan—like a predator who refuses to take the hint. My pulse quickened despite my blockers. He was already stepping toward me, slow, confident, smirk curling, as if he had every right to corner me.

I pivoted instinctively, moving toward the exit. "Excuse me," I said, keeping my tone clipped, professional, but the tremor in my pulse betrayed me just slightly.

Rylan mirrored me. "Wren. You're not just going to—"

Before he could finish, Marchand appeared, a solid presence between us. He raised one hand, blocking Rylan with a calm authority only he could wield. "Step back, Beckett. She's leaving."

Rylan hesitated, lips twisting, then nodded once, a silent acknowledgment of defeat for now. Security flanked him, and I exhaled quietly, forcing my pulse to slow as I slipped past. Marchand's eyes met mine briefly, just enough to reassure me, and I didn't need words.

Outside the arena, night had fallen. Cool air hit my face, almost shocking after the heat of the hotel and pressrooms. Security paced me as I walked briskly, the click of my boots on pavement the only sound except for the distant buzz of traffic. I kept my head down, blockers working overtime, and avoided any glance toward the parking lot where I knew Rylan might linger. The guards were professional, keeping an eye out until I was safely in my car.

By the time I reached the cabin, my body was still simmering under control, each step a small victory. I knew the guys would start their post-game celebration soon. Normally, I'd make an appearance—share a toast, a cheer, even a small laugh—but not tonight. Not after this week. Not after the Finals, the heat, the closeness, the way Rylan's presence gnawed at the edges of my restraint.

But I couldn't just vanish without leaving a bread-crumb. My fingers shook slightly as I punched in Roan's voicemail. I kept my voice low, teasing, playful, yet full of the tension I couldn't otherwise release:

"Same place as last time... and consider this an open invitation to chase. I'll be the omega on the run... claim me if you can."

I hung up, letting the words linger in the air like a spark. No one would expect it, not after the championship. It was a promise, a challenge, a tease—but most of all, it was mine.

Inside the cabin, I poured a glass of water, layered on extra blockers, and sank into the couch. The silence felt like salvation, a distance I desperately needed. My pulse still hummed beneath the surface, but for the first time all day, I allowed myself to relax just a little. I had survived the Finals. I had protected the team.

Soon... very soon, I hoped. They would come for me.

As I promised Roan, we'd settle this between the four of us.

I hoped.

THIRTY-NINE

The morning after the finals always hit differently. Normally, it was hangovers, scattered champagne bottles, and that hollow kind of exhaustion that comes after you've climbed a mountain you weren't sure you could survive.

This time, though, it was quiet. Too quiet.

We'd celebrated late. Like, *obscenely* late. The locker room had turned into a blur of champagne sprays and beer cans, Rhett leading a round of shots before Marchand cut him off for trying to drink from the trophy again.

When the party rolled over to the owner's suites, Roan had been his usual stoic self, taking it all in, watching over the guys like a proud, bruised sentinel. And me? I'd parked myself between him and Rhett, shoulder throbbing, half-grinning through the pain because, hell, we were *champions*.

But even as the night rolled on, one thing kept needling at the edge of my mind.

Wren never showed.

At first, it was easy to explain away. She probably got

buried under post-game press, coordinating with Marchand or handling the interviews. She always worked harder than any of us, and she'd been running on fumes for weeks. But then the night stretched on. The crowd thinned. The trophy made its way around the room twice. And still, no Wren.

By the time the bar lights came up, Roan was frowning into his glass like it had personally offended him. Rhett, who'd spent most of the evening alternating between jokes and borderline-decent karaoke, finally slumped into a chair and muttered, "You think she ditched us?"

"No," Roan said immediately. "She wouldn't."

That was the truth of it. Wren wasn't the type to just... disappear. Not without a reason.

I rubbed at my aching shoulder, already half-bracing for the scolding she'd give us when we finally saw her again—*because of course she'd find a way to make us feel like the idiots for worrying. God, she had talent and I adored her for it.*

That's when Roan's phone buzzed.

He frowned, thumbed the screen, then froze. The faintest sound leaked through the speaker—a low, playful tone that sent a pulse of adrenaline straight through me.

"Same place as last time... and consider this an open invitation to chase. I'll be the omega on the run... claim me if you can."

For a moment, the three of us just stared at each other, the words hanging in the air like a live current. My pulse kicked up, shoulder pain forgotten. I didn't even try to hide the grin spreading across my face.

"She didn't," Rhett said, but the gleam in his dark eyes said he *knew* she absolutely had.

"Oh, she did," I murmured, already feeling the thrill of it deep in my chest. It wasn't a biological tug, not with me, but it was still there sharp and electric because it was a challenge from *Wren*.

Brilliant. Beautiful. Breathtaking. From the classic cut of her sleek blue-black hair to the sharp intelligence in her whiskey-colored eyes, and the silken softness of her pale skin that never seemed to hold a tan—Wren captivated me. Just *thinking* about her was enough to make me hard.

Yet, my admiration for her smarts and my physical reaction to her body did not add up to the full sum of my feelings.

I loved Wren Foster.

Pure and simple.

Every delectable inch of her. I'd have loved her if she was alpha, beta, or omega. I needed her like I needed my next breath of air. She needed us too.

No doubt existed within me. If she hadn't, she'd have *never* sent that open invitation. Framed as a challenge with her impossible mix of control and chaos, she dared us to come after her on *her* terms.

Roan's jaw tightened, the smallest hint of a smile ghosting at the corner of his mouth. "She's at the cabin."

Rhett straightened immediately. "We're going after her, right?"

There wasn't even a pause. "Yeah," I said. "We're going."

One nod from Roan, all captain's calm and quiet command. "We give her a head start. Then we chase." Yet, there was a certain relish in his voice and his eyes. Despite his vaunted control, he was no less enticed than we were.

Laughing, Rhett tugged on a jacket. "Oh, she's not going to make it easy, is she?"

"She invited us this time," I reminded them both, heart thudding as anticipation tangled with something deeper, sharper, *real*. "She even gave us a clue. But do we really want her to make anything easy for us?"

Steady and knowing, Roan met my gaze and smiled slowly. "That's part of what makes her worth it."

Just like that, even the most dominant of our trio confirmed this wasn't about instinct, or dominance, or even the echo of the finals still burning through our systems.

It was about *her*. It had *always* been about her. Our omega—our Wren—who never let anyone define her except on her own damn terms.

RHETT

I couldn't stop grinning. Which, given the situation, probably said a lot about how messed up my head was.

Because, sure, normal people woke up the day after winning a championship, nursed their hangovers, kissed the trophy, maybe ugly cried a little in private. What did *we* do?

We packed up our gear, loaded into Roan's SUV, and decided to chase our omega into the goddamn wilderness.

Totally normal Tuesday behavior. I couldn't fucking wait.

Roan drove, jaw tight, eyes on the road like he was plotting a military campaign. Jay sat shotgun, shoulder still taped but looking about ten pounds lighter since we'd heard Wren's message. He was trying to play it cool, but every few minutes, his mouth twitched like he couldn't stop smiling either.

As for me, I sprawled in the back seat, boot tapping, heart thundering. That voicemail was still looping in my head like a song you couldn't shake.

"Same place as last time... and consider this an open invitation to chase. I'll be the omega on the run... claim me if you can."

It hit so hard that it rewired my pulse. I laughed under my breath. "You think she practiced that line?"

Jay snorted. "Doesn't sound like practice."

"No," I said, leaning back, letting my grin stretch wide. "It sounds like a goddamn challenge."

Roan's hand tightened on the wheel, and I could *feel* the energy rolling off him, not anger, not really, but something deeper. A heat that had nothing to do with the truck's vents.

"Wren doesn't do anything by accident," he said. Cool confidence kissed every single word. Sometimes I wanted to just poke him, like one would a bear, to see what would make him snap. Other times, I appreciated his control and leaned on it when my own frayed. Today? I wasn't sure which I wanted more.

"Yeah, no kidding," I muttered. "Woman throws down a gauntlet and disappears into the mountains like some kind of mythic creature. What are we supposed to do, *not* follow her?"

Jay shot me a look over his shoulder. His longer hair, fell over his forehead. Man needed a haircut, but he did messy bedhead well. Bastard. "Pretty sure that's the point."

I barked out a laugh. "Then we're already playing by her rules. God, she's good." A shiver went through my system. The craving for her had never really gone away, even when I worked to contain the reaction. With her permission, it boiled up to the surface and I didn't have to leash any of it.

The highway rolled by in silver streaks of early light. The mountains loomed ahead, dark and endless, the same ones we'd chased her through before. That memory was sharp and wild—Wren bare in that cabin, her body flushed pink with need and heat, her eyes blazing and the scent of her *heat* pounding into my pores.

She'd invited us back.

My blood was thrumming. Every nerve wired for motion, for *her*. I wanted to see her. Talk to her. Hell, I wanted to bury my face against her neck and just *breathe*. But first, we would play this game, we would bond our omega, and she would be a part of us forever.

Roan's jaw flexed again. The man looked like he was holding the universe together with willpower alone.

"So," I said, leaning forward between the seats, voice light, "what's the plan, Cap? We get there, we split up, we sniff her out? Or we play it slow, all dramatic, let her think she's got the upper hand?"

"You really can't help yourself, can you?" Jay turned toward me, smirking.

"What?" I grinned. "I'm contributing to strategy. I'm like—team morale."

"You're a distraction." Roan huffed out a sound that might've been a laugh.

"Exactly," I said. "And distraction's a *valid tactic*."

Truth was, the humor helped. It always did. Kept the edges from cutting too deep. Because underneath the jokes, the teasing, the easy charm—my blood was boiling. The wildness in me wasn't quiet anymore. It wanted her. Wanted *us* together.

Yeah, maybe that scared me a little. Because for all the jokes I cracked, all the smirks I threw around like armor, I knew one thing for sure: when it came to Wren, I didn't just want to chase. I wanted to *catch*.

Jay twisted the radio knob absently, static humming. "You think she's already there?"

I glanced out the window, the pine trees thickening as

we climbed. "If she's not, she will be soon. She's too smart to leave a trail she doesn't want us to find."

Roan nodded once. "Then we'll find her."

"We're bonding her, right?" I had to ask. We had the chance before, when her heat had been so out of control, she would have done whatever we asked. Begged us to bond her if we'd forced it.

Not that we *ever* would have. Roan had the right of it, leashing us, so that we filled her need and took nothing from her. Not then. Now? Now, she'd opened the door and I wanted to dash through it.

"Yes," Roan said. One syllable. Firm. Unyielding. "All of us." He shot a look at Jay. "You're in this."

"Damn straight." Jay gave a hard nod of his own. "She's *ours.*"

I smiled at that, the absolute certainty in their voices. The way they both declared it like a promise, an oath.

Outside, the horizon split open into a wash of gold light. The mountains rose up to meet us, sharp and endless and alive.

"Guess it's official, boys," I said, stretching, heart hammering as that wild, electric heat rippled through me again. "The chase is on."

Beneath all the laughter, all the bravado, there was this truth sitting heavy in my chest, what happened next would change all of us. We would mark her, take her, and when it was right, we'd knot her. She would be ours forever then. No one else for us and no one else for her.

I couldn't fucking wait.

"Don't suppose you'd consider driving faster?"

Roan didn't answer, at least not verbally. He did, however, put his foot down and my grin seemed to just grow.

We're coming, boots. Then you will be...

ROAN

The storm was coming in fast. You could smell the metallic tang of rain on the air, clouds boiling dark and low over the ridge. The trees were already whispering, restless, and the gravel popped under the truck's tires as we pulled up.

Her car was there.

That simple fact hit me like a punch and a relief all at once. The jolt of *she's here* cut through the rest of the noise in my head. The cabin sat tucked beneath the pines, just like before, weathered wood gleaming faintly with the last streaks of sunlight. The same porch. The same damned stillness. But this time, every nerve in my body felt tuned to her.

She was close. I could *feel* it.

We climbed out, the three of us quiet for once. Rhett's grin was gone, replaced by that sharp-edged focus he only wore in a game or in a fight. Jay rolled his shoulder, wincing, still sore, but he wasn't complaining. The silence wasn't awkward. It was electric. We all knew what this was.

The door creaked open under my hand. The cabin smelled like dust, wood, and Wren.

Christ, her scent was everywhere. Thick and warm, sliding through the air like silk. My control went tight, a muscle pulled too far. It wasn't just heat. Not this time. No, it was *her*. Every ounce of focus and defiance and quiet fire that made her who she was. I wanted to roll in it, breathe it, *live* in it.

Jay swore softly. "She was here. Recently."

"Yeah." Rhett's tongue clicked against his teeth. "And she was planning something. You feel that?"

I did. The faint hum of her challenge, like static on the air. Wren hadn't run. No, she'd taken *us* into account when she *crafted* this chase. She was so incredibly ours. It was just a matter of time.

I dropped my gear bag and pulled on the mask, the world narrowing, scent sharpening, every inhale a map of her. She'd been near the back door. She'd stepped on the porch. She'd—

The next scent hit me like a blade.

Rylan.

I froze. The name tasted bitter in my mouth. His scent wasn't old, less than a few hours. Not mixed with hers, but close enough to twist something deep in my gut.

"Son of a bitch," I muttered, voice low, raw.

Rhett's head snapped up. "What?"

"Rylan." I turned toward the porch, eyes narrowing on the faint scuff marks near the railing. "He's been here."

Jay's tone dropped, deadly calm. "There's no car."

"I know." My pulse pounded, heat crawling under my skin. "But he's here. Or was. Maybe on foot."

Rhett's mask came down slow, his shoulders rolling, that predator energy rippling through him. The humor was completely gone. What was left was something feral.

"Motherfucker followed her," he growled. "He followed *our omega.*"

The word hit like a match to gasoline. Ours. He didn't mean it lightly, and neither did I. The air seemed to shift, thick and humming. Jay's usually easy calm hardened, his jaw tight. I could feel the edge of his anger, cool but lethal.

"This isn't a game anymore," he said.

"No," I agreed. My voice came out rough, the alpha in me surfacing, sharp and unrelenting. "It's not."

For a second, no one spoke. The storm rolled closer, thunder low and distant. My instincts screamed. Hunt. Protect. *Claim.*

I turned toward them, mask settling into place, vision tunneling to purpose. "Find her," I ordered. My tone left no room for doubt or hesitation.

Rhett released a snarl, far more animal than man. Jay's eyes, barely visible beneath the mask, were cold steel.

"No mercy for him," I added. I didn't have to say it twice.

"Didn't plan on any." Rhett's grin was in his voice, a razor now. Jay just nodded, a dark promise flickering behind his eyes.

The storm broke as we stepped off the porch, icy rain starting to hit the earth. It wouldn't be long before it turned into sheets. Lightning split the sky, and I scowled. The rain would muddy her scent, distort his.

"We're connected," I reminded them. "The bond is there, we just have to seal it. Use it." Before my restraint snapped, I needed them to remember because somewhere out there, in that endless stretch of wilderness, Wren was waiting for us.

And Rylan was hunting her. That combination was all I needed to let the alpha take over. We were done waiting. We were going after her.

Now.

FORTY

WREN

At first, it was freedom.

The kind that tasted like cold air and pine sap, like rain-soaked earth and adrenaline. My boots splashed through puddles, mud streaking my calves, my breath coming out in laughter I didn't mean to release. My heart was pounding, not from fear, but from *want*.

For once, I didn't fight it. The heat was coming for me — slow, sure, inevitable — and I let it.

The cabin was behind me, a quiet little ghost, and I'd left my blockers sitting uselessly on the counter. The choice hadn't felt monumental when I made it, but now it echoed through my body like a drumbeat. I hadn't gone back on the suppressors. I hadn't smothered the thing I'd spent months trying to control.

No. I wanted *them*.

Roan. Rhett. Jay.

The thought of them out there somewhere — strong, relentless, *mine* — made every nerve light up. The night air was damp and heavy with ozone, the scent of the storm building on the horizon. My skin prickled, temperature spiking from the inside out. The heat pulsed through me, low and deep and wild.

For the first time, I wasn't ashamed of it.

I was savoring it.

I'd spent so long pretending that this part of me was an inconvenience — a hazard, a liability, something that needed masking. But right now, out here in the trees, under the weight of the storm, it felt like *power*. Every exhale left a trail of my scent — sweet, ripe, undeniable — and I didn't bother to hide it.

Let them find me.

Let them chase.

Let them claim what was already theirs.

The first drops of rain hit my skin, sharp and icy, shocking against the fever simmering under the surface. The storm rolled closer, thunder crawling over the mountains like a living thing. I tilted my head back, laughed softly at the sky. I wanted to feel *everything*. The chill. The burn. The hunger.

But then—

Something shifted.

A new scent rode the wind.

Alpha.

For a second, my body reacted instinctively — a rush of heat, of anticipation, a surge of recognition that came before thought. *They're here.*

Except... no.

It wasn't Roan.

It wasn't Rhett.

It wasn't Jay.

This scent was sharper. Colder. Wrong.

Beckett Rylan.

The realization sliced through me like a blade. My

stomach dropped even as my pulse spiked. The rain came harder, cold needles against my skin, washing over me as if the storm itself wanted to strip away the heat that had just begun to bloom.

He was close. Too close.

The sound of him — the way he moved — I remembered it from the ice. Controlled chaos. A predator that liked to play before the kill.

Fear threaded through the heat, twisting it, warping it until it became something jagged and confusing. My body still wanted — that primal, aching *need* for an Alpha to find me, to *fill* me — but my mind rebelled. Every instinct screamed *not him.*

Not Rylan.

Not the one who had haunted the edges of my safety since the trade.

I stumbled backward, breath shaking, the wind catching my scent and flinging it into the storm. A curse broke from my lips. I should've kept the blockers. Should've waited for *them* before I—

Branches cracked somewhere behind me.

That smooth, mocking voice cut through the rain. "You really shouldn't run alone, Wren."

My heart lurched.

He was here.

And my body — traitorous, burning — didn't care that my brain was screaming *run.* It responded to the Alpha in him, to the biological gravity that made every Omega weak in the knees when cornered.

I forced my feet to move, mud slipping beneath my boots, pulse roaring in my ears. "Not you," I whispered, half to the storm, half to myself. "*Not you.*"

Because yes, I had invited the chase.

But not from the monster who thought he could claim me out of spite.

The fear built fast — sharp, dizzying — but under it was still that molten, desperate ache for the *right* Alphas. The ones who had earned me. The ones I'd chosen.

So I did the only thing I could.

I ran faster.

And I prayed that Roan, Rhett, and Jay were already on my trail — because if Rylan reached me first, my heat wouldn't save me.

It would destroy me.

Cold was my only ally now.

It sliced through the heat haze wrapping around my body, clearing the edges of my thoughts like glass through fog. Every breath burned, lungs raw from running, but I needed that pain and clung to it. It reminded me I was more than my biology.

The rain came harder, pelting my skin like needles, soaking through my clothes until I was shivering. Good. Let it drown my scent. Let it bury me from him.

The storm was my camouflage. My absolution.

Mud clung to my boots as I pushed deeper into the trees, the terrain getting rougher, steeper. I used the terrain like I'd learned as a kid. Uphill for distance, downhill for speed. Keep your head low. Don't waste energy doubling back too early. Make your trail unpredictable.

But the bastard was still close.

I could feel it, that pull. That *alpha gravity.* My instincts didn't care that it was the wrong scent, that the wrong voice had whispered my name through the storm. My body still responded to him in flashes of raw, stupid heat. A cruel biological betrayal.

No. Even as wrong as it felt, my body responded to it.

Damn it. I refused to betray them. To betray *me*. Not like this.

My mind warred with every primal impulse that begged me to stop, to let the alpha find me. I forced my legs to move, heart hammering like it wanted to escape my ribs.

Lightning cracked overhead, so bright it painted the forest in white for half a heartbeat. In that blink, I saw movement down the slope. A dark figure, broad shoulders, purposeful stride. Beckett Rylan.

Too close.

My throat tightened. I bit down hard on my lower lip until I tasted copper, grounding myself in the pain.

Focus, Wren. You've run before. You've survived too long to give in now.

I veered sharply to the left, ducking through a stand of birch trees where the wind swirled unpredictably. I scraped my hand deliberately against a branch, and left a faint blood scent. A lure. Then I doubled back, crouching low, fighting against the trembling in my limbs as I pressed through the undergrowth in the opposite direction.

Rain hammered the earth, turning everything slick, but I welcomed it. The mud would swallow my tracks soon enough.

Another flash of lightning and another glimpse of Rylan further upslope now, heading toward the false scent trail. My breath hitched in relief.

For a moment, I could almost hear Roan's voice in my head, that calm command he used when the ice got tense: *Keep your head. Control what you can. Don't panic.*

I tried. God, I tried.

But the storm wasn't just rain anymore. It was a living wall of wind and thunder, screaming through the pines. I could barely see five feet ahead. The temperature dropped so fast my teeth began to chatter, the heat inside me battling the cold until it felt like my skin couldn't decide which way to burn.

My gear helped, barely. The waterproof layers were meant for media scrums, not mountain hunts, but the rain had found every seam, every zipper. My fingers ached from the cold.

A branch snapped behind me.

Not the storm.

Him.

I bit back a sound, ducking low, pressing myself against a fallen log slick with moss. The air was heavy, full of scent and ozone and fear.

Then, barely more than a whisper, his voice cut through the dark. "You honestly thought they'd find you before I did?"

My pulse spiked.

He was playing with me. Drawing it out. Beckett Rylan didn't just chase for dominance, he *enjoyed* the hunt. He'd been hunting me since our first meeting. I'd always managed to cut him off and avoid him. Now? Especially after losing the Apex Trophy to the Howlers, he wanted me scared, trembling, pliant.

But I wasn't prey. Not for him. Not for *anyone.*

I crouched lower, heart hammering, forcing shallow, silent breaths. My muscles shook with the effort of holding still. The icy rain kept falling, thick and relentless, masking scent and sound.

A gust of wind shifted, and suddenly I caught something welcome on the breeze, faint but unmistakable.

Roan.

A heartbeat later — Rhett.

Jay.

Their scents threaded through the storm, tangled and wild and *theirs*. Relief hit so hard my knees almost buckled.

Still, I didn't move. Couldn't risk leading them straight into Rylan's path. I needed to draw him off just a little longer.

I slid forward on my stomach, pushing through wet leaves until I reached the edge of a slope. What had been packed in snow before was all mud, leaves, and debris. Soon, it would be ice slicked and crystalline. Below me, though, was a narrow ravine, swollen with runoff from the storm. Dangerous, fast-moving water, but it would break my trail completely.

Decision made, I exhaled once, hard. "Come and get me, asshole," I whispered, and threw myself down the incline.

The cold hit like a fist. The current grabbed me, tearing my breath from my lungs as I fought to surface, clawing against the pull of water and mud and panic.

But even through the chaos, I had one thought — one, steady pulse in my mind that burned hotter than the heat still raging in my body.

Find me, Roan. Please. Jay. Rhett. Find me before he does.

The current slammed me against a rock hard enough to drive the air from my lungs. My world narrowed to water and thunder and the raw, searing cold that clawed through every inch of me. I couldn't tell which way was up. Couldn't breathe. Couldn't think.

Then—impact. A second splash, heavier, deliberate. A shape cutting through the current.

No.

Panic ripped through me, sharp and immediate. I kicked backward, heart pounding against my ribs like a trapped bird. My mind screamed *Rylan,* even before I could see him—his voice echoing through memory, through fear, through every instinct that said *run*.

But then—warmth.

Hands found me. Strong. Steady. Familiar.

I caught a flash between lightning strikes: honey-brown skin, dark curls plastered to his forehead, those impossible dimples half-hidden behind a grimace.

Rhett.

Relief hit so fast it hurt. My muscles went slack for a heartbeat as a choked laugh—or maybe a sob—escaped me.

"I got you, boots," he shouted, his voice rough and breathless but full of that infuriating, unbreakable confidence.

My fingers caught the strap of his gear, and I kicked hard, fighting the current beside him. The rain lashed our faces, the current tried to tear us apart, but we clawed for the bank together. Every inch forward felt like wrestling gravity itself.

We hit the shallows, half-crawling, half-dragging each other onto slick, stony ground. My body trembled, heat and cold battling until I wasn't sure which would win. Rhett's hand stayed on my back, grounding me through the chaos.

Lightning split the sky again—white and merciless—and in that flash, I saw him.

Rylan.

Standing on the shore like a nightmare given flesh, rain streaming down his face, eyes burning with something unholy.

My stomach dropped.

He moved fast—too fast—and before I could shout a

warning, he kicked out, boot connecting with Rhett's ribs. The impact sent Rhett skidding back into the water with a growl that wasn't human anymore.

"Rhett!" I screamed, scrambling to my knees, fingers clawing at the mud.

But Rhett wasn't down.

He twisted with the current, teeth bared in a snarl that would have frozen blood, and his hand shot out—grabbing Rylan's ankle in one brutal motion.

The shock on Rylan's face lasted only a second before Rhett *yanked*.

Both men crashed into the torrent, a tangle of limbs and fury and raw Alpha dominance, the storm swallowing them whole.

I staggered toward the edge, heart pounding, rain in my eyes, throat raw from shouting.

The water roared louder than any voice. Lightning turned the world white again.

And then I saw movement—two shapes, locked together, fighting the current and each other in a violent, swirling blur.

"Rhett," I whispered, uselessly. My voice vanished in the storm.

But even through the fear, even through the rising panic, something else flared deep inside me. A heat not born of biology this time—something fiercer.

They came for me.

And they weren't about to let Rylan take me without a fight.

The storm was everywhere—inside me, around me, inside *them*. The roar of the water drowned everything, but I could still hear them—Rhett's snarl, Rylan's curse, the splash and struggle as the river became an arena for something older than rivalry.

My knees sank into the mud at the water's edge. I shouted his name again and again, throat raw, hands trembling so hard I could barely keep myself upright. Every flash of lightning gave me glimpses: Rhett's arm locking around Rylan's shoulder, Rylan twisting, throwing a wild punch that barely missed. The current caught them both, dragging them farther downstream.

I started forward before I could think, boots slipping.

Then—hands. A grip on my shoulders.

"Stay with her!" Roan's voice cut through everything, sharp, commanding, and for one wild second, my chest cracked open with relief because he was *here.*

He didn't wait for an answer, just kissed me hard and swift. The burn of his mouth on mine a brand. Then he dove straight into the current, a blur of motion and muscle and controlled fury.

Jay's hand found mine, fingers fisting tight, holding me to him as the storm tried to pull the world apart. His body was shaking—from the cold or the adrenaline, I didn't know—but his grip didn't falter. "He's got him," he said, voice barely audible over the wind. "He's got him."

Roan wouldn't let Rhett fight alone. He'd back him. They'd get Rylan together. Jay and I moved together along the bank, following the violence that tumbled downstream. I could feel Jay's pulse thundering against mine, his own scent edged with protectiveness that blanketed me.

The rain turned to ice. Literal shards of it. It cut against my skin as the wind howled through the trees. Downriver, two bodies broke the surface—Rhett and Rylan—crashing against the rocky edge. Rhett was up first, mud-slick and wild-eyed, chest heaving, teeth bared in a snarl that looked more wolf than man.

Rylan pushed to his feet, spitting blood, eyes locked on Rhett. He lunged again. Then Roan was *there*.

He hit Rylan like a breaking wave, the force of it echoing through the storm. The sound—the *impact*—ripped through the air, a sickening mix of water and bone and rage.

"Roan!" I screamed, though it wasn't fear, not exactly. It was everything at once—terror, pride, heat, *love*.

Jay pulled me back just enough to keep me from slipping back into the water, but my eyes never left the three figures in the downpour.

It wasn't a hockey fight. It wasn't even a hunt. It was primal, raw, and absolutely personal.

Rylan swung first—fast, desperate—but Roan took the hit and drove through it, using that controlled strength that made him the leader he was. Rhett came in behind him, cutting off Rylan's retreat, a silent, brutal echo to Roan's precision.

Two against one, but there was no mercy in it.

Another hit. A roar. Then the sound of a body hitting the rocks hard enough to make my stomach twist.

Lightning split the sky, blinding white, and when the world came back into focus, it was over.

Rylan was down.

Blood mixed with rain, running in dark streaks across his face. He was breathing—barely—but he wasn't getting up again.

Rhett stood over him, chest heaving. Roan, soaked, shivering, and eyes burning with alpha fury, stared down at the man who'd stalked and hunted and *tried* to take me.

"Stay down," Roan said, voice low and dangerous. The kind of voice that promised consequences if he didn't.

For once, Rylan listened.

Jay's hand tightened around mine. "It's done," he said, his voice barely above the rain as we hurried toward them. "It's over, Wren."

But my pulse didn't slow. My body shook—heat, cold, adrenaline, and the overwhelming weight of what had just happened.

Rhett looked toward us, tracking our movements as we got closer. His dimples ghosted faintly on his face, despite his exhaustion. I could hear him clearly even if he didn't say a word. *Told you I had you.*

Then Roan turned, the storm of his eyes matching the rage of nature around us, but he found my gaze as we closed in. He was steady, fierce, and so damn *alive*. He was promise in human form. I said come and claim me.

They were here.

They were claiming me.

I nodded once, chest tight, heart hammering.

Because I believed them. The threat of Rylan was over, but nothing between Jay, Roan, Rhett, and me ever would be.

Inside, my soul exulted.

FORTY-ONE

ROAN

The bastard was after her.

That's the first thing I saw when we burst through the trees— Beckett Rylan, former Howler and eternal thorn in my damn side, in the water with Wren, trying to catch her like she was a prize he'd won instead of a woman he was about to break.

My pulse went feral.

Rhett got to her first, and getting her out of the water before he went after Rylan once more. He slammed his shoulder into Rylan's chest, all muscle and rage. I barely remembered the sound — a crack, a grunt — before they slammed into the rocks. I followed after them. Jay already had Wren. She was safe, he would protect her. Right now, all I wanted was to savage the son of a bitch who hurt her. Who'd *hunted* her and *wanted* to hurt her.

The fight didn't last long. Beckett Rylan was great at bullying those weaker than him, but not us. He didn't have the strength or the dominance to take on one of us, much less both. We dragged him up onto the shore, all of us soaking wet and him unconscious. The temptation to just leave him there to freeze to death was real.

Finishing him off was also an option visible in Rhett's feral eyes. I shook my head once and Rhett grimaced. "I know," I told him on a growl. "Call the sheriff's office. Report him for assault."

"Fuck, that's going to be paperwork."

I could hardly blame Rhett for the snarl. Not when I felt it too.

"Tell them our omega is in heat, and we're bonding. He's their problem, not ours." Identifying Wren as our omega in paperwork could cause some problems, but I didn't plan on us being here for them to take her name. "If necessary, we'll stop by in a few days once we're free. They can handle him until then." If that meant he sat in their jail cell, well, how sad for him.

Leaving Rhett for a moment, I stalked back to where Jay held Wren. Knowing Jay had her was one thing, yet a very primitive part of me *needed* to see her, touch her, to assure myself she was safe. She was ours—*mine*, dammit and I needed to assure myself she was fine.

She was shaking, soaked through, her hair plastered to her face like riverweed. Christ, she'd gone into the water. Her lips were pale, her skin clammy. I could smell the cold on her — that sharp, metallic edge — but underneath it, the unmistakable sweetness of her heat. Faint, but rising. Damn it all.

"Jay, get her to the cabin," I ordered, my voice coming out rougher than I meant. "Now. Get her warm. We'll take care of this."

He hesitated for half a second, his beta instincts all tangled up with protectiveness. Biological status aside, Jay adored her every bit as much as we did. But one look at me and he nodded. Wren swayed, and I caught her just long enough to steady her.

"Roan..." she chattered, voice trembling like broken glass. "What do you mean by... take care of?"

I cupped her chin, cold skin beneath colder fingers, and tilted her face up until her eyes met mine. Gods, those eyes. Copper infused whiskey like thawing ice.

"Trust me," I said.

Then I kissed her. Not long, not deep, just enough to soothe us both. To remind her we were here, and she was safe, *mine*.

Her lashes fluttered. Her lips, trembling and a little blue, curved the smallest smile. It cracked open something raw in my chest I didn't even know I'd been holding.

"As much as I'd like to kill him," I said against her mouth, "we won't. Not this time."

Her soft *thank you* landed somewhere deep, not just words, but a thread. Acceptance. Bond. She was in my blood, because of course she was. It was how we'd known she'd needed us before. Why we'd pursued the thread to find her even when we hadn't understood.

Alpha. Beta. Omega. Her designation had never mattered to me. She was mine. She would always be mine. We would be hers. Today—we would seal that bond permanently. After we dealt with the asshole.

"Go," I told Jay again, and this time my voice left no room for argument. He slipped an arm around her and started toward the cabin, both of them half-stumbling through the mud hardening with ice. It wasn't quite the snowy landscape it had been, the rain had melted a lot but this storm would bring more to blanket the frozen landscape. Wipe it clean.

But even through the cold and the chaos, her scent was

a slow blooming, molten sweetness curling through the air. Her heat was coming on fast now. Probably as triggered by us as we were by it.

Jay would handle it, for now. He'd keep her warm. Ease her. Rhett moved past me, caught Wren's hand before she could leave entirely. He didn't say a word, just bent, brushed his lips to hers. Rougher than mine. Fierce. Like he needed to taste her to believe she was alive. Not that I could blame him.

She made a small sound that was half sigh, half command. "Don't be long."

God help me, that tone nearly undid me.

Rhett and I exchanged a look, a silent agreement older than any team we'd ever played on.

"Wouldn't dream of it," I murmured.

Then we turned back to Rylan.

He was dragging himself up, blood on his teeth, eyes burning with something ugly and stupid. The kind of look a man wore when they've already lost but can't admit it.

"Didn't think you'd get here so fast," he spat.

"Didn't think you'd be dumb enough to come near what's mine," I said, stepping closer, cracking the ice off my gloves one finger at a time. "Guess we both underestimated something."

Rhett laughed, low, dark, dangerous.

For a heartbeat, the forest went still. Just the wind whispering through the pines. In the distance, I could imagine the cabin door closing behind Jay and Wren. We weren't that far if one took a direct route. Still, I trusted our beta with her. He would never let anything happen to her.

Standing there with my promise to her sitting heavy in my gut, I eyed Rylan. "Sheriff coming?" The question was for Rhett and surprise flickered over Rylan's face. He spat out blood.

"Sheriff? You're so—"

I didn't let him finish the comment, I just slammed my fist into his face with every ounce of my strength behind it. The feeling of bone crashing into bone vibrated up my arm. I probably broke a knuckle or three. But I absolutely broke Rylan's jaw. He dropped like a sack of rocks, crumpling into a bloody, silent pile.

That was better.

Promising to not kill him didn't mean I needed to listen to his bullshit.

"You're sure we can't kill him?" Rhett believed me, but his grumble almost made me laugh. I got it. I really did.

"If he ever touches her again," I said, swearing it in blood. After we bonded her, after she wore our scent? "I'll gut him without hesitation and we'll be within our rights."

Laws were strange things. Unbonded omegas had fewer protections than the bonded. As archaic as that was, I also understood that played a huge role in Wren's choices. She wanted to live her life on her terms and not be dictated to by assholes like Rylan. That she chose to let us bond her? Invited us to?

That was a gift I would treasure for the rest of my life.

"Good." Rhett nodded. "The sheriff is on his way. Soon as we scent him..."

Agreed. Once the sheriff was here, Rylan was his problem. As Wren's soon to be bonded alphas, we could press charges against Rylan easily enough. This wasn't team rivalry or league politics, it was just blood and consequences.

She was ours.

Always.

RHETT

The sheriff looked like every small-town cliché ever written — big hat, thicker mustache, and that drawl that could stretch a syllable into a sermon. I used to roll my eyes at men like him. Still kind of did, honestly. But right then? I could've kissed him.

Not for his charm. For the simple fact that he was *not* Rylan.

He nodded like he'd seen this kind of thing before, alphas who went too far, omegas who got caught in the mess, and the rest of us trying not to tear the world apart in response.

"Press all the charges you want," he said, his voice like gravel and tobacco. "Boy's lucky you didn't kill him outright."

I almost laughed. *Lucky* didn't even begin to cover it. If Roan hadn't been the one holding the line, Rylan would've been fertilizer under the pines by now.

Then came the part that made me grind my teeth.

The sheriff tipped his hat toward the cabin in that lazy way of his and said, "If she's yours, best finish bonding her right quick. Make it official. Save everyone the headache later."

Alphas will be alphas, that was the subtext. Boys will be boys. A little omega panic, a little violence, nothing the world hadn't seen before.

It should've pissed me off more than it did. Maybe it did. Right now it was a low, simmering thing in my gut that wanted to argue with the whole damned structure of how we'd built. But Roan's hand brushed my shoulder, a subtle touch, and the fire cooled just enough.

"Let it go," he murmured under his breath, eyes forward.

He was right. Wren was what mattered. Everything else could burn.

By the time the sheriff and the ranger climbed back into their truck, my head was already somewhere else. Or more accurately on *someone* else.

Wren.

The thought of her hit me all at once, low and deep and visceral. She was alive. Safe. Waiting.

For us.

We didn't talk on the way back to the cabin. Didn't need to. The air between Roan and me was charged, humming with the same single thought: *claim her.*

Snow crunched under our boots, wet clothes sticking to our skin. The moment we stepped inside, heat from the cabin's fireplace hit us, all rich and smoky and thick with the scent of *her*. Her heat had deepened, lush and heady, curling through the air like a drug.

Then I heard it.

Her cry.

A sound that made my heart slam against my ribs and my cock go hard in the same instant.

It wasn't a cry of pain. Oh, no. It was that soft, broken sound omegas make when they're *coming undone.*

Jay was with her. Good. Smart man. He'd done what we'd asked, warmed her up, eased her through the beginning of it.

Still, the possessive part of me, the alpha in me, snapped awake like a wolf hearing the dinner bell.

"Rhett," Roan warned, voice low, steady. Always steady.

I shot him a grin. "Not doing anything stupid. Just... fast."

He smirked, but I saw the same hunger flicker behind his eyes. Then he went around, checking every lock, every window. That was our Roan, methodical, protective, the kind of man who made sure the world stays outside before letting his heart loose. I wasn't built that way. My pulse was already racing ahead of me, already in that bathroom, with her.

Steam poured from under the cracked door. The scent of Wren, sweet and slick and wild, filled every inch of the cabin. When we pushed the door open, it was like stepping into a storm.

She was there, braced against the tile, hands on the wall, water pouring over her back. Her hair clung to her skin, her body trembling in that way that wasn't about cold anymore. Jay was behind her, mouth at her neck, one hand gripping her hip.

Her head turned, just slightly, and our eyes met.

Bam.

There it was.

That spark. That *recognition.*

The walls she'd built since the first day we met, the cautious smiles, the guarded scent, the way she'd pull back every time one of us got too close, was gone. Melted away under heat and want and the absolute trust of knowing she was ours.

She *beamed.* Not shy, not hesitant. Radiant. Like she'd been waiting for us to get here.

Holy shit, the pulse of her scent hit me square in the chest. Mine. Ours. I stepped forward, peeling off the last of my soaked shirt, boots thudding on the floor. Roan was right behind me, his gaze dark and focused, every line of him set with intention.

Wren moaned, low, throaty, and something primal in me answered.

Yeah, the sheriff had said *finish bonding her right quick.*

For once, I wasn't about to argue with authority.

Because right then, standing in that haze of heat and steam and her, I knew exactly what came next, every instinct in me roaring to life.

She was our home and we were done waiting.

WREN

The last heat had driven me close to madness, my body out of control, and my mind eroding under the weight of biological demand. This time? It was just as damn intense. Jay's touch helped to quiet some of the wildness as he stroked my skin while he stripped me. Once under the shower, he'd used his fingers to massage an orgasm out of my quivering body before he thrust into me.

The near punishing force of his strokes as he *moved* within me had robbed me of breath. No, there was no knot, or even the anticipation of one. But it was Jay and he was mine, and my body seemed to understand what my soul needed. No sooner had he filled me once, than he thickened again. His harsh breaths against my throat were music. He cupped and massaged my breasts, until I began to clench around him again and then he let out a pleased little hum and began to move again.

There was no relenting from his possession. Just on the cusp of another orgasm, I opened my eyes to find Rhett and Roan there. A purr vibrated deep within, a sultry release of sound that echoed *mine.*

And they were mine. All three of them. They'd come for

me and we were here. All of us. Jay bit me as he came this time and I flipped over the edge with him. The hot jet of his release pulsed inside of me and warmed me. His scent would be there, mingling with ours even as he marked my throat.

I would wear their marks, their scent, and I would be claimed in every way. Still trembling, I wasn't quite ready for Jay to let me go, but Roan and Rhett were right there, steadying me. The scent of them filled the steamy air and a wave of want crashed through me.

Even as Roan tilted my head back to take possession of my lips in a kiss that branded my soul, Rhett's hands were everywhere else, teasing, stroking, and making me alternate between shivering and moaning. My slick and Jay's release slid down my thighs, but Rhett caught both on his fingers and pressed them back inside of me even as he began to massage my clit.

They moved me and maneuvered me, Roan sliding in behind me even as Rhett lifted me. There was no patience in them and even less in me. I dug my nails into Rhett's shoulders as he pushed into me without any warning or preparation. He fucked me right through the wet of Jay's cum. Roan was pushing into my ass, all slicked up. The pressure was unbearable and perfect. Where I might have expected pain before, my body seemed to understand exactly what we needed even as they filled me with such demand that I tried to start moving.

A slap against my thigh, the sting rocketing through me.

"Patience." Roan's order snapped through me, the command made me whimper but Rhett kissed me and robbed me of the sound.

"Shh," Jay said, soothing as he massaged me. His calming touches were full of so much care, easing that ever tightening coil within me. His encouragement what I needed. I wanted so much. Needed so much and for all their patience, I wanted them to just *move* and take me now. Claim me.

"We have you," Roan said, his voice low, rough and vibrating. My heartbeat was a wild drum inside of me. "You're ours."

That declaration was enough to almost make me come right then and there. Rhett nipped my lower lip, once, twice, and then kissed me again on the third. He was almost brutally soft, nipping and licking alternately as he and Roan stroked me everywhere. I forgot whose hands were where as their cocks filled me.

"Always making it a challenge," Rhett moaned into the kiss, his smirk audible.

"We wouldn't have you any other way," Roan added, the absolute devotion stealing my breath and then there were no more words. They were thrusting, alternating in a push pull that stretched me in the most carnal ways and they took turns kissing me, even Jay slipping in there as he teasing my clit and pinched a nipple in between deep tongue tangling kisses.

I arched into *them*, the hot pulse of their need mingling with mine. My chest pressed to Rhett's, my back against Roan's, Jay's hands easing me into a rhythm I couldn't find alone. I was theirs. Every tremble, every gasp, every slick whimper spilling from me belonged to them.

Roan leaned in closer, his teeth a promise against my throat. "This... this is what you want, right? Say it, Wren."

"I do," I breathed, voice trembling, voice strong. "I want this. I want... all of you."

Rhett chuckled low in my ear, his growl a hot promise. "That's my girl. Mine. Ours."

The reverent motions turned punishingly primitive. Their hard thrusts staking a claim as they stabbed into me deeper and deeper. They were etching themselves into my soul, moulding my body to theirs and stretching—oh fuck. So much stretching. They were huge, too much, so much and the cries began to escape me on every push and pull.

Every wall I had built, every hesitation, every ounce of doubt — gone. I was theirs, and the clarity of it made me dizzy with relief and desire.

Roan bit down hard, his teeth breaking skin right over the spot Jay had bit me and then Rhett bit me on my other shoulder, an echo of how they'd bitten me before.

The pain of pierced flesh, blood, cum, slick...and I vanished into a conflagration, going up in flames as they kept me rocking between them. Sobs of pure pleasure escaped me as something deep inside snapped into being, a feeling that had always been there. Half-formed, maybe, but present. Now it sealed to titanium. Their scents embedded into mine.

The room became a storm of heat, wet skin, whispered devotion, teasing laughter, and moans that echoed off the tile. Each press, each thrust, each claim was love and need and possession all at once. Jay's hands guided, massaged, eased me into the rhythm, letting me ride the waves instead of falling into them blindly.

When their knots ballooned, I shattered, and the world blacked out entirely. It took time for me to surface. Some part of me aware that they were still inside of me, still stretching me to breaking, their knots so full that I would never not feel them with every breath again.

"Maybe should have thought about this before," Roan said on a husky chuckle.

"Fuck it," Rhett said, a naked kind of joy in his voice. "We can stand here forever. She feels so fucking good."

"She does," Roan agreed, but it was Jay's soft amusement that prodded me into opening my eyes. His smile was right there and I realized what the issue was.

We were still in the shower, naked, standing and they cradled me between them, Roan and Rhett had me impaled on their huge knots and something like delight just unfurled within me. There was an inescapable peace in my pleasure, in their pleasure and even as I found myself still wanting them, it was a kind of raw sensuality that carried so much emotion, I wanted to cry.

"Always have to challenge us," Jay said, an echo of Rhett's earlier words and I almost giggled.

Me. Giggling.

Who would have thought?

"You *like* that, don't you?" I whispered back, voice shaking, my pulse thundering like it could break ribs.

"More than anything," he breathed before nuzzling a kiss. "How are you doing?"

Every nerve, every cell, every beat of my heart was fused to theirs and Jay was in there too... I could feel him, feel his *love* and the intensity of it had a tear sliding down my cheek.

"Delirious," I murmured. "Will it be like this each time?"

"No idea," Roan admitted, but there was so much depth in his voice, I could hear his delight at the idea of discovering it with us.

"Can't wait," Rhett agreed, dipping down to steal a kiss of his own.

I was theirs and the rightness in that claim settled inside of me. Completely, irrevocably theirs.

451

"Jay?"

"I'm here," he promised.

But I just grinned, delighted. "When these brutes release me, I want you again—only I want to ride you this time and look down at you as you come."

"Anything you want," he said.

"Anything?" It was as much a confirmation as a dare to all three of them

"Oh yeah," Rhett said, his grin a wicked thing. "I have a lot of ways I want to fuck you too, Wren."

"And we want you like this," Roan said against my throat. "Every day for the rest of our lives—as long as you're up for it."

A real laugh escaped me this time, and it came out so full and throaty, the guys all stilled as they studied me.

"What?" Jay finally asked and I couldn't help it, I grinned so hard, it hurt.

"I think I just won my Apex Trophy."

Their groans were punctuated by laughter.

"Nope," Rhett said without missing a beat. "That takes the best of seven and this was just one."

Oh. A real shiver went through me. "Bring it on," I said. "I can take you."

"Yes," Roan said in a low growl. "You can."

FORTY-TWO

JAY

Three days later, the world still felt like it was tilted on some sort of sweet, drunken axis. Not from booze — though yeah, maybe a little — but from everything else. From the cabin, from heat and wet skin and whispered promises that echoed in our bones. From Wren.

She was *ours*.

After we'd dropped her car off at her place, we were sitting in the back seat of Roan's SUV with her hand curled over mine. We had a lot of details to work out for later, but we'd get there. I could feel the pulse of her, the scent of her bonded to ours, and every damn nerve in me buzzed like I'd had a hundred cups of coffee and a thousand heartbeats at once. She kept stealing glances at me, a little grin curling the corner of her lips, and I swear she could make my chest ache with nothing more than a look.

"I want to stop," she said, voice determined, fierce. Eyes bright. "Get my arms tattooed. I want your marks. I want everyone to know I'm yours."

I couldn't help but grin. Hell yes. That was my girl, unashamed, untamed, and utterly committed.

Roan's laugh rumbled from the driver's seat, deep and amused. "Good. Let them look. You're ours. Everyone should know."

Rhett leaned back from the front passenger seat, smirking, fingers brushing her arm. "And I'll be damned if I'm letting you wear ours and not *me*."

I chuckled, shaking my head. "Guess that settles it, then."

She crossed her arms, glaring playfully at us, and added, "I'm also not quitting my job. I'll fight anyone who tries to make me."

The grins on Roan and Rhett's faces were instant, mirrored by me. My shoulders relaxed. "Damn right you will," I said. "We've got your back. All of us. Every step."

Her fingers found mine again, squeezing, and I could feel it, her trust, her strength, her stubborn streak that had been hers long before any of us arrived in her life. She wasn't a trophy. She wasn't a prize. She was *Wren*. And the Howlers? They needed her. We needed her.

When we arrived at the tattoo studio, she didn't hesitate. Walked in like she owned the place. Like she *owned* herself. Roan and Rhett flanked me and her, all of us grinning like idiots under the bright fluorescent lights, every one of us buzzing with that same high — the cabin, the claiming, the proof of our bond that we were about to make permanent.

And when it was my turn to sit down, Wren's marks on my arms, matching hers, I felt something deep and steady click into place. Roan was right there, one arm brushing mine, eyes glinting with that same smug pride. Rhett leaned in, fingers brushing the other side of my arm, murmuring, "Pack, Jay. Pack forever."

I laughed, breathless, almost in tears. That's exactly

what it felt like. A pack. Sealed. No hesitations. No half-measures. Where one went, the others would follow.

Forever.

Wren's hand covered mine again as the ink started, hot sting, pressure, and pure, irrevocable devotion all at once. And all I could do was smile and squeeze her fingers back, because every mark we wore, every line of ink pressed into our skin, said the same thing:

We are each other's. No one else. Never apart.

By the time Roan, Rhett, and I had our matching tattoos done, the four of us were laughing, grimacing, and marveling at the permanence of it all. Wren's eyes sparkled at the sight, fierce and beautiful. And I knew, no matter where life threw us, no matter the jobs, the Howlers, the town, the world, we would always find each other.

Pack. Bonded. Ours.

Forever.

HOWLERS CELEBRATE APEX TROPHY WIN; PR HEAD WREN FOSTER ANNOUNCES BONDING WITH KEY PLAYERS

By Madison Kline, Sports & Lifestyle Correspondent

The Howlers are still riding the high from their thrilling 4-3 victory over the Vultures in the Apex Trophy finals. Game 7 showcased everything fans had hoped for: Roan Whittaker, team captain and Alpha forward, led the offense with precision and power; Rhett Navarro, ace goalie, kept the Vultures at bay with several jaw-dropping saves; and left wing Jay Kim brought speed and strategy that kept the Howlers in control.

But the celebration isn't just about the ice. Just a few days after the championship win, Wren Foster, the Howlers' head of PR, made a surprising announcement: she is now bonded to Whittaker, Navarro, and Kim. The revelation came during a press event for the team's post-season activities and was met with equal parts astonishment and excitement by fans.

Team owner Adrien Marchand addressed the news with characteristic pragmatism. "Designations don't dictate talent or skill," he said. "Wren Foster is every bit a Howler, and her leadership as PR head is just as vital as Roan, Rhett, and Jay on the ice. This is a team — on and off the rink — that works because it's balanced, committed, and bonded. Why change a good thing?"

The bonding of Foster to three of the team's star players has sparked discussion in the league and among fans. Could this pave the way for other omegas in professional sports leadership roles? Perhaps. But for now, the Howlers are focused on celebrating their victory, planning for the next season, and embracing a unique dynamic that has already strengthened the team both publicly and personally.

Fans are quick to support the quartet, with social media buzzing with messages of excitement and curiosity. The Howlers may have won the Apex Trophy, but the bond of their team — both on and off the ice — could be their greatest championship yet.

With Foster's leadership and the team's star players fully aligned, the Howlers are poised for a future as unstoppable off the rink as they are on it.

HOWLERS WIN APEX TROPHY — AND WREN FOSTER JUST SHOOK THE WHOLE LEAGUE

By: IceFans Daily Team

Okay, let's just take a moment. The Howlers *did it*. Game 7 against the Vultures went down to the wire, ending 4-3, and honestly? We're still recovering from the heart-stopping saves, insane goals, and pure Alpha-level energy from Roan Whittaker, Rhett Navarro, and Jay Kim. Our Howlers. Our champions.

But hold onto your helmets, because just a few days after the champagne settled, the *real* shocker came from none other than Wren Foster — the team's PR head. Yep, the brains behind the Howlers' off-ice magic just dropped the bomb: she's bonded to Roan, Rhett, *and* Jay. All three. At the same time.

The fan reaction? Predictably chaotic.

"Wait... what? Quadruple bonding? That's... actually amazing." — @IceQueen88

"Wren Foster is officially *untouchable*. Can we get a Wren + Howlers merch line already?" — @SkateAndBake

"I knew the Howlers were a team, but now they're literally a pack. Love it." — @GoalieGoals

Team owner Adrien Marchand gave us the official word, and honestly, he's got the right attitude. "Designations don't dictate talent or skill. Wren Foster is every bit a Howler and just as vital to the team as Roan, Rhett, and Jay. This is about balance, commitment, and loyalty — on the ice and off it."

Social media exploded with hashtags like #HowlersPack, #WrenIsOurs, and #QuadBond, and fans are already embracing the surprise. Honestly, it's kind of beautiful: Wren is fierce, brilliant, and unafraid to claim her spot, and now she's publicly part of the core of the team in every possible way.

Could this open doors for other omegas in the league? Maybe. Could it inspire other teams to rethink what it means to have a bonded pack off the ice? Definitely. But for now, the Howlers are celebrating their Apex Trophy win, their chemistry, and the bonds — literal and metaphorical — that make this team unstoppable.

So yeah, pack mentality isn't just a saying anymore. It's a *way of life*, and Wren Foster has just taken it to a whole new level.

FAN REACTIONS: THE HOWLERS' QUADRUPLE BONDING GOES VIRAL

@IceQueen88 – "Wait… Wren Foster is bonded to Roan, Rhett, AND Jay?! Quadruple bonding is officially canon. My heart can't."

@GoalieGoals – "Rhett Navarro saves goals, Wren Foster saves the team's PR… now they're literally a pack. #HowlersPack"

@SkateAndBake – "Can we talk about Wren wearing their marks?! This is peak Alpha/Beta/Omega drama and I LOVE IT. #QuadBond #WrenIsOurs"

@AlphaOnIce – "Never thought I'd see an Omega as fierce as Wren publicly claim *two* Alphas *and* a Beta. Respect. #PackGoals #NextSeasonCan'tComeFastEnough"

@FanaticForward – "Roan, Rhett, Jay, Wren = ultimate Howlers dream team. Apex Trophy wasn't enough, they had to flex their pack chemistry too."

@HotTakeHockey – "Wren Foster: PR genius. Team: Champions. Bonding: Surprise of the century. Fans: Losing our minds. Honestly, same."

@WolfPackForever – "This is so cute it hurts. Wren isn't a trophy, she's the glue. Now the Howlers are unstoppable on AND off the ice. #PackLife 🐺🤍"

Team Comment: Roan, Rhett, Jay, and Wren have yet to post a group pic, but sources say they're "celebrating privately and enjoying the chaos they caused online." Fans are... losing it.

AFTERWORD

So... yeah. That happened.

If you've made it this far, thank you for coming on this snowy, primal, emotionally unhinged journey with me. Writing this book was equal parts exhilarating and terrifying, mostly because it was my very first time stepping into the Omegaverse—and once again, the characters refused to behave quietly in the corners of my brain.

Wren and the Howlers surprised me in the best way. I didn't plan them. They simply showed up, made themselves at home, and started talking all at once. And honestly, what else am I supposed to do when the voices won't shut up? I write the story. That's just how this works.

This might have been my first Omegaverse, but definitely won't be my last.

If you're looking for something similar in a paranormal vein, you might enjoy **Shackled Souls**—a completed fated mates reverse harem where the heroine is very much *not* on board with being anyone's destined anything. (Turns out I have a bit of a soft spot for FMCs who push back against fate.)

Whether you came for the heat, the masks, the chaos, the found family, or the feelings, I hope this story gave you something that stuck with you. Wren certainly did with me—and I have a feeling the Howlers aren't done making noise just yet.

Until next time,

xoxo

Heather

Website:
heatherlong.net
Reader group:
facebook.com/groups/heatherspack

About Heather Long

I *love* books. Not just a little bit, but a lot. Books were my best friends when I was growing up. Books didn't care if I was new to a town or to a class. They were always there, my trustiest of companions. Until they turned on me and said I had to write them.

I can tell you that my own personal happily ever after included writing books. I've always said that an HEA is a work in progress. It's true in my marriage, my friendships, and in my career. I am constantly nurturing my muse as we dive into new tales, new tropes, new characters and more.

After seventeen years in Texas, we relocated to the Pacific Northwest in search of seasons, new experiences, and new geography. I can't wait to discover what life (and my muse) have in store for me.

Maybe writing was always my destiny and romance my fate. After all, my grandmother wasn't a fan of picture books and used to read me her Harlequin Romance novels.

Follow Heather & Sign up for her newsletter:
www.heatherlong.net
TikTok

Also by Heather Long

82nd Street Vandals

Savage Vandal

Vicious Rebel

Ruthless Traitor

Dirty Devil

Shamelessly Loyal (Novella)

Brutal Fighter

Dangerous Renegade

Merciless Spy

Reckless Thief

Fierce Dancer

Dirty Dancer

Bay Ridge Royals

Shamelessly Loyal (Novella)

Battle Lines

Deceptive Truce

Wicked Surrender

Violent Chaos

Desperate Victory

BLOOD Brothers

Burn

Lure

Own

Oath

Dare

Blue Ivy Prep

Problem Child

Mad Boys

Party Crashers

Money Shot

Bravo Team Wolf

When Danger Bites

Bitten Under Fire

Cardinal Sins

Kill Song

First Chorus

High Note

Last Word

Chance Monroe

Earth Witches Aren't Easy

Plan Witch from Out of Town

Bad Witch Rising

Fevered Hearts

Marshal of Hel Dorado

Brave are the Lonely

Micah & Mrs. Miller

A Fistful of Dreams

Raising Kane

Wanted: Fevered or Alive

Wild and Fevered

The Quick & The Fevered

A Man Called Wyatt

Going Royal

Some Like it Royal

Some Like it Scandalous

Some Like it Deadly

Some Like it Secret

Some Like it Easy

Heart of the Nebula

Queenmaker

Deal Breaker

Throne Taker

Lone Star Leathernecks

Semper Fi Cowboy

As You Were, Cowboy

Shackled Souls

Succubus Chained

Succubus Unchained

Succubus Blessed

Shackled Souls (Omnibus)

STANDALONES

Kiss of Fate (w/Blake Blessing)

Taste of Karma (w/Blake Blessing)

I'll Be Home... (w/Tate James)

Overexposed (w/Tate James)

Switchboard Duet

Talk to Me

Don't Let Go

Untouchable

Rules and Roses

Changes and Chocolates

Keys and Kisses

Whispers and Wishes

Hangovers and Holidays

Brazen and Breathless

Trials and Tiaras

Graduation and Gifts

Defiance and Dedication

Songs and Sweethearts

Legacy and Lovers

Farewells and Forever

Hellos and Happily Ever Afters

Untouchable What If

Rules, Roses, and Rivals

Letters, Lace, and Lies

Wolves of Willow Bend

Wolf at Law

Wolf Bite

Caged Wolf

Wolf Claim

Wolf Next Door

Rogue Wolf

Bayou Wolf

Untamed Wolf

Wolf with Benefits

River Wolf

Single Wicked Wolf

Desert Wolf

Snow Wolf

Wolf on Board

Holly Jolly Wolf

Shadow Wolf

His Moonstruck Wolf

Thunder Wolf

Ghost Wolf

Outlaw Wolves

Wolf Unleashed